Secrets
from the Past

Center Point
Large Print

Also by Barbara Taylor Bradford
and available from Center Point Large Print:

Breaking the Rules
Act of Will
Playing the Game
Letter from a Stranger

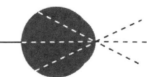

**This Large Print Book carries the
Seal of Approval of N.A.V.H.**

Secrets from the Past

BARBARA TAYLOR BRADFORD

CENTER POINT LARGE PRINT
THORNDIKE, MAINE

This Center Point Large Print edition
is published in the year 2013 by arrangement with
St. Martin's Press.

This is a work of fiction.
All of the characters, organizations, and events
portrayed in this novel are either products of the
author's imagination or are used fictitiously.

The text of this Large Print edition is unabridged.
In other aspects, this book may vary
from the original edition.
Printed in the United States of America
on permanent paper.
Set in 16-point Times New Roman type.

ISBN: 978-1-61173-724-0

Library of Congress Cataloging-in-Publication Data

Bradford, Barbara Taylor, 1933–
Secrets from the past / Barbara Taylor Bradford. — Center Point Large
Print edition.
pages cm
ISBN 978-1-61173-724-0 (Library binding : alk. paper)
1. Family secrets—Fiction. 2. Life change events—Fiction.
3. Large type books. I. Title.
PS3552.R2147S45 2013
813′.54—dc23
2013002138

For Bob, with all my love

Author's Note

I have been a journalist all of my life. I started my writing career on the *Yorkshire Evening Post* in Leeds. I became a cub reporter when I was sixteen, women's page editor at eighteen, and graduated to London's Fleet Street when I was twenty. I was fashion editor of a women's magazine before returning to newspapers at twenty-one, as a feature writer for *The London Evening News*. I have always been at home in a newsroom and was happy to go back to one.

Although I have spent the last thirty-odd years writing novels, I have continued to be a journalist and still write for newspapers and magazines. I owe a lot to journalism, and to other journalists, not the least when doing research for this book.

I am particularly indebted to those war correspondents and war photographers who have so courageously covered the wars in the Middle East over the past few years. The Arab Spring began in December of 2010, when a young Tunisian man, Mohamed Bouazizi, set himself on fire in protest of his mistreatment by a local policewoman. He ignited the revolution in his country and brought down the Tunisian government, which fell after his death in January of 2011.

After uprisings broke out in Tunisia, they quickly spread to Egypt, Libya, and then Syria.

Being a fan of news shows, I constantly watched television coverage, and voraciously read newspapers and magazines. I wanted to know as much as I could about the Arab Spring in the early part of 2011, since I was about to start writing this novel featuring a woman war photographer.

In the summer of 2011 my husband and I were in France, and my routine remained the same. I read every newspaper available every day, and part of the day we were both glued to the television set, watching the coverage on Sky News, the BBC, ITN, CNN, and the American networks when we could get them. The Libyan war was at its height that summer, and we witnessed it without being actually there in Libya.

I could not have written the Libyan section of this book without the television coverage by such correspondents as Lara Logan of CBS, Christiane Amanpour of CNN, Richard Pendlebury of the *Daily Mail*, and Marie Colvin of *The Sunday Times*, and her photographer, Paul Conroy. Their graphic reporting was extraordinary and it gave me the information and photographs required to create the scenes of the Libyan war for this novel.

I was stunned when the courageous Marie Colvin was tragically killed in Homs, Syria, on February 22, 2012. She will be mourned forever by her family and friends, her colleagues and fellow journalists, myself included. Intrepid, intelligent, and humane, she was a woman who had defied the odds for years. Her brilliant reporting of war atrocities saved many lives, and we will all remember how she insisted that she had to get the truth out so that the world knew what was happening. She succeeded. And died for it. And for that reason, among others, Marie Colvin will never be forgotten.

Contents

PART FIVE

PART SIX

EPILOGUE

Secrets from the Past

Part One

SNAPSHOT MEMORIES
Manhattan, March 2011

In my own very self, I am part of my family.
—D. H. Lawrence: *Apocalypse*

Memories of love abound,
In my heart and in my mind.
They give me comfort, keep me sane,
And lift my spirits up again.
—Anonymous

One

It was a beautiful day. The sky was a huge arc of delphinium blue, cloudless, and shimmering with bright sunlight above the soaring skyline of Manhattan. The city where I have lived, off and on, for most of my life was looking its best on this cold Saturday morning.

As I walked up Sutton Place, returning to my apartment, I began to shiver. Gusts of strong wind were blowing off the East River, and I was glad I was wearing jeans instead of a skirt, and warm clothes. Still shivering, I turned up the collar of my navy blue pea jacket and wrapped my cashmere scarf tighter around my neck.

It was unusually chilly for March. On the other hand, I was enjoying my walk after being holed up for four days endeavoring to finish a difficult chapter.

Although I am a photojournalist and photographer by profession, I recently decided to write a book, my first. Having hit a difficult part earlier this week, I'd been worrying it to death for days, like a dog with a bone. Finally I got it right last night. It felt good to get out, to stretch my legs, to look around me and to remind myself that there was a big wide world out here.

I increased my pace. Despite the sun, the wind was bitter. The weather seemed to be growing icier by the minute, and I hurried faster, almost running, needing to get home to the warmth.

My apartment was on the corner of Sutton and East Fifty-seventh, and I was relieved when it came into view. Once the traffic light changed, I dashed across the street and into my building, exclaiming to the doorman, as I sped past him, "It's Arctic weather, Sam."

"It is, Miss Stone. You're better off staying inside today."

I nodded, smiled, headed for the elevator. Once inside my apartment I hung up my scarf and pea jacket in the hall cupboard, went into the kitchen, put the kettle on for tea, and headed for my office.

I glanced at the answering machine on my desk and saw that I had two messages. I sat down, pressed play, and listened.

The first was from my older sister, Cara, who was calling from Nice. "Hi, Serena, it's me. I've found another box of photographs, mostly of Mom. Looking fab. You might want to use a few in the book. Shall I send by FedEx? Or what? I'm heading out now, so leave a message. Or call me tomorrow. Big kiss."

The second message was from my godfather. "It's Harry. Just confirming Monday night, honey. Seven-thirty. Usual place. Don't bother to call back. See ya."

The whistling kettle brought me to my feet and I went back to the kitchen. As I made the tea I felt a frisson of apprehension, then an odd sense of foreboding . . . something bad was going to happen . . . I felt it in my bones.

I pushed this dark feeling away, carried the mug of tea back to my office, telling myself that I usually experienced premonitions only when I was at the front, when I sensed imminent danger, knew I had to run for my life before I was blown to smithereens by a bomb, or took a bullet. To have such feelings now was irrational. I shook my head, chiding myself for being overly imaginative. But in fact I was to remember this moment later and wonder if I had some sort of sixth sense.

Two

The room I used as an office was once my mother's den years ago. It was light, airy, with large plate-glass windows at one end. She had decorated it in cream and deep peach with a touch of raspberry; I had kept those colors because they emphasized its spaciousness and I found them restful.

In fact I had pretty much left the room as it was, except for buying a modern desk chair. I loved her antique Georgian desk, the long wall of bookshelves which held her various decorative objects and family photographs as well as books.

At the windowed end of the room my mother

had created a charming seating area with a big comfortable sofa, several armchairs, and a coffee table. I headed there now, carrying my mug of tea. I sat down on the sofa, sipped the tea, and, as always, marveled at the panoramic view spread out before me . . . the East River, the suspension bridges, and the amazing skyscrapers that helped to make this city so unique.

The windows faced downtown, and just to my right was the elegant Art Deco spire of the Chrysler Building and next to it the equally as impressive Empire State. The city had never looked better, had made an unusually spectacular comeback after the bombing of the World Trade Center in 2001.

I realized, with a small jolt of surprise, that it was ten years ago already. The anniversary of that horrific attack would be this coming September.

What mattered, though, was that the new tower was on the rise. One World was already on its way up, would keep on going up and up and up, until it reached 1,776 feet, that well-known number not only commemorating Independence Day, but also making One World the highest building in the Western Hemisphere.

That particular September remains vivid in my mind, not only because of the heinous crime which had been committed, but because we were all here together as a family. In this very apartment, which my mother had bought thirty years ago now, around 1980, just before I was born.

My mother, who had an amazing eye for art and architecture, had a predilection for buying apartments and houses, which is why my sisters and I had grown up all over the world: New York, London, Paris, Nice, and Bel Air. My grandmother used to say we were like gypsies with money.

My father, who loved to tease my mother about anything and everything, would point out how proud he was of himself, because he had never felt the need to indulge himself in this way, had never invested money in bricks and mortar, and never would.

My mother's pithy answer was always the same. She would point out that despite this, he managed to somehow commandeer most of the closets in their different homes, in which he would then hang his extensive collection of beautiful, very expensive clothes. This was true, and they would laugh about it, as always enjoying being together, loving each other, the best of friends.

Suddenly, I saw them in my mind's eye. They were true blue, those two. True to each other and to us . . . my twin sisters, Cara and Jessica. They are eight years older than me and used to boss me around, albeit in a genial way. My father called us his all-girl team, and he was so proud of us. We were such a happy family.

That September of 2001 my father was in New York, not off somewhere covering a war, and so was his best friend and partner, Harry Redford. They had been pals since childhood; both of them had been born and brought up in Manhattan, had gone to the same school, become photographers together, then partnered up and roamed the world, plying their trade.

My father and Harry had founded Global Images in 1971, a photographic agency which was managed by Harry's sister, Florence, since the two men were not always in New York. My father and Harry were joined at the hip, and he was very much part of the family, loved by all of us. Dad's *compadre*, my mother's protector and champion, and an avuncular presence in our lives, always there for us no matter what. And these days he was my best friend as well as my god-father. He had always treated me like a pal, was never condescending, and I'd been his confidante since I was eighteen . . . he told *me* first when he was getting a divorce from Melanie, his first wife who was too temperamental, and then on his second divorce from Holly Grey, who was jealous of any woman who looked at him. And many did. He usually brought a girlfriend when he came to Nice.

The weather that last week of September and first week of October had been glorious. Indian summer weather. Balmy, soft, with light blue skies, sunshine, and no hint of fall.

Even though we were all angry, shocked, and

sorrowing because of the brutal terrorist attacks on New York and Washington, we were able to draw enjoyment from each other's company, and also comfort from being together at this frightening time.

Cara and Jessica had flown in from Nice, where they lived at the old house up in the hills, in order to celebrate their twenty-eighth birthday in October.

Before 9/11 we had been to see Broadway plays and movies, eaten at my father's favorite restaurants, most especially Rao's. There had been a great deal of family bonding during that period, and now, when I look back, I'm happy we had this special time together.

My mother's mother, Alice Vasson, and her sister, Dora Clifford, had come in from California to celebrate the twins' birthday with us. The two of them were staying at the Carlyle hotel, but they were mostly at the apartment during the day.

My mother, an only child, nonetheless had a great sense of family, and reveled in such occasions. This made us happy, especially my father, and particularly since my mother wasn't in the best of health during this period. Being surrounded by those who loved her helped to make her feel better, and she was more radiant and happier than I had seen her for a long time.

My grandmother and great-aunt had been instrumental in developing my mother's career, and, not unnaturally, they couldn't help boasting a bit, taking bows. They had made her into a mega-star, one of the greatest movie stars in the world.

Their tall tales and antics amused my father no end, and made him laugh; my mother merely smiled, said not a word, her expression benign. And we girls, well, we just listened, once again awestruck, even though we'd heard these yarns before.

I sighed under my breath, remembering my grandmother and great-aunt, the roles they had played in our lives, and I thought of their deaths, and the other losses over the last few years . . .

When someone you love has died, everything changes. Instantly. Nothing will ever be the same again. The world becomes an entirely different place . . . alien, cold, empty without the presence of that person you love.

When one quarrels with a loved one, there is often a reconciliation, maybe a compromise, or we go our separate ways. If a friend or relative decides to live somewhere else, in another place, it is easy to reach out to them, speak on the phone, send e-mails or text. In other words, to remain part of their lives is not difficult at all.

Death does not offer that consolation.

Death is the *final* exit.

Memories. Those are what I have in my heart, abundant memories that will be with me until the day I die. They are founded on reality, on things that actually happened, and so they are true. And because of this they offer real solace.

My father died eleven months ago. I was in total shock, filled with sorrow, grief, and guilt. A terrible guilt that still haunts me at times, guilt because I did not get there in time to tell him how much I loved him, to say good-bye.

I was late because of a missed plane in Afghanistan. Only a paltry few hours too late, but it might as well have been a month or even a year. Too late *is* exactly that.

When death came, that sly pale rider on his pale horse, he relentlessly snatched his prize and was gone. Suddenly there was nothing. A void. Emptiness. A shattering silence. But inevitably the memories do come back. Very slow at first, they are nonetheless sure-footed, and they bring a measure of comfort.

The book I have been writing for the last few months is about my father. As I delve into his past, to tell his amazing story, he comes alive again. He was quite a guy. That's what everyone says about him. Quite a guy, they tell me, admiration echoing in their voices.

My father, John Thomas Stone, known to every-one everywhere simply as Tommy, was one of the world's greatest war photographers. Of the same ilk as the famous Robert Capa, who died when he stepped on a land mine covering the war in Vietnam.

Until my father appeared on the scene many years later, there had never been many comparisons to the great Capa. At least not of the kind my father inspired.

For years Tommy cheated death on the front line, and then unexpectedly he died. At home in his own bed, of natural causes . . . a second heart attack, this one massive. He was gone, just like that, in the flick of an eyelash, without warning. No prior notice given here.

It was the suddenness, the unexpectedness of it that did the worst damage to me. Aftershock. My father, who was given to using military lingo, would have called it blowback, and that's what it was. *Blowback.* It felled me.

My mother, Elizabeth Vasson Stone, died four years ago, and I was devastated. I still grieve for her at times, and I will always miss her. Yet my father's death affected me in a wholly different way. It crippled me for a while.

It could be that my reaction was not the same because my mother had always suffered from poor health, whereas my father was strong and fit. Invincible, to me. That perhaps was the difference. I suppose I thought he would live forever.

My sisters still believe I was our father's favorite child. Naturally, I've continued to deny this over the years, reminded them that I'm the youngest, and because of this perhaps I was spoilt, even pampered a bit when I was growing up.

Traditionally, there is always a lot of focus on the baby of the family. But despite my comments, I'm well aware they are right. I *was* his favorite.

Not that he ever actually came out and said this, to me or anyone else. He was far too nice to hurt anyone's feelings. Still, he made it clear in other ways that he favored me, implied I was his special girl.

He would often remark that I was the most like him in character, had inherited his temperament, many of his quirky ways, and certainly it pleased him that I was the one daughter who had followed in his footsteps, and become a photographer.

I had a camera in my hand when I was old enough to hold one. He taught me everything I know about photography, and very importantly, how to take care of myself when I was out there working in the dangerous world we live in today.

My father impressed on me that I should look straight ahead, be on the alert and ready for the unexpected. He pointed out that I must keep my eyes peeled in order to spot danger, which could spring up anywhere, especially in a war.

It was from him that I learned how to dodge bullets when we were in the middle of a battle, how to make rapid exits from disaster zones, and seek the best possible shelter when bombs were dropping.

My father was a man the whole world seemed to love. Very easily he could invoke a natural charm that was totally irresistible. People were immediately drawn to him, smitten, men as well as women, and he was fiercely intelligent and charismatic. My mother said that he gave something of himself to everyone, and that they felt better for having met him.

That he had good looks was immaterial. It was his charm and outsized personality that captivated everyone. Those who worked with him knew how dedicated he was to his job. He feared nothing and no one, plunged into danger whenever it was necessary to get the most powerful images on film. He was also helpful to his colleagues and those who worked with him in the field, a friend to all.

Over the past few months, as I've done research for my biography of him, I've talked to a great many people who knew him. Almost all of them told me that there was something truly heroic about Tommy, and I believe they are right.

I idolized my father, but during the course of this week, I have suddenly come to understand that I *idealized* him as well. And yet he was a man, not a god, with plenty of the faults, flaws, and frailties all mortals have. In fact, being a larger-than-life character, I'm quite certain he had more than most people.

But when I was growing up he was the miracle man to me, the maker of magic who forever took us captive with his charm, who brought laughter, fun, and excitement to our lives.

I leaned back on the sofa, closed my eyes, listened to the quiet in this quiet room where I work, thinking of my father. And in the inner recesses of my head I heard my own voice, and words I had spoken to my sisters twenty-one years ago. Quite suddenly I could hear myself telling them that our father was Superman, a magician, a miracle maker all rolled into one.

I saw Jessica and Cara in my mind's eye, as they were then, staring back at me as if I was a creature who had just landed from some far-distant planet. Disbelief flickered in two pairs of dark eyes focused on me so intently.

At the time I was only nine, but I recall how I suddenly understood that they viewed Tommy differently than I did. That's why they were puzzled by my words. They couldn't see inside our father the way I could . . . they didn't know the man I knew.

Our mother was with us that afternoon. She was seated under the huge umbrella on the terrace of the house in the hills above Nice. She had laughed and nodded. "You're right, Serena. What a clever girl you are, spotting your father's unique talents."

The twins had jumped up, laughing, had leapt away in the direction of the swimming pool. They were boisterous, athletic, sports-addicted. I was the artistic one, quiet, studious, a bookworm, paying strict attention to every detail of my photographs, like my father.

It was Jessica and Cara who physically resembled Tommy, something which has always irked me. They had inherited his height, his dark hair and warm dark eyes; I didn't look like him or anyone else in the family. Certainly not my mother, who was very beautiful.

Once my sisters had disappeared and we were alone on the terrace, my mother beckoned me to come and join her. I had flopped down in the chair next to her, and she had poured a glass of lemonade for me. We had talked for a while about my father, the magician as I called him, and then unexpectedly she had confided a secret . . . she told me that he had enchanted her, captivated her the moment they met.

"I couldn't take my eyes off him, and I've only ever had eyes for him since. You see, I fell under his spell. And I'm still under it," she had murmured, then she had abruptly turned, stared down the length of the terrace.

My father had suddenly arrived with Harry, and, as usual, there was a flurry of excitement. They had hurried toward us carrying lots of shopping bags from posh boutiques, and when they came to a standstill my father had announced, "Presents for our girls."

He had rushed to hug my mother and then me, and so had Harry. And later Harry had taken pictures of me with my parents. One of them was deemed so special by my mother she had had it framed.

I opened my eyes, came out of my reverie, and stood up, hurried over to the bookshelves. I found that remarkable photograph at once. There we were . . . the three of us. My father stood behind my mother's chair. He was bending forward, his arms around her shoulders, his face next to hers. I was crouched near my mother's knee and she had her arms around me, holding me close to her.

We were all smiling, looked so carefree. My handsome father, my lovely mother, and me. "My little mouse," she used to call me sometimes, and with great affection. It was her pet name for me. But often I've thought that I am a bit mousey in appearance, with my light brown hair and gray eyes. But in this picture, taken so long ago, I realized that I looked rather pretty that day, and certainly very happy.

Picking up the silver frame, I stared at the image of us for the longest moment, marveling yet again at my mother. The camera loved her. That's what my father used to say, and everyone else, for that matter. And it did. She was truly photogenic, and it was one of the secrets of her success. As usual, she looked incandescent.

My mother, a movie star of the greatest magnitude, in the same league as Elizabeth Taylor, had been beautiful, glamorous, beloved by millions, a box-office draw, fodder for the gossip press. One of a kind actually, and like the other Elizabeth, larger than life. My mother had remained a huge star until her death.

Three

In the kitchen I was attempting to do three things at once: heat a can of Campbell's tomato soup, toast a slice of bread, and call my sister in Nice, when the other line began to shrill. I swiftly ended my message to Cara and took the incoming call.

Much to my surprise, it was my sister Jessica.

"Hi, Pidge," she said, using the nickname she had bestowed upon me when I was a child, a nickname no one understood except me. "What's up? How are you?"

"Hey, Jess! Hello!" I exclaimed enthusiastically, happy to hear her voice. "I'm pretty good, and where are you, actually? You sound as if you're just round the corner. Are you in New York?" I was hoping that she was; Jessica and I had a very special relationship and I hadn't seen her for some months. When she was with me, I was immensely cheered up.

"Not exactly, but kind of . . . I'm in Boston on business. Meetings yesterday and this morning. Now I'm done I thought I'd jump on a shuttle, spend the weekend with you, if you're not caught up with a lot of other stuff. I can't be *this* close and not see my darling Pidge."

"I'm not doing anything special, and I'll be mad at you if you don't come. What time will you get here?" I asked.

"I don't know. I'll head out to the airport now, get the first flight available. I'll probably be there in a few hours, but I've got my door key, so don't worry if you have to go out."

"I'm not going anywhere. Hightail it to the airport and get here as fast as you can," I ordered, bossing her for a change.

"I'll be there in three shakes of a lamb's tail," she shot back, using a familiar expression we'd grown up with. Our English grandmother, Alice, had been unusually fond of it, had used it constantly, much to our irritation most of the time.

There was a small silence and then we both burst out laughing before we hung up.

The toast had gone cold, the soup looked congealed, so I threw everything away and started again. I made some peanut-butter-and-jelly sandwiches, a childhood standby, and a mug of tea, and took everything to my office where I ate at my desk, as I usually did at lunchtime, a bad habit picked up from my father and Harry.

Later, I went to Jessica's room and looked around, wanting to make sure everything was in good order. It was, thanks to Mrs. Watledge, who came in twice a week to clean and do odd jobs for me, and she always dusted every room in the apartment, whether it had been used or not. Much to my pleasure, she was fastidious.

Jessica had left in a rush the last time she was here. I had hung up the clothes she had strewn around on pieces of furniture and put away all the scattered shoes once she was gone, and Mrs. Watledge had vacuumed, polished the furniture, and changed the bed linen.

I saw there was not a thing out of place, and that would please Jessica, who was normally the neatest of the three of us. A crisis in the auction house she owned in Nice had necessitated her unexpected and swift return to France last November, hence the messy room she had so blithely abandoned without a backward glance, as usual focused on the problems in Nice.

I was thrilled my sister was coming for the weekend. Although she and Cara had once teased me unmercifully, as the much younger child of the family, things had eventually leveled off as I grew older.

We became the best of friends, the three of us, very bonded, and we are still extremely close. We share this apartment and the house in Nice, which our mother left to us equally. The two places were our parents' main homes for many years. Their special favorites and ours; the ownership only passed to us after our father's death last year, which was the stipulation in her will.

Closing the door of Jessica's room, I went to the kitchen and checked the refrigerator. Mrs. Watledge filled it up with basic items and bought a fresh roasting chicken from the butcher every Friday.

There was plenty of food, and if my sister felt like eating out we could go to Jimmy Neary's pub on Fifty-seventh, or the French restaurant, Le Périgord, at Fifty-second and First. Two old favorites of ours where we'd been going for years, starting when we were teenagers.

I wandered down to the office, sat at the desk, and opened the top drawer, staring at the two cell phones and the BlackBerry.

I knew there would be no messages. I never used the BlackBerry these days, only ever took a cell phone with me if I intended to be gone for several hours.

Grimacing at them, I reached for my Moleskine notebook and closed the drawer firmly. Those devices reminded me too much of the front line.

I gave up covering wars eleven months ago, and have no intention of ever walking onto a battleground again. The mere thought of this sent an ice-cold chill running through me, and I shivered involuntarily.

For eight years I had been lucky. But I had come to believe my luck wouldn't last much longer. And I'd grown afraid . . . afraid to put on my flak jacket and helmet and head out to some no-man's-land on a far-flung distant shore, my camera poised to get the most dramatic shot ever. Fear had taken hold of me bit by bit by bit.

When you're afraid you don't function with the same precision and skill, and that's when you're truly putting yourself at risk. I understood all this. The game was over for me.

Flipping through the pages of the Moleskine, I came across some jottings I had made during the week, regarding the year 1999. I needed to talk to my sisters about that particular year, and what we'd all been doing then. I had a photographic memory, but several months of that year were somehow missing in my head. Jessica would no doubt remember.

I pulled the manuscript toward me and glanced at the one section which continued to trouble me. As I pored over the pages I realized that only my father appeared in this long chapter. Obviously it was the reason I was worried.

His family and friends needed to occupy those pages as well, didn't they? *Yes,* I answered myself.

A sudden thought struck me. I jumped up, went

to one of the cupboards built in below the bookshelves, and looked inside. Stored there in stacks were many photograph albums which had been carefully put together by my mother.

I pulled out a few and glanced at the dates. The years 1998 and 2001 were there, but not 1999 and 2000. So they must be in Nice. The albums ran up to 2004, and some were even much earlier, dated in the early nineties. All would come in useful, but they were not helpful to me at this particular moment.

Four

I took the two albums I wanted to review and carried them over to the sofa. Balancing the one marked "1998" on my knee, I opened it, and a smile immediately flashed across my face.

In the middle of the first page my mother had written: MY THREE DAUGHTERS GROWN UP.

When I turned the page my smile widened. There were a number of snapshots of Jessica, which had been taken by my father. She had been twenty-five years old at that moment in time, tall and arresting.

I gazed at the images of her, thinking how beautiful she was, gorgeous really, with her glossy black hair framing her heart-shaped face. Her large black eyes were full of sparkle and she was smiling broadly, showing perfect white teeth. Our grandmother had called it "the smile that lights up a room."

What a knockout she had been. The snaps were taken in the summer of that year; Jessica had a golden tan, was wearing a white cotton shirt with the sleeves rolled up, and white jeans. She looked even taller because she was in a pair of high wedged espadrilles.

On the following pages were shots of her taken outside Laurent's, the well-known auction house in Nice that the ancient owners had, somewhat ridiculously, allowed to become run-down and decrepit. Jessica had bought it with my parents' help.

I saw how cleverly my father had told the story of Jessica's first business venture. He had documented almost every step, showed her supervising the restoration and remodeling of the Belle Epoque building, working on the outside and in the interiors. His picture story showed me how diligent she had been in bringing it back to its former architectural glory.

Stone's, as she had named it, became, under her direction, one of the most technically modern and digitally up-to-date auction houses in Europe. And a most glamorous venue. And it had happened because of her vision, talent, hard work, and determination.

The pièce de résistance of my father's brilliant picture story was the next section, devoted to

Jessica's opening night. My sister had inaugurated Stone's with a grand auction—the contents of our mother's Bel Air house, which our mother had recently put on the market, plus selections from her haute couture clothes by famous designers. Also in the auction were pieces from our mother's collection of jewels, from the world's greatest jewelers.

The auction had been a sensation, had broken all records, and the publicity for Stone's had continued to roll ever since. It was a big hit then, and still is now, is considered to be one of the most important auction houses in the world.

Now there *we* were, me and Cara, our images captured on the next few pages of the album. I stared at them eagerly, had forgotten how special we looked on that gala evening. We were in attendance to boost Jessica's confidence, and cheer her on, wanting to make her opening night a big smash. Naturally, it was a family affair.

I peered at the pictures; we were dressed to the nines. Transformed. So glamorous, so beautiful, or perhaps we only looked that way because of Dad's superb photography, plus the skillful professional help from our mother's makeup artist and hairdresser. I wondered who we were trying to impress? Or which men to attract?

Cara, as dramatic in appearance as her twin, was wearing a clinging, royal blue silk gown, with a plunging neckline. The dress showed off her hourglass figure to perfection, and she had never looked so sexy before.

Jessica had chosen her favorite color, daffodil yellow. She appeared sleek and elegant in the chiffon dress which fell in narrow pleats to the floor, was somewhat Grecian in style. Her black hair was swept up on top of her head, and she was wearing diamond chandelier earrings, which our mother had loaned her for the event.

I gaped when I saw the pictures of myself. I was in scarlet, and now I remember how brave I had felt, choosing the red silk strapless sheath. I certainly pulled that one off, I thought, continuing to study myself, filled with surprise. *Seventeen.* I had been seventeen that year, so young, so innocent . . . it seemed so long ago.

Of course, we were overshadowed by our mother, as was every other woman who attended the auction, blotted out by her staggering beauty. She was, quite simply, *incandescent.* With her shimmering blond hair, exquisite features, and turquoise blue eyes, she was incomparable in those photographs.

That night she wore a sea-foam bluish-green chiffon gown, and aquamarine-and-diamond jewelry. As I looked at her image now I heard again the many compliments she had received, remembered how delighted she was. After all, she was fifty-nine at the time, although she appeared years younger.

When I came to the last section of the album I found myself staring at pictures of my father, which had been taken by Harry.

Tommy Stone. As dashing as ever, and glamorous in his own masculine way. He was in an elegant tuxedo, the white dress shirt accentuating his tan. He had cut quite a swathe, as I recall, with women swirling around him as they usually did. In the picture he stood next to Mom, his arm around her waist, surrounded by his daughters.

There were several different shots, and then a series of new images, starring Harry, as debonair as his pal Tommy, wearing an impcccably tailored tux. Those two had always known how to dress well when not rushing off to war zones in fatigues.

Harry was standing next to my mother, and we were on either side of him. I peered at Harry, a sudden rush of affection swamping me. He was smiling hugely, as proud of Jessica as we were. Whatevcr would I do without him? He had been my mainstay since my father's death, the person who was there for me anytime, night or day, constant, caring, and full of wisdom.

I sat up straighter on the sofa, asking myself where Jessica's husband, Roger, was? There were no pictures of him in this album.

I sat staring into space for a moment, focusing on that gala evening of long ago, and then everything came back to me. He hadn't been there that night because he was in London. His absence had infuriated everyone.

Poor Roger. My memories of him were pleasant. He was a nice man, kindly. I was suddenly filled with pity for him as I realized he hadn't stood a chance in that family of ours, now that I thought about the situation in hindsight.

Roger Galloway, an Irishman of considerable charm and good looks, somehow "got lost in the shuffle," was the way Cara had once put it.

He was an artist, but worked as a set designer at theaters in Dublin and London, and was frequently away. I know Dad had liked Roger, yet he had genuinely believed the marriage was ill-fated.

"They're poles apart," Dad had once muttered to me, looking decidedly glum, even troubled. My mother had overheard this comment, had frowned, glanced at me worriedly. But she had not said a word. However, at the time I believed that she felt the same way as Dad. They thought alike.

Whatever the reason for the split, Jessica had kept it to herself. She had said very little to me, and Cara was also kept in the dark. I'm positive our mother knew the full story, although she never revealed anything to either of us. My mother was very good at keeping other people's secrets, very reliable in that way, and loyal, discreet. "I keep my mouth shut," she once told me. "I've no desire to cause trouble or play God."

One day Roger disappeared forever. Just like

that he was gone, and Jessica moved back into the house in Nice to live with us, having left their rented apartment for good. Eventually, they were divorced. *Amicably*. At least, that was what I heard through the family grapevine.

The whole family loved the old manor up in the hills above the city, with its white, ivy-clad walls and dark green shutters, terraces, orange groves, and beautiful gardens, hence its name, Jardin des Fleurs.

My mother had bought the house in 1972, when she was thirty-three, just a few months after she had married my father. It became her favorite place to live over the years, and I have long accepted that it was the one place she was truly happy and at ease. It was also near the international airport in Nice, convenient when she had to fly off to work.

Finally closing the album, I placed it on the coffee table and stretched out on the sofa, closed my eyes, thought of my mother. Our mother. Tommy's wife. Harry's best friend. My grandparents' only child. *Elizabeth Vasson*. One of the greatest movie stars the world had ever known.

I remember once asking her, when I was about seven or eight, if she *liked* being a movie star. I'll never forget the intense, perplexed look she gave me. "I've been a movie star all my life," she had replied, frowning. "What else would I do?" I had no answer for her; I was only a kid.

By the same token, a few years later, I was foolish enough to wonder out loud if she *minded being so very famous.* Once again she threw me a puzzled stare. "I've been famous for as long as I can remember. Fame doesn't bother me," she had answered.

What she had said on both occasions was true. She had first become famous when she was fourteen months old. Born in London in May of 1939, she was a beautiful baby with a marvelous gurgling smile, silky blond curls, and those unique turquoise blue eyes.

Her photograph was on the label of a new baby food being introduced, and very soon my mother was the most famous baby in England. Every pregnant woman hoped her child would be a girl, and as beautiful as Elizabeth. Very soon the new brand of baby food was as famous as the child herself. And it still is.

By the time she was five, she was a successful model for children's clothes; in 1948, after the end of the Second World War, Elizabeth was in her first movie. When it was released in 1949, it was a big hit. Everybody had gone to see it because of her. She was ten years old, and the new child star.

Several films followed, once again big hits, and then Kenneth and Alice Vasson packed their bags, and took their talented and beautiful child to Hollywood, where they believed she should be, and where they were certain she belonged.

The Vassons went to stay with my grand-mother's twin sister, Dora, who had married her G.I. Joe boyfriend, Jim Clifford, after the war. Dora and Jim lived in Los Angeles, which was Jim's hometown, and where he was connected. He was a young lawyer working in a well-established show-business law firm. Jim, intelligent, street smart, and savvy, had a keen eye and saw endless possibilities and opportunities for his wife's beautiful and talented niece, whom he fully intended to represent.

The Vassons had jumped at the chance to go to America. They had agreed to stay for three years at least, but in fact they never left.

At fifteen, my mother appeared in her first Hollywood movie. A star was born overnight, and that star never looked back. Not for a single second.

The sound of the front door banging made me sit up with a start. Pushing myself to my feet, I rushed down the corridor to greet my favorite sister.

Five

My sister Jessica has always been very special to me since my childhood. Even when she was teasing me or being bossy, I never felt angry, nor did I ever bear a grudge, because I knew there was no malice in her. She was, and is, benign by nature and has great warmth.

I once asked my mother why everyone seemed to love Jessica so much, and my mother answered that Jessica was a good person, that people instantly perceived this, and also knew she had a heart of gold.

Since I was quite little at the time, I immediately had an image of a gold heart, similar to my mother's locket, and for ages I was certain my sister had one just like it embedded in her chest.

Later, when I was grown up and earning a living, the first present I bought Jessica was a gold locket, which she still treasures. If I am with her, and if she happens to be wearing it, we exchange a knowing smile; one of the many good things about having sisters are the lovely memories we share.

Although Jessica looked like my father, had his dark hair and eyes, it was from our mother that she had inherited certain qualities. My mother's grace, her loving manner and optimistic nature. Jessica had an aura of happiness surrounding her; I didn't know anyone who was as upbeat as Jess. She always seemed to be in a good mood, held the belief that tomorrow would be far better than today.

When I hurried into the hallway Jessica was hanging up her long camel overcoat and a red wool scarf in the closet, and she instantly swung around when she heard my footsteps.

Immediately, she took hold of me and hugged

me close. "Hi, darling, it's good to be here. I've missed you."

My spirits lifted as usual. "And I've missed you too, Jess. Why didn't you tell me you were coming to Boston?"

"Only because I didn't want you to be disappointed, if I couldn't make it to New York," she answered, and beamed her dazzling smile at me. "As it turned out, things went quickly, and here I am for the weekend." Grabbing the handle of her suitcase, she rolled it behind her, walking toward her room.

The moment she entered she began to chuckle. "I see you cleaned up after me, thanks for that, Pidge. What a mess I left behind in November. So sorry about that."

I laughed with her. "I understood. Your mind was focused on your problems in Nice."

I sat down on a chair and watched my sister as she unpacked her carry-on, hanging up a black trouser suit, two white silk shirts, and a black sweater. As usual, she traveled light, the way our father had trained us. Although it worked with us, he was never able to make the slightest impression on our mother, who considered six suitcases to be the minimum for a weekend.

"I missed a call from Cara earlier today. Apparently she found some of Dad's pictures, and some of Mom she was really taken with, that I might want to use in my book," I confided.

"Yes, they are great," Jessica said without turning around, placing underwear and small items in a chest of drawers. "We've been looking at Dad's collections in his studio, and there's a treasure trove there. We've left everything the way it is, since you're the best judge, Serena. We want *you* to review everything."

"I will when I come to Nice in a couple of months."

Straightening, Jessica turned around, and frowned. "A couple of months? I thought you were planning a trip earlier than that?"

I detected something in her voice, a flicker of concern behind her eyes, and wondered if everything was all right. Had Cara become depressed again? She had been very low since her fiancé had died. Her fiancé's fatal accident had deeply affected her. I was about to voice this thought, and changed my mind. I said, "I'll get there as soon as I can, Jess, I promise."

"How's the book coming along?" she asked, closing the drawer.

"I'm pleased with most of it. There's just one chapter that needs work," I answered, and rose. "I'm going to make coffee. Do you want something to eat? Are you hungry?"

"Not really, but I'd love some coffee, Pidge." She threw me a smile before going back to the carry-on and the last of her unpacking. "I'll meet you in Mom's den in a few minutes."

"Okay." I didn't bother to correct her. She still referred to it as our mother's den, sometimes even called it Mom's sitting room, and it had been both.

It was now my office, but even I associated it totally with our mother. It was the room in the apartment where I spent the most time.

"I'd forgotten all about this album!" my sister exclaimed ten minutes later, when I walked into my office carrying the tray holding coffee and cups and saucers.

"Leaf through it, Jessica, it's great! I can't believe the way we all look," I answered, and placed the tray on the coffee table. Glancing at her, I added, "Even Dad was impressed with us that night of your gala. He took great pictures."

Jessica was already turning the pages, staring at all the photographs, and laughing out loud at times, exclaiming about some of the images of herself and Cara and me.

I poured coffee for us both and sat down in a chair opposite her. "That's a lovely picture story Dad did, the way he took shots of you at every stage of the remodeling of the auction house. And you look great. We all do. Especially Mom."

"That's true. Why were you interested in this particular album?" she asked, finally closing the album, putting it back on the coffee table.

"I was actually searching for the 1999 album," I explained. "Because I need to know what we were all doing in 1999. You see, I need more information for that one chapter that needs rewriting. Do you remember anything much about that year?"

Jessica took the cup of coffee I was offering, and sat back on the sofa. "I certainly do. Aside from it being my first year in business, I got a divorce from Roger. Cara finished building her second large greenhouse. Dad was off in Kosovo, anyway somewhere in the Balkans, covering a war. And you and Mom were not too happy with each other."

Her last statement startled me and I sat up straighter, stared at her. "I don't know what you're talking about," I responded, shaking my head. "Mom and I weren't quarreling."

"That's true, you weren't, but she wasn't too happy with you, Serena. Have you forgotten how angry she was with you?"

I was speechless for a moment, but my mind raced. After a long pause, I said, "Mom was never angry with me ever, Jess. You must be mixing me up with Cara."

"No, I'm not. Mom was definitely angry with you in 1999. I know because I witnessed it. Do you want me to tell you about it?"

I could only nod.

Six

Jessica's announcement that I'd had a quarrel with my mother had not upset me, but it had taken me aback. I was certain she was mistaken, filled with disbelief as I sat waiting for her to explain.

After quietly scrutinizing me for a few seconds, she said softly, "I didn't mean to upset you, Pidge."

"I know that, Jess, and I'm not upset."

"But, darling, you look . . . *stricken.*"

"Do I?" I frowned. "Well, I'm not, I'm floored because I have no recollection of this incident. I don't remember Mom being angry with me, nor was I with her. *Not ever.* It was Cara she had disagreements with, or have you forgotten that?"

"No, I haven't, and you're absolutely correct. Mom and Cara often did have little upsets from time to time. But I honestly think you've simply forgotten the incident because—"

"I've a very good memory. And you know that," I cut in. "A photographic memory, Dad called it," I reminded her.

"Perhaps you haven't *forgotten.* Maybe you've *blocked* it out instead. Because you didn't, don't, want to remember something as distressing as a quarrel with our mother."

She held me with her eyes, and I knew she

wasn't being difficult or arbitrary, only wished to help me. She had always been kind, loving, and in a way much more than Cara had, who was extremely self-involved. Unless there was a crisis. Then Cara was the best at coping.

After a moment, somewhat reluctantly, I said, "Maybe you're right. I must have blocked it out. And we're going back a long time. To 1999."

Jessica now said in that same kind, warm voice, "You know, you were very special to Mom and Dad, Serena, and being born eight years after us, you were a much-wanted baby. And therefore you were Mom's little princess, a bit pampered and cosseted by her. And as you grew older Dad treated you like the son he'd never had . . . that was a unique relationship."

This was said without any rancor or jealousy. I knew she was just being truthful, matter-of-fact.

"More like a pal," I remarked, "and I was a bit of a tomboy. But Mom cosseted all of us, Jess, not only me. That was her nature, she was very loving and devoted to Dad, you, and Cara. And to Granny and Aunt Dora. That was the way she was, she was like . . ." My voice trailed off, and I shook my head, at a loss.

Finally I explained, "I know this might sound odd, because Mom was so beautiful, but she was like an earth mother. That was the wonderful quality she had, the way she gave her love. She was the most giving person I've ever known."

"I agree with you," Jessica answered, and leaned forward. "We've been lucky, having had such great parents, Pidge. I'm very aware you had a tranquil relationship with our mother. But I also *do* know a situation developed between you and Mom that year."

I remained silent, angry with myself for not being able to remember this incident. I felt like a fool. Maybe my sister was right; I'd blocked it out, obviously because I couldn't bear to have anything mar my memories of my relationship with Mom. We had been so close. "Two peas in a pod," Dad used to call us.

As if reading my mind, Jessica said, "I'd like to tell you about that particular day, so that you understand. I don't want your happy memories of Mom to be overshadowed. So can I tell you?"

"Yes," I answered. "Go ahead."

Jessica did not speak, sat staring at me. It struck me that there was a flicker of apprehension in her eyes.

"Go on, tell me, Jess. If you recall an incident between Mother and me, then obviously it happened. I know you wouldn't make something up, you silly thing!"

"Of course I wouldn't!" she exclaimed, horrified at the thought. "I've always told you the truth, and Cara too. Although sometimes, in the past, she hasn't been honest with us, has she?"

"She never lied, but she did omit to tell us

things. But she doesn't do that now. Or does she?"

"No, she doesn't. Quite the opposite," Jessica responded and laughed. She took a deep breath, and began. "The incident you had with our mother was at the end of September in 1999, the year you're so curious about. We'd spent most of the year in Nice, with Dad and Harry coming and going from front lines. Do you remember that?"

"Yes, I do. Granny and Aunt Dora were in Europe, and came for a visit. Dad and Harry went to Kosovo. The war had finally ended in June. They went back at the beginning of September to photograph the aftermath of the war. You were in the middle of your divorce. Cara was building her orchid business, finishing the second large green-house. And I was photographing her activities for Dad, doing a picture story. Like the one he'd shot of you the year before."

"You know a lot," my sister exclaimed, sounding pleased. "Anything else?"

"I did speak to Dad on the phone, and it *was* a Saturday, I just remembered. I told him the shoot with Cara was going well. And that's about it. Oh, wait, there was one other thing. I did say that I wanted to come with him and Harry the next time they covered a war."

Jessica nodded. "That was it. Your comment to Dad. You hung up, and Mom asked you what you'd meant about covering a war. You told her that you had definitely made your mind up to become a war photographer, and wanted to work with Dad and Harry. To be on the front lines with them. She sort of went crazy, and she was really angry. She said she wouldn't permit it. That she had worried about Dad's safety all of their married life, that she wasn't going to go through hell again, worrying about her youngest daughter getting killed."

I had paid attention to every word Jessica had just uttered, and I really did not recall this outburst. Finally, I said, "I just don't remember that conversation."

Jessica picked up her cup, didn't say anything for a while.

I poured myself another cup of coffee, and glanced out of the window. The sky was beginning to darken over the East River. It looked as if it would be a beautiful night . . . cold clear sky which undoubtedly would be filled with stars.

At last Jessica broke the silence. She said, "What did you do for the rest of that Saturday, Serena?" She stared at me intently.

I shrugged. "I don't know, probably went on taking pictures of Cara doing her stuff with the orchids."

"I can fill you in," Jess said. "I was with you and Mom that morning, on the terrace. Dad rang from Kosovo. I spoke to him, passed the phone to Mom, and she gave it to you, after she finished speaking with him. I was working on my notes, for a catalog I was preparing, when all of a sudden holy hell broke loose. Mom was becoming rather agitated for her. You burst into tears and fled." Jessica paused. "Don't you have any recollection of this?"

"No, I don't. What happened then?"

"You didn't come back for lunch. Later it began to rain hard and there was a thunderstorm. Mom was getting anxious about you, because Cara said she'd seen you on the drive when she was returning from the greenhouses."

"I don't think I left the grounds."

"Mom decided to go and look for you. She found you in your room, and spent the afternoon with you."

"I see. When was everything all right between us?" I asked quietly.

"That same evening. Mom took the three of us out to dinner, and all was tranquil. It was as if nothing had happened."

"I see. I must admit, it really bothers me that I can't remember any of this." I got up, went to sit next to Jessica on the sofa. "You must be right. I guess I did block it out."

"I think so, Pidge." She squeezed my hand. "Well, Mom did eventually relent, didn't she? She let you go off with Dad and Harry to cover a war. You were twenty-one by then."

"We went to Afghanistan. And one day, some years later, again in Kabul, I missed a plane and

56

didn't get back to Nice in time to see Dad before he died." Unexpectedly, tears came into my eyes. I blinked them away, took control of my emotions. Naturally Jessica noticed. She had never missed a trick in her life.

She put her arms around me, consoled me, stroked my hair. But after a few minutes she jumped up, pulled me to my feet, and said briskly, "I bet there's a fresh chicken in the fridge for the weekend, following Stone family tradition."

I laughed. "Of course there is."

"Then let's go and make *poulet grand-père*, the way Lulu taught us. If you've got all the ingredients."

"I do. Except some of them will have to come out of cans."

Lulu, the housekeeper at Jardin des Fleurs, had taught Jessica to cook, and when I was old enough I was allowed to go into the kitchen with her, also to be taught the art of French cooking by Lulu.

Cara never joined us. She was busy in the gardens, which she loved. In fact she was addicted to flowers, plants, and nature. Eventually she became a brilliant horticulturist, and when she was older she specialized in growing orchids.

For the last ten years she had supplied her fantastic exotic orchids to hotels, restaurants, and private clients on the Côte d'Azur, and was renowned.

And so when I was growing up it was just me

and Jessica who stood next to Lulu in the big old-fashioned kitchen. Over the years, the jovial Frenchwoman taught us the basics of French cooking and helped us to hone our skills.

And we learned to prepare many of her specialties, *poulet grand-père* being one of them. It was a simple dish composed of a chicken roasted in a pan in the oven, reclining on a bed of sliced potatoes and chopped carrots, along with mushrooms and tomatoes.

Picking up the tray I followed Jessica out of my office. Once we were in the kitchen, I opened cupboard doors and looked inside. "Canned tomatoes and mushrooms," I announced. "And I know Mrs. Watledge bought potatoes and chicken broth the other day."

"Then we'll be fine." Jessica glanced at her watch. "It's already five, so let's have a glass of wine, shall we?"

"Why not? There's a bottle of Sancerre in the fridge." As I spoke I went to get it, and also took out the chicken, carried both over to the island in the middle of the kitchen.

Jessica opened the wine, and I prepared the chicken, smearing butter all over it and placing half a lemon in the cavity. At one moment I said, "We've been so busy talking about the past, you never told me about your trip to Boston. Do you have a new client?"

"Yes, I do," she replied, and filled two glasses with white wine, handed one to me. "He's a lawyer, you wouldn't know him. His widowed mother just died and left him her fabulous villa in Cap d'Ail, plus a collection of valuable furniture and art. She'd been married to a Frenchman for years. Anyway, my new client is the sole heir, and he just signed with me. Stone's will be holding the auction later this year. It's going to be very special, because of the Art Deco furniture and Post-Impressionist paintings."

"Congratulations!" I said, lifting my glass.

We clinked glasses.

Jessica leaned forward and kissed my cheek. "You're the best sister in the world."

Seven

At last I was in a yellow cab and on my way to meet Harry Redford for dinner. I'd had a difficult day, trying to do my rewrite, and I had given up at the end of the afternoon. Frustrated, I'd put the chapter away until tomorrow; I needed time to think about it some more, and also about the year 1999.

I was glad to leave the apartment. It had been so sad and empty without the joyful, buoyant presence of my sister. Jessica had left this morning, very early, to catch the eight-thirty British Airways flight to London. She had some meetings there before returning to Nice to prepare for her upcoming auctions.

Fortunately, First was not clogged with traffic tonight, which was a big relief, and the cab moved at a good pace up the avenue. I was running late, and the restaurant was way uptown in East Harlem. Harry and I were having dinner at Rao's, which stood on the corner of East 114th Street and Pleasant Avenue.

It had always been my father's and Harry's favorite restaurant in Manhattan. They had started going there in the 1970s, had the same table every Monday night since then, a table which they "owned."

When they were away covering wars, or out of town on other assignments, their families and friends got the chance to use the table, and were thrilled to do so. Over the years, Rao's had acquired a special kind of mystique and glamour, some of this due to the celebrities who often went there, and it was virtually impossible to get a reservation because of the regulars.

Tommy and Harry had become good friends with Vincent Rao and his wife, Anna Pellegrino Rao, over the years, and they were shocked and saddened when Vincent and Annie both died in 1994.

Since then Rao's, owned by the same family for over a hundred years, has been run by Frankie Pellegrino, Annie's nephew, and his cousin Ron

Staci, who both owned it now. It is exactly the same as it has always been . . . warm, welcoming, and fun. Dark wood-paneled walls, permanent Christmas decorations around the bar, pristine white linen cloths, and a jukebox playing softly in the background combine to create a cozy atmosphere.

It was Frankie who greeted me affectionately as I pushed open the door twenty minutes later to be enveloped in a warm blast of fragrant air . . . the mingled smells of traditional Italian cooking. It was exactly seven-thirty, and I wasn't late after all.

Frankie had known me since I was ten, and he gave me a big bear hug, and said, "Welcome, Serena, we've missed you."

After I'd hugged him in return, I said, "I know what you mean, but it's only been two weeks."

"It seems longer," he shot back with a grin, leading me past the open door of the bustling kitchen situated near the front door. We chatted as we walked through the room toward the booth which was ours every Monday night.

Harry was already standing, beaming, as I hurried toward him. "You're a sight for sore eyes!" he exclaimed, kissing me on the cheek, holding me close for a moment. He was always exactly the same, with a warm and pleasant personality, a graciousness that was unique.

We sat down opposite each other in the booth. "Sorry about not joining you for the last couple of weeks," I apologized. "But I really had to isolate myself, to move ahead on the book."

"I know that, Serena, and you don't have to explain or feel badly about it. I've always told you, it's not possible to be a committed writer and a social butterfly. One or the other occupation usually has to go."

He glanced at the package I'd placed on the seat next to my bag. "Is that for me? Are those the first chapters you promised to give me? That you want me to read?"

This was said with great eagerness; I noticed his eyes were bright with anticipation. He was the one person who had encouraged me to write a biography about my father, and actually believed I could do it. He was my biggest booster and always had been. But then I was like the daughter he had never had, and we were close.

I said, "I've brought you the first seven chapters that I think are okay. Those are enough to give you a taste, aren't they?"

"More than enough. I can't wait to get into them."

"I want you to be honest with me, Harry. It's important that you tell me the truth."

"Of course I will," he promised, and ordered two glasses of white wine from one of the genial waiters. Turning back to me, he went on, "It would be unfair if I lied to you, just to please you. Now wouldn't it?"

"Yes," I agreed.

He leaned back against the banquette and nodded approvingly. "You look good, Serena. Very good in fact. Never better."

"Work helps. I've been keeping myself busy with the book, and Jessica cheered me up. It was a lovely surprise when she showed up unexpectedly, out of the blue."

"I'm sorry she couldn't come tonight," he murmured, meaning it. Harry loved Jessica and Cara as well as me.

"She was disappointed not to see you, but she couldn't cancel her meetings in London, and changing her ticket would have been difficult."

"I understood. And I told her this when we spoke on the phone."

The wine arrived and we said cheers in unison as we touched glasses.

As I relaxed and sipped the cold wine, I studied Harry for a few seconds, thinking that he looked fit. He would be sixty-nine this year, yet appeared so much younger. There were not many lines on his face and he was tanned. He had a lean look about him, bright blue eyes, and salt-and-pepper brown hair.

Harry interrupted my thoughts when he said, "I ordered the mixed salad, the roasted peppers you've always loved, pasta pomodoro, and lemon chicken. How does that sound?"

I laughed. "You're just like Tommy; he always ordered far too much."

"Just taste a bit of everything. You can take the rest home if you want, to eat another day, it'll sustain you while you're writing," he suggested in his charming, lovely way.

"Thank you, Harry, but no thanks. I have to be careful these days. I'm sitting at a desk a lot."

"Ah yes, the curse of all writers, Serena," he responded with a laugh.

Leaning across the table, I now said, "I'm trying to remember as much as possible about 1999, Harry. Jessica has given me some of her recollections. What about you? I know you and Dad were in Kosovo, weren't you?"

He was holding his glass of wine, and he stared down into it for a moment or two. When he lifted his head, looked across at me, I saw the bright blue eyes had darkened, were suddenly filled with a hint of sorrow.

At last, he said quietly, "I remember the hell of that particular war. Tommy and I were there from March to June. It was tough, a lousy war. But then all wars are lousy. We were about to get out in May, but changed our minds. We stayed on. The cease-fire came in June, after the NATO and UN intervention, and we finally left. Your father went back to Nice. I came to New York. I'd wrenched my back, helping some desperate women push a broken-down truck, filled with wounded and dying children, to safety. I knew I had to get the best medical treatment, which is why I came back to Manhattan."

"Then you went again to Kosovo in September, didn't you?"

"Yes, we did. Your father thought we should cover the aftermath of the war, and I agreed. We went to Sarajevo as well. Later we flew to Nice for Thanksgiving, as I'm sure you remember."

"I do. During that period, did you hear anything about Mom being angry with me? Upset with me?"

"Elizabeth was disturbed because you wanted to be a war photographer like us. So Tommy told me, anyway."

"That's right, she was. Jessica reminded me on Saturday. And here's the weird thing, Harry. I don't recall this incident. That troubles me a lot."

"You more than likely wiped it out, because you didn't want to remember. It was obviously painful . . . you were so close to your mother, and she adored you, Serena. She was obviously a bit panicked when she thought you were going to go off to the front lines. Because of the danger to you. But Tommy reassured her, and she calmed down eventually."

"And let me go in the end."

He gave me a faint smile. "You'd come of age. You could do what you wanted, and she knew that. Better to acquiesce than throw a fit. And we promised her we'd look after you. Make sure you were safe at all times. And *I* had to call her every day, as well as Tommy."

Before I got a chance to respond, plates of delicious-looking food started to arrive, along with a bottle of white wine.

"Come on, take some of the red peppers," Harry said, smiling encouragingly as he helped himself to the salad. I did as he suggested, and as we ate we chatted about other things, and in particular Global Images.

"There's something I need to talk to you about," Harry suddenly said a short while later, after we'd eaten the main course. "Something important."

His voice was normal but his expression had turned very serious and there was that worried look in his eyes, a look I knew. "What is it? Is there something wrong?"

"Sort of . . ." His voice trailed off, he took a sip of wine, and stared off into the distance for a moment.

"Harry, please tell me. Tell me what's wrong."

He took hold of my hand resting on the table, clasped it, gave me a penetrating look. "When you told me you wanted to write a biography about Tommy, do you remember what else you said?"

"I said I wanted to write it because I needed to honor my father. Is that what you mean?"

"Yeah, I do. Now I want you to do something else to honor your father."

"What?"

"Let me explain something first. Years ago your father came and got me out of Bosnia. He'd left before me, because Elizabeth was sick and she needed him. I'd stayed on, and then I just wouldn't leave, even though I should have. He came and took me out . . . *forced* me to come out before—"

"You want me to get somebody out of a war zone, a danger zone," I interrupted, my voice rising slightly. I stared at him intently, felt a chill running right through me as it suddenly hit me where this was leading. "You want me to go and get Zac. This is about Zac North, isn't it, Harry?" Before he even responded I knew it was.

He took a deep breath, squeezed my hand tighter. "It is. But I don't need you to get him out of Afghanistan. He's out—"

"If he's out, then he's safe," I exclaimed, cutting in again.

Harry nodded in agreement, then continued, "But he's in very bad shape, Serena. On his last legs, strained, exhausted, anxiety-ridden. I sent Geoff Barnes in from Pakistan to get him out, and he did manage it. But Geoff says Zac's in a deep depression, not well, in need of care. He thinks Zac is at an emotional low. As he put it, Zac's a dead man walking."

"Where is Zac now?" As the words left my mouth I knew exactly where he was. I exclaimed, "He's in the bolthole, isn't he?"

Harry nodded, his eyes still clouded with worry.

I blew out air, shook my head. "I can't go. I don't want to go. Besides which, he'll bang the door in my face the moment he sees me. We haven't spoken for eleven months."

"He won't do that, Serena. I promise you. It was Zac who asked for you. He said there was no one else who could do it, who could help him."

"He's got a family on Long Island, Harry. And you know that. Parents, a sister, a brother."

"They can't help him . . . he needs someone who's been there, who knows about war, who's suffered through it, lived through the sheer hell of it, seen the death, the blood, the devastation . . ." His voice trailed off, and he sighed.

"I can't go. I just can't," I said, my voice tearful, wobbling. "That row we had in Nice after Dad's funeral was horrendous. He was so violent verbally. Angry. I'm sorry, Harry, but I still blame him. It was Zac's fault we missed the plane from Kabul. And all because he wanted to get a few last pictures."

"I'm sorry, too, honey, I shouldn't have even asked you to do it. That was very stupid on my part. You don't need this right now." He took hold of my hand again. "I'll think of something, talk it through with Geoff Barnes, come up with a solution."

I nodded, bit my lip. "Let me think about it," I murmured against my better judgment. "Let me sleep on it."

Harry was silent for a moment, staring at me. Then he said in a low voice, "No, honey, I don't want you to go. It was wrong of me to suggest it, to load this responsibility on you. It's my problem, and I'll solve it."

Much later that evening, back at the apartment, I discovered I could not sleep. Nor could I think straight. I was far too agitated and distressed about Zac, and about myself and my reaction to Harry's request.

Zachary North needed me and I'd said I wouldn't go and help him. And yet he was the only man I'd ever been in love with, and whom I would always love in a certain way. Even though he had broken my heart.

I was aware, deep within myself, that Harry really did want me to go to Zac's aid, otherwise he wouldn't have asked in the first place. He had changed his mind when he had seen my reaction and my reluctance.

My father would certainly want me to go, I knew that without a doubt . . . because of the camaraderie, the dependency, and the loyalty that war photographers shared. They were always there for each other. But I couldn't go, because I was afraid of Zac, the effect he had on me.

I was afraid of my own emotions. But I should go. I would go.

Part Two

PERSONAL CLOSE-UPS
Venice, April

There is nothing new except for
what is forgotten.
--—Attributed to Mademoiselle Bertin,
milliner to Marie Antoinette

Only I discern
Infinite passion, and the pain
Of finite hearts that yearn.
—Robert Browning:
"Two in the Campagna"

Eight

I had been wrong to refuse Harry, who had actually spoken the truth when he had said I was the only person who could help Zac, because I was accustomed to wars, knew what they did to those who lived in the middle of them on a regular basis.

Zac's family couldn't help, no one could except another veteran of wars . . . another photo-journalist.

And that was me.

And so I went.

I put aside my qualms and fears, packed my carry-on, and took a night flight to Italy on Wednesday afternoon. Alitalia at 5:30 P.M. out of JFK, with a layover in Rome the following morning. I would be arriving in Venice at 11:25 A.M. European time.

I glanced at my watch, which I had changed to local time before dozing off during the night. It was exactly five minutes to eleven. Another fifty minutes of flying and I would be there.

My plane would touch down at Marco Polo airport, where Geoff Barnes would be waiting for me. He would tell me as much as he could, as much as he knew, and then I would be on my own.

Harry had reassured me that Geoff would stay on for a few days if needs be, and if I thought it

73

was absolutely necessary. Once I knew I could manage alone, Geoff would hightail it back to Pakistan.

I was relieved he did not have to go to the badlands of Helmand Province in Afghanistan in Zac's stead. No one should have to be there anymore; it was an intolerable place. The Taliban was everywhere, intent on slaughter.

I told Harry that if Geoff did stay in Venice for longer than a couple of days, he would have to move out of the bolthole and into the Bauer Hotel. The bolthole was too small, especially since I would be dealing with Zac . . . a Zac in great distress. Harry had agreed with me that this was the only way to go.

The bolthole. I knew it well, had stayed there a number of times with my father and Harry, and with my parents. And also with Zac on numerous occasions. It was a medium-sized apartment which Tommy and Harry had found in 1982.

They had rented it for several years from Louisa Pignatelli, the woman who owned the small building located just behind the Piazza San Marco, and who lived on the floor below.

Global had bought the apartment from her in 1987, because it was such a useful "stop-off" place for photographers constantly on the move, like Tommy and Harry and others working for Global.

Venice was the perfect city, the key city, because

it was so strategically placed, right in the middle of a cluster of European countries and a stone's throw away from the Balkans just across the Adriatic Sea. It was in a direct flight path to Istanbul, countries of the Middle East, and Africa. Venice was considered to be the best link between East and West by those who circulated in and around this area of the world.

The bolthole served as a welcome resting place for all of the Global guys, who often wanted to touch down after grueling months in a war. They needed to recuperate, did not always have time to get to home base before taking off on another assignment.

Although it was not large, the apartment was adequate, and quite comfortable. There were three small bedrooms, two bathrooms, a little galley kitchen, and a living room. After they had bought the apartment my father and Harry had been smart, had furnished it simply, but with comfortable sofas and chairs, a table and chairs for meals, and, of course, television sets, which were always on for continuing world news.

When there was no one from Global staying at the apartment, Claudia, Louisa's daughter, had it thoroughly cleaned and made sure all the bed linen went to the laundry. She diligently watched over the place with an eagle eye, and took care of it in general.

I had spoken to Geoff yesterday, and he had

assured me he would be outside customs waiting for me. I knew Geoff well and he was reliable. I'd had to depend on him in the past and he'd never let me down yet. I trusted him to tell me the truth, and I knew he would level with me about Zac.

Last night, as I had settled down in this seat after dinner, I'd tried to fall asleep without success. My mind kept zeroing in on Zac.

I first met him when he had come to work for my father and Harry at Global. I was nineteen and he was twenty-six, and I didn't like him at all.

He was bumptious, conceited, and full of himself, or so I thought. Certainly that day he had been strutting around the New York office, showing off because he'd just won some award. This was in the spring of 2000. We didn't meet again until later that summer, when he came to stay at the house in Nice, much to my dismay.

However, I was pleasantly surprised. He was a different person altogether, warm, disarming, very friendly, and extremely funny. He had a great sense of humor, and poked fun at himself in a most self-deprecating way that kept me laughing.

He stayed with us for several days and in that time I fell head over heels in love with him and he with me. It was a mutual meeting of the minds, and we were on the same wavelength, although we did not link up with each other for some time.

It became serious in 2004. I was twenty-three,

Zac was thirty, seven years older than me and much more experienced in every way.

It was a passionate affair, and romantic. It was also a bumpy ride at times. But we made it together for six years. Our breakup had been at the edge of violence, verbal violence at least. Zac had a temper. A nasty temper. It had alarmed me, frightened me. I knew he was the love of my life and yet I was certain it would never work. I hadn't spoken to him for almost a year.

Now I was on my way to help make him well again, if I could. I sensed I had quite a task ahead of me. And I wasn't sure I would succeed.

Nine

I passed through passport control and customs very quickly, and as I went out of the restricted area I spotted Geoff immediately. He was a Californian, tall and lanky, with streaky blond hair and a tan. Because of his height he was easily visible amongst the small group of people who were waiting for other passengers in the arrivals hall.

Waving to him, I moved forward, dragging my carry-on, and within a few seconds we were greeting each other with a warm hug.

"Hi, Serena, I'm glad you're here," he said as he took my case, rolling it along next to him, guiding me toward the exit. "Did you have a good flight? Get some sleep?"

"I only dozed." I looked up at him worriedly. "How is he, Geoff? How is Zac really?"

"Not good, honey, but maybe not as bad as you're probably imagining. No wounds, but he's done in, exhausted, fucked out, to be truthful. Not suicidal though, and I told Harry that. But listen, kid, he is very depressed, so silent. He hardly says a word."

Geoff paused, threw me an odd look before continuing in a worried tone, "I don't think he has the strength to speak. That might sound weird, but he won't eat, he doesn't sleep. He's badly in need of your care, I know that. And he did ask Harry to get you to come here."

Geoff's words troubled me. I swallowed. My mouth was dry. Finally, I managed to say, "Do you think he should be in a hospital?"

"I sure as hell do, but you won't get him to agree. I couldn't. Neither could Harry, when he spoke to him on the phone. I guess you'll just have to get him on his feet and back to health in the bolthole. Because he won't move from there. I gotta tell you, that's a given."

"I understand," I answered, but I was filled with dismay. I cleared my throat. "He can be very stubborn. How do you get somebody to eat? To drink—" I cut myself off as a thought struck me, and I looked up at Geoff, asked swiftly, "He's not dehydrated, is he?"

"I don't think so, he has been sipping from the

bottles of water I've given him." Geoff shrugged. "You can only make a proper judgment when you see him."

I was more alarmed than ever and telling myself not to panic. Yet I did feel a sense of panic and anxiety, even a hint of fear.

Geoff and I walked out of the exit door of the arrivals building, and he led me toward the private water taxi stands. "That's ours," he said, and indicated one of the motorboats. "I came over on it, had the guy wait. He'll take us to the Piazza San Marco."

I nodded, glanced around.

It was a gray day, the sky murky, laden with bloated clouds, and there was a hint of rain in the air. But then March and April were the rainy months in Venice.

I was glad to be off the plane and breathing fresh air, and it *was* fresh, much cooler than I had expected. I loved Venice, had come here often with my parents and sisters, and we had always had the best times.

Still, I didn't have that sense of excitement I usually had when I arrived in this ancient, beautiful city of light and water. And I knew at once this was because of my mission, the task ahead of me.

For a moment, I wished I hadn't come, and then immediately chided myself for being so apprehensive and cowardly. I could handle this, I could get Zac better, there was no doubt in my mind about that.

Well, there was just a little bit of doubt, but I was now going to stamp on it, grind it under my foot. I was going to be positive and determined, just like Jessica was when she had a challenge to meet.

The owner of the water taxi held out his hand, guided me onto the boat. I forced a smile, thanked him as he helped me down the steps and into the large cabin. A moment later Geoff was ducking his head, coming inside after me, taking the seat opposite.

The driver began to back out, edging his way into open water, maneuvering the boat skillfully, as all of these Venetians seemed able to do with their eyes closed. Staring at Geoff, I asked, "What about the food situation at the bolthole? Did you manage to go out and buy anything?"

He gave me a look that verged on the scornful, and exclaimed, "This ain't my first rodeo, lady. What do you take me for, a greenhorn?"

Geoff laughed as he said this with a mock cowboy twang, and I laughed with him.

"No, it ain't your first rodeo, I know that, pal, but I figured you'd been a tad busy since you got here," I retorted.

"I have stocked up. Claudia stayed with Zac, had coffee with him the day after we arrived, and I went out to the market, picked up lots of items, per Harry's instructions."

"What did you buy?" I asked.

"Pastas, canned stuff, lots of fresh fruits and vegetables, the kind of things you like to make soup with, again per Harry's advice. And Claudia did the rounds for me early this morning, bought fresh bread, cheese, butter, milk, oh, and two chickens and chicken bouillon for your soup."

"My famous chicken-in-the-pot," I muttered almost to myself, and then remembered how much Zac liked it. I focused on Geoff again, and added, "Thanks for doing the shopping, I'm grateful."

"My pleasure. I also want you to know that I've booked myself into the Bauer Hotel, moved my junk over there already. You must be alone with Zac. You'll succeed much better without me hovering over the two of you. And if there's any sort of emergency, I can be there real quick, and there's also Claudia downstairs."

"Oh," I said. "Oh, okay, that's fine." But was it? I wondered.

"Don't sound so concerned, Serena, you'll see, he'll respond to you better than he has to me." He leaned forward, focused his intelligent gray eyes on me. "It's you he wants with him, you he depends on, you he needs."

I made no response, just gazed at him.

Geoff exclaimed, "Hey, I'm not copping out, don't think that! I really believe it's better that I'm out of the way. He's still in love with you, take my word for it, and once you're there, he'll become calm."

"Isn't he calm?" I asked anxiously, envisioning a rampant Zac, angry and upset the way he'd been when we'd broken up eleven months ago. "Is he agitated? Excited? What state is he in?"

"None of those you've mentioned. He's . . . well, sort of nervous, moves around a lot, doesn't seem able to sit still for long. Goes from one room to the next. But he's not yelling and shouting, nothing like that. I told you, he doesn't speak much. He's very closed in. Remote, very distant, as if he's in another world."

Oh God, I thought, perhaps he's in catatonic shock. Some kind of shock, anyway. Why isn't he talking to Geoff? They've been through a lot together, they're war buddies, veterans of battle on the front line. Which is why Harry sent him to get Zac out. What am I going to do for him? How can I bring him back? Get him to be more normal? And how will I get him to eat and sleep?

Geoff must have read something in my expression, the look in my eyes, and he reached out, put his hand on my knee, said in a low, reassuring voice, "You'll be fine, honey, stop chewing it over. Zac needs *you,* and you'll succeed where nobody else could."

"I hope so," I sighed, shook my head. "I'll give it a try."

"Your very best bloody try," Geoff asserted and squeezed my hand.

The water taxi dropped us off at the jetty near the Piazza San Marco, and we walked across the piazza slowly and in silence.

We were both lost in our own thoughts. I was recalling the times I had come here in the past, such happy times with my family, or with Zac, the two of us alone. Often I had been here in the height of the summer when the piazza was jammed with tourists from all over the world. But this was not the tourist season and it was less crowded on this chilly April morning.

There were some people moving ahead of us, heading for the shops on the Frezzeria or Florian and Quadri *caffès*. Other tourists were sitting at the small tables in the square, watching the passersby and the pigeons fluttering around or gazing at the magnificent Basilica di San Marco, marveling at its beauty and whiling away the morning until lunchtime.

Geoff and I headed for a far corner of the piazza and the narrow cobbled street where the bolthole was located. Unexpectedly, Geoff came to a sudden standstill and turned to me, taking hold of my arm. "Listen," he exclaimed, "I forgot to tell you one thing. I must warn—"

"About what?" I asked, cutting across him.

"Zac and television. He has all the sets on at

the same time on different networks. And he's watching them constantly." He grimaced. "He's watching one or the other, night and day, and he gets furious if you try to turn one off. So don't do it. Humor him, okay?"

I nodded. "What's he watching?" I asked, and knew the answer before Geoff spoke.

"War coverage, of course. General news. But mostly war coverage. He's addicted to war, Serena."

"I know that," I said. My voice was a whisper.

We reached the building and went up to the third floor in the small, rather narrow elevator. When we got to the door of the bolthole I stood staring at it. Geoff was staring at me. Waiting.

Finally I said, "Okay." I took a deep breath, added, "I'm okay. Let's go in."

Ten

Noise from the various television sets bounced off the walls of the apartment, but when Zac saw me standing in the doorway he immediately turned off the one in the living room and got up out of the chair. The other TVs in the bedrooms continued to drone on, but they were at least muted to a certain degree, created only background noise.

I put my handbag on the table, shrugged out of my pea jacket, draped it around a chair back, walked toward Zac. He had remained standing near the TV, had not moved, and his eyes were riveted on me.

To say I was shocked by his appearance would be an understatement. I was appalled. He had lost a great deal of weight, which somehow made him look taller, and his face was gaunt. I could see that quite clearly even though he had a lot of stubble, had obviously not shaved for days on end. His brown hair had lost its luster, looked gray, and strangely dusty, and there was an air of exhaustion about him. He appeared diminished; even his green eyes were dulled, had lost their sparkle, and his mouth was pinched.

As I walked forward he came toward me, and a moment later my arms went around him. I held him close. He was so thin I could feel his bones through his shirt, and my heart ached for him, for his suffering. A split second later I experienced such a rush of love and tenderness I was startled at myself.

War had taken its horrendous toll on him, and I knew I must make him better, bring him back to life, to what he had been before. Whether there would be a future for us I did not know, nor did it matter at this moment. What I wanted was to get him well, no matter what. That was my aim, and my reason for being here.

Releasing him, I took a step away, turning my head. His clothes were dirty and they smelled.

And so did he. Taking several deep breaths, I said, "Harry sent me."

"I asked him to," Zac replied. "Thank God you came."

A few seconds earlier, out of the corner of my eye, I had noticed Geoff rolling my suitcase into one of the bedrooms, and now he suddenly reappeared, came to join us in the middle of the room.

"How about coffee?" he asked genially, looking from me to Zac. "I could use it."

We both nodded, and I said, "With milk and sweetener, please, Geoff."

"Coming right up," he answered, and walked off into the kitchen.

Taking hold of Zac's hand, I led him to the big overstuffed sofa, and we sat down. I couldn't quite make out the expression on his face . . . I didn't know if it was one of longing, weariness, or pain, and then almost immediately his face crumpled. He started to cry. He brought his hands to his face as he wept.

After a moment he took control of himself again, and wiped the tears away with his fingertips, shook his head, looking regretful.

"I'm sorry, I didn't mean to break down, Pidge," he apologized, using Jessica's nickname for me, the only other person allowed to do so.

"It's all right, it's all right." Moving closer, I put my arms around him, wanting to console him, but instantly drew back, again almost gagging. One thing was certain, I had to get him out of these filthy clothes and into a shower as soon as possible.

Now my eyes roamed around the room. His cameras were on the table, his flak jacket laid on a chair, his holdall on the floor nearby. He was all set and ready to roll, to hightail it back to another war, wherever the hell it was, I thought dismally. He'd even go back to Afghanistan, the most hellish place on earth. The smell of cordite, blood and sweat, exploding roadside bombs, Marines being killed relentlessly. A foul battleground.

He was addicted to war, the adrenaline rush, as so many of us were. I had been, but had managed to extract myself from the front line before it was too late, as my father had before me, and Harry as well.

If you didn't get out you were burned to a shred like Zac was now. Ashes to ashes. Dust to dust, I thought, and shivered involuntarily.

Geoff brought out mugs of coffee and handed them to Zac and me, returned to get his own. When he came back he was carrying his mug and a plate of cookies, which he put down on the coffee table.

We drank our coffee in silence. Finally, I said quietly, "As soon as you're up to it, Zac, I want you to have a bath, or a shower, whichever you prefer."

He threw me a swift glance, and all of a sudden there was a stubborn set to his mouth. He said, "Tomorrow's fine."

"No, it isn't," I answered in the most business-like tone I could muster. "Your clothes stink, and so do you. No cleanup, no Serena. I'll check in to the Bauer . . . where nobody smells."

"That bad, is it?" he said, and glared at me.

"I'll say! And now that I'm here, and only at Harry's behest, remember, you'll have to live by my rules."

"I see."

"I hope you do." I rose. "Shall I run a bath, or will you take a shower?"

He slumped down into the cushions on the sofa, a morose expression settling on his face. He was unresponsive. Leaning his head against the pillows, he closed his eyes, ignoring me.

I decided, in that instant, that the only way to deal with Zac and get him back on his feet and healthy was for me to get tough and stay tough. If I showed any weakness he would endeavor to manipulate me. And he was good at manipulation, as I knew only too well.

Being tough was necessary, but I also had to use the threat of leaving. That would frighten him into submission, persuade him to do what I wanted. I knew he truly needed me at this particular time, otherwise he wouldn't have buried his pride and asked Harry to ask me to come here.

Geoff looked at Zac, then across at me, and raised a brow.

Making a decision, I said, "I'm glad I didn't unpack, Geoff. Come on, let's get my bag and go to the Bauer. I'm hungry, so I'll check in there, and then we can have lunch on the terrace."

"A shower," Zac announced from the depths of the huge sofa. "A shower's easier right now." As he was speaking he pushed himself to his feet. I thought he looked slightly groggy.

I watched him walk across the room, and I realized he was limping. That old shrapnel wound from years ago was more than likely acting up. "Do you need help?" I called after him.

"No," he grunted and went into the bathroom he was using, banging the door behind him.

I turned around, and said to Geoff, "That's a relief. His clothes stink. Why didn't you warn me?"

Geoff looked at me askance. "And frighten you off? No way, kid. Anyway, I can only say that he cheered up the moment he saw you. I think he's trying to behave as normally as possible. Obviously he doesn't want you to leave. Sometimes at night—" Geoff cut himself off, and sat down again in one of the armchairs.

"What is it he does at night?" I asked, taking the chair opposite, staring at him, wondering if Zac was suffering from nightmares or flashbacks. More than likely he was.

"He has bad dreams, Serena, so be prepared. He shouts and screams and calls your name quite a lot . . . sometimes he's yelling for Serena, sometimes he uses the nickname Jessica gave you . . . *Pidge.*" Geoff now gave me a thoughtful look, then frowned. "What does that mean, Serena? Pidge is an unusual name."

I sighed, staring back at Geoff without speaking. I had always been secretive about Jessica's nickname for me, why I'll never really understand.

"Go on, tell me," Geoff encouraged, obviously riddled with curiosity.

Suddenly I made my mind up to tell him. He was intrigued, wanted to know, and I was grateful to him for risking his life by going to Helmand Province to get Zac out of that highly dangerous zone.

"I've never told anybody, not even Zac knows," I explained. "I'm going to tell you though, but you must keep it a secret."

"I will. Go on then, tell me. I'm all ears. I really wanna know."

"When I was little, Jessica started to call me Smidge. That comes from the word 'smidgen,' which means a small portion, a little bit . . . I was a *little bit* to her. She used it affectionately, but I hated that name and objected most voraciously. So at my request she dropped it, started to call me Pidge, which is short for 'pigeon.' She told me she chose it because a pigeon is a small chirping bird, just like me. But keep it quiet, okay?"

"I will," Geoff answered. "I'm flattered you told me, although I don't know why it's such a big secret. It's not such a bad nickname."

I smiled at him warmly. I liked Geoff and he had been a good friend to me over the years. "Little girls like to have secrets, you know . . . and I've maintained the secret over the years."

He smiled back, winked. "I get it, and your secret is safe with *moi*. But about Zac, he's improved already. I think he has relaxed because he feels safe with you here. I'm beginning to feel optimistic about his recovery."

I sat back in the chair, brought my hand to my mouth, reflecting on what he had just said. I knew Geoff was correct in one thing—Zac *had* relaxed as soon as he saw me, and he was talking, if only in short takes. But he wasn't the same Zac. He *was* diminished and there was a fragility about him; immense sorrow was reflected in his eyes. He'd seen so much, far too much over the years, and he was drowning in pain. His behavior was calm on the surface, but I recognized he was extremely stressed inside. Hence the bad dreams Geoff had referred to, and which hadn't surprised me.

"What's worrying you, Serena?" Geoff asked, breaking into my troubled thoughts.

I wanted to be honest with Geoff, so I told him the truth. "I'm pleased you're optimistic, and that you see a change in him because I'm here. Still, I do think he's very stressed out, on the edge, filled with anxiety."

"He is, but I feel easier about leaving you here alone with him."

"I'm comfortable being around Zac, Geoff. I'm not very big, but I can defend myself if he suddenly goes nuts." I realized how droll I sounded, and despite the seriousness of the matter, I couldn't help laughing.

Geoff grinned, and shot back, "You could blow him over with a few puffs, he's so weak."

"Not quite. But he does seem docile. I know he's a bit grumpy, doesn't want to bestir himself, but that's exhaustion, isn't it?"

"It is, yes. As I told you, he hasn't slept since I brought him out. Once he's cleaned up, you might be able to get some food into him, some of your chicken-in-the-pot. And a bit of food in his belly will help him to sleep. Food and sleep, that's what he needs right now."

"I'm going to start preparing my chicken-in-the-pot," I announced and stood up.

Geoff followed me out to the kitchen, explaining, "Let me show you where I dumped all the food."

Eleven

When I brought Zac to the bolthole for the first time, we had used this bedroom because it was the one my parents used, and my favorite. He had glanced around with interest, and made a remark about how much my parents were in love and yet slept in twin beds. He obviously thought this was strange.

There was a Stone rule: We didn't discuss private family matters with outsiders. But I do remember now that I had been oddly embarrassed that day, had felt obliged to explain the reason to Zac. And so I confided that my mother had had a rare form of osteoporosis, which necessitated that she sleep in a single bed for her comfort.

He had been sensitive enough not to ask any further questions, and I had not volunteered any more information. I did not wish to go into personal details about my mother's health. I felt that simple explanation was enough.

Ever since that first visit together we had continued to use my late parents' bedroom. In any case, the two others were also furnished with twin beds. Essentially, the bolthole was maintained for Global photographers and photojournalists, so that they could get a bit of much-needed R & R, and was not for romantic interludes.

Tonight the room was still, quiet, and nothing

stirred except the flimsy white curtains flapping against the glass. I'd opened the window earlier to let in fresh air, and a breeze had blown up.

I was wide awake and listening attentively. I sensed Zac was awake as well. I was hoping he would eventually fall asleep, knowing I was here with him. Earlier this evening, I'd managed to get him to sip some of the soup and eat a bit of the chicken, although not enough to satisfy me. At least his stomach was not entirely empty.

What did please me was his cleanliness. He had showered, shampooed his hair, and thankfully it was now his natural glossy brown again, and not that strange dusty-gray color. It was long, but that was of no concern. He had even shaved, had nicked himself with the razor, but he had made the effort. After his shower, he'd put on a pair of Harry's pajamas and a terrycloth robe, which Geoff had found for him.

After Geoff had gone off to the Bauer Hotel, I pottered around in the kitchen, watched my chicken bubbling, called Harry to report in, then spoke to Claudia downstairs, to say hello and thank her. After that, I unpacked my bag. For the remainder of the day, and the evening, Zac was glued to the TV, but he kept the sound low, and he seemed calm, and much less uptight.

Instinctively, I knew it was best to keep everything as normal as possible, low-key, with no pressure of any kind. By allowing Zac to be himself, to do whatever he wanted, he would feel more natural and at ease.

And it worked. He had begun to speak a little, although he did not say very much, and I chatted back casually, avoided asking any questions. Harry had warned me not to probe, just to accept that he had come out of Helmand Province because he was tired, weary of being on the front line in Afghanistan.

Eventually my eyelids began to droop, but I wanted to stay awake for as long as possible, to be there for Zac. And so I began to make a mental list of things to do tomorrow.

I must call Harry twice, morning and evening, that was mandatory. He insisted on knowing what was happening with Zac, and, just as importantly, how I was coping.

I had to let Jessica know where I was, and what I was doing. That was also mandatory, another Stone rule. We must know each other's where-abouts. Dad had drilled that into us. And I *must* speak to my other sister, Cara. Not only about Dad's pictures of Mom, but about the dummy of the photographic book she had recently found, one which my father had started but not finished.

Cara. My mind focused on her. She called herself the middle sister, because Jessica had been born first; she had been the second twin to pop out ten minutes later.

It was Cara who had explained our mother's

bone condition to me, when I was old enough to understand. What Mom actually had was osteoporosis, usually considered an old woman's disease. Our mother had a rare form of it, and this had been triggered by her pregnancy, which is when a woman's bone density drops, and especially if she breastfeeds.

Mom was thirty-four when the twins were born, and she had breastfed them. Also, she had low peak bone mass to begin with, her doctors had told her at the time, and this had not helped.

Cara had gone on to explain that when I was born, eight years later, Mom's condition was under control, thanks to medication, although she was not permitted to breastfeed me.

I was grateful that Cara enlightened me about tricky or complicated family matters. She usually plowed ahead, even if she thought it was something I might not want to hear, and told me the truth. She always said it the way it was.

She was very matter-of-fact, pragmatic by nature, and slightly more reserved than Jess. They looked alike, resembled Dad, and she shared Jessica's dark and glowing beauty.

I loved Cara, just as I did Jess. She made me laugh a lot, and this was because of her pithy observations, often about people we knew, and her frequently caustic comments about life in general.

As a child, Cara had spent a lot of time with our

grandmother, my mother's mother, Alice Vasson. She was the only grandmother we had. Our father's parents, David and Greta Stone, had died long before we girls were born.

Granny Alice had a repertoire of old sayings to suit almost every situation; Cara had picked them up when she was little, had kept using them ever since, and they were now part of her vocabulary. Her three favorites were: "That's going to put the cat among the pigeons"; "I'll be there before you can say Jack Robinson"; "Waste not want not." That last saying I often threw back at Cara, because she was no more thrifty than Jessica and I were.

It struck me that perhaps I had failed Cara, in a certain sense. I hadn't been around enough for her after Dad died; she and Jessica had suffered as I had, and had been grief-stricken as well, and I'd been nursing my wounds and my guilt in New York when I should have been with them.

Cara, in particular, was vulnerable these days because of her fiancé's death two years ago. Jules Nollet had been killed in a skiing accident when they were on vacation in the French Alps. And that was the reason I believed Cara was frequently depressed. Jessica agreed with me. All Cara did these days was work in her orchid business. My thoughts ran on and on about Cara. I worried about her . . .

I must have fallen asleep. Suddenly, I awakened with a start.

Zac was calling, "Serena, Serena!"

I struggled up, threw the bedclothes back, and jumped out of bed, rushed over to him. "What is it? What's wrong?"

"I'm cold. *Freezing.*"

Turning on the bedside lamp, I looked down at him. His face was chalk white, his eyes red-rimmed, and he was shaking uncontrollably, huddled under the duvet.

Immediately, I pulled the duvet off my bed and laid it on top of him, then ran and closed the window. I pulled open a drawer in the chest, found two hot-water bottles, as I knew I would, and a pair of thick wool bed socks. Our mother believed in them, made all of us wear them when we were growing up, and there was a drawerful here, bought by her years ago.

After untucking the sheets at the bottom of Zac's bed, I managed somehow to pull the socks onto his feet, which were icy. Picking up the hot-water bottles I went to the kitchen, put on a kettle of water to boil, ran back to the bedroom. "Are you feeling warmer?" I asked, bending over him in concern.

"No," he mumbled, and I noticed that he was still shaking.

I was alarmed and a little frightened. Was he

coming down with an illness? Or was this a manifestation of his exhaustion and lack of food? He was also stressed out and filled with anxiety, not in good shape at all. I hovered over him, uncertain about what to do to help him, other than get his body temperature back to normal.

The whistling kettle pulled me into the kitchen, and after filling the hot-water bottles I returned to the bedroom. I placed one close to his chest, the other against his back. "The hot-water bottles will help, you'll soon be warmer," I murmured.

He grunted something unintelligible.

I remained at the bedside, wondering what else would help him. Then I suddenly remembered there was nothing like another person's body heat to warm someone who was freezing cold. I went to the other side of the bed, got in, lay close to his back, and put my arms around him. With a little maneuvering, I managed to put my body partially on top of his, hoping my body heat would do the trick.

He continued to shiver for a while, but then slowly and very gradually the shivering became less and less. I remained on top of him, my arms holding him until he finally dozed off.

Not much time elapsed before he was breathing deeply and evenly. Finally I got out of his bed, went and turned off the lamp, praying that he would sleep through the night.

• • •

To my relief he did. When I woke up just before seven the next morning Zac was still sleeping soundly. Slipping into my robe, I let myself out of the bedroom quietly, and went to the kitchen, where I made a pot of coffee, scrambled eggs, and toast.

Carrying the tray back to the living room, I took it over to the table at the far end of the room, and began to eat.

My mind was focused on Zac and his life. I realized that he had met Harry and my father in 1999 . . . there was that year again. They were all in Kosovo in September and naturally he knew who they were, was in awe of them, he told me later. Harry and Tommy took a shine to the young photographer, and he became, over time, Harry's protégé. He was given a job at Global in 2000 and had become the star photographer over the years.

He was not a novice when it came to war, I thought now, sipping my coffee. He'd already done a lot, seen a lot of bloodshed and devastation on the front lines all over the world by the time he met Dad and Harry. He was a young veteran meeting old veterans . . . two men who had had more than their fair share of luck when it came to survival.

Tommy and Harry had become war photographers in the early 1960s, and neither of them had ever taken a hit, nor been wounded. What luck, I thought, and I was unexpectedly rather pleased that my father had died in his own bed, and not covering a war.

If he'd had to die, at that moment in time, he had done so in the best place of all, with two of his daughters with him.

I was finishing my scrambled eggs when Zac suddenly appeared, bundled up in the terrycloth robe, looking rumpled. "Hi, Serena," he said in a slightly hoarse voice, and paused near the kitchen door. "I'll get a mug of coffee."

"Hi," I answered. "Do you want me to make you some eggs?"

"Not sure," he mumbled, and disappeared into the kitchen.

A moment later he sat down at the table opposite me with his coffee. "Thank you," he said, staring across at me, "for last night." He cleared his throat several times, then went on, "I don't know what was wrong with me, but I was icy cold. I've never experienced anything like it before."

"You were freezing. I must admit I was worried. But I managed to get you warmed up." I studied him for a moment, noting that he did look more rested, and his face was less taut. I added, "In my opinion, what you had was some kind of reaction to exhaustion and lack of nourishment. That's why you should try and eat a little of something, Zac."

He nodded. "Maybe scrambled eggs then?" he asked hesitantly. "If it's not too much trouble."

"Not at all," I answered, rising, taking my plate, and heading for the kitchen. "Back in a minute," I called over my shoulder.

I couldn't help smiling wryly to myself, as I set about beating four eggs in a bowl. *If it's not too much trouble,* he'd said, after asking me to come all the way from New York to take care of him.

As I returned to the living room, with his eggs and toast on a plate, I noticed that he had not turned on the television set. Silence is golden, I thought, well pleased that the room was quiet and peaceful.

He ate half the eggs and a little bread, and drank the coffee, but he didn't say much, still appeared somewhat remote, cut off from me. At least his body was relaxed, and he was totally calm if uncommunicative.

I made a little conversation. I told him about Jessica's new client, her trip to New York to see me, and mentioned that I was making progress on the book. He listened, nodded, and even smiled several times, made a few noncommittal comments.

He was not the Zac of old, the intense, passionate, talkative photojournalist with an opinion about everything and a great sense of humor. He was toned down, a little out of it, listless, I decided, preoccupied even. On the other hand, he was in control of himself, and that was the most important thing of all.

Give it time, I told myself. You've only been with him for a day and a night, for God's sake. Every day he'll improve, and he'll soon be his old self.

How wrong I was. I had no way of knowing that morning that trouble was on its way.

Twelve

"Do you mean you're not going back to Pakistan this week, or never ever going back?" I asked Geoff, frowning as I stared at him, puzzled by his statement of a moment ago.

"Never going back, honey. Yep, I'm outta there, and I told Harry I wanna stay out. No two ways about it, Serena, I've had it."

"I understand," I said, genuinely meaning this. "There comes a moment when enough's enough. I felt like that last year, I knew I had to quit the front lines. I lost my nerve. I'm sure of that. And when that happens you've no alternative."

Geoff nodded, was silent for a moment, sipping his iced tea, his eyes reflective as he glanced around.

We were sitting on the terrace of the Bauer Palazzo hotel, overlooking the private dock and the Grand Canal. It was Tuesday morning and I had been in Venice for five days.

Earlier, I had taken Zac to the barber's shop, the one which Tommy and Harry had used whenever they were in Venice, because he had decided he needed his hair cut this morning. A good sign, I thought, and I had called Geoff, suggesting we all have lunch once Zac was finished.

Geoff had been agreeable, and suggested we meet here at the old Bauer Palazzo, which was next door to the more modern Bauer Hotel, where he was staying.

As we sat here together enjoying being outside on the sunny morning, I was feeling relaxed. Zac had been relatively normal, not his old self yet, but not manic, nor agitated in any way. Also, much to my relief, he was eating every day. Not a lot, but he was putting some food inside himself. He slept constantly, slipping out of the living room, and going to bed.

I remember that Dad often slept like that when he came back from covering a war. Total exhaustion took over. He usually had to crash. And often so did I, when I returned from a battleground.

I was thankful that Zac had not had any really disturbed nights so far. Several times he had woken up shouting, and calling my name, but these few incidents did not alarm me. I knew my presence here was helping him, and I was gratified that I had come. It seemed to be paying off. I prayed it was.

Geoff turned to me, put his hand on my arm. "Listen kid, I know Zac's been relatively quiet since you got here last Thursday." He nodded to himself, then said slowly, "I wonder if that strange attack, when he was so icy cold, frightened him? Perhaps it made him focus on his health, kinda brought him up short."

"Maybe you're right," I answered. "He's never really talked about it with me. I explained that I thought it was a reaction to fatigue, lack of sleep and food, and he agreed. He's doing okay, Geoff. I know that."

"I trust your judgment, Serena, and I'm glad he's not drinking or glued to the TV set. Booze, and war reportage seen secondhand tend to agitate him no end." Geoff gave me a penetrating look. He said, "Do you think he's got post-traumatic stress disorder?"

This comment took me aback. "I haven't seen any real signs of it yet."

Geoff nodded, took a sip of his iced tea. "I witnessed a few strange things when I brought him out of Afghanistan . . . the pacing around, the sleepless nights, the agitation, the awful fucking nightmares, and the boozing. There were times when he really did attempt to drown his sorrows. And by the way, Harry has wondered about his condition."

"I know, I've discussed it with Harry, and he said I should humor Zac, that I must allow him to rant and rave, to weep, and to get his rage out. As you and I well know, when we come out we all have pent-up emotions, anxiety, anger, frustration, despair. Being witness to too much killing, too much death doesn't help much."

There was a silence, and Geoff looked off into the distance again, and then he drew closer, leaned forward. "Listen, I am developing really bad feelings, and I'm very aware, after a few days living a normal life here, that I do have to jump ship. *Pronto*. My time is up on the battlefield."

"Then it's the right moment to go," I said in a firm voice. "That's when you lose your edge, when you start to dither, or question what you're doing. That can be dangerous, Geoff, one mistake and you're dead."

"I know. Zac mentioned that he'd been covering wars since he was twenty-one, that's sixteen years, a helluva long time. I've only been at it for seven and lately I've felt pretty rotten most of the time. I don't want to end up like Zac, burnt out, just a shell of what I was."

"I understand, and I must say I've certainly been one of the lucky ones," I responded. "Eight years on the front. But my father and Harry sent me out a lot. Dad made me go back to Nice for breaks, they both deemed it necessary. And anyway, my mother insisted on it."

Geoff volunteered, "You're not very damaged, Serena, in my opinion anyway. In fact, I'd say you're pretty damned good. I've often wondered if your father or Harry ever suffered from PTSD. Do you know?"

"They both did, at different times, so they've told me. But they coped, they got out, cooled off. My father went back to Nice very often because of Mom's fragile health. And Dad once brought Harry out of the Balkans. So Harry told me the other day. From Bosnia. He was in a bad way. Dad and Harry took a very long break after that."

"They needed it, I bet."

"You know, Geoff, Dad and Harry had Global Images to fall back on, a business to run, when they got out of the front lines, and they both did other photography for a time. What are you going to do? I hope you're not leaving Global, Geoff."

"No, I'm not. Harry said I should take a month off, longer if I needed it, to think about my future. And he definitely wants me to remain with the agency. I'm staying here in Venice for a few more days, I want to get myself really rested. Then I'm going back to California to see my daughter. As you know Chloe lives with my ex-wife. It's all very amicable. And I do need to touch base with them, have a big dose of normality. I want to put this monstrous world out of my mind." Geoff looked at his watch. "I wonder where Zac is?"

"Oh, he'll be here any minute," I answered, attempting a nonchalance I did not feel. I hoped I was right.

Thirteen

As Zac walked across the terrace toward our table, my throat constricted and a wave of emotion washed over me unexpectedly. He looked so young from a distance, appeared to be just like he was when we first met long ago, eleven years now. And for a moment I was thrown back in time.

A decade dropped away, and I recalled how I had fallen in love with him during a very special summer in Nice. What an extraordinary summer it had been. Idyllic, romantic, filled with laughter and happiness.

He had been endearing, loving, and thoughtful. Although he was handsome, it was his charm and intelligence which captivated me. I enjoyed being with him, and we had a lot in common. In particular, we shared a love of photojournalism, especially war coverage.

Of course I had not been on the front line then, but he had, and he shared so much about it with me, and his experiences, and we very quickly bonded. He's my soul mate, I had thought, and he had felt the same way about me. When we became serious about each other, four years later, we had both believed it was going to last forever. But that was not meant to be . . . we had finally parted bitterly last year.

As he drew closer, I noticed that Dad's favorite barber, Benito, had given Zac the best haircut. It was short, stylish, and youthful, and Benito, being an excellent barber, had obviously applied his skills to Zac's face, had shaved him; Zac's cheeks were smooth, free of stubble, and he appeared less tense.

I smiled inwardly. Zac was wearing my father's ancient black-leather bomber jacket, which had definitely seen better days. It was years old, had become communal property, was borrowed by everyone who stayed at the bolthole. I'd even used it myself at times.

With the worn, cracked leather jacket Zac had on an open-necked white shirt and dark slacks; the casual outfit added to his air of youthfulness.

When he finally drew to a standstill, squeezed my shoulder, half smiled, I noticed the tightness around his eyes, the wrinkles, and now that he was close up I was aware of his overall weariness. Yet he was calm, obviously wanting to behave as normally as possible. He had control of himself, that I knew.

Before I could say anything, Geoff was on his feet and hugging Zac, who returned his embrace. I noted the affection between them, the respect they had for each other. They had always been good buddies, and it was genuine loyalty and concern that had compelled Geoff to get him out of Helmand Province when he was in trouble, despite the danger and risk Geoff was exposed to in that terrible place.

Zac sat down between Geoff and me, glanced at the iced tea and said, "I'd like a glass of white wine, I think."

I was silent; I felt a spurt of panic. Wine was dangerous. If he had one glass he could easily end up drinking a whole bottle. I glanced at Geoff, signaling my alarm with my eyes.

Geoff took charge at once, in that swift and efficient way he had of dealing with things. "Let's have a glass of champagne instead of white wine. That's gonna be great on this sunny morning in Venice, Italy, on a very peaceful day away from bloody bombs and bullets." He glanced at me. "Don't you think so, Serena?"

I agreed at once. "What a grand idea! We can toast your liberation, and champagne's great for a celebration. Let's make it *pink* champagne."

"Fine by me," Zac said, then asked, "What liberation? What celebration?" He looked at Geoff quizzically, seemed puzzled.

"I'm outta Pakistan for good, Zac. I'm not going back," Geoff explained in a determined voice as he beckoned to the waiter. After ordering three glasses of pink champagne, and asking for the menu, he continued, "I told Harry I'm retiring from the front line, Zac. He agreed I should, if I felt strongly about it. And naturally he agreed, he understands that an unenthusiastic war photographer is a liability to Global, not to mention to himself. He puts himself at risk."

"Why now, suddenly?" Zac asked, frowning.

"Because I realized when I brought you out of Afghanistan that I was gonna end up like you in the not-too-distant future. I'm quitting before I become a basket case. Or get myself killed."

Zac was silent, just nodded.

I said, "Once you feel that way you've got to leave. As I did."

I had the feeling Zac was a little startled by Geoff's words, and mine, but he did not really show it. After a moment he turned to Geoff, asked, "But what will you cover, if you're not a war photographer? That's what you've done all your life."

"I don't know, to be honest," Geoff answered. "Right now, I'm planning to go to California to see my daughter, get a bit of R & R. I'm not making any special plans, it's too soon. I wanna take it easy for a while."

Zac was silent again, his expression thoughtful.

I said, "You might want to create some sort of photographic series, Geoff. Harry suggested I should do that, since I do want to continue being a photographer. World famine was a subject I was considering."

Zac glanced at me swiftly, said very pointedly, "I thought you were writing a book about Tommy's life."

"I am. Harry was just thinking ahead, looking for something I could do when I've finished the book."

"Don't you want to run Global Images with Harry? After all, you own half of it now," Zac remarked.

"I've no interest in doing that. Florence has been in charge since the beginning, and personally I think she should remain in charge. I'd only be a spare wheel. Besides, I don't want that kind of job. Can you just see me in an office?"

"No, I can't," Zac exclaimed, and then laughed for the first time since I'd arrived in Venice.

Geoff and I began to laugh with him, and we toasted each other with the pink champagne, which the waiter had just placed on the table. And then a moment later, Zac startled me, and Geoff I think, when he announced he was hungry.

"It's the fresh air," Geoff said. "Getting out, going to the barber's shop, and the walk over here. It's done you good, Zac, we'll have to do this more often."

"How long are you staying?" I asked curiously.

"Another few days." Geoff gave me a knowing look, and picked up the menu. "I'm gonna have a bowl of spaghetti bolognese, but hey, Zac, the fish is good, so is everything on the menu. What tempts you?"

"Not sure. Maybe gnocchi, or lasagne. Mom makes the best lasagne . . . I grew up with Italian food, you know."

"Yeah, you told me before. So, look at the menu, and let's order."

Zac and I both followed Geoff's lead and chose spaghetti bolognese as our main course, with tomatoes and mozzarella to start.

Much to my surprise and annoyance, Geoff ordered three more glasses of pink champagne when he asked for a bottle of sparkling water. But I kept my mouth shut, just sat back in my chair, picked up my half-empty flute, and sipped the champagne that remained in it.

Geoff and Zac began a conversation about Italian food and their favorite dishes, and whilst this took me by surprise, I was pleased Zac was opening up in this way, talking again. His dissertation about Italian food was not new; he had had many with Frankie, when we had been at Rao's for dinner.

Zac was half Italian. His mother, Lucia, had been born in Italy and brought to America as a baby, when her parents had emigrated. His father, Patrick, was of Irish descent. But to me it was his Italian side that appeared more dominant in him: He spoke the language fluently, and his dark good looks were Latin. His eyes were Irish, though, at least that's what I thought. They were a luminous light green when he wasn't exhausted.

For once Zac ate his lunch, and obviously enjoyed the food. Geoff and I did too. We skipped dessert, but had two coffees each, and Zac insisted on paying the bill when it was time to leave.

Before we left the restaurant, I phoned Harry in New York, checking in with him around three o'clock European time as I usually did. It was nine in the morning in Manhattan and Harry was delighted to speak to Zac and Geoff, to hear both of them sounding well, and he was a happy man when he hung up.

Geoff wandered off to the Bauer Hotel next door to the old Palazzo, and Zac and I walked through the streets, heading for the Piazza San Marco. We didn't say much as we strolled along, but at one moment Zac took hold of my hand, and squeezed it. I squeezed his, and looked at him. He stared back at me, and a soft smile played around his mouth, then he leaned in, kissed my cheek. "Thanks, Serena, thanks for coming to Venice, thanks for everything."

"I was glad to come, if a little concerned. I didn't know what I was going to find."

"I haven't been so bad, have I?"

"No, you haven't. Not too many nightmares. I was worried about you when you had that strange attack, when you were so icy cold last week."

"I'll never know what that was," he answered, shaking his head, looking baffled. "Exhaustion, being very stressed out after leaving the front line, as you suggested."

"Perhaps," I agreed, and looked at him again.

"Today you're the best you've been since I got here. And I know now it was rest and food you needed, among other things."

"I enjoyed my lunch," he told me, and squeezed my hand again.

We had reached the piazza, and Zac suddenly said, "Let's stop off at Florian's and have a drink."

"All right. But not a drink, Zac," I replied, and instantly knew I sounded uptight, and I was annoyed with myself.

"That was just a turn of phrase," he responded, his voice even. "So an ice cream, a Coke, a lemonade, a coffee, a glass of water. *Anything.* It's just too nice to go back to the bolthole yet, and this square is full of memories for me. Isn't it for you too, Serena?"

I did not speak for a moment, and then I said softly, in a low voice, "Very many memories, Zac," and I felt my heart lurch. I was suddenly a little afraid. Not of him but of myself and my reaction to him, and what might happen between us.

Fourteen

In the past, when we had been in love and together, Caffè Florian had been a favorite place. We had come here every day and now here we were again. Florian's was still the same but we were not. We had changed.

Despite the sun it was a cool afternoon, and a wind had blown up, and so we sat inside at a cozy table near the bar. Zac ordered coffee, but I suddenly fancied a vanilla ice cream. As I ate it slowly Zac couldn't keep his spoon out of the dish, kept dipping it in and spooning dollops of ice cream into his mouth.

At one moment, he glanced at me, and asked, "Have you ever let another man eat food from your plate? Or, as in this instance, a dish?"

I shook my head, endeavoring not to smile, detecting a hint of normality surfacing . . . his jealousy about unknown men. Actually, nonexistent other men. "No," I said at last.

He glanced at me out of the corner of his eye, and murmured, "Good. It's very intimate."

"I know."

"Do you mind? That I've always done it?"

"No, I don't, and listen, it's a privilege only you enjoy."

He gave me a funny little smile, sat back comfortably in the chair. "I don't know exactly why, but I've always loved this place. Perhaps because it smacks of another era, from a time gone by."

"I'm sure you're right. I feel the same way," I said, thrilled that we were actually having a proper conversation, one that wasn't stilted or awkward. "My mother told me that the original eighteenth-century décor had been carefully preserved, that Florian's was one of the first cafés in Europe to serve coffee, when it was considered to be an exotic drink." I looked around. "It does have a special warmth, it's very welcoming, sort of quaint."

"I loved your mother's bits and pieces, as she called all that information she had tucked away at the back of her beautiful head," Zac remarked. "She was such a lot of fun."

I nodded, smiled at the memory of her. "She used to say she was a fountain of information nobody needed or cared about." I picked up my glass of water, took a swallow, gazed at him for a moment.

I saw him clearly, as he was now, and there was something of the old Zac about him this afternoon. His color was better, his eyes unexpectedly brighter, and the sharp angles of his face had softened. He was obviously relaxed, and it was visible in the way he held his body, as well as in his face.

Suddenly, he said, "You're staring at me, Pidge. Is something wrong?"

"No, something is good," I responded quickly. "I think you're much less uptight, and it shows. Ever since I arrived in Venice you've had strict control of yourself, as if you were afraid to be you, to be who you really are."

"I know, and I'm still in control."

"But you're not so rigid this afternoon." I eyed

him carefully, and a smile broke through, when I added, "It's as if you have loosened the tight rein you've had on yourself, and decided to trust me."

"If I didn't trust you, I wouldn't have asked Harry to persuade you to come!" he exclaimed, giving me an odd look.

"He didn't have to do much persuading."

"I would've been in a mess if you hadn't agreed," he said after a moment, now looking at me intently. "I'd have been lost. Your presence is very soothing to me, Pidge, even healing. I really believe I need you to help me get through this difficult period."

"I think so too," I agreed, and went on carefully. "How did you know you had to get out? Did something happen? Go wrong? Or did Harry decide to pull you out? He's not discussed it with me, nor has Geoff. They sort of left me in the dark, actually. Are you able to talk about it? Or would you prefer not to? Is it too hard?" I asked, the questions tumbling out of me. Questions I'd wanted to ask for days.

"I can talk. I want to talk about it, and about other troubling things. That's what I told Harry . . . that you're the only person who would have a clue, would be able to properly discuss the front line and war reporting. Because you'd been there, seen it all, been as heartsick and as numb as me at different times."

He paused, shifted slightly in his chair, and continued speaking in such a low voice I could hardly hear him. I leaned closer to him, not wanting to miss a word.

"I feel so rotten at times, Serena, so devastated I can hardly stand myself. There's a remorselessness about war that is chilling. And it kills the soul. Yet I've gone back time after time, and I don't know why."

"Because you had to, Zac," I answered. "Because of your honesty and humanity, and the need you have to tell the world the truth about brutal regimes oppressing people, and to expose the terrible suffering in war zones. You're a photojournalist, as I am, and that's what we do."

I reached out, took hold of his hand. "Except that there comes a time when we can't do it anymore, because we're too battered, exhausted, and disillusioned. Those are the reasons I stopped, and they're yours."

He nodded, squeezed my hand tightly. "Something happened one day, and I just couldn't stand it anymore—" Unexpectedly, tears filled his eyes, and he blinked, cleared his throat. "I can't discuss it, go into details, not at this moment, mostly because we're here at Florian's. I know I'll cry . . ."

I continued to hold his hand. "I understand. You don't want to weep in public. So we'll save it for later. Whenever you want. Anyway, from what I gather, you told Harry you wanted out. Am I correct?"

"Yes. I had to leave the front, I knew it was the time I had to go. I didn't feel well, physically or mentally, and I realized I needed help. Harry said he'd come in and get me, and I told him not to. He suggested Geoff, and I agreed at once. And fortunately for me, so did Geoff. He came in within twenty-four hours, and he never flinched."

"He's a good guy. You seemed startled earlier, when he said he wasn't going back to Pakistan."

"I was for a split second, and then I knew he felt like I did, burnt out. And also mentally bludgeoned by what he'd witnessed."

"You asked him what he was going to do, once he'd left war photography, and he didn't really have an answer for you. But it troubles *you*, doesn't it? You're facing the same dilemma," I suggested.

A small sigh escaped. Zac nodded. "Yep. I am. We're in the same boat, he and I. Totally at a loss, I guess."

"I think you can only deal with that when you are feeling better, Zac, when you're back on your feet. I know you have a lot of troubling stuff to deal with, to get out of the way first. When the time comes, you'll understand what you want to photograph, what kind of life you want to lead."

"I guess so. But sometimes I wish I had a hobby,

something I could throw myself into . . ." He let his voice trail off, looked suddenly troubled, his eyes sad.

"You need a release from war coverage, something that takes your mind off the conflict, the blood and bullets, dead troops, maimed civilians caught in the cross fire. We all do, actually. All that destruction is mind-boggling."

"Do you have a hobby these days, Serena?" he asked, sounding interested in knowing about me and my life.

"There's the biography I'm writing about Dad, that's not exactly a hobby, but I am enjoying it." I laughed a little hollowly. "Well, most of the time. The thing is, I really do want to continue writing. But to be honest, I wish I could find another occupation, or a hobby, something to throw myself into. Jessica loves sailing, mucking around on boats, and she always has."

"That's what Marie Colvin does, that's her passion when she's not covering wars," Zac told me, referring to the famous war correspondent we both knew. "I love being on boats myself, maybe that's something I could try eventually . . . as a pastime."

"You once told me that you used to go sailing with your father, in Upstate New York, and—"

"That's right!" he exclaimed, cutting across me. "We had a log cabin near the Finger Lakes. In fact Dad still has it. Anyway we all used to go up there for weekends but I was the only one who went fishing with Dad."

I smiled, pleased to see that fleeting glimpse of pleasure crossing his face as he said this. It was obvious he had good memories about those days of his youth.

We lingered at Florian's, enjoying the friendly and familiar surroundings, escaping, in a sense, into the past, when we had been happy together. We both ordered tea, and went on talking about all kinds of things. This was the first time in the five days that I had been here that he had been as normal as this, and it pleased me. It was a good sign.

All I wanted was for Zac to get better. In my own way, I loved him. We had once been so close it was hard not to have feelings for him. But at the same time I realized I could never become romantically involved with him again. I had grown wary, cautious, and self-protective over this past year.

There was no viable future for us together, despite our attraction for each other. That was still there, I was very well aware of this, and it wasn't just me. Zac felt it too, I was sure, and he had swiftly moved out of my parents' bedroom in the bolthole, which we had shared for the first couple of nights. He had not said a word, and neither had I. And I understood why he had gone back to the other bedroom. Close proximity was unnerving.

Helping Zac to get better was one thing, falling under his fatal spell was something else altogether. What if he went back to the front? And he might feel the compulsion to go to bad places, where disasters were constant, or because he wanted to put himself in danger for the thrill of it. Or to test himself. That could become a disastrous cycle, one I wanted no part of at all.

Immediately, I pushed this unacceptable idea to one side. I knew he fully understood he could never go back to the battlefield. He would have to find a different area of photography to focus on, one which was much less dangerous.

It was almost as if he had read my mind when he said, "I guess I could follow in your father's footsteps."

I was puzzled. "What are you getting at?"

"For the last few years of his life, Tommy took pictures of presidents, politicians, royals, celebrities of all kinds. Maybe I could do that. What say you?"

Ready to seize on anything that was not physically dangerous for him, I exclaimed, "That's brilliant! Dad enjoyed shooting those pictures."

"The thing was, he managed to get pictures of them in funny, amusing, and unusual poses. He obviously persuaded them to do stuff they didn't normally do. That's what made the photos so great."

"You could do it, Zac, you're a natural to step into his shoes," I told him, and I meant this.

"I'll think about it." He paused, suddenly looked worried when he went on: "You don't really want to shoot a series on world famine, do you?"

"I don't know, to be honest. It interests me, and yet it would mean facing a lot of women and children suffering, and that's heartbreaking, as you well know." I made a face, added, "On the other hand, people should know how much famine there is around the world."

He nodded, but his face was glum, even slightly disapproving, I thought.

"Like you, I'm looking for something to do. I have the book to finish about Dad's life, and then I might work on a photographic book Tommy started but never completed. Cara and Jessica found quite an extensive archive at the house in Nice. Loads of photographs Dad had taken over the years."

"Hey, that would be wonderful!" He sat up straighter, a smile glancing across his face. "It would be another great tribute to Tommy."

"That's what my sisters said."

Zac settled back, drank his tea, and after a few moments of contemplation, he said, "Can I ask you something, Pidge?"

"You can ask me anything."

"Why is it that some combat photographers come out done in, shattered like I am, and others don't?"

"To be honest, I don't know," I said. "We're up front with the troops, and just because it says 'press' on our helmets and flak jackets it doesn't mean we're not going to get shot at. We're often targeted because we *are* the press. Let's face it, we're in the trenches with the troops. Some photographers handle that well. They can seemingly cope forever. Others just can't."

I shook my head. "Let me correct myself, most of us can't cope. Not in the end. Because we've witnessed too much horrific stuff. And you know that a lot of troops return home suffering from post-traumatic stress disorder, as well as some combat journalists."

"I don't have PTSD," he stated, looking at me intently.

"But you are shattered, Zac. You will soon get better, though."

"I hope to God I will." He glanced around Florian's, almost as if to reassure himself where he was, then muttered, "We get hooked on war, don't we?"

"We do. All of us. That adrenaline rush is very addictive. But the smart ones get out. Eventually. And stay out, if they know what's good for them, and they lead safer lives."

He was silent for a moment or two, then he leaned closer, said quietly, "I can't go back, Serena. Whatever you might think, I just can't hack it anymore."

A surge of relief ran through me. I was convinced he meant every word and that he would not change his mind.

We had been sitting in Florian's for hours, and when we finally left it was early evening. We walked back to the bolthole in silence. But that had never been a problem for us, our silences were compatible.

I glanced around, feeling relaxed. Venice had that effect on me. The piazza was much less crowded because of the hour; the wind had dropped and it was a pleasant evening.

I looked up. The sky had changed, had deepened to a soft pavonian blue, and the fading light bathed everything in a hazy softness, as if a gauze veil had been draped over the ancient buildings.

Venice was calm, seemed otherworldly in the twilight. I had always loved this place from my childhood, and it held happy memories for me. I suddenly realized it was a good place for Zac to recover, and I was happy Harry had thought of putting him in the bolthole.

At one moment, Zac took hold of my hand when we were in the middle of the square, swung me around to face him.

"What is it?"

"What happened to me? To you? To us, Serena?"

I was silent for a second, then I said, "Life."

"What do you mean?"

"Life got in the way. It changed you, it changed me."

"Do you mean it also split us up?"

"Sort of, yes. We're victims of Life, and all the nasty tricks it plays on people. Life frequently comes up to hit you in the face."

"Can it be repaired?" he asked quietly.

"What?"

"Our relationship?"

I stiffened involuntarily, and did not answer at first. Finally, I said in a low, noncommittal voice, "I don't know . . . I'm not really sure, Zac."

He nodded.

We started to walk across the square again. As we approached the street where the bolthole was located, he said in a soft, loving voice, "I still have feelings for you."

When I did not respond, he asked, "Do you?"

"Certain feelings, yes. However, the most important thing is for you to get better, Zac. Only then can we think about our past relationship." I was careful not to mention the future.

"Understood," he said.

We went on up the street in silence.

Fifteen

When the noise first started and I woke up with a jolt, I thought, for a split second, that someone was banging a nail into a wall to hang a picture. Then, as it grew louder, and more intense, I decided it must be filtering in from outside. But no, it wasn't.

The noise was actually coming from the living room, just beyond my bedroom door. When I realized this, I leapt out of bed, snapped on the light, struggled into my robe and slippers, and ran to the door. I yanked it open to find myself facing a room full of blazing lights. Every lamp was turned on.

Much to my shock and horror, Zac was standing in the center of the room in his pajamas, looking demented, angrily bashing the television set to pieces with a kind of manic concentration. And what was that he had in his hands? A frying pan? I was astonished. I didn't even know we had one. Pushing this unimportant thought to one side, I rushed toward him, exclaiming, "Zac! Zac! Stop it! Stop doing that! At once! You'll wake Claudia. She'll be up here any minute wanting to know what's going on."

I took hold of him firmly, put my arms around his rigid body. He stared at me blankly. I saw how glazed his eyes were, and his face was wet with tears.

"Oh, Zac," I whispered against his shoulder. "You're suffering so much, I'm so sorry. I'll try to help you in any way I can. Come on, give me the frying pan."

He pulled away from me, gaped at me once more, almost angrily now, and then, with something of a grand flourish, he threw the copper frying pan onto the floor and made a motion to walk away from me.

Before he could take one step I shrieked, "Stop! Don't move!" I had just noticed he was in his bare feet. "You'll cut your feet on that mess," I warned him.

The floor where he stood was strewn with twisted metal, broken glass, wires, and components that go into the innards of a television set. I had an unexpected flash of Richard Burton as Shannon, the defrocked priest, in the movie *The Night of the Iguana*, cutting his feet to shreds when he stepped on broken wine bottles near his bed.

"I'll get your shoes," I said, hurrying into Zac's room, shouting over my shoulder, "Just stay there. Don't take a step."

He didn't.

When I came back he was still standing in the same spot. He did not say anything to me, nor did he look at me; his gaze was directed at the floor and the detritus surrounding him, as if he was surprised to see it scattered there.

Walking carefully, I pushed bits and pieces of glass and metal to one side with my feet, until I'd made a small space in front of him, where I placed his loafers. "Slip your feet into them," I instructed.

Once he had done so, I guided him over to the sofa, forced him down onto it, and took the seat next to him. He appeared to be in a weakened state; he fell back against the cushions and closed his eyes.

I sat holding his hand, not sure what to do to help him, other than to keep him calm. I had no idea what had brought this on. Had he been watching the news? Following reports of the Arab Spring? The various uprisings spreading through the Middle East, after a young Tunisian man, Mohamed Bouazizi, had set himself on fire last December, and died in hospital in January?

I knew from Geoff that Zac had watched the unrest and violence developing, was aware of the troubles infecting other countries. But he'd promised me he would not watch any more coverage. Had he had a nightmare again? Or one of those horrific flashbacks, when a bad experience replays itself, and is just as engulfing as the real event? I just didn't know what had affected him. How could I?

Certainly something had set him off, made him genuinely angry. But that was easy to do. Anger lurked beneath the surface these days; he was angry at tyrants and dictators, politicians and governments. And terrorists and insurgents. Overall, he was stricken by the horrors of the world we, as photojournalists, lived in day and night on a constant basis.

Zac had covered too many wars in too many countries in the past sixteen years. It was no wonder he was full of rage and sadness and despair. We all suffered from a kind of numbed exhaustion when we finally came out, stunned by war.

He had taken his all-seeing camera to Sierra Leone, Somalia, Ivory Coast, Israel, Palestine, Lebanon, Kuwait, Bosnia, Kosovo, Iraq, and Afghanistan, to name some of the places he'd worked. The thought of what he must have witnessed boggled the mind. I had seen a lot myself, but I hadn't been with him until Afghanistan and Iraq. He had seen much more over many more years, double the time I'd been a war photographer, in fact.

I had a tissue in my pocket, and I pulled it out, patted his cheeks, which were still damp with tears.

Instantly, he opened his eyes, looked at me with a degree of intensity. "Serena?"

"Yes, Zac?"

"What happened?"

I shook my head. "I'm not sure why you were doing it, but you were beating the television to death, and the noise woke me up. You were hell-bent on destroying it, and there's the mess you made. Over there. I just guided you out of it."

He followed the direction of my gaze, then looked at me, bit his lip, as if he were baffled at himself. Worry was suddenly reflected in his eyes; he was chagrined.

I said, "Were you watching the news? Did you get hooked on the coverage of the Arab Spring? What's been happening in Egypt? And the Mubarak regime? Or were you focused on Afghanistan?"

"No, none of that. I told you I wouldn't focus on war or the uprisings, or the Middle East. In fact, I *promised,* actually. And I kept my promise to you, Serena."

I nodded my understanding. "But were you watching TV?" I fastened my eyes on his.

"I was, yes, but nothing to do with news. I was zapping around, flicking different shows on and off, not really paying attention to anything in particular. I just couldn't sleep. That's why I got up, came in here, watched for a while, had a glass of milk. I never went near a news show."

"So what made you smash the TV?" I wondered out loud.

He was silent, sat staring at me, and then finally he said, in a low voice, "I had a flashback. A bad one. I guess I just went berserk. I became angry. It got the better of me . . . I suppose I was in a rage."

Before I could say anything his face crumpled

unexpectedly, and tears welled in his eyes, slid down his cheeks. He brought his hands to his face, endeavored to control himself, to choke back the sobs. But he couldn't manage that. And so, embarrassed I think, he turned away from me, rested his head on the wide arm of the sofa, and wept.

I moved closer to him, put my hand on his back, stroked it for a while.

Eventually, I said quietly, "Don't try to control yourself because of me, Zac, or hold the tears back. Cry everything out, and as much as you can. It really is the only way to deal with grief. And I know you're grieving. You're full of sorrow and heartache."

He mumbled something I couldn't quite catch, and then he began to sob as if his heart was broken. And I think it was. I knew the flashback had been powerful and that it was tearing him apart. He was awash with pain.

I also understood that I must leave him here alone, give him his privacy, not encroach on him. And so I slipped away, went into my bedroom until he needed me.

As I walked into the room I noticed the clock on the bedside table. It was two in the morning. I was about to call Harry in New York and then I instantly changed my mind. I didn't need to report in. I was a big girl. I could handle this situation on my own without any advice.

I knew Zachary North inside out and upside down. Nobody knew him better than I did. And that was why he had wanted me to come here . . . to help him assuage his grief and to cope with his mental state. He understood himself well enough to know he needed to heal and that I was the one to lead him in the right direction.

I closed my eyes and tried to sleep, but images of the front line in Afghanistan filled my mind. The sound of gunfire, shells bursting, roadside bombs exploding, the rumbling sound of helicopters hovering overhead. The noise was incessant, barely let up until it was dark. But even then there were noises—sounds of firing, explosions as snipers roamed around and an insurgent accidentally stepped on one of their bombs and was blown to bits. The stink of sweat and gunpowder and blood. The dead and the wounded. These images rolled in my head, and I wondered how I had managed to live through these nightmarish years, dodging bullets and bombs, rushing in, camera poised, to get the ghastly shots, to show the world what was happening. There was always fear because of the ever-present danger, but I had pushed it aside to do the work. But sometimes the fear was crippling. Somehow, I overcame it.

Sixteen

I insist on buying a new television set, to replace the one I smashed," Zac said. "I spoke to Claudia on the phone, when you were in the shower, and she's given me the name of the best shop, it's not far from here."

I nodded in agreement and picked up my bag from the coffee table. "Come on, then, let's go," I said, walking across the room toward the front door. I had seen that obdurate look on his face many times before, and I knew not to argue. The best thing was to agree to do what he wanted.

He gave me one of his lopsided smiles, rare at the moment, and we left the apartment together. When we stepped outside into the street, I was surprised how warm it was, quite balmy, with no breeze, for once. The sun was shining, and it felt good to be out of the bolthole, mingling with people, seeing the world.

We walked along, side by side, in silence as usual, lost in our own thoughts. I was relieved he had finally made reference to the TV set he had destroyed, and hoped that once the new one was installed he would tell me more about the awful flashback, which had set him off five nights ago.

So far he had been reluctant to discuss it. I had asked him about it only once; when he had shaken his head, looking grim, I had instantly let the matter drop. He would tell me when he was able to do so, in his own time, of that I was certain.

After I had filled Harry in the following day, his instructions had been to leave it alone, and therefore I had.

"So Geoff's coming back tonight," Zac suddenly said, turning to look at me, as we walked through the Piazza San Marco, which was busier than ever today; but not as busy as it would be at the end of April . . . full of tourists for Easter.

"That's what I told you earlier this morning," I answered. "What I didn't say was that he wants us to have dinner with him. Tonight. At Harry's Bar. He's not staying long, just a few days and then he's off to L.A."

"Did you accept?"

"More or less. I said I'd be there, but I had to check with you. I added that I was sure it would be all right. He said to tell you he's not taking no for an answer, and that he's already made the reservation at Harry's Bar. From London."

Zac laughed. "Just like Geoff. And of course I'll go with you. Did he confide in you? About his decision?"

"No, he didn't. I'm well aware Harry's eager for him to take over Global's London office, and if Geoff's as smart as I think he is, then he will."

"It's one way for him to make up with his ex-wife," Zac pointed out, looking at me through

136

the corner of his eye. "He's keen to do that, isn't he?"

"Yes. He's constantly told me that Martha couldn't take it when he was covering wars. But he says they still care for each other, that she might give the idea of a reconciliation a chance . . . if he's running the London bureau for us, and has no dangerous assignments."

Zac nodded. We strolled on. He seemed deep in thought, remained silent until we reached the shop Claudia had recommended. It was in a narrow street, and within seconds Zac was inside speaking rapidly in perfect Italian to the man whose name he had been given. *Luigi.* An old friend of Claudia's, who would make a good price, she had assured Zac. It looked to me as if the two of them were already hitting it off.

I left Zac and Luigi to their deal-making and wandered around the store, not really interested in any of this complicated equipment.

In fact my mind was elsewhere. I was worried about Jessica. Last night Cara had phoned to tell me Jess had fallen at the auction house that afternoon, had taken a bad tumble down a short flight of steps. Apparently nothing appeared to be broken, but Jess was going to have more X-rays this afternoon at a clinic in Nice.

Another reason for Cara's call had been to find out when I would be arriving in Nice. Dad had died on April 22 last year, and I'd promised my sisters I would be there with them on the first anniversary of his death. To celebrate his life, and to remember him proudly and lovingly.

Our mother's birthday had been in May, and I'd planned to be with them anyway that month. Ever since her death, four years ago, we usually celebrated her on the day she had been born.

When I told Cara I wanted to bring Zac along, she had agreed that this was fine. Yet she hadn't been able to resist saying, "I'm glad he's feeling better, but just remember, Serena, a leopard doesn't change its spots."

I had laughed, then jokingly told her she shouldn't take our grandmother's old sayings too seriously. She had joined in my laughter, and then said she really would like Zac to join us to honor Dad. "Because they cared so much about each other."

I didn't want to let my sisters down, and I wanted to go. Later today I would break the news to Zac that we would soon have to leave the bolthole and go to Nice. I had already been in Venice for over two weeks . . . how quickly the time had passed.

Glancing across the shop, I noticed how animated Zac was in his discussion with Luigi. I also realized he looked so much better physically.

He had put on weight, mainly because I had played on his love of his mother's Italian food, and what better place to find it than here in

Venice. He had been sleeping better, and his face was less gaunt. That tautness had left him, just evaporated.

Oddly enough, after the night of the flashback he had had fewer nightmares and bad dreams, and seemed more tranquil. Certainly I had not witnessed any anxiety, agitation, or panic attacks.

It struck me now that he was well enough to travel, and my sisters would certainly be able to help, should he show any signs of PTSD. After all, they had grown up with a war photographer for a father, and Tommy had suffered bouts of it from time to time. Zac kept saying he didn't have it, but how did we know it was so? He hadn't seen a doctor.

There were other reasons why I wanted to go to Nice. The bolthole was a wonderful convenience, a useful place to have. However, it really only worked for a few days, a week at the most. It was confining, which was why I had made Zac come out with me every day, to do things, go to other parts of Venice like Murano, the Lido, and Giudecca.

We even went sightseeing again, even though we had done that long ago. We ate at small restaurants and cafés, where I encouraged him to indulge in the food he had been brought up on.

I believed that when we got to Nice I could get Zac involved with the picture book my father had never finished, as well as his photographic archive. I felt these projects would give Zac an interest, be a distraction for him.

And lastly, I missed my sisters, longed to spend time with them in the place I had always loved, my mother's house in the hills above Nice, Jardin des Fleurs.

"Let's go to Florian's for lunch," Zac said as we eventually bade farewell to Luigi and finally left his shop.

"I'd love it," I answered. Zac was obviously well pleased with the deal he had made for the new flat-screen TV, which would be delivered and installed tomorrow.

"Why not today?" I asked as we walked down the street.

"Because it's such a nice day, and I want to be out doing things," Zac answered. "I've been feeling so much better, and today I really have some of my energy back."

He took hold of my arm and went on, "You've done me good. Been good for me, Pidge, and so has Venice. It's a relaxing place, nonaggressive, ancient, comforting." He smiled at me, leaned closer, kissed my cheek. "I feel great, and you look good, Serena. Very beautiful."

My heart sank. Suddenly I was acutely aware of him, conscious of his close proximity. I had to admit that off and on I'd worried about my attraction to him. There had always been something different about Zac North, something unique in him which made my head spin.

As we sat down at one of Florian's outdoor tables, I cautioned myself to be wary of him. On my guard. I mustn't fall into his arms again. If I did I would be lost. Irretrievably lost.

"Shall we have a glass of champagne?" he asked. "To celebrate."

"Celebrate what?" I asked, puzzled. I frowned at him.

"Anything you want," he said. "The great deal I got on the TV set, Geoff's sudden return, dinner at Harry's Bar, my improved health, both mentally and physically."

He took hold of my hand and smiled at me. "Or we can celebrate being here together again, at one of our favorite places, enjoying the beautiful spring weather."

I felt a sense of dismay trickle through me. I recognized the flirtatiousness in his eyes, the warmth of the smile still playing around his mouth, that irresistible charm floating to the surface of his being. Grasping this opportunity, I said, "Or we could celebrate our upcoming trip."

Obviously I had startled him. Zac gaped at me. "Upcoming trip? Where are we going? Not New York, I hope."

I shook my head. "No, we're going to Nice. At least, I have to go there. I thought you might come with me. Cara and Jessica would like that, and we can celebrate Dad's life together. On the first anniversary of his death."

He looked chagrined. "I was the one who caused you to miss the plane from Kabul that day. Are you sure you want me to come?"

"Yes, I do," I responded in my most reassuring voice. "Cara reminded me how much you and Dad meant to each other, and in certain ways you were like a son to him."

"Oh no, no, no! That's not me. That's you, Serena!" he exclaimed. "And you're very well aware of this."

I ignored his comment. "Let's have champagne to celebrate being alive, and being good friends again." As I spoke I slipped my hand out of his, rummaged around in my bag for my cell phone, found it, put it in my jacket pocket.

Zac beckoned to a waiter, ordered two glasses of pink champagne, and then said, "Those are great reasons to celebrate, and I'm glad we've made up."

I didn't immediately answer, wondering where this was leading, filled with apprehension. Did he think that my saying we were good friends meant our relationship was back in place?

A variety of emotions assailed me for a few seconds . . . fear, anxiety, and worry, which I tried to push aside. If any of these feelings showed in my face, Zac did not appear to notice.

He sat back in the chair, relaxed and at ease,

and, much to my amazement, he seemed to be like his old self. Did my presence mean so much? Had I really helped the healing to begin? I had no answers, and I decided to relax, to let things take their course.

When the champagne arrived we toasted each other, clinked glasses, and chatted, and after a short while Zac requested the menu. We ordered a selection of the small tea sandwiches and fancy pastries, because we weren't very hungry, and a pot of English breakfast tea with slices of lemon.

Once the waiter disappeared, I turned to Zac and said quietly, "I haven't had a chance to tell you this, Zac, but Jessica fell yesterday afternoon. In the auction house. Nothing seems to be broken, but she's getting more X-rays done this afternoon. Cara said I shouldn't worry, but I do."

I took my cell out of my pocket and put it on the table. "I'd like to have this here, if you don't mind; I don't want to miss Cara's call."

"No, I don't mind, and hey, I wish you'd told me before. Why is Jess having X-rays? Didn't they take them yesterday?"

"Yes, they did. But she's not felt quite right since the fall."

"Understandable. It's probably just shock, but listen, do you want to leave tomorrow? Fly to Nice? I'm okay with that, Pidge, if you do. I'll come with you."

"That's a thought, and thanks for offering."

"Whatever you want to do is okay by me, and I'm sorry about Jessica's accident."

"Cara will tell me exactly where it's at. She's known for her bluntness, and she's not at all afraid to break unpalatable news to anybody," I said dryly.

Zac threw me a knowing look, took a sip of champagne, then slid down in his chair, his face upturned to the sun, his eyes closed.

I glanced around thinking how truly beautiful it was today. The light in the piazza was dazzling, the sky a clear, unblemished blue, with no clouds visible. The ancient buildings appeared to gleam golden in the brilliance of the day.

To think that the basilica was built in the ninth century, as were the other buildings here . . . there was an ageless quality about them, as well as a certain kind of theatricality . . . but then that was part of their magic.

My father used to say that Venice lived up to J. M. W. Turner's paintings of this city and its waterways, and he was right. If anyone had captured this light it was Turner; no artist had ever bettered him, or painted Venice in his way.

I drifted with my thoughts, lost for a short while in the past . . . I remembered how once my mother's picture hat blew away, floated across the piazza, carried by a sudden gust of wind.

We were sitting somewhere near here, enjoying our ice creams, and the hat had just whirled and swirled away. Our mother had half risen in her chair, then swiftly sat down again, having realized she would be recognized at once if she drew attention to herself by running after her hat.

It was Cara and I who raced across the piazza, chasing it, and finally catching it. Waving it in the air, laughing as we ran back to her, looking triumphant, I recall now.

Following Zac's example, I closed my eyes, and turned my face to the sun. Behind my lids I could suddenly see my mother's face . . . as she had looked that day, dressed in pale pink and white, her light blond hair a golden halo around her exquisite face, her blue eyes the color of the sky.

I had loved my mother so much, we had all loved her. And she had loved us in return. It was that particular summer we had moved out of the bolthole and into the Gritti Hotel, because my mother decided we needed more space . . . much more space. Especially for her luggage. We were all growing irritable, and had agreed with her at once. I now remembered it had been 1992, and I had been eleven years old . . . so long ago . . .

It was during lunch that my cell began to buzz. I seized it at once. "Serena here."

"It's Cara, darling. All is well. Thankfully, no broken bones. Jessica's good, and she wants to speak to you."

"Hi, Pidge," Jessica said a moment later, sounding perfectly normal.

"Hello, Jess, are you really all right?" I asked worriedly.

"I am. *Honestly.* I think what happened is that I was in shock after the fall. It . . . well, it sort of surprised me, the way I went down. It jolted me, actually. But I haven't broken anything, I promise. Cara says you'll be here in a day or two, or thereabouts."

"About the twentieth, if not before," I responded. "And thanks for calling, Jess. I must admit I was concerned, worried about you."

She began to laugh, then said through her laughter, "Remember what Mom used to call you?"

"Many things," I said, laughing with her. "Which name are you referring to?"

"Not a name really, but she did often say that you were a professional worrier. She was joking, of course."

"No, she wasn't," I shot back. "She was serious. She used to say I was so good at it I was like a professional."

A loud burst of Jessica's laughter echoed down the phone, and I was laughing too as I hung up.

Seventeen

As we walked down the Calle Vallaresso toward Harry's Bar at the far end near the Grand Canal, Zac suddenly grabbed my hand, swung me to face him. He stood staring at me without saying a word.

"What is it?" I asked, frowning, because he looked so serious.

He didn't answer me, just pulled me forward into his arms and held me close to him. After a moment, he released me, and said in a low voice, "I'm always so happy when I'm with you, Serena. I wonder why that is?"

Surprised by this question, I raised a brow, then said, "Is it because we are extremely compatible? When we're not having a big row?"

"I guess that's it. Compatibility." A wry expression struck his mouth briefly, and was instantly gone. "We don't have many rows," he protested, scowling at me.

When I didn't say anything, he asserted, "You know we don't."

"Perhaps not. But when we do have one, it's very tempestuous, wouldn't you say?" There was a smile on my face when I said this, a hint of amusement in my voice.

He immediately picked up on my tone, and laughed, looked relieved.

I took his hand in mine, and we went on walking down the street. He fell into step with me, and said, "We'd better not go there right now, discuss our disastrous rows. Why spoil this tranquil mood?"

"I agree. Let's forget about our quarrels of the past, and move on, Zac. Let's have a nice evening with Geoff, and give him a great send-off."

Zac nodded. "I'm pleased we're meeting him at Harry's Bar, it's one of my favorite places."

"Mine too," I replied, and a second later I announced, "And here we are." Pushing open the door, we went inside and were immediately greeted by one of the waiters we knew.

Geoff was already there, seated at one of the best tables at the back of the room. He immediately jumped up when he saw us being ushered toward him. We hugged, kissed, and greeted each other warmly, and I couldn't help thinking how well Geoff looked tonight. There was a sparkle in his eyes and his normally slightly dour expression had been erased. He looked relaxed and easygoing for once. I bet he's taken the job in London, I thought, as I sat down. I hoped he had.

"I'm having a Bellini," Geoff said. "What would you like, Serena? Zac?"

I said, "I'd love a Bellini, too, please, Geoff, and why don't you have one, Zac?" Peach juice and prosecco wine would do him no harm, I decided as I said this.

"I will. That'd be great. Thanks, Geoff," Zac said.

Once Geoff had ordered the drinks, he announced, "I enjoyed being in London, it was great, and the guys at Global are the best. Tops. But I'm not sure I can take the job—"

"Why not?" Zac cut in peremptorily, his voice rising. "It's an ideal place to be. You get to cover the whole of Europe from there. You shouldn't pass on this one," he added, looking suddenly concerned.

"Are you hesitating because of your ex-wife?" I asked.

"I think so, Serena," Geoff answered. "I explained that to Harry earlier today. I do wanna try for a reconciliation with her. I miss Chloe, and she needs a dad . . . *me*. Not some other guy."

"Is there another guy in the picture?" Zac asked swiftly, staring intently at Geoff once more.

I was startled by this question, and Geoff looked as if he was too. He said, "Not that I know of, but Martha's young, attractive. Who knows what could happen." He sighed. "Having a normal life these past couple of weeks, being here with you two, and then going to London . . . well, to be honest, I wanna keep living this way. No more wars, I gotta tell you that. War is a dangerous game, and I'm not up to playing any longer."

"You don't have to tell me," I said, and paused when the drinks arrived.

After we'd toasted each other, I continued, "What has Martha said about the idea of moving to London with you?"

"I haven't told her about that possibility yet. I needed to go there, meet the guys, look things over," Geoff explained. "Get the lay of the land, so to speak."

"But you have discussed a reconciliation with her, haven't you?" Zac now asked, leaning forward across the table, his dark eyes focused on Geoff with great interest and also concern.

"Some time ago, yes. And she said she'd consider it if I wasn't putting myself in danger anymore. In other words, she wanted me to quit the front lines."

"Geoff, London's the best place for you!" Zac exclaimed. "For one thing, there's no language barrier, and everything else is pretty much the same as the States. Martha and Chloe would fit in."

"Well, maybe not," Geoff replied. "London's not California."

"But she'd get used to it," Zac shot back. "You ought to talk to Martha immediately, get things settled as soon as possible."

"I agree with Zac," I said. "What are you waiting for, Geoff?"

"To be honest, I'm going to call her tonight. Don't forget, it's nine hours' time difference between L.A. and Venice. I just hope she really does want to reconcile . . . I certainly do. I can't think about much else these days."

"Then you must convince her," Zac told him. "Make her understand how much you need her."

As he said this to Geoff, Zac glanced across at me, and smiled that endearing lopsided smile of his. I found myself smiling back, and then sat up straighter in the chair, fully aware that Zac's inbred charm was surfacing once more. Reconciliation was on his mind. I glanced across at a waiter and silently mouthed, "Menus, please."

"And what are your plans?" Geoff asked, looking from Zac to me.

"We're going to Nice next week," I explained. "I promised my sisters I'd be there for the first anniversary of Dad's death, and Harry agrees Zac should come with me. Anyway, I think we've both had it with the bolthole. It can be very confining, as you well know."

"It can," Geoff replied. "And how's your health?" he went on, turning to look at Zac. "All okay?" He threw Zac a penetrating stare.

"A few bad dreams. One lousy flashback, but I'm doing better than I expected, aren't I, Serena?"

"Yes. You're doing good."

Zac went on. "I don't have PTSD, Geoff, so I don't think I need medical help. And I'm okay to travel."

"That's great news!" Geoff exclaimed with a

wide grin, obviously thinking we had made up.

I did not say a word, simply smiled benignly, and accepted a menu from the waiter. I ordered carpaccio, the thinly sliced raw beef with slivers of parmigiano cheese, and grilled branzino; Zac and Geoff selected the same first course, and ordered risotto primavera for their main dish.

Once the order had been taken and we were alone again, Geoff turned his attention to me. "If I don't take over Global's London office, why don't you do that, Serena? You and Zac together, I mean."

I was somewhat taken aback by this suggestion, and gaped at Geoff. I think Zac was also startled, but he was the first to answer. He quickly jumped in, and exclaimed, "That's not a bad idea, Geoff, not bad at all!"

This comment surprised me, and I said in a businesslike voice, "I can't see you sitting in an office, running Global Images, Zachary North. You'd last a day. Not even that. Half a day. *Maybe.*"

"Yes, I'm afraid you're correct," Zac answered. "But London is a good jumping-off spot. Aside from covering the U.K. from end to end, we could go to Russia, all of Europe, and Africa."

"There's some truth in what you say, but it doesn't excite me," I announced in a firm voice.

Zac was silent, sipped his Bellini.

Geoff changed the subject. He began to talk

about his ex-wife and the idea of moving back to California permanently, to be close to her and their child. But only if London did not appeal to her. I knew he was genuinely serious about this. He'd often talked to me about her in the past, and I'd always understood how much he missed her, and Chloe in particular. I couldn't help thinking how smart he was being. He had chosen life over possible death . . . certainly over endangerment, and that was a good thing. On the other hand, was reconciliation a fantasy?

Geoff ordered another round of Bellinis, and then the carpaccio was served, and Zac and Geoff began a long conversation about football. And I fell down into my thoughts as I ate, preoccupied with my own future as well as Geoff's.

I hoped that Zac had digested Geoff's words about his reasons for quitting, and that they had made an impression on Zac. He was after a reconciliation with me, of that I was quite positive tonight. He had made it clear, without really coming out and saying it. Would it work? Only if he didn't go back to being a combat photographer.

Would he become bored? Restless? Would he succumb to the need to be in danger? The need for that adrenaline rush? I wasn't sure. How could I be? He wanted and needed to expunge those terrible memories of death and destruction and move on. And I would help him as much as I could.

As I listened to him, watched him, I found myself falling under Zac's spell once more. There was no one like him. He was as much an original as my father had been, and just as charismatic. And he *was* the only man I had ever really loved. Still loved, if I was honest with myself.

Would it work if I went back to him? Wouldn't I be walking back into danger? Perhaps. But wouldn't I regret it one day, if I didn't try?

Later, on our walk through the piazza, heading for the bolthole, Zac stopped abruptly, and pulled me into his arms. He kissed me passionately, pressing me into his body. I responded, clung to him as if never to let him go. We went on kissing. I was dizzy with desire, wanting to be in bed with him. Then, suddenly, I thought: No! I can't do this.

Part Three

REVEALING ANGLES
Nice, April

The beauty of the world has
two edges, one of laughter, one
of anguish, cutting the heart asunder.
—Virginia Woolf: *A Room of One's Own*

If two lives join, there is oft a scar.
They are one and one, with a shadowy third;
One near one is too far.
—Robert Browning: "By the Fireside"

Eighteen

My mother used to tell us that she had an innate ability to walk around a house or an apartment and "sniff it out." She genuinely believed that the walls of a dwelling place sucked in the history of those who had lived there over the years, and whose lives had created the atmosphere that prevailed.

We girls knew she was truly happy when she began to smile as she prowled around a room, and suddenly announced that it lived and breathed. We were fairly positive we would probably move there at some point in the future.

One day, when I was about thirteen, I had asked her to explain this belief of hers. She told me that people put their imprint on a dwelling without realizing it, and that this imprint lasted forever. She had then added, "Haven't you heard that expression 'If only walls could talk,' Serena?"

She had smiled in that lovely, enigmatic way of hers, and added, "I think everything that happens in a family, good, bad, happy, or sad, lingers within the home forever. Marriages, births, deaths, sickness . . . every place has seen joyousness, success, failure, and unhappiness. And has perhaps even witnessed something horrendous like a murder, or some other terrible tragedy. Yes, the sheltering walls know everything."

Certainly my mother had left her indelible imprint on Jardin des Fleurs, as my father had also. But it was my mother's spirit, her joie de vivre, and her deeply rooted love for the old manor house that pervaded every room, and the gardens.

My mother had first seen the house in the hills above Nice when she was making a movie in the south of France. This was in 1970, when she had left her third husband. It had been an acrimonious divorce, and she had been relieved to leave Hollywood for a while to make the film abroad.

She had been taken to Jardin des Fleurs by Louise Obrey, her devoted friend and longtime makeup artist, whom she always used whenever she was filming in England or France.

The house was owned by Louise's friend, Pauline Doumer, whose husband Arnaud had founded a renowned cosmetic company and had run it until his death. Apparently, she had been captivated by Jardin des Fleurs from the first moment she saw it, and had returned with Louise several times to attend dinners given by Pauline Doumer. Two years later, in 1972, Pauline died, and when the house came on the market Louise let my mother know at once.

As it happened, my parents, then just newly-weds, were in Paris and they had flown to Nice immediately. "I wanted to 'sniff it out' again," Mom had explained to me and Jessica one day, when she was reminiscing about the early years of her marriage to Dad and their grand romance, which had never waned.

"And what was it that you sniffed?" Jessica had asked, her eyes riveted on our mother.

"Love," my mother had answered instantly, without a moment's hesitation. "Love in all its splendor, in all its different guises and colors. Your father felt it too, as well as that warm, welcoming atmosphere, an overall feeling of peace and tranquility. So I bought it." She had laughed and blown a kiss to Jessica, confided, "You and Cara were conceived the very first night your father and I slept there. I've never told you that, but it's true."

Zac and I had arrived from Venice last night. And now here I was, back at Jardin des Fleurs, sitting in the famous octagonal room located at the top of the main staircase. Jessica and Cara loved this room as much as I did. Aside from being the personification of our mother's taste in decorating, it was, in a certain sense, *our room,* where we had confided in her, shared our secrets, our troubles, asked her advice, and passed many happy hours with her . . . all of our lives in fact, until the day she died. It was her private haven, but we were always welcomed.

The walls were painted that strange pale green faintly tinged with gray, a color that only the French seem able to mix correctly. The polished parquet floor was bare except for a lovely old Aubusson rug in front of the fireplace, where a sofa and two French chairs were grouped around an antique coffee table.

A *bureau plat*, the flat-topped French desk my mother preferred, stood in front of the high, arched window. There were other French country pieces scattered around, echoing the decorative theme of the entire house . . . French Provençal for the most part.

My father painted as a hobby, and some of Tommy's better watercolors were arranged on one wall; above the fireplace hung a full-length, life-sized portrait of my mother. It had been painted by Pietro Annigoni, when my mother was about twenty-seven, and it was my favorite of all the portraits of her.

In the painting she stood in the foreground, posed slightly sideways and gazing into the distance. Behind her was a delicate garden landscape and a faded, high-flung sky. My mother looked absolutely beautiful, ethereal in a pale blue evening gown and a filmy cape made of pale blue organza. The artist had captured that unique, enigmatic quality which my mother had possessed, the faraway, dreamy blue eyes, the mysterious smile, the serenity . . .

I suddenly sat up straighter and glanced at the door as it opened.

My sister Jessica came in, exclaiming, "There

you are, darling, I thought I'd find you up here."
Her arched black eyebrows drew together in a
frown as she walked toward me. "Are you all
right, Pidge? You look troubled."

"I'm fine," I answered, smiling at her, thinking
how smart she looked this morning, in narrow
navy pants and white cotton shirt, her only
jewelry a watch and gold hoop earrings. As she sat
down, I explained, "I was daydreaming and
thinking about Mom."

"What about her?" Jessica asked, pushing her
flowing black hair away from her face, looking at
me questioningly, a dark brow lifting.

"Nothing of any great importance. But from the
moment we got here last night, I've felt the love in
this old place. And just now I was remembering
Mom's theory about atmospheres, and how she
believed that the walls knew everything."

A smile spread across Jessica's face. "When I
look back, and think about Mom, I realize how
clever she was. But also somewhat quirky at
times, I've got to admit that. The problem was
her great beauty, Pidge. Nobody really got past
her looks. They were just stunned by them. And
yet there was quite a brain behind that gorgeous
face."

Jessica's dark eyes were suddenly glistening,
and I was aware she was remembering our mother
with love in her heart, and I thought, for a split
second, that she was going to start crying. But she

didn't, although she remained silent for a moment or two.

Before I could say anything, she continued in a steady voice, "She was priceless at times, wasn't she? And she was mostly right about everything, including houses."

"Yes, she was," I answered, still thinking about Mom myself, and missing her. I suddenly felt as if she were here with us in this room. So strong was the feeling, I glanced around, fully expecting to see her.

Settling back in the chair, my sister changed the subject when she said, "Zac looks better than I expected, Serena, and he's still quite the handsome son of a gun! But I could see he was bone weary, and there's a pinched look to his face. He was very relaxed when you arrived though."

"He was, and he still is. He was happy to go running with Cara. He needs the exercise, he says, and also to let off steam. It'll do him good," I told her.

"You didn't confide much on the phone from Venice, but I suppose privacy was a bit of a problem, in the confines of the bolthole, wasn't it?"

"It was. Although I knew he didn't mind when I was talking to Harry about his health. Zac understood how worried Harry was about him, and still is."

"And I've been worried about you!" Jessica

exclaimed. "I haven't forgotten some of the problems Dad experienced. Does Zac have PTSD?"

"I don't know. But you shouldn't be concerned. If Zac does have it he would never hurt me. And it's a pretty well-known fact that post-traumatic stress disorder doesn't *usually* manifest itself in violence toward others, only violence against oneself. Although there have been exceptions to this rule, I guess."

"I think I probably knew that from Dad or Harry."

"Zac's doing okay at the moment, Jess. He's trying hard, striving to be as normal as possible. And I think that's because he wants us to get back together." I paused. I always told Jessica how things were in my life; she empathized with me, and was never judgmental.

Jessica leaned forward, asked in an earnest voice, "Do you want to get back with him? If you did, where would it lead in the end?"

"I don't know where it would lead. And I'm not sure I want us to get back together. I couldn't cope if he insisted on going back to the front line. I could only handle it if he led a normal life, like Dad and Harry did eventually." Shaking my head, I finished, "Frankly, I don't know how our mother managed, all those years of worrying about Dad's safety."

"And yours, I might add," Jessica pointed out.

"Mom was always a bit agitated inside, when Dad and you were covering a war, at least that's what I believed then, and I do now. Mostly she kept it to herself, and never complained, but she *was* constantly worried."

"I'm sure she was," I replied. "But I wanted to be a war photographer so badly, and I was so driven about it, and you know how selfish the young can be."

She nodded, obviously agreeing with me, and asked, "Are you still in love with Zac, Serena?" As usual she got straight to the point in that very direct way she had.

"I do have feelings for him, yes. After all, we were together for a long time. I do love him, care about his well-being—"

"Don't fudge it, Pidge. I'm talking about *being in love,*" she interrupted, and repeated, "Are you in love with him or not?" Her voice had become an octave higher.

"One day I think I am, the next day I believe I'm not," I explained. "And what I was trying to say a moment ago is that I have loving feelings for him."

"Oh pooh to that! Come on, darling, it's me you're talking to, remember. In my opinion, you're still in love with Zac, but you're also angry with him. You just haven't let go of the anger you felt when you broke up. He was pretty nasty verbally, volatile, and let's not forget that I heard most of his rant."

She paused, gave me a loving look, and added, "It's all right to be in love with him, you know. I would never interfere in your private life, and neither would Cara."

I slumped down in the chair. "I've got to admit I've done nothing but dither about him since I arrived in Venice. I guess I'm worried that he might want to continue being a combat photographer, and that would not sit well with me."

"I'm not surprised you feel that way. He came out of this last battlefield a very disturbed man, from what you've told me. Has he had any more of those flashbacks?"

"No, only the one I told you about on the phone. He still hasn't offered any details about that, nor has he confided what horrendous memories brought it on."

Jessica nodded, rose, went across to the window, stood looking out at the gardens. After a few seconds she returned to the fireplace, and sat down next to me on the sofa. "I'm so glad you're here, Serena, and Zac too. There is something healing about this house, just as Mom always claimed there was."

"Yes, I know that, and talking of healing, how's Cara been lately? Is she still grieving for Jules?"

Jessica said, "A little, and the good thing is she's not so depressed anymore. So I think she's finally making progress."

"She certainly seemed elated when we arrived last night."

"She was happy to see you, Pidge, and Zac. She's always had a soft spot for him," Jess said.

"I know." I gave my sister a pointed look, and went on carefully, "I wish Cara could meet someone, and you too. Aren't there any nice men on your horizon?"

Jessica let out her marvelous, full-bodied laugh, and exclaimed, "Unfortunately not. But I'm okay with my lot in life, Pidge. I enjoy running the auction house, and I have a nice social life here, and in Paris, when I go there. And I'll meet somebody one day. Mom always said that when you're looking for a man there's never one around. So I'm not looking. In the meantime, I'm thrilled you're here, and I'm behind you all the way, whatever you choose to do about Zac. You can always count on me."

"I know that, and I always listen to you, take your advice," I replied, and this was the truth.

A smile flickered on her face, and she said softly, "In the last year of her life, Mom spoke about you often, Serena. I've not told you this before, but she asked me to always look after you. Because I was the eldest, and you were the youngest of her daughters, and it was my responsibility. That was the way she put it. I promised her I would, and that I would always have your back. That expression amused her a lot,

166

she said I was using Dad's military lingo, and she liked that."

I was so touched I couldn't speak for a moment. I felt tears prickling the back of my eyes, and I moved closer, put my arms around her, held her tightly.

She hugged me in return, and against my hair she said, "You were the child she had wanted for so long, and thought she'd never have. She used to say you were her little one, and the treasure of her life."

I didn't speak. I couldn't.

We held each other close for a long time.

Nineteen

After Jessica went off to do the marketing in Nice, I strolled into the gardens, heading for my father's studio at the far end of what our grandmother persisted in calling "the front lawn." We all knew what she meant. It was English terminology for a beautiful lawn at the front of a house. But in this instance ours was at the back, falling away from the long stone terrace. Nonetheless, Grandma insisted on calling it the front lawn despite our teasing.

It was only eight-thirty, but it was already a lovely morning, soft, balmy, with a light breeze floating on the limpid air. The bouncy white clouds in the bright blue sky were highlighted by pale sunshine. I loved these pretty days in the south of France, so typical of late April, when it was not too hot.

I glanced around as I walked down the path, instantly aware of the glorious display of flowers everywhere. It was Cara's handiwork. As hard as she slaved in her orchid business, workaholic that she was, she made time to team up with Raffi, our longtime gardener, who had adored my mother. Mom had created these gardens; Cara was following in her footsteps, and doing a great job. She had made it a labor of love, I could see that.

I hurried on, passed the swimming pool, veered right, and approached my father's studio. I smiled to myself as I paused at the pergola which ran down one side of the stone building.

My father and Harry had built this structure; I held on to one of the supporting poles, closed my eyes, stood perfectly still. In my head I could hear the sound of their hammers, explosive bursts of laughter when they joked with each other, as I now recalled the scenes of them at work. My throat tightened with emotion and I swallowed hard, momentarily carried back in time for a few seconds.

The pergolas were of their own design: four sturdy poles securely planted deep in the earth, topped by a roof made of wooden lattice and covered with ivy. When it grew up around the poles and onto the lattice, which it did in abundance, the ivy eventually made a lovely, leafy green roof, and offered much shade.

Over the past twenty-odd years they had constructed three pergolas on the property, and my mother, good sport that she was, always smiled in delight when a new one unexpectedly appeared, and exclaimed, "Oh, Tommy, angel, how lovely of you to do this. It's perfect to keep me cool. Thank you. And thank you, too, Harry darling."

This was always said with such conviction we all believed every word she uttered, forgetting she was the ultimate actress. But I noticed, over the years, that Mom hardly ever sat under any of the pergolas, preferring a large umbrella to protect herself from the sun. Occasionally, I wondered why no one else noticed, but perhaps they did and simply kept quiet.

Moving on, I took the key from my pocket, unlocked the door, and went into the studio. It had four big windows, and light streamed into the large room. It was exactly the same as it had been in September, when I was last here.

I walked around, touching certain items lovingly, looking at the many photographs, drifting down to the long built-in credenza where all of Dad's light boxes stood in a row. Six of them lined up, so that he could easily view a quantity of photographs at the same time, making sequences that worked for his picture stories.

Everything was in its given place. My sisters

169

had not touched a thing, nor would they ever. Neither would I. His studio looked as it always had . . . as if he had just walked out, gone up to the main house for lunch or dinner. If only that were true.

I went and sat in his chair, a chair I had loved as a child. Because it was an office chair it was on casters, and with a slight push it easily rolled across the floor. It also pivoted around.

I used to sit on Dad's knee and he would give me "a whirl" as he called it. Now I did the same for old times' sake, swinging around in the seat, then rolling over to the window and back.

The chair was teamed with a large Parsons table, which he used as a desk, and it was loaded with Dad's favorite mementos and objects. Also there were four of his favorite photographs of Mom, Jessica, Cara, and me lined up next to each other, which he himself had taken.

I leaned back in the chair and stared at them. The pictures had been shot in the garden here, the summer before Mom had died. Four years ago. I felt a rush of sadness, a longing for her. I stood up, walked across to look at the table full of awards which Dad had won for his dramatic and evocative photographs. Then my eyes lifted to the wall above the awards, where he had hung pictures of himself and Harry in danger zones, and also in Paris: there were some of me and Zac with him. And alongside were photographs of Mom in all her movie-stardom glamour, and other celebrities and actors, writers and journalists of some repute.

And a sudden thought struck me: He'd had a good life. *A grand life.* Tommy Stone had had it all, no doubt about that. This thought made me feel happy, and I was also glad he had died here at Jardin des Fleurs, as Mom had, and not on a battlefield far away.

Under one of the windows my sisters had set up two folding card tables. A large cardboard box stood on each. On one lid a label told me that this contained Dad's unfinished book. It was called COURAGE; the other box was marked MISCELLANEOUS, and therefore told me nothing. A smaller box was labeled VENICE, and that was all.

I stood for a moment with my hand on the box containing Dad's book, thinking about the contents, and I was going to lift the lid and look inside. But I changed my mind. There was no point getting involved with it until after Easter. Today was Wednesday; Harry would be arriving tomorrow, and the day after was Good Friday. It was also the anniversary of my father's death . . . in two days' time he would have been dead for one year . . .

Sighing, I turned around and walked toward the door, swallowing hard once more, fighting back the emotions rising up in me. Then I closed the door on Dad's private domain. Locked it.

As I slipped the key into my jeans pocket, my cell began to vibrate against my other leg. I pulled the phone out, opened it, placed it against my ear.

"Serena here."

"It's me, Serena."

"Hi, Harry! And good morning. How's little old London town?"

"Still standing," he answered swiftly, and hurried on, "Is this a bad time? Do you have a few minutes to talk?"

"I'm fine. I was just waiting for Cara and Zac to come back from their jogging. Actually, I was looking around Dad's studio. It's just the same."

"I'm sure it is. Listen, I've a problem, and need to discuss it."

"Tell me what's wrong."

"As you know, I'd asked Geoff Barnes to fly to London and hold the fort for me for a couple of days, before flying off to L.A. Well, now he's not going to L.A. and I wondered—"

"Not going to see Martha and Chloe? Why not?" I cut in, sounding surprised.

I heard Harry's long sigh, and it spelled trouble, but before I could say anything, he continued, "It's Martha. She doesn't want him to come. At least not to stay for a month. A quick visit to see Chloe, that was always okay. But when he said he was taking a month off to be in California, and also that he wanted her to move to London with him, she said she couldn't do that, and that he shouldn't come to see them. Or rather, he could come for a couple of days for a visit, but that was all."

"There's another man!" I exclaimed, instantly convinced of this. What else could it be?

"Well, aren't you the smart cookie!" Harry responded. "Trust you to figure it out in an instant."

"So I'm right?"

"You are. Naturally, he's hurt, and obviously it came as a surprise. And this is my problem . . . I don't want to leave him alone in London over a holiday weekend. Annie Stewart says she can handle the office perfectly well, and I was toying with the idea of bringing Geoff with me to Nice. How do you feel about that?"

"It's all right with me, Harry, and I don't think the girls would object. Friday is a special day for us, of course, remembering Dad. But Geoff's part of the Global family. And anyway he knew Dad for years. So my answer is yes, bring him with you."

"I was pretty sure you'd say that, and thanks, Serena."

"Is he very upset?" I asked, frowning to myself.

"Hurt, as I said before, and taken aback. But as I pointed out to him, he has been divorced from her for quite a while. So to be honest, I was a bit surprised by the way he reacted. After all, he'd been making *assumptions* they could get back together."

"And how! And creating his own scenario, daydreaming in a way. Poor Geoff. Well, we'll cheer him up. So when will you be here? Shall I come and get you?"

"I've ordered a car to meet us at Nice airport, so you don't have to, Serena. And we should arrive about three o'clock. So we'll be at the house around four-thirty or five depending on the traffic."

"I'm so happy you're coming, Harry, and so are Jess and Cara. It'll be like old times—" I stopped as I said this, annoyed with myself. "Well, not quite," I added miserably.

"No, not quite that, darling, but it'll be comforting, being together. And we'll remember Tommy with a lot of love in our hearts, and fantastic memories of him, and Elizabeth, too. She's part of all this, part of Friday's celebration of Tommy's life."

I went and sat on a chair under the pergola, thinking about Geoff. It was astonishing to me the way people behaved. Geoff was smart, down-to-earth, and dependable. And yet he had held a strange fantasy in his head . . . the idea that his ex-wife would come back to him if he changed a dangerous job for a safe one.

Martha had been terrified he would get killed as a combat photographer, and I understood that perfectly well. But there were obviously other reasons for the divorce, not just the one thing. Separations between couples were caused by many things as a rule. And why wouldn't there be another man looming on the horizon? She was young, good-looking from the photographs I'd seen of her, and she was exceptionally bright, according to Geoff. But then he was prejudiced. And delusional perhaps?

My thoughts were interrupted by Cara shouting out, "Cooee! Cooee!"

I looked up and saw her flying down the hill pell-mell, a slender figure in a black track suit, her black hair held back with the usual scrunchy. As she drew closer I saw that she was perspiring heavily. Behind her, a bit in the distance, I spotted Zac trailing along, looking totally depleted.

As she drew to a standstill, Cara fumbled in her pocket, pulled out a tissue, wiped her face. "That was a helluva run, and I hope I haven't been too excessive with Zac."

I laughed, mostly because she looked so worried, and obviously she knew very well she had overdone it with him.

"He'll live," I said, my eyes focused on him. "But he doesn't look so good at this moment."

"Oh dear," Cara exclaimed, and turned around, stared at him.

A second or two later, Zac finally joined us. He was soaked to the skin, I could see that, and he looked unusually pale, and rather diminished.

I jumped up and went to him, took hold of his arm. "Are you all right?" I asked anxiously, peering at him.

"Exhausted. But I'll be okay," he answered, with a forced smile. "She's pretty damn fast, that sister of yours!"

"I'm sorry, Zac," Cara said, smiling at him somewhat ruefully. "I didn't mean to take you through your paces quite as fast as that."

He nodded, and began to walk toward the house.

I followed behind him with Cara. I said, at one moment, "How about some hot coffee and breakfast, Zac?"

"God no! I'm wet through and as sticky as hell. I'd like a shower first and a bottle of Evian. Then I'll have breakfast with you."

"It's a deal," I said.

"I'll join you now," Cara said. "I need to talk to you about something."

Twenty

Whenever Cara announced that she wanted to talk to me about something I usually became instantly alarmed, especially when she spoke in a somber tone, as she had just now. Inevitably, she had bad news to impart. And I wasn't in the right frame of mind to hear that this morning. I sought peace and quiet.

I followed her into the small alcove which

adjoined our large country-style kitchen, a comfortable spot to have a drink, a snack, or to read. We both sat down on the banquette and put our mugs of coffee on the oak table.

Immediately, I said, "I have something to tell you, Cara, so I'll speak first, if you don't mind."

"Go ahead. What do you want to say?" she asked, looking across at me, lifting her mug, drinking the coffee eagerly.

"Harry called me just before you appeared in front of me on the hill. He wants to bring Geoff Barnes with him tomorrow. I said that was okay, and I hope you agree."

I then went on to explain about Geoff, Martha, and the situation that had apparently just developed in L.A.

Once I had finished, Cara said, "I don't know about Jess, but it's all right with me," and then she jumped up, went into the kitchen, saying over her shoulder, "I need a glass of water. Back in a minute."

I sat relaxed on the banquette, and bit into a croissant, enjoying it, because for once I'd spread butter and raspberry jam on it. To hell with my diet this morning; I needed a treat once in a while.

When she returned with her glass of water, Cara picked up where we'd left off. "As I said, I don't mind Geoff Barnes being here for Dad's memorial evening tomorrow. If I remember correctly, he's been part of the Global team for years."

"What do you think Jess will say?"

"I doubt there'll be a problem, Serena." After finishing the glass of water, she continued, "Actually, it's Jess I want to talk to you about."

There was such a strange look on her face when she said this, I peered at my sister intently, quickly asked, "Is there something wrong?"

"I don't know, there could be . . . as far as her health is concerned."

"What are you getting at?" I was suddenly worried about Jessica, and pressed, "Is she ill? What's the matter with her?"

"I suspect she might have the same rare osteoporosis that Mom had," Cara announced, leaning back against the cushions, and staring at me knowingly.

"But Jessica's not pregnant. Or is she?" I gave her the benefit of a long hard stare, knowing she would tell me the truth. She never avoided being the bearer of bad news. Cara claimed she had to be absolutely honest, couldn't pull any punches, and this was the truth, she never did. Nonetheless, it seemed to me that she derived a certain pleasure from bringing unsettling news to us all.

"I'm certain Jessica's not pregnant," Cara said, finally answering my question. "She would have told me; however, lately she's complained of aching bones, tiredness in her legs, and don't forget that fall she had in the auction rooms recently."

I leaned forward, focused my steady gaze on Cara, said pointedly, "But she didn't break anything, and if she has that rare kind of osteoporosis, surely she would have broken at least one bone, don't you think?"

"I do, yes, there's some truth in what you say, Serena. But she has complained a lot about her aches and pains, and so I want you to do something for me, and—"

I cut in, "What do you want *me* to do?"

"Talk to her. You are always able to get through to her. So please, ask her to have a few tests, X-rays, that sort of thing. And before you say I should do it, I want you to know she doesn't listen to me about anything, not anymore."

"Oh come on, Cara, I know she listens to you," I exclaimed. "You're twins, joined at the hip, closer than any two people I know. It's always been that way. I remember Mom once telling me that even as babies of only six months you were very aware of each other, that when she laid you side by side in a cot you held hands with each other."

Cara shook her head. "It's better you talk to her. She definitely pays attention to what you say. Look, she wouldn't even listen to me about Allen Lambert."

"Who's Allen Lambert?" I asked, baffled.

"Her boyfriend."

"Jessica has a boyfriend!" I was genuinely

startled and I knew my voice had risen shrilly. Why didn't I know about him?

"Yes," Cara answered. "I can't say he's my favorite though, and when I said I wasn't so keen on him, she bit my head off, and walked out of the room."

"She hasn't breathed a word about him to me, and I must admit I'm surprised about that." I felt a small pang that she hadn't confided in me.

"So am I," Cara agreed, giving me an odd look.

"How long has she been seeing him?"

"About a year, but sort of off and on. He travels a lot and he's not always around."

"But who is he? How does she know him?" I probed, riddled with curiosity.

"He lives here, and also in London, and she's known him for about five, six years. But I guess she only started seeing him twelve months ago."

"What's he like?"

"Quiet, doesn't say a lot, sort of wimpy, come to think of it. But rather good-looking, in a blond English way. He has some sort of PR company, or maybe he's in advertising, I'm not sure."

"Has she invited him to Dad's memorial evening?" I wondered out loud.

"I rather doubt it, I think she sees tomorrow night as a very personal dinner, just for family. It'll only be the three of us, Zac, and Harry of course. And now Geoff Barnes, but he's from Global, kind of family in a sense."

"I understand. And perhaps I'll meet Allen Lambert over Easter weekend, and look, Cara, I am going to tell her you mentioned him to me. Because I want to know more about him, and I'm going to ask a lot of questions."

"You can tell her. I don't care, it's not a secret that she's seeing him. Maybe she'll be more forthcoming with you."

"Do you think she's really involved with him? You know, serious about him?"

Cara shrugged. "I've no idea, as I said, she doesn't say much, plays it close to the vest."

"Is he available? He's not married, is he?"

"No, he's not married. But he was. He's a widower." Cara made a moue with her mouth, and shook her head. "His wife died in some sort of strange way . . . in Africa."

I was about to ask a few more questions when Zac strolled into the kitchen. He had showered and shaved, and his hair was still damp. He was wearing blue jeans and a white T-shirt, looked fresh, well groomed, and this pleased me.

I stood up and walked toward him, asking, "Do you want me to make you some eggs, Zac? Or will you settle for a croissant with your coffee?"

He swung around when he heard my voice, and smiled lopsidedly. "A croissant's fine." As he spoke he poured himself a mug of coffee, and reached for the milk.

Cara came strolling out of the alcove with her

empty cup and glass, and after putting them in the dishwasher she said, "See you both later. I've got to clean up and go to the greenhouses."

I nodded, watched her go. I couldn't understand why she seemed so disapproving of Allen Lambert. Did she know something bad about him? Did he have a reputation? Had she been trying to warn Jessica about him? I was puzzled, and I aimed to find out about him.

Twenty-one

S o you think Geoff has been deluding himself about Martha, and what she feels for him? Is that what you're saying?" Zac asked, half turned toward me in the car seat.

"You've got it," I said without taking my eyes off the road. I was driving into Nice, where Zac wanted to go shopping for a few items, and there was heavy traffic this morning. "He longed to be reconciled with her so much, he believed she wanted that too. But obviously her interests have turned elsewhere."

Zac let out a long sigh, and remained silent for a moment or two. Then he said, in a low voice, "Poor sod. He'd set his heart on it, so it must have come as a terrible shock. And telling him over the phone. Jesus! That wasn't nice."

"Remember, they are divorced, and have been for several years. He was living in a dream world, frankly. I think he'd convinced himself that she'd come back to him, start again, if he left the front lines. But two or three years is a long time for a young woman to be divorced and alone," I pointed out.

"You're right, Serena, but I can't help feeling sorry for him."

"So do I. Anyway, Cara knows I told Harry that Geoff could come for the weekend, and she made no objection. Neither will Jessica."

"I'm glad Harry's doing that, bringing him here, and we'll try and cheer him up. He's a good man, and I'll never forget what he did for me, coming to get me out of that risky hellhole in Afghanistan." Zac straightened in the seat, and went on, "And what are Geoff's plans after this weekend? Do you know?"

I shook my head. "Harry had asked Geoff to hold the fort in London, until he got there to make a few more changes in management. He's sent Matt White to cover Pakistan, in Geoff's place, and he has to decide who'll run the London bureau, until Geoff officially takes over. If he's still prepared to do that."

"But surely he will. There's not much for him in California, if his ex-wife is hooked up with another guy."

"I hope he'll take London, but Harry told me Geoff's been thrown for a loop. I'm not worried about the London bureau, there are a couple of people who can run Global equally as well as Geoff. Things'll be all right there, no matter what."

"Pete Sheldon's pretty good. He could step in anywhere."

"I agree. Harry and Geoff will be arriving late tomorrow afternoon. Harry's already ordered a car, so we don't have to meet them at the airport. Tell me about your run with Cara. How was it?"

"*Great.* She ought to enter the New York Marathon next October. Talk about speed, she goes like the wind. I couldn't keep up with her for very long. I guess I'm out of shape. But the run did me good, Pidge. I said I'd go with her tomorrow. Running helps me to let off steam."

"I'm glad." I drove on, silent, wondering whether to repeat Cara's conversation about Jessica. Immediately, I decided not to, following the rules I'd been brought up with: We kept family matters to ourselves. Instead, I said, "I'm going to park the car in Lulu's little driveway. You remember our old cook, don't you?"

"I sure do, best food I ever had, except for Mom's. And she lets you do that, does she?"

"I'm not certain that she's aware there's a car there, or that it's mine, she's very old now. But her daughter Adeline is still working for us at the house, running it. And her other daughter, Magali, comes in to help when we have guests or if Jessica is giving a special dinner or cocktail party. It was

Adeline who told me to make use of their drive a long time ago. She's already called their house this morning, spoken to Lulu's caregiver, told her that I'll be parking there for a bit."

Zac nodded. "It certainly saves driving around Nice looking for a parking spot. When we've done my bit of shopping I'd like to go to the Hotel Negresco, for old times' sake, buy you a drink. I used to go there with Tommy. After that we can find a bistro for lunch. Okay?"

"That'd be great, Zac."

I peered ahead, drove carefully, paying attention when we entered the city. There was a lot of traffic today, because Easter was looming, and although the French took this religious holiday seriously, they also celebrated it with great spirit.

Lulu's house was in a small back street behind the Promenade des Anglais, and after I had parked, I walked with Zac toward Vieux Nice. The old town was much the same as it was in medieval times, with narrow bustling streets and ancient buildings. We soon found various shops for Zac to purchase T-shirts and underwear, and then we headed toward Cours Saleya, where we passed the flower and vegetable markets, and lots of busy cafés.

As we wandered on, heading toward the seafront, Zac suddenly said, "I'd like to get gifts for Jessica and Cara. What do you think they'd like?"

I was taken aback for a moment, but then said,

"They're hard to buy for, Zac, even I have a hard time wondering what to get. I think your best bet is perfume."

"I'd like to do it this morning, Pidge, before we go back to the house. Give them a gift each tonight."

"No problem," I replied. We strolled out onto the beautiful Promenade des Anglais, which was built by the English colony living in Nice in the 1800s. Lined with palm trees, it was wide, stretched for three miles along the seafront, and most of the best hotels were located there, as well as many boutiques.

Turning to Zac as we approached the Hotel Negresco, Nice's grandest hotel, I said, "Dad always told us this was a fairy-tale castle when we were little. And it does look like one, don't you think? All white, with its fanciful dome and balconies."

Zac nodded, gazing up at the hotel. "It sure does, and let's go to the bar and toast him. I always enjoyed my little sojourns here with Tommy. It's one place I got to know a different side of him."

Once we were seated in the bar, I told Zac to order mimosas, because the orange juice counteracted the champagne. "I've got to drive us home, remember?" I explained, when he stared at me, frowning. But I was also concerned about Zac's consumption of liquor. He didn't always know when to stop, and drink affected him badly these days.

He suddenly smiled at me, nodded. "Hey, that's what Tommy used to order!" he exclaimed, and beckoned to a waiter.

Within minutes we were toasting my father, and then Zac settled back in the chair and recounted a few anecdotes about him, and their adventures together, and he did so with a certain glee.

I had heard them all before, but I listened attentively, relieved that Zac was his normal self. During the night he had shouted a lot and been restless.

Before we left Venice, I'd phoned Jessica, told her I wanted Zac to use the room which adjoined mine, and which had once been used by my nanny when I was a toddler. Jessica had agreed this was a good idea. Certainly, with the door open, I could hear him, as I had last night. I had gone in, but he was suddenly quiet, and under the covers. After a few seconds, I'd left.

Against my better judgment, I allowed him to order two more mimosas, and we sipped them, still talking about Dad. At one moment I asked him where he wanted to have lunch, mentioning a number of bistros we knew. I thought it was time we left the bar.

"Oh, let's stay here," he answered, offering me that endearing lopsided smile. "I don't mean here in the bar, but outside on the terrace. Why go searching for a bistro when we're in the best place in town?"

He said this in such a jaunty way, I couldn't help laughing. But in my heart I knew that he didn't want to bestir himself; it was a common occurrence these days, almost as if he didn't have the strength to move. On the other hand, perhaps he was just tired from jogging with Cara.

It was four o'clock by the time we got back to Jardin des Fleurs, and the first person I ran into was Jessica. She gave me her usual dazzling smile as I walked into the kitchen, where she was busy preparing dinner.

I knew at once she was making one of her specialties, boeuf bourguignon . . . beef stew in red wine with bacon, onions, and mushrooms. She usually did most of the cooking, was sometimes helped by Adeline when we had guests, but I noticed Lulu's daughter was nowhere in sight at the moment.

I smiled back as I walked over to the long oak kitchen table in the middle of the floor, where Jessica was preparing vegetables. There was a delicious smell of beef and bacon floating in the air, and my mouth began to water.

"I can smell that we're in for a delicious dinner tonight," I said, sliding onto one of the tall stools at the opposite side of the table, gazing at my sister.

"Beef stew. I know it's one of your favorites, that's why I'm making it, Pidge." As she spoke she looked toward the door expectantly. "Where's Zac?"

"He went upstairs to rest. We've been shopping in Nice, buying a few things for him, but he seemed a bit done in when we'd finished lunch."

"That's possible. But he does seem in control of himself. A bit quiet, not his usual exuberant self, but he's been through a lot."

I sat studying Jessica, wondering how to broach the subject of her new boyfriend, feeling a little awkward.

She saved me the trouble, when she put down the wooden spoon she was holding, and said, "I haven't told you about Allen Lambert, Pidge, because there's not a lot to tell. It's not a big romance, nothing like that. What it is, actually, is a very nice friendship."

I stared at her, said nothing.

Jessica began to chuckle. "I see you're surprised I'm aware Cara talked to you about him . . . well, you know what she's like. Gossipy. She came and confessed she'd been blabbing to you about Allen, when I got back from the auction house an hour ago. I think she felt guilty for chattering behind my back. I told her to forget it, all families do that . . . gossip about each other, I mean."

"Well, I don't!" I exclaimed a little heatedly.

"Please don't be upset, Serena, I know you're

probably feeling hurt because I didn't confide in you, but honestly there's nothing to confide. If I was involved in a big romance, you'd be the first to know."

"Cara said I should talk to you, persuade you to go and have more medical tests, Jess. She thinks you could have inherited Mom's osteoporosis."

I saw sudden anger in Jessica's dark eyes, and she exclaimed, "She's too much! The cheek of it! Why did she come to you? We've discussed it at length, she and I, and I went for the additional X-rays the day after my fall, and I gave you those results when you were in Venice."

"I know. I guess she still worries about you."

Jessica gave me a steady look, but there was a hint of annoyance in her voice when she said, "I assure you I'm not sick. I'm very healthy, in fact."

"Don't let her get your goat! You know she expresses opinions even when she doesn't know anything about the subject she pontificates about."

Jessica let out a long sigh, and picked up the wooden spoon, stirred the bowl. "I do know she used to omit telling us things years ago."

"But she's never lied, to my knowledge. So why would she lie to me about you now?" I said.

"What lies?"

"She says you're constantly complaining about having tired legs and aching bones."

My sister shook her head. I could tell from her expression she was exasperated. "She's exaggerating. I admit I did complain about my aches and pains, but that was just after I'd fallen."

"Let's move on. I guess she told you Harry's bringing Geoff Barnes with him tomorrow, and that I'd said he could."

"It's fine with me, as you knew it would be. Geoff's part of Global Images, so he's family."

She took the bowl of vegetables over to the sink, filled the bowl with water, and placed it on the countertop. Then she turned off the stew, and returned to the table. Removing her apron, she came around the table, and took hold of my hand. "Come on," she said, "let's go and sit in the garden, and I'll tell you all about Allen Lambert."

"All right," I said, following her. And I couldn't help wondering about the Englishman Jessica was involved with. Was he a cad, as Granny would have called him? One of those men who have a dangerous aura?

Twenty-two

We went and sat in the pergola which Dad and Harry had built not far from the kitchen. Their idea was that we could have alfresco meals in the summer. The food was in close proximity, and that made life easier for everyone, cooks and helpers alike.

I sat down, and then lifted my eyes, looked up at the Alpes Maritimes. The range of mountains which soared above the gardens was magnificent, and very beautiful, whether covered in greenery as they were now, or frosted with snow in winter.

When I was little, my father had told me that the mountains were the guardians of our house, and that we would be safe always, because we were protected by them forever. He had had so many tales to tell, and I had listened attentively, and believed every word.

As I believed Jessica. I'd never known her to tell me a lie in her life. She was my favorite sister, and I was close to her. I loved Cara, but she had certain traits that irritated me, and I was aware she also irritated Jess at times, even though they were twins and extremely close, so very connected. Cara wasn't a bad person, she was just complicated, and sometimes strangely remote, distant. It was as if she wasn't part of us, part of the family, at times.

Jessica broke into my thoughts, and asked, "Are you worrying about Zac, Pidge?"

I glanced at her; she looked concerned. "No, I'm not. Why do you say that?"

"You seem very thoughtful; *pensive,* actually."

I shook my head. "I was thinking about Cara . . . she gets to me occasionally."

"I know. She does to me, too, and she did to Mom, as well. But she's fine. Deep down, she loves us, couldn't bear to be without us. She cares as much as we do, and in a crunch she'd be there, defending us with all her might. She'd take a bullet for us."

"I know that, I really do. So go on, tell me about Allen Lambert. And don't leave out a thing."

She burst out laughing, in her usual cheerful, exuberant way, and leaned back in the wicker garden chair. "All right, here goes. I've known Allen for six years. He works for a PR firm in London, where he has a flat. But he also has a house in Nice. His mother died when he was a child and his father remarried. His stepmother was French, and so he spent a lot of time here in his childhood, and when he was grown up. After his parents died he decided to keep their house in Nice. He spends many weekends here, and the summer. I first met him socially, and later he did some PR work for Stone's."

"When did you start going out with him?"

"We occasionally had dinner over the years, but we've grown closer these last few months, and we're seeing more of each other. Still, it is just a friendship."

"I was startled when Cara told me about him."

"I'm not having a love affair with him, Pidge, which is why I didn't mention him when I was in New York. He's just a friend."

"Cara doesn't like—" I stopped abruptly, could've bitten my tongue off. I didn't want to be a tittle-tattle, or repeat what Cara had said to me.

Jessica was far too smart, knew I'd been about to confide.

She said, "I know Cara doesn't like Allen. I think that's probably because he's rather reserved, not a man given to making a fuss. She has no clue what he's actually like, Serena, because she hasn't spent any real time with him. Her judgment's flawed because she doesn't know him."

"And what is he like?" I asked.

"He's a lovely person, attractive, but a bit reserved, as I just said. Nonetheless he has a great sense of humor, and he's cultured, well educated, and just a little complex."

"In what way?" I asked, my rampant curiosity getting the better of me.

"I suppose I should have said that his life's been complex in a certain way. His wife was killed in Africa."

"Cara mentioned that. What happened to her? And what was she doing in Africa?"

"Felicity ran a not-for-profit organization. Some sort of charity created to provide aid to deprived African children. She was on a trip with members of her team, and they died because they got trapped between two factions who were fighting each other in a bloody war. It was eight years ago."

"Oh my God, Jess, how awful! Allen wasn't in Africa with her, I guess?"

"No, he wasn't, he was working in London. He kissed her good-bye at Heathrow Airport and never saw her again."

"Where did she die?"

"In Sudan."

"So are you saying his life's been complex because he's not recovered from his wife's death?" I asked, staring at my sister, frowning. Eight years seemed a long time to grieve.

"Not exactly. He's over it now. But I do think her death does sometimes come back to haunt him, and he feels guilty, blames himself for letting her go to such a dangerous place. And in the middle of a violent civil war."

I nodded, then asked, "Does he have children?"

"No, they didn't have kids, and believe me, he's very thankful for that, considering what happened to Felicity."

"I can well understand that." I let out a heavy sigh. "What terrible things happen in life. You just never know what dreadful tragedies strike at people, what people sometimes have to bear."

"No, you don't, and when we first met he hardly ever mentioned it. But he did tell me all about it eventually, and I'm glad he did. I understand him much better now." Jessica glanced at me and smiled. "You'll like Allen, Pidge."

"Am I going to meet him?"

"Of course. I invited him to lunch on Easter Sunday, and he can't wait to meet you." Before I could answer Jess started to laugh, changing our slightly somber mood. "You'll never guess what he calls Mom."

"Did he know her then?"

"Not well. He met her around the time he met me, and he refers to her as Grace Monroe."

I stared at her, did not answer for a split second and then I too began to laugh. "Because Mom was a cross between Grace Kelly and Marilyn Monroe? That is what you mean, isn't it?"

"Yes, it is. Of course, he's right on target. Dad always said that about her himself, ladylike but loaded with sex appeal."

"I like the sound of Allen Lambert. But where do you two stand exactly?" I pushed, wanting to get to the heart of the situation.

"I'm not sure about his feelings, I know he likes me a lot, and is attracted to me, and we do enjoy being together. I have a feeling he's becoming a little emotionally attached, certainly more involved with me and on a new level."

"And what about you?" I probed.

She cocked her head on one side, and a playful smile flickered on her mouth before she said, "I think I'm kind of falling for him, Pidge."

I grinned at her. "I'm so glad I'm here. I'm going to push the two of you into each other's arms and over the edge."

"The edge of what?" she asked, looking slightly puzzled.

"The edge of the pit of love. Down you'll go, and you'll both be ecstatic, I promise you."

Twenty-three

Jessica returned to the kitchen to finish preparing the beef stew, and I went upstairs to look for Zac. I found him in my bedroom, sitting on the sofa, staring at the television screen.

His face was pale, and he had a stricken look in his eyes. As I closed the door and walked toward the sofa, he glanced across at me, picked up the zapper, and clicked off the TV.

"You're upset, aren't you?" I said in an even voice. "You've been watching news from Libya, and the rest of the Middle East."

"I have, yes," he agreed. "But I'm not so much upset as *dismayed*. Uprisings in so many countries, fighting in the streets, angry, distressed civilians frantically fighting trained professional soldiers, which can only end up badly . . . all this rotten killing . . ." His voice trailed off, and he sighed, exasperated and troubled, no question about that.

I sat down next to him on the sofa, and he took hold of my hand. "I just can't stomach it anymore, Serena. The whole world has gone mad. It's become a battlefield . . . there's violence and bloodshed everywhere you look." He stopped abruptly, leaned back, rested his head against the sofa, and fell silent.

I thought he looked tired, drained even, and very sad. The short time he had been sitting in front of the television, digesting the latest news, had done him in, I decided.

Zac had been so much better this morning and over lunch, almost his old self again. Then it suddenly struck me that he was not upset because he wasn't over there covering the events, but because he was filled with sorrow that this turmoil was happening at all.

Turning to him, wanting to express my understanding of his grief, I saw that his light green eyes were filled with tears. He started to say something, but couldn't quite get the words out. His mouth began to tremble, and he brought his hands to his face, started to cry; I saw the tears leaking through his fingers.

"Oh Zac, how can I help you?" I asked gently, putting my arm around his shoulders, moving up closer to him, longing to make him feel better. He began to sob and held on to me tightly, as if he were drowning. And in a way he was . . . drowning in pain and heartache.

At that precise moment something shifted in me. I knew without a shadow of a doubt that I loved him completely. He was the love of my life.

There was no way for me to turn away from this knowledge, or deny it any longer. I loved Zachary

North with every fiber of my being. I wanted to be with him always. To spend the rest of my life with him. No matter what happened, whatever he chose to do, we must be together, to love and cherish each other for as long as we lived.

I knew now that I had been in denial for the past year. Jessica had been right; she had said earlier that I was filled with anger about Zac's behavior a year ago, when we had broken up. Now that anger had mysteriously dissipated, was entirely gone. Just like that, in a flash. What I felt was total love for him. I understood him, and his predicament—disillusionment and a sense of loss. I wanted to make him whole again, to restore him to himself, to help him build a future.

Eventually, the sobs quietened, finally subsided, and he wiped his face with his fingertips, shook his head. "Sorry," he mumbled. "So sorry, Serena."

"It's all right. I understand, I really do."

"That's why I wanted to be with *you,* and no one else. I need you. I trust you absolutely, and I feel safe with you, because . . . well, because I know you're trustworthy, loyal, dependable, an honorable person. You have such integrity, Serena, like no one I've ever known. And I love you for everything you are."

I didn't respond. I couldn't. I was touched by his words, knowing how sincere he was being. After a split second, I said, "Dad once told me that the impact of war on the human psyche is overwhelming. And you have been overwhelmed in Afghanistan. Fortunately, you knew you had to get out before it was too late. It's devastated you, leaving the front, but you did the right thing."

He stared at me intently for a long moment. "Tommy was right, and so are you. And yes, it *was* time . . ." He paused, took a deep breath. "I want to tell you about the flashback I had when I smashed the television set in Venice. Can I?"

"Yes, tell me. I've been wanting to know. If you unburden yourself it will help you, Zac, I'm certain of that."

"When I woke up that night, in the bolthole in Venice, I thought I was back in Helmand Province, where I'd been embedded for some weeks with a platoon of Marines, out on patrol near a remote village," he explained. "We were on the edge of the village, in an old building. A lot of heavily armed insurgents were out there, snipers mounting round-the-clock attacks on us. Very heavy attacks. I knew two young Marines, one from Brooklyn, the other from Connecticut . . . Mitch Johnson and Joe Marshall—"

Zac's voice choked up and his mouth began to tremble. But he swiftly managed to regain his control, continued slowly, "Mitch and Joe went out on a recce. The lieutenant in charge needed more information, so a reconnaissance it was." Zac paused, blew out air, ran his hands over his face nervously.

"You don't have to go on, if it's too painful," I said softly.

"It's okay. I'm okay," he said, and after a short while he continued steadily, "I was with the lieutenant, Jack Bentley, from Los Angeles. Our eyes were riveted on Mitch and Joe as they moved down that dangerous road toward the village. They went very slowly, and with enormous caution. A corporal and a bunch of Marines standing near us had their rifles poised ready for action and covering Joe and Mitch, watching their backs. Suddenly an improvised explosive device went off, and then another. Those roadside bombs were everywhere on that road, and lethal. Mitch and Joe were upright one moment, down on their backs the next."

Zac stopped, swallowed hard. "The lieutenant acted at once, instantly radioed for a medevac. We were very lucky, one of the Black Hawk choppers was already close, and it came in quickly."

"Was the chopper able to land safely?" I asked, knowing how frightening and tricky the situation must have been, not to mention dangerous for the pilot and medics on the chopper.

"It was tough going," Zac replied. "As you know, the medevac chopper is not armed, but is always accompanied by another aircraft that is. As usual, the insurgents were shooting at both. Somehow, the pilot of the medevac heli managed to get it down into the landing zone safely.

Without any incidents. The lieutenant and some of the Marines ran forward to help move Mitch and Joe, and the medics got them into the helicopter and out safely, heading for a nearby medical facility."

Zac blinked, coughed behind his hand, and I saw the tears glittering in his green eyes once more. After clearing his throat a few times, he said quietly, "The lieutenant told me he didn't know if they were going to make it . . . Joe had lost a leg and had a spinal injury, and Mitch had a gaping hole in his chest—" Abruptly, Zac broke off, jumped up and went into my bathroom, closed the door behind him.

I was certain he had gone there to weep again, seeking his privacy, needing to be alone. And I understood all the reasons why. I had been on the front line for years. I myself had been where he was emotionally at this moment. I knew how raw and distressed he must be, remembering everything, reliving what he had witnessed that violent morning in Afghanistan . . . thinking of the horrific injuries those two young Marines had suffered.

That was why I truly was the only person he could talk to, because I understood what he had been through. His parents and his siblings loved him, no doubt would want to help, but they had not had any experiences on the front line, nor did they know what combat was really like. I was the veteran here, and I could empathize with him, comfort him, and hopefully pull him through.

As he had been recounting what had happened, I had visualized everything in my mind's eye. The Black Hawk chopper coming in, accompanied by an armed aircraft escort for protection. I knew only too well that the insurgents never paid any attention to the Red Cross emblem painted on the underbelly of the medevac chopper, even though under international law these helicopters are supposed to be off-limits when it comes to enemy fire, because of the Red Cross insignia.

But it meant nothing to them, even though medevacs would transport insurgents who had been injured as well as civilian Afghan adults and children hurt by an IED, or caught in the cross fire. They took them all to medical facilities to be looked after.

I understood Zac's raging emotions and what he was going through, and my heart ached for him. All I wanted now was to help him to heal, and to get to a better place in his mind and heart.

The bathroom door opened, and he walked out, obviously in better shape. He certainly looked calm as he came and sat down on the sofa, a faint smile flickering for a fleeting moment.

"I'm sorry I lost it, Serena," he said. "I don't exactly know what happens, but unexpectedly I feel overcome and I start weeping. I can't help it, and then I'm embarrassed. A man shouldn't cry like that."

"Yes, a man should cry!" I exclaimed. "And I'm glad you did, and do. And that you will again, if you are moved to do so. Men and women are quite different in many ways, yet we certainly share the same emotions about things." I grabbed his hand, held it tightly.

He remained quiet, digesting what I'd said.

"You mustn't be embarrassed or ashamed of crying, Zac," I continued. "You're human, and we're all affected by life, by its heartaches and sorrows. And also by its joys and triumphs. Always remember that."

He inclined his head slightly, obviously agreeing. He then moved closer. "There's something else I have to tell you . . ." He paused, looked into my face. After a moment, he said in a low voice, "I'm still in love with you, Serena. I wanted to tell you that in Venice, but somehow I felt you didn't want to hear it. At least not then, and I lost my nerve."

I was taken aback, startled that he was announcing this, and with such conviction. I didn't speak, simply stared back at him, seeking the right words.

"Could we . . . can we? Start all over again?" he asked me, his voice tense.

I still didn't say anything, just looked into those green eyes, realizing how serious he was being, and sincere.

"Do you remember what I used to say to you?" he said. "Come with me and be my love, and I will all the pleasures prove? Well, I do want that . . . I want you to be my love, and I will make you happy."

"Don't, Zac, please don't, you'll have me in tears," I whispered.

"No tears, Pidge. Only kisses." He leaned in to me and his lips brushed against my check. "I'm in love with you more than ever, you know."

When I was silent, he said, "Don't you believe me?"

"Yes, I do," I finally replied. "Geoff told me."

"Is that why you believe me? Because Geoff Barnes told you?" Unexpectedly he began to chuckle, shaking his head, then he put his arms around me and held me close. "So, can we start all over and do it right this time?"

"Yes," I said, and I felt my love for him flowing through me, and I knew this would never change. I would be steadfast always. "I'm still in love with you too, Zac," I finally told him. "And I will be for the rest of my life."

He released me, sat back, stared into my face, his own full of relief. "I can't begin to tell you how much I've longed to hear you say that." He paused, and a reflective look crossed his face. After a moment's hesitation, he continued, "I'm sorry, Serena, for all the things I said last year. For the hurt and pain I caused you. I want to spend the rest of my life making up for that, and loving you as you deserve to be loved."

We talked for a little while longer, opening up our hearts to each other. He said things to me I never thought I would hear, and I did the same, and we were both happy about this. Finally we had cleared the air, settled things between us. We were on a new journey together.

Unexpectedly, I felt the need to get out of the room, to go down to the gardens. It was now late afternoon; night would soon be encroaching, and I wanted to catch those moments before the sun finally set. It was beautiful at this time of day on the Côte d'Azur.

I jumped up, gave Zac my hand, and said, "Come on, lazybones, let's go to the terrace and have a lemonade." I grinned at him. "To celebrate our reconciliation."

"Lemonade it is," he agreed and gave me his lopsided smile.

We went downstairs together. The house was perfectly still. Nothing stirred. Nobody was there. I knew Cara would still be at the greenhouses, and Jessica was probably resting in her room. As we went into the kitchen my nose twitched, and Zac exclaimed, "Wow! That smells good. What's cooking?"

"A beef stew," I answered, walking over to the refrigerator. I took out the jug of lemonade, filled two glasses, and then we went out to the terrace.

"Just look at that sky!" Zac exclaimed. "It's full of golden fire."

"I know. It usually is at this time of day. The Magic Hour, that's what they call it in Movieland. And it was Mom's favorite time of day."

"Yeah, I remember that, remember how she loved to come and sit here, and it is the Magic Hour indeed, wonderful for filming . . . especially a romantic scene."

"My mother liked you a lot, Zac, she always said you reminded her of my father."

"Did she really?" He sounded surprised. "That's quite a compliment. And I hope I am, like Tommy, I mean. Well, I do know one thing. I'm a one-woman man, just as he was. He never had eyes for anyone else but your mother."

"I know," I said, and, for a reason I didn't understand, I suddenly shivered. Gooseflesh ran up my arms. Somebody just walked over my grave, I thought, conjuring up one of Grandma's old sayings. I pushed the saying away, not liking the thought of it at all.

Twenty-four

A little while later, we walked down to the studio, stopping off in the kitchen to get the key out of the green-glazed jug on the mantelpiece.

As we went inside the studio, Zac looked around and said, "It's exactly the same, isn't it? Tommy might have just gone up to the house to see your mother . . ." He broke off, staring at me.

I nodded. "I thought that when I was here this morning. Perhaps because his presence is really and truly in this room. After all, he occupied it for many years, and somehow he left a lot of himself behind."

Zac walked over to me, and took my face in his hands, gazed deeply into my eyes. "I'm so sorry I made you miss the plane," he said quietly. "Truly, truly sorry."

"It's all right," I said. "It happened, and perhaps it was meant to be."

Zac leaned forward and kissed me on my cheek, and then he put his arms around me and brought me forward, holding me tightly against him. I clung to him. "Oh, Pidge," he murmured, "I do love you so."

"So do I, you," I answered.

He sighed against my hair and added, "This is where we made love for the first time. Do you remember?"

"How could I ever forget?" I looked up into his face, and I knew mine was full of yearning. My desire for him was suddenly rushing to the surface, and I saw at once he felt the same; longing was etched across his face, reflected in his light green eyes.

Moving away from me, Zac walked across to the door and locked it, came hurrying back. Wrapping his arms around me once more, he said softly, "I want to make love with you, Serena. Do you? Will you?"

"I do. I will."

Holding on to each other, not wanting to separate ourselves, we went over to the big old sofa and sat down together. Zac began to kiss me . . . my forehead, my eyelids, my face, and the side of my neck. His mouth was on mine, tenderly at first, and then he was kissing me passionately. I felt waves of heat flowing through me and I wanted him desperately, just as I knew he wanted me.

Somehow we managed to struggle out of our clothes, hardly moving, and within a couple of seconds we were naked, stretched out together on the sofa, our arms wrapped around each other, needing to be close . . . as close as possible.

Zac caressed me tenderly at first, as he always had. He was an expert lover, thrilled me with his gentle touching and stroking, which inevitably became more forceful and insistent. Eventually I reached out to him, and we began to make love as we had in the past, without haste, languorously, and it was as if he had never been away from me.

We were natural, at ease, comfortable with each other, and I knew nothing had changed between us. Zac was a sensual man who aroused the sensuality in me, knew my body as well as he knew his own, knew how to please me. I longed to have him inside me, possessing me, loving me . . . and especially in this private place which was so meaningful. I was glad we were being reunited here, where it had all begun seven years ago. I smiled inwardly. I had been fairly innocent, inexperienced, and Zac had been my very willing teacher, and an expert one at that.

His mouth devoured mine, and I responded with ardor. My hands smoothed down over his shoulders, went up into his thick hair, then onto his neck. He was kissing my breasts; his hands began to roam over my body, exploring, learning every part of me yet again. Unexpectedly, a moment later, he took me to him urgently, and with great swiftness, making me gasp in surprise.

"I've yearned for you, Serena," he whispered hoarsely against my neck. "Oh God, how I've wanted to be with you like this. I've missed you so much."

"So have I . . . wanted you . . . missed you . . . ," I answered, and it was the truth.

He lifted his head, looked down at me for a moment, as if he was surprised we were here together like this, making love. I touched his face with my hand, my eyes holding his, and he gazed back, and it was almost as if we were looking deeply into each other's souls.

Kissing me passionately, holding me close, Zac

began to move against me, and we were both overwhelmed by desire, discovering our urgent need for each other. And we were filled with ecstasy as we left everything behind and soared into a glittering place together, a place we had visited before.

Twenty-five

It was Friday, April 22, and the first anniversary of my father's sudden death. By chance, it also happened to be Good Friday, and a religious holiday around the world.

Harry had arrived yesterday, bringing with him Geoff Barnes. After dinner last night, Harry and I agreed to meet this morning. Early. To chat about a few things we had not been able to discuss with others present, during dinner and afterward.

And so I was up early, left Zac sound asleep in my bed, and came downstairs to make coffee. Once it was ready I put it on the tray with milk, sweetener, and mugs, and carried it down to the studio.

Even though it was already a sunny morning at seven o'clock, the grass was still laden with dew, and my sandals, bare feet, and the edges of my jeans were soon soaked as I walked across the lawn.

But I didn't care about the wet grass. I was

happy I was here in this lovely old house where I had grown up, surrounded by those whom I loved, and who loved me: Harry, my godfather, best friend, and the unique link to my father; my darling sisters, whom I adored; and Zac. My lover. My true love.

There had been a strange moment the other afternoon, when, irrationally, I wondered what I was doing in the studio, making frantic love with Zac, when I had hated him for a year, had vowed never to see him again, and had blamed him for that missed plane.

But there I was, naked and stretched out under him, oblivious to everything but him. At that moment caring only about what we were doing to each other. Nothing, no one mattered. Only him. And me. Together like that. A man and a woman joined in sexual pleasure.

That he turned me on, filled me with a hot raging desire that rendered me weak with longing when he kissed me, were not good enough reasons. Or were they? *Yes.* Because no other man had ever made me feel that way. But the real reason I was with him on the sofa was because I was in love with him. As he was with me. We wanted each other, needed each other, and we were both aware that we were meant to be. It was our destiny, he had said that afternoon. I also understood that I had not stopped loving him at all. I'd simply obscured that love, because I was angry with him. Anger had built a wall between us. I had torn it down.

Once inside the studio, I put the tray on the coffee table and glanced at the sofa, smiling to myself, my thoughts still caught up with Wednesday afternoon, here with Zac. Much later that night, in the comfort of my bed, he and I had made love again, more passionately than ever, and then we had talked late into the night.

At one moment, Zac had confessed that he had been disappointed when we hadn't made love in Venice, which to him was the most romantic place in the world, and full of memories of our early years together. I had explained that it hadn't been the right time for me then, but that it was now. And this had clearly pleased him, erased that earlier disappointment.

Suddenly Harry arrived, came striding into the studio, a wide smile on his lean face. Immediately, he took me in his arms and hugged me, kissed my cheek. I clung to him for a second, truly happy he was with us for the weekend. We stepped away, and the love we had for each other was reflected on our faces. He and I had depended on each other for years, even when Dad was alive, and we were extremely close. Harry had been married twice, but had never had any children, and he said I was like the daughter he had never had. We had worked together, been on the front lines, and in danger. Like Dad, Harry had protected me in every way he could, had my back at all times.

He said, "We can't be sad today, Serena. Tommy wouldn't like that. He'd want us all to celebrate that he'd been here on this planet, because he was the first to say he'd led a charmed life, had lived it to the full, had been truly blessed."

"I know he would," I answered, and sat down on the sofa, poured coffee into the two mugs, adding cream and sweetener.

Harry joined me, and went on, "I know he was far too young to die. Seventy's considered no age these days. Just let's be glad he died far away from the bombs, the guns, and the violence of war. That he was here, where he had spent so many wonderful years with you and your sisters and your mother . . . in this beautiful and peaceful place she created."

"I thought that myself the other day," I said. I picked up the mug, took sips of my coffee, and after a moment, I went on, "I want to ask you something, Harry . . . Jessica was wondering if she should invite a friend tonight. Allen Lambert. She wasn't sure." I told him about Allen, at least as much as I knew, explained their relationship, and then finished, "He knew Dad, not very well, but he did know him, and Mom, and I told her she should invite him. Particularly since she's become more interested in him lately. She was still a bit hesitant, uncertain, so I said I'd ask you. What do you think?"

"Tell her to ask him to come, Serena. I'm sure Cara won't object, and certainly I don't. Why would I?" He gave me a pointed stare. "You're looking odd. Do you think Cara won't want him to come?"

"No, I don't." As I said that I wondered if she would be annoyed. But I added, "She won't care either way."

"When does she get back from St. Tropez?"

"She told me she'd be home around five. She's leaving two assistants behind to make sure everything's in order on Saturday, which is when the wedding reception is taking place. At the villa of the bride's mother." I smiled. "The entire place is going to be filled with Cara's exotic orchids. It's a big job for her, and she's worked hard, being such a perfectionist."

"That she is." Harry drank some coffee, and leaned back, relaxing.

I glanced across at him, thinking how great he looked, trim, healthy, and in good shape. Moving on from Cara, I said, "Although Geoff was rather quiet last night, I thought he didn't seem all that upset. How's he been?"

Harry pursed his lips, shook his head. "He vacillates, to be honest, honey. One minute he's depressed, the next accepting the situation. Then suddenly he takes the blame. Becomes guilt-ridden because he believes he neglected his ex-wife and Chloe. But look, he'll be fine. And here's the good news for us." Harry smiled when he explained, "Geoff's decided to stay with Global, and he'll be running the London bureau, which makes me happy, as it should you. He'll do a good job."

"That's great!" I exclaimed, as relieved as Harry obviously was. Our London office was an important part of the Global Images network, and needed a strong manager, which I knew Geoff would be. He would also become chief photographer, taking on the important assignments in the U.K. and Europe. I then thought to ask, "Is he going back to L.A. first? To see his ex-wife and Chloe before he takes over?"

"No, he's not. He wants to get settled in London, and then he'll make the trip. But he'll only stay a few days." Harry sipped his coffee, was silent, looking reflective.

I had the feeling he was about to speak to me about Zac and I sat back against the cushions and waited.

Eventually Harry leaned forward, and focused his bright blue eyes on me. "Zac is very calm and together, Serena. I told you that you'd do him good. He's not only on an even keel and like he used to be, but he actually seems *happy*. He was positively euphoric last night. You're back together, aren't you?"

"Does it show?"

Harry laughed. "It sure does, and I'm happy if you are, Serena."

"I am. I put all my doubts about him to one side because I suddenly realized how much I love him, and that this won't change. I'm stuck with him . . . for better or worse."

Harry's head lifted alertly, and he stared at me, his eyes narrowing. "Are you going to marry him?"

"He hasn't asked me."

"Not yet. But he will."

I didn't respond.

"Take my word for it," Harry now asserted. "And also my word on this—he won't go back to the front line. It's over for him. He's lost his edge completely, and he's totally aware of it. He's no fool."

"I know. He's really doing okay."

"He told me he'd filled you in about the flash-back . . . and he told me all about it, too."

I said quietly, "I really believe it helped him, unburdening himself to me."

"It did." Harry cleared his throat, and quietly added, "Those two young Marines didn't make it. They both died from their wounds."

A feeling of dismay settled in the pit of my stomach. "He didn't tell me," I said in a saddened voice. "And I didn't dare ask."

Harry sighed. "He's okay. The one thing that still worries him is that you haven't forgiven him for making you miss the plane from Kabul . . . that you didn't get here in time to say good-bye to Tommy."

"I thought I'd made it clear that I don't blame him. Not anymore."

"Better tell him again." Harry moved closer, took hold of my hand, his eyes focused on me. "I've said this before, and so have your sisters. Tommy understood you were on your way, and then he had that massive second heart attack—" Harry cut himself off, unable to finish the sentence, choked by emotion.

"You miss him very much, Harry, I know that."

"Every day. And I will for the rest of my life. We worked together for over fifty years, and we knew each other since we were young boys, as you well know. Tommy was my best friend as well—"

His sentence remained unfinished and I saw the tears glittering in Harry's eyes. I was still holding his hand. I squeezed it, and we sat there for a long time, not speaking. And I knew he was thinking of Tommy, just as I was.

My father and Harry had always been there for each other, and I know it was Dad, with Mom's help, who got Harry through his two divorces. Not to mention some of his tumultuous love affairs.

Twenty-six

My sisters and I had decided we must get dressed up and look glamorous for Tommy's memorial dinner tonight. Our mother had been glamour personified, and Dad had always had a predilection for lovely women who put themselves together well: It was our way of honoring him.

Jessica and Cara were elegantly dressed more often than not, because they were in business. I was the one who was usually wearing trousers and a T-shirt, a pant suit, or my combat gear. I'd put the latter away a year ago, and I would never use those camouflage pants, combat boots, and that flak jacket ever again.

Now I sat in front of the mirror at my dressing table, adding finishing touches to my eye makeup. Before I put on my dress, I sprayed myself with Ma Griffe, one of my preferred scents, which Mom had sometimes used.

After slipping on my red dress, I stepped into my Manolos, a pair of red high-heeled satin pumps. I loved these shoes, and they matched my silk dress. This had a V-neck, softly gathered skirt, and long sleeves that flared out slightly from elbow to wrist.

I never wore much jewelry, but I treasured the tank watch my parents had given me for my twenty-first birthday. Designed for evening wear, it had a black satin strap and tiny diamonds around the face. I admired it again as I put it on. The earrings I had chosen for tonight had been left to me by Mom, and they were diamond flowers with a pearl drop, and I wore them proudly because they had been hers.

Looking in the mirror one last time, I decided I wasn't so mousey after all. I had been outside a lot in the last few weeks, and my brown hair had become sunstreaked. It had an overall blond sheen, was glossy and soft around my face. For once I was quite pleased with my appearance.

Walking across my bedroom, I went into Zac's room, which adjoined mine, to tell him I was going downstairs.

Zac was sitting in a chair, newspapers and magazines scattered on the floor. These he had bought earlier, when he had gone with Harry and Geoff for lunch in Nice. I was happy the TV wasn't on.

Glancing up, he was slightly startled at the sight of me, and did a double take, then exclaimed, "Wow!" and jumped to his feet, still staring at me. "Wow again! You're spectacular tonight, Serena. Just fantastic."

"Thank you," I replied, smiling back at him.

"You look very sexy in red."

"The dress was Mom's. She gave it to me a few years ago," I answered. "It's one of those dresses that never date. Probably because it's so simple. Her clothes fit me, you know, and I often borrowed her stuff."

He grinned at me, a mischievous look flashing across his face. "One thing's for certain, your sisters could never get into her clothes. They're far too tall, bigger in build altogether. That should please you, Pidge, since I know how much it irks you that they look like your father."

I laughed. "It's true, they do, and certainly I don't. But then I don't look like Mom either."

"Actually, I disagree. You *do* have a look of Elizabeth at times," Zac said. "It has to do with a certain whimsical expression that occasionally flickers on your face, and you are the same height she was, and you do have her build."

"Do you really think I have a look of Mom?" I asked eagerly, staring at him.

"I do, Serena, I honestly do." He walked over, took my hand, held it high, twirled me around. "You'll be the star tonight."

"Oh, I don't know about that," I answered quietly, but I was pleased by his reaction.

"Oh, I do," he shot back, and winked flirtatiously.

"You're prejudiced."

"Listen, Pidge, I'm glad we're not going out, that we're having dinner here tonight."

I glanced at him quickly, frowning. "You say that in a funny way, Zac. What are you getting at?"

"The way you look, the earrings you're wearing. You'd be in danger if you put one foot outside the door. You'd need a handful of bodyguards, and not only because of the diamonds."

I couldn't help laughing, then I explained,

"Jessica, Cara, and I decided to get dressed up, you know how Dad liked us to look glamorous. And so we took some of Mom's jewelry out of the safe . . . actually earrings she'd left us in her will."

Zac threw me a questioning look. "I thought all of your mother's jewelry was sold. When Jessica held that auction at Stone's years ago."

"The bulk of it was, but actually Mom had some other lovely pieces left, which are kept here for safety."

"I understand," he murmured, and drew me into his arms. Against my hair, he said, "Mmmm. You smell delicious. Let's go to bed."

"Don't be silly. I've got to go downstairs to help my sisters," I replied, kissed his cheek. "You don't have to come down for another hour," I told him as I closed the door behind me.

Jessica was alone in the peach sitting room. As I hurried in, asking her where Cara was, she swung around to face me. "She'll be down in a minute or two," she answered, smiling.

Walking toward me, Jess said, "Pidge, you look lovely. Red really does suit you."

"Zac just told me I look very sexy," I confided.

"He's right, and by the way, everything seems to be good between you. I'm glad you made the decision to get back together."

"I think it might well be a battlefield at times,

because we're both strong-willed and independent. But we also know when to call a truce. And hey, you look great, Jess. I love Mom's aquamarine earrings with your royal blue dress."

"Thanks. And it was Mom, of course, who said I should wear them with every different shade of blue, but never with black."

We walked over to the window and looked out at the terrace, and I said, "I think we're better off having drinks inside tonight. Those are heavy clouds out there. It might rain."

Jess nodded. "Stormy weather predicted."

I turned to her, and gave her a penctrating look. "Did you call Allen Lambert?"

"No, because he called *me* from London. He can't come to Nice before tomorrow night, because of some business. So I never mentioned the dinner this evening. What was the point?"

"He is coming to lunch on Sunday, isn't he?"

"He is, and he can't wait to meet you."

"Let's light all these little votive candles, and when Cara comes down she'll place the orchids where she wants them."

Once we'd finished with the candles, Jessica asked, "Should I light the fire? What do you think?"

"Absolutely. There's a bit of a nip in the air tonight, and anyway I like a fire, it's so welcoming, cheerful."

Whilst Jessica hovered around the fire with the

box of matches, I walked around the sitting room, looking everything over.

The room was typical of our mother's decorating. It was a mixture of peach, cream, and pale blue, with bright accent colors of scarlet and delphinium blue in the cushions. Big overstuffed sofas and several French antique bergere chairs gave the room a comfortable welcoming feeling, and the porcelain lamps and lovely paintings added to its overall charm.

I paused when I came to the dark-wood Provençal table placed against a wall. Earlier, we had arranged our favorite photographs of Mom and Dad on it, and as I stood gazing at their images I found myself choking up. I swallowed, moved away swiftly.

Once I'd composed myself, I turned around and noticed my sister watching me. Cocking my head on one side, I asked, "Why are you staring at me so intently?"

"You're like Mom. There you are, checking that everything's in order, just as she used to do before guests arrived."

"I guess I picked up the habit from her." I swung around as Cara hurried across the hall, her high heels clicking against the wood floor.

I thought she looked her very best tonight, and told her so as she walked into the sitting room. She was wearing an emerald green silk cocktail dress and emerald-and-diamond chandelier earrings, which had been Mom's. Her black hair was in an updo, to show them off properly.

Jessica said, "You look great, Cara. You and Serena have done Dad proud."

"And so have you, Jess," Cara said, and then laughed. "I was going to wear white tonight. I'm glad I didn't. We would have looked like a flag."

There was a moment's pause, before she said in a more serious tone, "Our earrings would bring a great deal of money if they were auctioned off. Why don't you do that, Jess? Have an auction of all the stuff in Mom's safe? We could certainly make good use of the money."

I was astonished by these remarks, and I looked from Cara to Jessica. I realized I was not the only one surprised. Jessica was obviously taken aback by Cara's words, and was staring at her twin.

Although I wanted to know more about why we needed money, I decided it would be wiser to keep my mouth shut for the moment. Trust Cara to be the bearer of bad news as usual, I thought.

Jessica finally answered. "I'd planned to speak to you and Serena next week, Cara. About holding an auction. But I hadn't wanted to go there until after the dinner tonight. Since you've brought it up now, I have to tell you I think it's a good idea. None of us wears any of Mom's jewelry, because the pieces are too important and valuable. And it's just too dangerous today anyway, unless we're at a private party."

"I agree," Cara said. "It's all sitting there in the safe, not doing anybody any good, and we do need the money."

"Why do we need the money?" I asked, jumping right in, and sounding a little shrill. "And why haven't you told me this before?"

It was Jessica who answered at once, in a soothing tone. "We don't need money to live on, Pidge. I have a good salary from Stone's, and the auction house is doing well, is in profit. And Cara's in the same position with her orchid business. We need money for the house, it's very old as you know, and needs a lot of work. Sections of the roof are leaking, the plumbing is worn out, and all kinds of things need replacing. That's why we could use some extra cash . . . for Jardin des Fleurs."

"I understand," I said. "So go ahead, plan an auction, Jess."

Cara exclaimed, "Well, I'm certainly glad I brought up the idea of selling the jewels, and thank God we're all in agreement. We'll talk about it tomorrow. Right now, I need to deal with the orchids." She walked over to the crate of plants in the doorway.

"Let's you and I go into the kitchen," Jessica announced, taking hold of my arm. "I have Adeline keeping an eye on things, but I'd better go and check the rack of lamb."

As we walked out together, I wondered if my

sisters had told me the truth. Did they really need the money for repairs to the house? Or were they short of cash themselves? And were their businesses doing as well as they said?

They would never lie to me. On the other hand, they were both protective because I was the youngest, and they had been known to fudge things in the past for that reason.

Twenty-seven

I've read the chapters again, Serena," Harry said, "and you're off to a good start with the biography of Tommy. Just keep going, honey." He touched his champagne flute to mine and beamed at me. "And congratulations."

I took a sip of the pink Veuve Clicquot, and felt a little rush of pleasure at his words. "I'm so thrilled you like it, Harry. You're the only person whose judgment I really trust."

"I've made a few notes that might be useful to you, I'll give them to you later, and you know I'll help you any way I can. And I also hope you can get back to your writing soon."

"Next week, I think. Zac's going to start working on Dad's photographic book, and I believe that will be good for him. It's something for him to focus on."

"He needs that, although he seems to be coping well. Better than I thought he would." He drew me to him, gave me a hug. "You're the best, Serena, just like Tommy. Loyal, dependable, and constant. I had a good talk with Zac over lunch today, and he finally agreed to see Dr. Biron, admitted that he needed medical help." Harry gave me a knowing look, went on. "That's a good sign. I told him Daniel Biron helped me and your father. He's a great psychiatrist, and he has a good under-standing of post-traumatic stress disorder, better than any other doctor I know."

Harry's cell began to ring and he stepped over to the coffee table, picked it up, stood talking for a moment or two.

I realized at once that it was the London office calling him, and that it was Annie Stewart just checking in with him before going home.

We were standing in front of the blazing fire in the peach sitting room, just the two of us. Once again, I thought how good Harry looked. He was wearing dark gray trousers; a blue, open-necked shirt; and a deeper blue cable-knit cardigan I'd given him for Christmas.

Once he'd clicked off his cell, I told him about the discussion I'd had earlier with the twins, about Mom's jewelry and auctioning it off.

A look of surprise flickered in his deep blue eyes for a moment. "Well, why not? The world has changed. Only celebrities wear stuff like that these days." He grinned. "Also the Chinese. Luxury goods appeal to them, and especially jewels. She should get good prices if she focuses on the Asian market."

"That's exactly what Jess was saying when I was in the kitchen with her. So we're definitely going to do it."

"I'm all in favor, and listen, if Jessica needs the money to do the repair work immediately, I'll give it to her."

"No, no, that's not necessary, and anyway, I can advance it, if she needs it now." I threw him a pointed look and asked, "Did Dad ever mention to you that the roof needed repairs?"

Harry shook his head. "No, but your mother and I had a discussion about her jewelry a couple of years before she died. She had thought of having another auction, but she changed her mind. She said she'd decided to leave the remaining pieces to her three girls, just in case there was ever a rainy day, as she put it. And I guess that's now."

I began to laugh and Harry did too, and said, "A leaking roof and bad plumbing would be the last thing on Tommy's mind, by the way, and you know that as well as I do."

"You're right. It was Mom who was usually on top of these things."

I heard the click-click of Cara's high heels again, and a moment later she swanned into the sitting room, moving elegantly across the floor. When she drew closer to Harry she broke into smiles.

"Why Uncle Harry, you look scrumptious!" she exclaimed and gave him a bear hug. "And that shirt certainly matches your eyes. Good choice."

"Forget the Uncle bit," he said, grinning. "You haven't called me uncle since you were four. And I must compliment you on these orchids." He swung his head, waved his hand at them. "They're spectacular, I've never seen anything like them. Where did these very colorful specimens originate?"

"Oh, thank you, Harry, and some came from Africa, others from South America, several from Asia. They're very rare." Cara paused, and turned around as Geoff walked into the room.

If Harry hadn't noticed it, I might have thought that I'd imagined it. But he said I hadn't, that he'd witnessed it too, the way Cara and Geoff looked at each other. Harry also said to me later that the most powerful exchanges can happen in a split second. Two people look into each other's eyes, and wham! They instantly understand they're on the very same wavelength. Nothing needs to be said. They've got it. And they get each other. Get where they're coming from.

And so there they stood, gaping at each other.

I can't believe this, Geoff of all people, I thought, as I rushed over to introduce them. "There you are, Geoff!" I exclaimed. "This is Cara, she was in St. Tropez when you arrived yesterday, and this is Geoff Barnes, Cara."

She thrust her hand out at him and said, "I think we've met before."

Geoff looked startled. He took her hand, flushed slightly. "Oh, but we haven't. I would have remembered you," he gushed. "I really would. You're . . . well, you're unforgettable."

I winced at his words, and stared at Cara, who was flushed also, and smiling at him in that simpering way of hers. I looked at Harry, my eyes wide in astonishment. He winked at me, crossed the floor to the ice bucket on the drinks table, lifted out the bottle of champagne, and poured two glasses, took them over to Cara and Geoff.

They thanked him, and Harry said, "Feast your eyes, Geoff." He paused, bit back a smile, as Geoff continued to gaze at Cara as if mesmerized. "On the orchids, Geoff. They're from Cara's greenhouses. Aren't they superb?"

"They sure are," Geoff said, continuing to focus on Cara, and lifted his glass. "Cheers," he said absently and barely glanced at the orchids.

Cara smiled, her manner coy once again. She said, "*Santé.*"

I looked from her to Geoff, and hurried away when Jessica came into the sitting room. I was somewhat alarmed to see her left arm bandaged. "What have you done? How have you hurt yourself?" I cried and peered at her intently.

"Oh, it's nothing, Pidge, I just bumped my arm on the fridge door. Honestly, it's okay, don't fuss,"

Jessica exclaimed, and went over to greet Harry and Geoff.

I watched her glide across the room, and then I slowly walked to the windows facing the terrace, stood looking out. It had started to rain, and in the distance I could hear the rumble of thunder. Lightning flashed intermittently. I wondered if a mistral was blowing up. It was still possible at this time of year.

Suddenly Harry was standing next to me; I turned to him. "Did I imagine that? Or did those two just glom on to each other in the most extraordinary way?"

"They did indeed."

"I can't believe it! Yesterday Geoff was down in the dumps because his ex-wife had taken up with another man. Tonight he's gazing at Cara like a hungry man about to devour a tasty morsel."

Harry chuckled. "I think he is hungry," he said softly, keeping his voice low. "And you've got to admit, she does look ravishing tonight."

"She does, that's true, but his behavior is unexpected. After all, he was so dour last night, I thought he would burst into tears at any minute. Now he's raring to go. This is crazy."

"You never know what people are going to do, Serena. Human behavior can be most extraordinary. That's why I'm no longer shocked by anything. But to tell you the truth, I am a bit surprised at Geoff's behavior myself."

"Cara hasn't looked at a man since Jules was killed two years ago." I shook my head. And I whispered to Harry, "I never thought she'd be interested in a tall, lanky Californian with streaky blond hair, and a twangy way of speaking. But as Granny used to say, there's no accounting for taste."

"The world is a funny place," Harry said. "We never know what's going to happen. Is there a grand plan to all of our lives? Or is everything random, accidental, happenstance? Who knows?" He moved away from the window. "I decided years ago to just let it all come at me, and I deal with it as it happens." He shrugged. "What else is there to do? And by the way, where is Zac?"

"I don't know." I frowned, put my drink down on a glass end table, and told Harry I was going upstairs to find out.

The moment I walked into my bedroom, and went through to Zac's room, calling out his name, I knew something was wrong. I could feel it in the air.

He was sitting on a chair, wearing his bathrobe, holding a hairbrush in his hand. He looked up and stared at me. I was certain he had been crying. His eyes were red and puffy.

"Zac, whatever is it?" I asked, sitting down on the other chair. I took hold of his hand. "Have you had a bad memory? A flashback?"

He shook his head. "No, I haven't. After my

shower I just started to cry, I don't know why. I just did, as I have in the past. I told you about that. And I couldn't stop. Not for a long time."

"I'm sorry. I know this happens unexpectedly. Do you want to stay in your room? I can tell everyone you're not feeling well. There's no problem, you know."

"There is for me, Pidge. It's Tommy's memorial dinner. Of course I can't miss it. And I don't want to. I'll be okay in a few seconds." He stood up, forced a smile. "I'll brush my hair, and get dressed. Go on, go down. I'll follow you shortly."

I also stood, put my arms around him, and held him tightly to me. "I love you," I said. "I'm here for you."

I ran downstairs, and returned to the peach sitting room. Harry and Jessica were in a deep discussion, more than likely about the idea of the auction, and Cara and Geoff were seated on the sofa closest to the coffee table.

I went to sit with them, listened to my sister talking to Geoff with great expertise about some of the orchids she had grouped together. There were several gorgeous and unique slipper orchids, some green and white, some in various shades of pink, and they looked beautiful grouped together in plain white porcelain pots in the center of the bronze coffee table. I noticed Geoff suddenly sniffing. He looked at Cara and frowned. "Why do

I smell chocolate?" he asked, obviously puzzled.

Cara smiled, looking very pleased. "I was waiting for you to notice. What you're smelling is this one here." She indicated a dark burgundy-brown speckled orchid on the lamp table next to the sofa. "It's called Sharry Baby, it's an *Oncidium*, and yes, it gives off a smell like chocolate. I just love it myself."

"I'll be darned," Geoff said, and gazed at my sister as if he was awestruck.

I saw Zac coming down the stairs, and jumped up, went to meet him in the hall. "Are you feeling better?"

"I'm okay, Serena," he answered. "I'll be all right. I've got it together."

I nodded, took his arm, strolled into the room with him. I was pleased that he was wearing an open-necked pristine white shirt with long sleeves. He had thrown a red sweater over his shoulders, and he looked relaxed, and somewhat collegiate in appearance.

Harry came over at once, carrying a glass of champagne for Zac, and the three of us stood talking near the window.

Not long after this, Jessica raised her voice slightly, and said, "I'd like to propose a toast. To Dad. Cara, Serena, will you both come and stand here with me, please."

We did as she asked.

Jessica raised her glass, and so did we. And the

men followed suit. In her clear, light voice, Jessica said, "Here's to Tommy, a man we all loved very much in our different ways. He died a year ago today, but he still lives on in our hearts, and he will never be forgotten. To Tommy."

We all said in unison: "To Tommy!" And drank our pink champagne, which had been his favorite, and thought our private thoughts.

Harry spoke about him, and so did Zac. I listened, and was pleased with their words. And then Geoff talked for a few seconds about Dad as well.

I did not want to speak at this moment, and neither did my sisters. We had discussed that earlier. Our time would come later. During dinner or afterward, whichever we preferred. We would talk about him in our own way, reminisce and relate anecdotes, and celebrate that he had lived, had been part of our lives.

Twenty-eight

Earlier, I had worried that the evening might become sad and tearful. But quite the opposite happened. Right from the start of dinner we laughed a lot. The numerous anecdotes the men told about Dad were amusing, and the next hour was filled with hilarity, whether it was Harry, Zac, or Geoff speaking. I thought they did this on purpose, not wishing to be sorrowful.

Jessica was sitting between Harry and Zac, ignoring her bandaged arm. She told me that she had had Adeline wrap it, in order to prevent the arnica cream she had used from getting on her silk dress. Nonetheless, I was keeping an eye on her, and Cara and I had not allowed her to serve the food or do anything in the kitchen.

The two of us had taken over, and with the help of Adeline, Lulu's daughter, we had managed things very well. Adeline, who had been the housekeeper here for many years, was small, dark-haired, and spry, flew around the kitchen like a woman half her age, and was always good-natured, willing, and a great cook herself.

The dinner Jessica had cooked was not complicated to serve. There was a salad, already plated, composed of artichoke hearts, tiny rock shrimps, and mandarin segments with a vinaigrette dressing, followed by rack of lamb with roasted potatoes and green beans.

At one moment, when dinner was almost over, Harry congratulated Jessica, told her the meal was a triumph, and we all toasted her. She beamed with pleasure, looked flushed, very happy.

Dessert was a *tarte tatin*, the upside-down apple tart, which she excelled at, and it was served with dollops of thick cream. It had been Dad's favorite, which was why she had chosen to make it.

The three men, who continued to tell stories

about Tommy for some time, kept us laughing, and then eventually we girls took over.

Jessica kept the merriment afloat when she launched into the tale of Dad having to learn as much as he could about boats and sailing, because of her love for the sea, her desire to become a sailor. She induced more laughter when she explained how he had grumbled, protested loudly at first, claiming he got seasick, that she must find a different interest. Of course, ultimately he had relented, had become a superb sailor, had taught her well. And he ended up loving the sea and boats as much as she did.

Cara spoke next, confiding that our father's greatest gift to his daughters was his talent for making each one of us believe we were extra-special to him. She pointed out how brilliant he was at that, since everyone was aware I was his favorite.

I protested with great volubility, denying this, but my protests were ignored.

Then Cara plunged on with her own favorite story about Tommy. Dad had made a tremendous effort to take her to the Chelsea Flower Show every May; when he couldn't go he always paid for this much-longed-for trip. Mom had accompanied her, if she was not filming, and Dad, too, when he was not covering a war. If they were both busy with work, Granny stood in. The famous flower show had been the highlight of her life at that particular time, had been the inspiration for her career, she finished.

My own special remembrances of Dad were many, but I chose to talk about the endless hours, days, weeks, and months he had spent training me to keep myself safe on the front line: how to dodge bullets, how to cleverly hide myself if necessary, and how to know when it was vital to vacate a combat zone, PDQ, he always told me.

This was not one of the stories which made anyone laugh, but they listened attentively, which pleased me.

There was a certain stillness around the table when I finished, and I knew that Harry, Zac, and Geoff were suddenly thinking of their own experiences, and remembering a lot.

Just after this, breaking the quiet mood which surrounded us, Jessica lifted her glass, and said, "Here's a toast to Mom, Tommy's other half."

"And the linchpin of his life," Harry added, lifting his wineglass, as we all did.

After the toast, Cara said, "She was the linchpin of our lives as well. Mom was Mother Earth, always there for us, and she never let her fame or career get in the way. She was always our mother, occasionally a movie star. And she had one rule, which was never broken. We were never allowed to be in the limelight, never photographed. We remained anonymous. She protected us in that way, because she wanted us to be safe."

Jessica looked across at me, and then glanced around the table. She said, "As the youngest, Serena got away with murder. And since she was also a bit cheeky, plus intrepid, she asked Mom a lot of questions . . . questions Cara and I would have never dared to ask." Smiling at me, she added, "Go on, Serena, tell us about the time you quizzed Mom about her many husbands."

Cara exclaimed, "Oh yes, I love that story! Go on, Serena, start talking."

I made a slight grimace, but began, "I knew Mom had had three husbands before Dad. Since she was only in her early thirties when she married Tommy, I asked her how old she had been when she married the first husband."

I took a sip of wine, and went on, "She told me she had married Andrew Miller when she was twenty-three. Mostly in order to escape from home. And for her independence. She soon discovered she couldn't stand him, and they were divorced within a year. She was twenty-five when she married David Carstairs. She was in awe of him, admired him. He was a famous director, and an intellectual. But that blew up, too, after four years. Her third was Malcolm Thompson. And she married him because he convinced her he wanted a family, like she did. But that didn't happen either—" I broke off, thinking I'd now said enough.

"Don't stop, Pidge!" Jessica exclaimed. "After

all, you're the one who knows about these marriages. She never discussed them with us."

"It was my understanding that Malcolm didn't really want a family," I said. "So the relationship became tumultuous and the divorce was acrimonious. Mom took off for France to make a movie."

"And then later she met Dad one day, and it was love at first sight," Cara finished for me with a triumphant flourish.

"That's the absolute truth," Harry interjected. "I was with Tommy when he met Elizabeth, and it was indeed love at first sight . . . a genuine *coup de foudre*. It was the most romantic and beautiful love affair I ever witnessed, and it lasted until the day Elizabeth died."

"And even after that," Cara asserted. "Dad never stopped loving Mom."

A short while later Jessica led the men into the peach sitting room, and Cara and I stayed behind to help Adeline clear the table, which we did with great speed.

At one moment, when Cara and I were alone, I moved close to her, asked, "What was all that about earlier with Geoff?"

"I don't know," she replied, shrugging her shoulders lightly. "He stared at me. I stared at him. And we connected in an uncanny way. I guess something clicked. How do you explain these

241

things?" She looked baffled, then gave me a diffident smile. "Don't you like him, Serena?"

"Of course I do!" I said at once. "He's been a good friend over the years. And it was selfless and brave of him to risk his life, going into Helmand Province to get Zac out the way he did."

"Yes, it was," she agreed. She stared at me intently. "We just glommed on to each other, I guess."

"No kidding!" I exclaimed.

She had the good grace to laugh at my sarcastic comment.

Cara and I finally joined the others in the peach sitting room. The storm was still raging outside, and Harry had banked up the fire. We all sat around the hearth, enjoying the warmth and coziness, sipping coffee and cognacs, and talking into the night.

Harry spoke again about Mom and Dad, and our parents' enduring love story, and we listened to him attentively, having always loved his "take" on them. After all, he had been their closest friend, and Dad's lifelong friend, part of our family always.

At one moment Harry came and sat next to me on the sofa. He took hold of my hand. "It's been a great evening, Serena, just the way Tommy and Elizabeth would have wanted it . . . a celebration of their lives. And there was nothing sad about it."

I simply nodded, suddenly feeling choked up. I gave Harry a quavery smile, and he put his arm around me, brought me closer to him.

He said softly, "Tommy used to say that we must never look back, only look forward, go forward and meet the new day. That's what you must do now . . . what we all must do."

Several hours later I awakened with a sudden start and sat up. Zac had left my bed at some point during the night, because he was restless, and shouting in his sleep. There was no sound now, but, nonetheless, I got up and went to see if he was all right.

He was sound asleep, no longer appeared restless. This pleased me. I was also gratified that he had been careful about his intake of alcohol, had drunk much more coffee than cognac after dinner. He was obviously keeping a check on himself. A very good sign, as far as I was concerned.

Returning to my room, I sat down on the edge of the bed. I was wide awake. Something was nagging at the back of my mind, but I couldn't pinpoint it. I looked at the clock, was startled to see that it was almost six in the morning. I felt a sudden compulsion to go downstairs, stepped into my slippers, pulled on my robe, and left the room.

A few seconds later I was walking into the

kitchen. All the lights were on and Cara was kneeling next to Jessica, who was prone on the floor.

"My God! What's happened?" I cried and rushed to my sisters, filled with alarm and concern.

Jessica explained, "I came down to make the coffee, and I don't know exactly what happened, but I tripped and fell. I think I sprained my ankle."

Cara said, "I got up to go running, but as I was getting into my track suit I felt that something was wrong with Jessica. So I rushed to her room. You know how twins are. When she wasn't there, I came down here. And sure enough, I found her on the floor, incapacitated."

"I'd just fallen a few minutes before," Jessica added. "And I was finding it hard to get up."

"We're going to help you," Cara said reassuringly.

Taking charge in her usual way whenever there was a crisis, she continued: "I'm going to bend down behind you, Jess, and put my hands under your arms. And Serena, I want you to stand on Jessica's right. Stand sideways and put your right arm in front of her, so she can grab your arm with both hands. Put your left arm around her waist, to keep her steady."

I did exactly as Cara had instructed.

Cara said to Jessica, "I want you to put your weight on your left foot as we attempt to pull you up. Okay?"

"Understood," Jessica answered, sounding strained, worried.

Bending forward, Cara put her hands under Jessica's arms. Jessica reached out to me, held on to my right arm tightly. I smiled at her encouragingly.

Somehow, with a bit of an effort, we managed to get our sister off the floor and upright. We helped her to hop over to the alcove, where she could sit down. But before she sat she put her right foot on the floor and took a step, and winced with pain.

"I have a feeling my ankle's broken." She sat down heavily on the chair.

As usual, Cara voiced her troubled thoughts immediately, but she was also echoing mine, when she said, "I'm afraid you probably do have the same type of rare osteoporosis Mom had. I think you must have more bone tests. In fact, I insist."

Jessica remained silent, simply nodded her assent.

Cara continued, "After we've had some coffee and toast, we'll take you to the hospital in Nice. To Emergency." She glanced at me. "I'm going upstairs to change, and I'll get some Aleve for Jess. Please make the coffee, Serena, and I'll be back before you can say Jack Robinson."

Despite the seriousness of the situation, Jessica and I both laughed, as we always did when Cara spouted one of Granny's old sayings.

As I prepared the coffee I prayed that Jessica did not have that awful disease which had so debilitated our mother. But it was hard to dispel my anxiety, and I found myself thinking the worst.

Part Four

A SINGLE FRAME
TELLS IT ALL

Nice–New York, May/June

> So absolutely good is truth,
> truth never hurts
> The Teller.
> > —Robert Browning:
> > "Fifine at the Fair"

> Truth stood on one side and Ease on
> the other; it has often been so.
> > —Theodore Parker

> Down in the flood of remembrance, I weep
> like a child for the past.
> > —D. H. Lawrence: "Piano"

Twenty-nine

For the first time in some years I was entirely alone at Jardin des Fleurs. Harry was back in New York. Geoff had gone to London to run Global Images. And everyone else had taken off earlier in the day.

Not too long ago, Zac had gone to Nice to keep an appointment with Dr. Biron, who had treated Dad, and Cara had rushed up to her two huge greenhouses, built on her hilltop land which adjoined the gardens of the house.

Jessica, needing to keep an appointment at the auction house, had asked Adeline to drive her to the city, and Adeline had been happy to do so. She was going to the market to do the shopping for the weekend anyway, and it presented no problem. Only Raffi, the gardener, was around somewhere in the grounds, plying his trade.

I was working at the dining room table, where Zac and I had set up our base. There were masses of photographs for Dad's war book, and the large round table offered plenty of space, and we had a useful overview of all the pictures.

The house was so quiet and still it was almost like being in another place altogether. I enjoyed the peace and tranquility because it was so conducive to work.

Usually there was noise from the kitchen, when

Adeline and her sister Magali were working there, and Jessica, a music lover, frequently had an opera or a movie soundtrack on the sound system. As for Zac, he had at least one television turned on downstairs, and I had come to understand that Cara and I were the two quietest people in the house.

Zac and I had been concentrating on the photographs for the book for over ten days. Within the first few hours of looking at them properly, and studying them, we realized how important they were. Actually, they were extraordinary . . . dramatic, savage, heartrending, and touching beyond belief. Many had moved me to tears, and every single one of them was brilliant.

Tommy had captured the relentlessness of war, and its evil; counterbalancing this was the power of peace. The photos of the military men and women showed their courage, compassion, and great humanity. There were many images of civilians, the ordinary people of the world, which were a tribute to their indomitability and the triumph of the human spirit. Those were uplifting, and needed to be in the book.

It was obvious that Dad had put a lot of time and effort into the dummy; he had selected the best photographs, had arranged them the way he wanted them to appear in the book. Zac and I only had a few more files to go through, and it wasn't a daunting task.

My father had always been efficient when it came to his work. He had identified every shot, left copious notes, and we had been thrilled that we'd been able to move ahead with such speed. Thanks to Harry and his connections, we even had a potential publisher in New York, who was apparently genuinely interested in the book, and this had spurred us on.

I was sorting through a file marked GULF WAR in large letters when I came across a truly dramatic picture, and as I studied it, I suddenly realized one corner of it was stuck to another photograph underneath. After attempting to separate them without success, I went and got a sharp knife from the kitchen, pushed it carefully between the two pictures where they were attached at the corner.

They came apart without any damage to either, and I was momentarily surprised to find the photo stuck to the war shot was one of my mother.

Well, not so surprised really, since there were hundreds of photographs of her in his studio. Dad had obviously been looking at this one of Mom when he was selecting photos for his book.

I gazed at her image . . . shimmering . . . incandescent . . . my mother at her best. I turned it over, and saw that it was stamped with the logo of Twentieth-Century Fox, and it was obviously a publicity still taken by one of the studio photographers. She was wearing a white dress, and I recognized it.

I sat back in the chair, still holding the picture in my hand.

The decades dropped away, and I remembered the day that this particular photograph had been taken.

Dad and I had gone to the studio to pick Mom up. She was working only half a day, and Dad was taking us both to lunch at the Bel Air Hotel before he left for New York.

I'd been to the backlot many times before, and always enjoyed being there, unlike Jessica and Cara, who never wanted to go. I loved the cameras, the giant arc lights, the dolly tracks, the commotion, and the excitement, all the marvelous ballyhoo of major movie-making at its best.

Heather Stanton, Mom's personal publicist, was with us that day, and she took us to one of the huge soundstages where Mom was shooting only one scene, and doing some stills. An easy day for her.

The moment I saw the red light flashing I knew we couldn't go inside. They were filming. Once it finally stopped, Dad pushed open the heavy soundproof door, and we went into the enormous soundstage beyond.

Mom was in the center of a group of people, and when she spotted Dad and me with Heather, she smiled at them, said her farewells. Then she came hurrying over to hug and kiss me, as she always did.

It was a well-known fact in our family that the studio heads loved Mom . . . she was known throughout the business as a real pro. Grandma had told me that Mom was never late, always knew her lines, and got on with it, without any fuss and bother.

Much later, when I was years older, Heather had confided that my mother wore her enormous fame with great humility, and that this was the reason she was beloved by every crew she ever worked with. And also for her warmth and friendliness.

I happen to believe that my mother's under-stated manner was also due to the many years she'd been in the business. She had been a child star before becoming a megastar, and she carried her fame rather casually . . . she was so used to it. And she never threw her weight around.

That day in the summer of 1986, when we went to pick her up for lunch, she was forty-seven, had recently celebrated her birthday in May. She didn't look her age, appeared much younger, her beauty and her figure still intact.

I was five, and attending kindergarten in Beverly Hills. We were living at Mom's old house, which she had owned since her first marriage, and had kept all those years.

My mother was shooting several major movies back to back. Her health was extremely good at this time, and apparently she wanted to make the most of it, to make money whilst she could.

Jessica and Cara were at boarding school in England, and I had my parents all to myself.

I can easily recall how they spoiled me. When Dad went off to New York, or to cover a war with Harry, Mom and I were alone in Bel Air, which I loved even more. There are many times I think about my early years, growing up in Hollywood, and I have nothing but happy memories.

I've always loved California, with its marvelous weather, palm trees, lush gardens, and beautiful houses, plus its casual, relaxed lifestyle.

When we were living there in the eighties, we went backward and forward across the Atlantic, from L.A. to Nice. Sometimes we flew to New York, stayed for a while at Fifty-seventh Street, and continued on to Nice to spend a summer at Jardin des Fleurs.

We *were* gypsies, just as Granny said so many times. Nonetheless, we were much-loved girls, and knew it. Both Dad and Mom were smart about verbalizing their feelings about us, and we responded in kind.

Once there had been Marilyn and Grace, but both those beautiful blond stars were dead. Marilyn had passed away in August of 1962 and Grace in September of 1982. Now there was only Mom in that league, and she was the reigning queen at that particular time. The shining blond beauty, the superstar at the top of her game.

I let thoughts of those days drift away, and,

needing to stretch my legs, I went out into the garden.

It was a beautiful day. A California day, I thought, glancing up at the perfect blue sky. I walked around the garden where, thirty years ago, Mom had planted palm trees, cultivated the flower beds, and flowering shrubs. It suddenly struck me again that this garden was very much like the one she had created at her house in Bel Air. I smiled to myself.

What an incredible afternoon it was. The air seemed to shimmer. The sunlight was intense. I went over to the far side of the lawn, stood looking out at the Mediterranean. Its deep blue vastness, as placid as a pond, appeared to merge into the sky, as if there was no horizon. Stretching into infinity, I thought.

Suddenly, I swung around as I heard a car coming up the drive. As if from nowhere, Raffi appeared, waving, calling my name, alerting me that we had a visitor.

I waved back, and walked toward the approaching car. I did not recognize it. Nor did I know who the driver was.

Thirty

The moment I viewed the car up close I knew exactly who the visitor was. *Allen Lambert.* Jessica had mentioned that he had a passion for vintage cars, and now I was staring at an old but highly polished light blue Jaguar parked in our driveway. It had to be his.

A moment later a man alighted, lifted his hand in greeting. I waved back and walked toward him. He reached into the car, took out a bouquet of flowers, and headed down the garden path.

There was a genial smile on his face; he was fair of coloring, rather nice-looking, and casually dressed in an open-necked blue-checked shirt, beige slacks, and a navy blazer.

As we both drew to a standstill, he thrust out his hand. "I'm Allen, and you must be Serena."

"I am, and it's lovely to meet you finally. I'm sorry I've not been around. When you came to see Jessica last week I was in Nice."

He smiled again, his blue eyes sparkling. "How is Jessica? I just got back from London at lunchtime, and I thought I'd pop up for a little visit."

"She's fine, but I'm afraid she's not here at the moment. She went to the auction house for a while."

"Oh dear, how silly of me not to think of

phoning her there. Quite frankly, it never occurred to me she'd be at work."

I noticed the flash of disappointment in his eyes, the way his expression changed, and I said, "Come on, let's go to the terrace and wait for her. She won't be long."

"Well, all right, if you're sure she won't mind . . ." His voice trailed off, and he now seemed somewhat hesitant about hanging around.

"Of course she won't. Anyway, she's probably on her way back already. Adeline was going to pick her up, once she'd finished the marketing. I'll give Jess a call on her cell, find out when she'll be back."

"Good idea," he said, his face instantly brightening.

We walked over to the terrace and up the steps. I said, "Sit down, Allen, make yourself at home. I'll go and grab my cell phone."

He nodded, offered me a warm smile. I already had the feeling that Allen Lambert liked my sister a lot, and that there was much more to this relationship than I'd realized. I was pleased as I hurried off. Once I was in the dining room I searched for my phone, and soon found it under a pile of photographs. I dialed Jessica's number and she answered immediately.

"Hi, it's me," I said. "Where are you, Jess?"

"Almost home. Why?"

"Allen Lambert arrived here a few minutes ago.

Apparently he just got back from London this morning, and he decided to pop up and see you. At least that was the way he put it."

"Oh God." I heard her long sigh echoing down the phone.

"What's the matter? Don't you want to see him?"

"I do and I don't."

"Now you're the ditherer, like I was about Zac."

"I know."

"I like him, Jess. I've only spent a few minutes with him, but he's so nice, very genial, and he's got an open, honest face. Actually, he's quite . . . dishy," I finished, meaning this and thinking: So much for Cara and her opinion.

"Yes, I agree, but I feel awkward when I'm with him at the moment," Jess replied.

"In what sense? I'm not following you." I was surprised by her comment. Jessica was normally at ease with everyone.

"I haven't told him about inheriting osteoporosis from Mom, that I'm taking medication. But I think I should be honest with him, don't you?"

"I do, yes. You should tell him if you plan to continue seeing him."

"I'd like to . . . but he might not want to see me." She suddenly sounded doubtful and a little sad.

I knew exactly where she was going with this, and I said firmly, "You must explain it, Jessica, and take your chances with him. If he feels he can't cope, then he'll obviously back off, move on. And good riddance to him. You don't need a wimp, do you?"

She burst out laughing. "Oh Pidge, there's nobody like you! And you're correct, a wimp of a man is no good to any woman."

"Listen to me. I don't think Allen will be put off. He doesn't seem the type to me," I asserted. "Besides which, osteoporosis is so treatable today, with all the new drugs available. I'm not trying to make light of it, I know it's worrying. But you must remember that Mom developed the condition over thirty-nine years ago, when she got pregnant with you and Cara. Things were a bit different then."

"I know. And I'm coping well, I believe. Okay, I'll tell him. I'll be home soon."

Allen was standing near the balustrade, staring out at the Mediterranean, and he swung around as I walked onto the terrace.

"It's a magnificent view from up here," he said. "Just marvelous. And what a beautiful sight the bay is today . . . so inviting with all the sailboats bobbing around out there. I'm sorry Jessica is a bit restricted by the cast on her leg. It would have been nice to go sailing this weekend."

"Oh, so you like puttering around on boats as much as she does, do you?" I asked, studying him with growing interest.

"I do indeed. I've been a sailor since I was a kid, following in my father's footsteps when I was growing up here. He kept a boat in the port and I inherited his love of the sea." Allen laughed and added, "I tend to be a bit of a workaholic, Serena, and it's been important for me to have another interest, one that gets me away from my desk."

"I know what you mean. Anyway, I just spoke to Jess on her cell, and she and Adeline will be here in a few minutes."

He nodded, suddenly looked much more cheerful. "How's your photographic book coming along?" he asked, and sounded genuinely interested.

"Very well. Zac and I are excited about it. Dad did a lot of work on the dummy before he died, and that's made our job much easier. Zac's in Nice, but he'll be back soon, too. Hopefully we can all have tea together."

I went and sat down under the umbrella and placed my cell phone on the table.

Joining me, Allen said, "I was so sorry about Jessica's accident, and that she had to cancel the Easter lunch. I was very much looking forward to meeting you and Zac. She's told me a lot about the two of you."

I grinned at him. "I do hope she left out the bad bits!"

"Of course she did." He leaned back in the chair,

and stared off into the distance for a moment, then asked, "How's Cara?"

"Fine, she's another workaholic, and I expect she's up at the greenhouses at the moment. Or seeing clients. But she'll probably be back for tea. It's a bit of a ritual here on Fridays . . . with the weekend about to start."

He leaned across the table, and pinned his deep blue eyes on me. "I have the distinct feeling Cara doesn't like me."

"I'm sure you're wrong," I answered swiftly, immediately hoping to dispel the impression he had. I wanted this rather nice man, who was interested in Jessica, to feel welcome in our family.

I added, "Cara's much more reserved than Jessica. Even though they are twins, they have different personalities. And she's been somewhat sad since Jules was killed." I made a small grimace. "You do know her fiancé was killed in a skiing accident, don't you?"

"Jessica told me. I was sorry to hear about it. What a tragic thing to happen."

"I think you're just picking up on Cara's sadness in general, and that curious reserve of hers. She's much less outgoing than Jess, you know," I continued, feeling the need to explain further.

"I'm glad I brought it up. You've made me feel better," Allen said, glanced toward the French doors leading into the peach sitting room. "I think Jessica's arrived," he announced, suddenly happy. He rose. "Should I go and greet her? Bring her out to the terrace? I've been a bit hesitant about trying to help her, Serena, she's so terribly independent."

"I know, but go ahead, go and get her!" I instructed, sounding a bit bossy.

Allen was smiling broadly as he walked through the peach sitting room, obviously anxious to see my sister. I liked him, and I felt he wasn't the type of man to be deterred by anything, least of all an illness that could be properly treated today. There was something very genuine about him.

As they came out onto the terrace I thought how good they looked together. Allen was tall, like Jess, and well built, and he seemed to be protective of her. They had similar interests, from what she had confided earlier. They both loved movies, the theater, music and opera. And he himself had just told me how much he enjoyed boats and sailing, just as she did.

Fingers crossed, I thought, and went to greet my sister. As I stared at her I realized there was a look of real happiness in her dark eyes. I had a feeling that everything would be all right between these two. She deserved a guy like this Englishman.

"I'm glad you finally met Serena," Jessica said to Allen as she lowered herself into a chair, and then a look of surprise crossed her face as he presented the bouquet. "These are for you, darling," he said.

"You spoil me," she said, still smiling at him as she smelled the flowers. "Thank you so much."

When I noticed the gilded smile, the joyous expression on her face, I knew with absolute certainty that she was deeply involved with this man, even if she didn't know it herself. Or perhaps she didn't want to admit it. I might have to enlighten her.

I decided to leave the two of them alone for a few minutes. "I'm going to help Adeline with the tea. I won't be long," I announced.

Jessica said, "Would you please ask Adeline to give you the bottle of pills we picked up at the pharmacy earlier? I need to take one with my tea."

"Yes, of course," I answered, understanding exactly what she was doing: alerting him she wasn't well.

Turning to Allen, Jessica went on. "I haven't had a chance to tell you this before, but I've been having some bone density scans, and other tests. Because of my two recent falls, and my broken ankle. You see, my mother had a rare form of osteoporosis, which I've apparently inherited, just as my doctor thought."

If Allen was surprised or perturbed to hear this, he didn't show it. "I'm sorry, Jessica. Fortunately, today doctors can work miracles with all the new medications now available."

"Yes, I know. And I'm not worried. My condition

is very treatable. I have great doctors, and I'll be fine."

Allen nodded, put his hand on top of Jessica's which was resting on the table. He smiled at her. "You will be fine. I'll make sure of that, I promise you."

They sat there gazing at each other, and my heart lifted. I knew I was right about him. He was one of the good guys. My sense of relief was enormous.

My mother had loved afternoon tea, and she had collected lots of tea paraphernalia over the years. Tea pots, milk jugs, cake stands, glass jam roll dishes, honey pots, jam pots, silver candy bowls, napkins, dainty forks, and beautiful old cake knives. Name it, we had it. It was all in the storage room with a collection of antique tea trolleys.

The room adjoined the kitchen, and now I went in and selected a trolley which had three tiers of glass shelves. It was probably Edwardian, and I particularly liked it because of the intricate metalwork, and the fact that the shelves were large and held a lot.

As I wheeled it into the kitchen, Adeline looked at me, and exclaimed, "*Mon Dieu*! Why that one?"

"Because it holds so much and we are five for tea, Adeline. Monsieur Lambert is here."

"*Ah oui*," she answered, nodding her head,

giving me a knowing and conspiratorial smile. The housekeeper was a romantic at heart.

"Before I forget, Jessica would like her pills, please. She said you had them."

"I'll get them. *Immédiatement.*" As she spoke she went over to the counter, rustled around in her bag. A moment later she handed them to me, and said, "It is fortunate I was smart enough to bake a lot of cakes for the weekend."

"You're a genius, Adeline," I said, laughing at her little display of vanity.

She paid no attention to me, rushed across the kitchen, selected the largest of the teapots, turned on the kettle, and hurried into the larder. I went to help her bring out a coconut cream cake, a jam roll, a chocolate roll with cream filling, eclairs, an apple tart, and a plate of cookies. Everything was mouthwatering and smelled delicious. Adeline had inherited Lulu's talents as a cook.

I was as fast as Adeline, and within ten minutes we had the tea made and everything loaded onto the trolley. I rolled it from the kitchen to the hall, through the peach sitting room, and out to the terrace. I gave Jessica her pills and I had just started to pour the tea when Zac came bounding up the terrace steps from the garden.

He greeted us both affectionately, and then Jessica introduced him to Allen. The two men began to chat in a desultory way at first, but they soon became animated and involved when they got onto politics and the turmoil that was happening in the Middle East.

I closed my ears to this chitter-chatter, and concentrated on being the perfect hostess, since Jessica had vacated that role for the moment. It was difficult for her to move around swiftly handing out cups of tea and cakes when her foot and ankle were in a plaster cast.

Jessica and I ate sparingly as usual, since neither of us was greatly interested in cakes and pastries. But the two men were thoroughly enjoying themselves, tasting everything and drinking endless cups of tea. I was glad they got on so well.

Twenty minutes later Cara came gliding onto the terrace, saying hello to everyone before flopping down into one of the chairs.

I glanced at her quickly, and I couldn't help thinking she looked pleased with herself, and wondered why. I also wondered what might come flying out of her mouth at any moment.

She delivered her first bombshell when she finished her cup of tea. Looking at me intently, she spoke in that somber voice of hers she used at times, and which I dreaded. "I have it on good authority that it is very likely you and I also have that rare osteoporosis which afflicted Mom, and which Jessica has inherited. We must have tests."

Swiftly, I looked at Jessica, saw how flabbergasted she was, and gave her a reassuring smile. I

266

myself was so furious with Cara I couldn't speak for a moment. She had exposed Jessica and her illness to Allen without knowing how much he knew about the situation.

I closed my eyes and took a deep breath, mortified that she had been so thoughtless, and careless. And yet I knew that she wasn't malicious, that she merely said what was on her mind without editing herself. She was worried that we had inherited it too. And so was I. Cara would never do anything to hurt Jessica or me intentionally; she wasn't a bitch. She was a nice person who never thought of the damage she might cause.

I opened my eyes when I heard Jessica say in a mild voice, "Perhaps that would be a good idea, Cara. Why don't you make an appointment for yourself and Serena with Dr. Colmar. I'm sure he'll fit you in, and as soon as possible, because you're my sisters."

"Thanks, Jessica, and we should go to your doctor," I said, and turned to Cara, threw her a pointed look. "I'll fit in with your schedule," I said somewhat coldly.

"I can't do it until later next week," Cara responded.

"Oh really, and why not? You're the one who made it sound so urgent." I frowned at her, and she knew at once that I was put out, annoyed.

Taking a deep breath, Cara explained, "Because

I'm going away for the weekend, and I won't be back until Tuesday night." She glanced around the table, as if this had been a special announcement. Actually, it was her second bombshell.

"Oh really, and where are you going? Is it a business trip?" I asked a little sharply, my eyes riveted on her.

"No, it's not." There was a moment's pause before she said slowly, "Well . . . I'm going to London."

On hearing this, Zac sat up straighter in the chair, chuckled, and asked in that teasing tone of his, "Don't tell me you're going to see our little lad Geoff. You're not, are you?"

Cara gave him a smile that was somewhat smug and knowing. She replied in a cool voice, "Of course I'm going to see Geoff. Why else would I go to London?"

"The Chelsea Flower Show, your favorite," I ventured, unable to resist saying this. I knew it would irk her no end, and it did.

She gazed at me with a certain amount of disdain when she answered, "That's later in May, as you well know, Serena. Geoff invited me, and I accepted. You know I don't like to travel unless it's necessary. I don't relish it at all, in fact. I did too much of it as a child. But I'm going because I want to see Geoff."

I was irritated by this retort about traveling, but I kept my mouth shut. Nonetheless, I wanted to slap her. Nobody knew better than I how much she had enjoyed traveling the world with our parents. Ungrateful, that's what she is, I thought, and glanced at Jessica.

Jessica took one look at my face and started to laugh. It was that wonderful, pealing laughter of hers that I loved so much. It rang to the rafters and it was infectious. We exchanged knowing looks and immediately I started to laugh with her, unable to resist my sister's good humor and jocularity.

It was Jessica who finally stopped laughing and spoke first. "I think that's lovely, Cara. I for one am delighted you're going to see Geoff. I know he likes you, admires you, and I think you'll have a lovely time."

Zac looked as if he was about to make some sort of pithy comment, and I shook my head, warned him with my eyes to stay silent. Which he fortunately did.

When my cell began to ring, I flipped it open. "Serena Stone," I said and rose, walked away from the table, saying, "Hi, Harry. How're things in New York?"

"All's well at the office. Where's Zac, honey?"

"Right here on the terrace with me. Why? You sound funny. Is there something wrong, Harry?"

"Let me speak to Zac, Serena. His phones are all turned off. Hurry up, honey, it's urgent."

"Just a minute." I looked across at Zac,

beckoned. "It's Harry, for you. He says your phones are off," I explained.

"That's right," Zac said, as he walked over to join me. "I didn't want any interruptions when I was with Dr. Biron in Nice."

I handed him my phone, took a few steps away from him, wanted to give him privacy.

"Hi, Harry, what's up?" Zac fell into total silence as he listened. I saw him stiffen, took note of his sudden deathly pallor. He looked shocked. "Okay, I'll do it now. Right away . . . thanks, Harry." Zac clicked off and stood gaping at me, speechless.

I could see he was stunned. "What is it?" I went to him, grabbed his arm, led him away from the table, took him along the terrace. "What is it?" I asked again, peering into his face. I could see how stricken he was.

At last he spoke. "It's my mother. She's had a stroke. She's in the hospital. Dad's been trying to reach me on my various cell phones. He finally called Harry. Dad wants me to get home as fast as I can. It's serious. I must leave immediately."

"I'm sorry, Zac, so very sorry. I'll help you to pack. We must get you on a plane tonight. Jessica has a good travel agency." I put my arms around him and held him close. "I'll get everything organized, and I'll come with you if you want."

Zac clung to me, gripped me tightly, but remained silent.

Thirty-one

Zac had left a week ago. He had gone to New York alone.

We had decided that this would be the best. He could stay out in Long Island with his family, focus on his mother in the local hospital, and help his father to cope. Also, with Cara going to London to see Geoff Barnes, I had not wanted to leave Jessica alone that weekend.

Today was Friday the thirteenth, which I did not consider unlucky as some people did. And I had had good news an hour ago.

Zac called to tell me his mother was much better, had recovered most of her speech. I was thrilled that she was making such good progress after her stroke, and it made me happy to hear him sounding so cheerful. It was a lucky Friday, as far as I was concerned.

When Zac first left I worried about him, asked Harry to be available if Zac suffered a sudden PTSD attack. Harry had acquiesced, but pointed out that Zac was now so totally focused on his mother, an attack was unlikely. And so far he had been correct.

I was making progress on Dad's book *Courage*. I had finished sorting out the last batch of pictures, and the entire book was now ready for shipment to New York. Because it was bulky,

Jessica had suggested a freight company she used, and I'd agreed. She had arranged for the large package to be picked up next week and it would be crated and sent to Harry at Global's New York office.

Currently I was sorting through the photographs in the box marked VENICE. Cara had told me they were incredibly beautiful, and she was correct. In fact, the photographs were so superb many of them looked like paintings.

I thought of the great English artist J. M. W. Turner, and the glorious landscapes and seascapes of Venice which he had created in the mid-1800s. It seemed to me that Dad had followed in his footsteps, had endeavored to capture similar images with his camera that Turner had put on canvas . . . the lemons, golds, and rusts of Turner's sunrises and sunsets, and the blues of his seas. The warmth and color of Venice made for wonderfully vibrant images on film.

The door of the studio suddenly opened, and I glanced up, surprised to see Cara standing in the doorway.

"Hi," I said, staring at her. "I thought you'd gone to London again. For another weekend with Geoff."

She shook her head. "Can I come in? Am I disturbing you?"

"No, you're not, and yes, come on in. I'm going through the Venice pictures, and you were right, they are truly amazing . . . *awesome*. More like oil paintings than photographs."

"I know. I'm beginning to realize what a genius Dad was with a camera." She gave me a small smile. "But then you've always known that, haven't you, Serena?"

I didn't comment. I got up and walked over to the sofa. I said to Cara, "I can take a few minutes to talk to you. Is something wrong? You look worried."

She followed me to the sofa and sat down in the chair opposite, leaning forward slightly, her elbows on her knees. She was totally focused on me, her expression intense.

"I know you're angry with me about last Friday, and I just wanted to talk. I'd like to clear the air between us, that's all," she explained.

"I'm not angry anymore, Cara. But I admit I was last weekend."

"But why? I'm not really understanding." She sounded puzzled.

For a moment I was nonplussed, taken aback that she didn't realize what she had done. That was very dense of her; on the other hand, I knew she was being truthful.

I said quietly, "You spoke about Jessica having osteoporosis in front of Allen Lambert, without giving it a thought. It was so careless of you. What if she hadn't told him? Don't you realize the damage you might have done?"

"But why does that matter? She's not serious about him. And why should she be?"

"Actually, Jess is serious. And I totally disagree with you. I think Allen's very nice. Anyway, that's beside the point. You can't be indiscreet, Cara, it gets people's backs up. It can also be hurtful."

Cara sat up straighter in the chair, shook her head, then sighed heavily. "I know what you're going to say—my mouth's always open and my foot's always in it."

"Another saying of Granny's, which does happen to be true when applied to you, Cara. You must edit yourself, take the feelings of others into account."

"I can't help being outspoken," she protested sharply.

"When I was growing up I was glad you were so open about things. Such as explaining Mom's osteoporosis to me. And also telling me all about sex. Even when I was far too young to really understand any of it." I began to laugh. "I know you probably meant well, believed I ought to be well informed for my own good. But you made it sound so . . . icky and gruesome." I started to laugh again, and so did she.

"Sorry about that," she said. "But I'm sure you overcame your problems when you met Zac. How's his mother, by the way?"

"He phoned a while ago, she's much better. She has her speech back. And thank God the paralysis has left her right side. He was very excited about her progress and how well she's doing. The whole family is relieved. And incidentally, you once said a leopard doesn't change its spots, but Zac has."

"I know. He's a different man. Geoff says Zac's lost his edge, that he won't go back to the front line."

"What's going on with you and Geoff *actually?*" I probed, wishing to change the subject, and also curious about her unexpected involvement with Geoff. To me it was a curious liaison.

"I guess you could say we're having an affair," she murmured in a low voice. "He's the first man I've met since Jules died that I can actually stand. Most men leave me cold, but there's something genuine about Geoff. He's totally sincere, and very caring. I suppose he's a bit square, but I like that about him . . . he's the real thing."

"What you say is true, Cara. But—" I broke off, hesitating, and then decided to finish my sentence. "I thought he was going to L.A. to visit his daughter. I'm sure you heard what happened, that you know the whole disastrous story."

"I do. I told him he was batting against the odds, and wanting to get back with his ex-wife was silly. That she was long gone, that's for damn sure. I suggested he bring his daughter to London for a visit, rather than go over there to see her. Why set foot in enemy territory?"

I couldn't believe she had said all this to Geoff,

and my stomach churned. Dismay rendered me momentarily speechless. Finally, I found my voice. "That might be tough on a little girl, don't you think? London's hardly California. Not only that, Geoff's working . . ." I let my voice trickle away, wondering why I had embarked on this complex tale of Geoff and his ex-wife. It wasn't any of my business. No, not strictly true. Geoff was one of our employees at Global and important to us.

Cara now said suddenly, "I offered Geoff another alternative. I suggested he could invite his daughter to come here with him. I think Chloe would enjoy spending a few days at Jardin des Fleurs."

I found it hard to disguise my astonishment, and I exclaimed, "Geoff has to run Global in London! He can't take off just like that!" I gave her a hard stare. "He has responsibilities to the agency."

"He could take a weekend off, surely? And I could look after Chloe here for a few days while he goes back to London."

This idea of Cara's alarmed me, and I wanted to end the conversation, nip it in the bud. So I said, "It seems you've got it all worked out in your head. But I'm afraid it won't fly." I suddenly wondered what Jessica would say about these plans, and was about to say this, but changed my mind. Instead, I asked, "So, have we cleared the air?"

"I think so. I'll try not to be so blunt in the future, and I'll apologize to Jess. What about the bone density tests? Shall I make an appointment for next week?" she asked, moving on abruptly, for once understanding I was irritated.

"Yes, but make it early in the week." I jumped up. "I'd better get back to the pictures of Venice." I was somewhat relieved she'd let the matter drop, and I hoped I'd got my message across about Geoff and his child. The fact that Cara even wanted a child around her astonished me; she worked eighteen hours a day most of the time, including weekends, and was so focused she was in another world.

Cara walked across the floor, turned at the door. "I think there's a lovely coffee table book in those pictures, Serena, but you'll need a few more, don't you think?"

"I agree, but you told me there are a lot of Venice shots in Dad's archives."

"Tons. Over there in the files in the credenza."

"I'll look for them in a while." I sat down at the desk, once more staring at Tommy's dummy.

Cara left the studio, quietly closing the door behind her.

I realized as I analyzed the dummy of the Venice book that it was actually much more complete than *Courage* had been, except for needing a few extra photographs at the end. Dad had called it *La Serenissima*, using the ancient name for Venice in its heyday when it was first a republic. It meant "the most serene."

After half an hour I got up and went over to the credenza which contained the built-in filing cabinets. In the top drawer "La Serenissima" was written on several folders, each one marked with a red star. This was Dad's usual way of indicating that the folder contained his favorite and preferred shots.

Taking them back to the desk, I looked at them all and was even more thrilled. They were staggeringly beautiful, and I understood that with the addition of these the Venice book did not require much work at all. I couldn't wait to tell Zac.

Later, when I went up to the terrace for tea, I saw that Jessica was alone. "Where's Cara?" I asked, joining her at the table.

"She's gone to see a client. Unexpectedly. She said we're not to wait for her, that she'll grab a cup of tea when she comes back."

I nodded, then told Jess about the conversation I'd just had with her twin and I left out nothing.

Jessica laughed when I'd finished my tale. "Well, it's true, she did take my breath away for a moment last Friday. I couldn't help thinking she was being rather dumb. But you've always known she's got a blind spot when it comes to people's feelings. She's too honest, that's her real problem, actually."

I nodded, and poured myself a cup of tea. "She says exactly what comes into her head. No editing. But listen, what's so amazing to me is her unexpected involvement with Geoff Barnes. You talk about having the breath knocked out of you when she blabbed about the osteoporosis. I was blown away when I heard about the affair with Geoff."

"I was, too. Flabbergasted." Jessica studied me for a moment. "I've thought about their involvement for the last few days, and come to realize that Geoff is a lot like Jules. Not in his looks, I'll grant you that. Jules was movie-star handsome, and Geoff's plainer in appearance. But he is much taller, fits better with Cara, in that sense. Anyway, Geoff has the same kind of niceness, which is what made Jules so warm, *likeable,* I guess that's the word. I think Cara sees that, understands that Geoff's character is underscored by the same kind of genuineness and reliability that Jules had."

"Now that you mention it, Geoff is a very authentic person. But I hadn't made the connection between Jules and Geoff, to be truthful. How do you feel about having Geoff and his daughter staying here?"

"Oh, I don't mind, Pidge, I really don't. Actually, I'm pleased about Cara and Geoff. She's had some really bleak, depressed days over the past two years, ever since Jules died. I want her to have a little happiness now. Anyway, the house is big, and it's nice to have company. And you'll be leaving soon, won't you? You've got to get back to work on Dad's biography, and now's the time, because you've finished sorting out *Courage*. And I think it's marvelous, by the way, it's going to be a great book."

Pausing, Jessica smiled. "That was a mouthful, wasn't it, Pidge? But you will be leaving me, and I'll miss you."

I heard the sudden sadness in her voice, and exclaimed, "I do have to go, yes, but I'll be back later in the summer. Zac wants to come with me, because he does have to write the text for *Courage*. We've only sorted the photographs and created sections so far, got them in proper order, the way Dad envisioned it. Also, Zac wants to try his hand at writing a memoir." I cocked my head on one side, and endeavored to suppress a smile, when I said, "We'll be back here before you can say Jack Robinson."

"I ought to throw this cupcake at you," Jessica cried, grinning as she picked it up. "I thought we promised each other we'd never use any of Granny's sayings."

"That's true, but I couldn't resist."

"When do you think you'll be leaving?"

"In about a week or ten days. I'm happy to tell you I have already found those additional pictures for the Venice book. I just have to create the last few sequences. And it's easier to do it here." I paused, gave her a pointed look. "And I don't want Zac to think I'm breathing down his neck in New York. I want him to devote all his time to his mother, all the time she needs him to help her get well."

"I understand. Cara mentioned she's going to make an appointment for you both to have the bone density scans. Early next week."

I nodded. "That's right. I told her to make it as soon as possible."

"I'd like to explain something to you," Jessica said, sounding tentative. Then she cleared her throat, and went on in a stronger voice. "Tell you about this rare form of osteoporosis I've inherited from our mother."

"Go ahead," I replied, and sat back in the chair, focused on her, feeling a little nervous unexpectedly.

"My condition has been caught early, which means I can lead a relatively normal life," Jessica explained. "And if you and Cara do have it, then you'll be pretty much in the same category as I am. You're eight years younger, of course, so you'll be better off than Cara and me in a sense. I just wanted to tell you that I take a drug called calcitonin, which slows bone loss, along with painkillers, and various calcium supplements."

"And they're helping, aren't they?"

"Yes, very much so. A lot of women who suffer

from osteoporosis are often treated with bisphosphonates, which are the most powerful drugs to slow bone loss." Jessica took a sip of tea, and went on, "But most doctors won't prescribe them for women who are still of childbearing age, like me, Cara, and you."

"Why is that?" I asked a little anxiously.

"Because the long-term effect of the drug on the developing baby's skeleton is not yet fully understood. It's all about not damaging an unborn child."

"I understand that completely, Jess. And you do feel all right, don't you? You're not in great pain, are you?"

"No. I'm really doing good. And incidentally, I'm glad I spit it out, told Allen. He's been so understanding, and it doesn't seem to bother him. It's made me feel much better, talking about it, being open and honest."

"I think he's serious about you, Jess."

A small smile played around her mouth. "I think he is too, and guess what?" She leaned across the table and said softly, still smiling, "And I am too. About him. I believe there's a future for us together."

"I realized that before you did!" I exclaimed buoyantly.

"So aren't you the clever one! Just like Mom. Always spotting relationships budding, affairs starting, and all that romantic stuff, and long before anyone else. So, Pidge, what about you and Zac? Where do you two stand?"

"We're together. We're serious. Actually, we've been talking about getting married next year."

"Why next year? Why not now?" she asked, a brow lifting.

"He wants to feel right about himself, his health, wants to be sure he's got his PTSD under control."

"That's understandable. On the other hand, don't leave it too long, Serena, don't let time slip away. Get married, make a home, get new careers, be together in the best way. You can trust him, because you and I know he's never going back to the front. And neither are you."

"You're absolutely right," I answered. "I'll never wear a flak jacket again."

Little did I know on that sunny May afternoon how wrong I was when I said those words. But then none of us knows what the future will bring, or the sorrow and pain we will encounter. What's in store for us is a secret.

Thirty-two

We went to the African Queen.

We put on our jeans, our best silk shirts, and sparkling fake earrings, and set off from the house, the three of us in a congenial mood. Cara drove us there . . . to the charming little port in

Beaulieu-sur-Mer where the famous old restaurant was located.

It had been one of our mother's favorite spots, and we had been going there for years, so what better place to celebrate her birthday. It was May 15, and if she had lived she would have been seventy-two years old today. I found that hard to believe. In my mind's eye she was the beautiful blond superstar of my younger years, and she always would be. My sisters felt exactly the same as I did. Our mother was forever young in our hearts.

Cara took the Moyenne Corniche to Beaulieu. The traffic was light, and she was lucky enough to find a parking spot on the port. This was helpful to Jessica, who was now wearing a soft cast on her foot and feeling better, but still couldn't walk far.

Our table was ready when we arrived, and the bottle of pink Veuve Clicquot, which Cara had ordered in advance, was waiting for us in a bucket of ice. As we sat down we were assailed by a cacophony of sounds—the chatter; the laughter; the rattle of china, crystal, and cutlery; the joviality in general—and the delicious smells emanating from the kitchen were mouthwatering.

The African Queen had always been a lively spot, and so popular it was often hard to get a table. But because of our long family history with them we were never refused.

A waiter came, opened the bottle, and poured

the champagne, and the three of us clinked our glasses and said, "Happy Birthday to Mom," as we had done for the past four years since her death. And then we sat and reminisced about her for a while, recalling her joie de vivre, her lovely quirkiness.

At one moment Cara glanced around, said sotto voce, "The posters are starting to look faded, don't you think?"

Jessica and I followed her gaze, and saw that she was correct. The walls were covered with framed posters of Humphrey Bogart and Katharine Hepburn in the old movie *The African Queen*, from which the local bistro took its name.

I said, "I could ask Harry to get them some new ones. He has a friend who deals in old movie posters and memorabilia. But maybe everyone likes the faded ones."

"That's more than likely," Jessica interjected. "I'd leave it alone, if I were you. I'm sure they know where to get the posters. These are not the ones they started with. This place has been open for thirty years or more."

"They've probably got a storage room full of them," Cara muttered, sounding cynical, and reached for the menu. "I'm having my usual," she announced, then glanced at the menu anyway.

We all ordered the same thing. To start, we selected warm white asparagus, now in season, with vinaigrette dressing, followed by *moules marinière pommes frites* . . . mussels steamed in a broth of white wine and served with French fries.

My sisters were in a good mood and both appeared to be happy. And so was I. Now that I had finished sorting the last photographs for the Venice book, I would soon be returning to New York.

Zac's mother was continuing to improve, and he was in good shape. He called me twice a day and sounded great, almost like his old self. Zac loved his family, felt a sense of responsibility to them; being in their midst and taking charge had undoubtedly distracted him.

Harry had said the same to me only last night, had remarked that Zac was so focused on his mother's health and his father's well-being, he didn't have time for his PTSD. But I knew Zac was missing me and wanted me to go to New York as soon as possible. And that was my aim.

As for Jessica and Cara, they were both following their hearts, and were engrossed in their romantic liaisons with Allen and Geoff, respectively.

This genuinely pleased me. I was now fairly certain Jess and Allen were going to end up together on a permanent basis. I wasn't sure about Cara and Geoff, although I knew how genuine and sincere Geoff was. I would have to wait and see what transpired between them.

Halfway through the meal, Jessica suddenly brought up the subject of the jewelry auction, when she said, "I'd like us to go through Mom's safe tomorrow, so that we can decide what to sell."

"I thought we were selling everything," Cara exclaimed.

"All of the important pieces, yes," Jessica responded. "But there are some smaller things, items which are less valuable. I thought perhaps we should each choose some of those things for ourselves, as keepsakes, for sentimental reasons."

"Whatever you want," Cara replied, and I nodded in agreement, then asked, "When are you thinking of having the auction, Jess?"

"Next spring. You see, it—"

"Why so far off?" Cara asked, cutting in, frowning at her twin.

"Because of the Elizabeth Taylor Auction. Christie's is holding that in New York this coming December, and right now part of the very extensive Elizabeth Taylor Collection is touring the world. I believe it's not possible for me to compete with that kind of ballyhoo."

"I agree," I said.

Jessica continued, "There are hundreds and hundreds of lots of jewelry, paintings, clothes, and accessories in Taylor's collection. It's immense. This aside, our mother's jewelry has to be photographed, properly evaluated, and documented, and I have to create a catalog. There's a lot more to an auction than you can imagine."

"You know your business better than we do," I said. "I trust your judgment, and I'm sure you feel the same way, Cara, don't you?" I fixed my gaze on my other sister.

"You're right, Serena, Jess is the boss." Settling back in the chair, she told her twin, "Whatever you do is okay with me." This was said in a soft voice, and she reached for her champagne and lifted it to Jess, then took a sip.

My eyes were still on Cara, and I realized she looked particularly beautiful. She wore her long black hair loose tonight. It framed her face, which seemed more delicate than ever, like a finely sculpted piece of alabaster. Her skin glowed and her black eyes were bright with life. She seemed happier than she had for years, and there was a tranquility about her.

"Are you going to marry Geoff?" I blurted out before I could stop myself. Jessica was sitting next to me, and immediately squeezed my knee under the table in warning, but did not utter a word.

Cara laughed out loud. This took me totally by surprise, because she was always so serious, even glum at times. Cara rarely ever laughed, and especially like this . . . so joyously, freely, uninhibited in fact.

I sat staring at her, dumbfounded, at a loss, not knowing what to say.

Finally, Cara spoke. "He hasn't asked me, Serena. You see, I've yet to meet his little daughter, Chloe. I know her reaction to me and mine to her is extremely important to Geoff. So I'm biding my time. Anyway, I don't want to rush into anything, we need to know each other a little longer. However, I'll be honest, I would consider it. We've discovered we're extremely compatible." She paused, looked at me and then at Jessica, added, "In bed and out of it."

Jessica broke into her pealing laughter, grabbing her twin's hand and squeezing it. "I'm so happy for you! And incidentally, that makes two of us . . . being compatible with our boyfriends, I mean."

"Three of us," I announced, laughing with my sisters, loving them both so much. They had always been part of me and would be for as long as we lived. They were loyal and devoted to me as I was to them . . . that was the way our mother had raised us.

Thirty-three

On Monday morning, Cara and I went to Nice to see Jessica's doctor and have our bone density tests. On Tuesday we sorted through Mom's safe and made an inventory of the important jewels. Later that same day we went through her three wardrobes of haute couture clothes, and did the same, listing everything.

Jessica said she would have the fashion expert at the auction house inspect the clothes, so that the best could be selected. They all looked fabulous to me, and I said so.

It was Wednesday afternoon that I stumbled across a selection of additional Venice photographs, and they made me catch my breath in surprise. And not exactly in a good way.

I was tidying up Dad's studio, putting everything back in the filing cabinet, when I noticed a blue folder on the bottom of the lower drawer.

Picking it up, I took it over to the desk, opened it, and looked at the photographs inside. The first few were of a young woman, scantily clad in a short greenish gray filmy chiffon dress, dancing in a huge room.

I realized the room was in a Venetian palazzo, because of the interior architecture, the Venetian chandeliers, and the few antiques scattered around.

The photos showed the young woman in motion, her arms held out, or floating around her, or above her head. Her body movements were graceful, her long legs shapely. It seemed to me she must be dancing to actual music, so convincing was she. The pictures were all lovely, especially those in color.

The young woman had long straight brown hair, but I could not properly see her face. It was obscured either by her hair, or her arms, or blurred because of her constant movement around the room.

As I continued to go through the blue folder, I saw to my surprise how the photographs began to change.

In several, the young woman had draped herself on a chaise longue, her legs parted in a suggestive way, or she had put them high up on the back of the chaise, the filmy dress falling away, and revealingly so.

It instantly struck me that there was something erotic about these particular photographs, and because Dad had taken them they were beginning to trouble me. Why had he taken them? What was his involvement with her? This was not his style. The pictures were somewhat intimate, and I knew it was this that made me feel uneasy, uncomfortable.

I turned one over and it had my father's typical caption on the back: A narrow strip of white paper, taped down at each end, and as usual the caption was typed. It read: *Val in perpetual motion.* The others read, *Val impatient; Val in flight.*

I frowned to myself, continued to peer at this young woman, face obscured, whom my father had photographed so assiduously. Fifteen shots so far. Quite a lot for Tommy Stone.

There were three left in the blue folder, and when I looked down at them I recoiled in shock. The woman's face was finally revealed. It startled me because it looked so familiar, and then I realized it was my own face that was staring back at me.

This woman called Val was sitting on the chaise, the dress artfully draped, and she was staring straight into the camera. And we bore a strong resemblance to each other. No wonder she seemed familiar. There were two more shots and they made me gasp out loud.

In the first, the young woman was naked, her belly huge. She lay stretched out on the chaise, her hands covering her crotch, and she was very pregnant.

In the second shot she was also naked, standing in profile, again showing her huge belly. Her face was turned to the camera, and she was smiling. It was a curious smile. Self-satisfied, perhaps?

One frame tells it all, I thought, remembering that favorite phrase of my father's. It was one he had used often.

Who was she? Who was this mysterious Val?

I turned the two photographs over. The caption for the reclining nude shot read: *Val waiting for Serena.* The second said: *Val and Serena.*

SERENA. *My name.*

Why was my name on these photographs?

Who was this woman?

I began to shake uncontrollably. The implication on the caption was obvious. This woman was pregnant with me. And since she had been photographed by my father it was apparent she was his lover. She was expecting his child, wasn't she?

One frame tells it all, Dad would say. This one told quite a story, didn't it?

I closed my eyes, unable to accept the mere idea that this woman had been carrying me. I was Elizabeth Vasson Stone's daughter. I knew I was. I had been her precious darling, the longed-for baby. Her treasure. I was *hers.* I was not the reason for this other woman's big belly.

Why had my father taken these photographs? What did this woman mean to him? And who the hell was she?

I pushed all of the photographs back into the blue folder, and sat back in the chair. I was still feeling shaky, unsettled, and a bit sick, as if I was about to throw up.

My mind raced. All kinds of dire thoughts were tumbling around in my head. I endeavored to make sense of the pictures, to no avail.

I knew suddenly what I must do. I grabbed the folder, left the studio, and ran up the garden path.

Jessica was working in her office next to the library. She had to see these pictures which so alarmed me, and so did Cara.

Jessica was at her desk in the little office when I burst in unexpectedly and she glanced up swiftly in surprise.

"I've found something horrendous!" I gasped as I rushed across to her desk.

Jessica was gaping at me, obviously startled. "Whatever is it, Pidge darling? Why are you so upset?"

"It's these photographs Dad took!" I cried somewhat shrilly, and dropped the folder on the desk in front of her.

I hovered, watching her face, as she went through the pictures. Finally, she looked at me. I saw that she was as stunned as I had been. Her face was as white as bleached bone, her dark eyes bleak.

"Where did you find this folder?" she asked shakily, her expression stricken. Her gaze did not leave my face.

I explained how I'd just come across it, and then said, "Look at the captions, Jess."

She did as I asked, and her face became even paler. She then studied the last two shots of the pregnant woman, shaking her head in obvious disbelief.

"Why would Dad take pictures like that?" I asked, staring at her. "And who is that woman? Do you know?"

She nodded. "It's Mom's cousin. Val."

I frowned. "Did you know her?"

"Of course. We all knew her. She is Aunt Dora's daughter, Granny's niece. Her name is Valentina Clifford, and she used to visit us occasionally when we were little."

"And did I know her?"

"Not very well, you were just a toddler. I think the last time she came to see us here was when I was eleven, so you must have been three."

I swallowed hard, asked hoarsely, "What happened to her? *Eventually?*" I sat down on the chair near Jessica's desk. "I can't remember her at all, so she must have eventually stopped coming."

Jessica leaned back in her chair, biting her lip. She was obviously racking her brains, and her expression had turned thoughtful. "I'm not sure why she didn't come again," she said at last. "I have a faint remembrance that she went off to cover some war or other, and she was injured, but—"

"Was she a war photographer?" I cried, interrupting her, suddenly growing more alarmed than ever.

"Yes. She worked at Global Images. With Dad."

So they had been buddies. I felt as if a lump of lead had settled in my stomach. "Did she die? Or what?"

"She might well be dead by now," Jessica answered. "However, I do know she didn't die from her injury. And now that I think about it, I believe she was in some sort of car crash in the war she was covering. She didn't take a bullet or anything like that. I think she was in a Jeep that overturned."

"When did Mom and Dad last hear from her?"

I probed. "Or see her? Can't you remember?"

"I can't, Pidge. But she didn't come to visit us after the accident. Cara and I were away at boarding school in England, and honestly I can't recall seeing her again. Anyway, don't you have any memories of her?"

"None at all." I stood up, walked over to the big bay window, looked out at the garden. A replica of Mom's Bel Air garden. My throat tightened. I swallowed hard, turned, and went and sat down on the sofa. I was flooded with anxiety.

Jessica was focused on me, and she said in a gentle voice, "The photographs don't mean anything, Pidge, truly they don't. Let's just destroy them, and forget all about them."

"The captions mean something," I said, suddenly fighting back tears. "My name is on two of the captions, Jess."

"That means nothing!" Jessica exclaimed heatedly, her voice rising. "Those photographs were obviously taken in Venice, which was once called La Serenissima . . . the Most Serene . . . which immediately leads to the name Serena. It's not necessarily a reference to *you,* many women are called after Venice. Besides which, there's no date on the pictures. They could have been taken ten years ago, or whenever."

I sat silently, not answering. I knew Jessica loved me, wanted to make me feel better, and her solution was to destroy the pictures and dismiss this incident as one of no consequence. But I couldn't do that. I was troubled by the images. And my name in the two captions. Before I could stop myself I burst into tears.

Within seconds Jessica was putting her arms around me, holding me close, endeavoring to soothe me. I began to sob, and eventually, when I had calmed down a bit, I whispered, "I don't want to be that woman's daughter. I want to be Mom's daughter, Jess. I've always been so proud to be part of her, to be *her* daughter. I loved her so much, still love her. I won't be able to bear it if Mom's not my mother. And what do those pictures say about Dad? And their great love affair? If the pictures are true? If he slept with that woman?"

Jessica answered me at once. "Mom and Dad *did* have a great love affair! All of their life together. And we witnessed it, Serena. You and me and Cara, their daughters. We grew up with it."

I nodded, held on to her hand tightly.

She continued to speak softly. "And if Dad did sleep with Val, so what? It was probably a one-night stand, when they were on the front line. Something like that. And anyway, you know what men are like. And just because a married man sleeps with another woman briefly, doesn't mean he doesn't love his wife. That's just the way men are."

I sat back, gazed at my sister. "I do understand what you're saying," I began and then my mouth started to tremble and the tears came once more. After a moment, I managed to add, "But Mom and Dad were different from everybody else. They had a big love, a grand love. They were true blue, so special . . ."

"What's wrong? What's happened?" Cara said in a loud voice, slamming the door behind her as she came rushing into the room, obviously filled with concern.

I looked up at her and tears slid down my cheeks and splashed on my hands and I couldn't get control of myself. It's the shock, I thought. I'm still in shock. I groped around in my pocket for a tissue, dried my eyes, and endeavored to get hold of my floundering emotions.

Cara came to me and took hold of my hand. "What's the matter, Serena?" she asked in the gentlest of voices.

I couldn't speak. I just shook my head.

Jessica said, "I want you to look at some pictures which Serena found a little while ago. They're very startling and upsetting. I'd like your opinion of them."

Jessica got to her feet, went to her desk, brought back the blue folder. She said to Cara, "There are captions on the back of some of them. But no date when they were taken."

Cara sat next to me on the sofa, and began to look at the pictures. When she came to the last few she exclaimed, "Oh my God! What the hell are these?" and she looked from Jessica to me, shock settling on her face. After a moment, she took a deep breath and said, "They're pretty damned strange, weird, don't you think? What in God's name was Dad thinking when he took these?"

Thirty-four

Y ou think Dad had an affair with Val, and that you're the result of that affair, don't you, Serena?" Cara said in her inimitable, very blunt way, giving me a penetrating stare as she spoke.

"I do," I replied. "Most of the dancing pictures are suggestive, and in two of the nude shots Val looks extremely pregnant. Also, my name is in the captions. What else can I think?"

Cara made no response.

Instead she got up, opened the French doors to the terrace, and said, "It's stifling in your office, Jess. Let's go and sit outside for a while."

"Good idea," Jessica answered, and followed Cara. I tagged along behind, immediately realizing it was so much cooler outside. Raffi had rolled down the canopy earlier in the day, and the terrace was shaded and pleasant, and there was a light breeze blowing up from the sea. I suddenly could breathe better, felt less constrained. Perhaps now that nauseous feeling would go away.

We sat down in the white wicker armchairs, surrounding a wicker coffee table, just a few steps away from the French doors and Jessica's office.

After a moment, Cara continued, "Look, I can't say I blame you for jumping to conclusions. The pictures are startling, even shocking, in a certain sense. They're also a bit odd, because those sort of photographs are not Dad's style. Are you sure he took them?"

"I've no way of knowing," I answered. "However, they were in his filing cabinet. The first of the dancing pictures are rather beautiful, could easily be his, but I'm not so sure about the pregnant nude shots."

Cara nodded in agreement. "If he did take those, then Tommy Stone was far ahead of his time, and rather daring. When was it that those pregnant nude shots of Demi Moore appeared in *Vanity Fair*?"

I shrugged. "I don't know."

"And I've forgotten," Jessica added. "Some years ago, though, and you're right, of course, Dad *was* ahead of his time, in many different ways."

Cara gave me an odd look, frowning, then murmured, "The Serena referred to in the captions might not be you, you know. Maybe Val was pregnant by her boyfriend, and had already chosen that particular name. There's another thing . . . those photographs could have been taken long before you were even born. Or after."

"I suppose so," I replied quietly, staring into

space for a moment, wondering exactly when Dad had shot them. In the distance, I could hear the birds twittering in the trees at the edge of the lawn, and beyond the sound of Raffi's lawn mower, and I closed my eyes for a moment, remembering other lovely summer days like this, when I had lingered here with Mom, drawing pictures while she read scripts . . . so long ago. My throat closed. I sat very still.

"Val couldn't be your mother, Pidge," Jessica announced, taking me by surprise.

I opened my eyes, sat up straighter in the chair, and stared at her. "What are you getting at?"

"*We* were here when you were born," she answered, and looked across at Cara. "You remember, don't you? You and I were at Jardin des Fleurs when Pidge was born here, on July 6, 1981. We were home from boarding school for the summer, and we went into Mom's bedroom to see our baby sister the day after her birth." Smiling at me lovingly, Jessica finished, "You were just two days old, Pidge, and a little pink poppet."

"She's right, Serena," Cara interjected. "And aside from Mom and Dad and you, and us, the only other person present was Harry."

Cara's expression changed, and she exclaimed, "Hey, what about Harry? You should call him, Serena, and ask him what he knows about the photographs."

"Why? What's he going to say? And maybe he

doesn't know about them." I shook my head vehemently. "Anyway, he'd never tell us a thing. Harry was devoted to Mom and Dad, and if there are some terrible secrets from the past he'll never divulge them, because he'd never betray Tommy . . . anything he knows he'll take to the grave."

"Yeah, you're right about that, I'm afraid. But I've just recalled something else." Turning to Jessica, Cara said, "Do you remember that year when Dad was in New York on business, and Mom was shooting in Paris, and Granny had to take me to the Chelsea Flower Show? You must remember it, because you were a stick-in-the-mud, you didn't want to come with me. The headmistress let me go up to London and I stayed with Granny at the Dorchester, and I went to the flower show with her and Aunt Dora."

"Yes, I do remember. I had some exams looming and stayed at school. When you got back you said Val had put the cat among the pigeons," Jessica answered.

"That's right! And it was because she got engaged to her boyfriend. What was his name? Wait a minute . . . it was *Jacques!* And he was a war correspondent."

"So you met him?" I asked, raising a brow, intrigued and curious.

"I did. He worked for a French newspaper, and Aunt Dora didn't like him," Cara explained.

"Talking of Aunt Dora, don't forget she was

Granny's twin, and they looked alike. There's the family resemblance," Jessica pointed out, smiling at me again.

"I hadn't thought about that. So did Val get engaged, Cara? Did she marry Jacques?"

"I'm honestly not sure. But I do know there was a big fracas because Aunt Dora objected." Cara gave me a small smile. "I've always loved that saying of Granny's . . . 'It's going to put the cat among the pigeons.'"

"No kidding," I said, shaking my head, thinking how she'd never stopped using it.

Jessica laughed and then told me, "I'm quite positive I never saw Val again. None of us did. She sort of disappeared."

"Maybe I should talk to Harry after all." I threw Jessica a questioning look.

"I don't think so, Pidge, leave it alone. Listen, I have to ask you something important. Where's your birth certificate? That will tell us a lot."

For a moment I was puzzled, and then it came back to me. "In the safe in New York. A couple of years ago, when Dad was living at the apartment, he mentioned that he'd put my birth certificate and some other family documents in the safe, plus cash, and he gave me the code number."

"So what did it say on your birth certificate?" Cara asked, standing up.

"I don't know, I never looked. At the time, I was going off on assignment, meeting up with Zac. I

303

had my passport, that was all I needed." I shrugged. "I'd always had a passport, so had you two. Let's face it, we did start traveling when we were just kids." I shook my head. "I guess the birth certificate wasn't ever at the front of my mind."

"So take a look at it when you get back to New York. I bet it says you were born here, and that it also gives the name of Mom's obstetrician."

Cara said, "Yes, do that. I'm going to get a bottle of water. Do either of you want anything?"

Jessica said, "A lemonade, please, Cara."

"I'd love a ginger ale," I said, hoping that this would make the sick feeling go away.

She watched her twin rush into the house, and then Jessica said to me softly, "I think you have to put all of this out of your mind, Serena darling. I really do. You've so much going for you at the moment, and Zac's waiting for you in New York. You have a life to live."

"You're absolutely right, and I will move on," I promised her, knowing how much she worried about me. "But there's just one other thing I want to ask you."

"You know you can ask me anything, Pidge. So go ahead. What is it?"

"Why do you think that Dad kept those photographs? And why on earth did he leave them lying around the way he did?"

"I've no idea why he kept the pictures, unless of course they were important to him. Or because he always kept his pictures from important shoots, and you know that he did."

"Of course I do, and he did keep everything. Copies, I mean. On the other hand, they were just there in the bottom of the filing cabinet, not even in a proper file. A bit careless, don't you think?"

For a moment Jessica did not answer, and then she said carefully, in a low voice, "No, not careless, Pidge. He forgot about them, I believe. In the last year of his life he became . . . *forgetful.*"

I sat up, leaned across the coffee table, my eyes focused on hers. "Are you saying Dad had dementia? Or something like that?"

"Dementia was starting to cloud his mind. In the last six months of his life he wasn't the same Tommy, he wasn't your magic man anymore, darling."

Tears filled my eyes; I blinked them away, brushed my eyes with one hand. "Why didn't you tell me?"

"If you'd been about to visit us, we would have mentioned it, but you were in Afghanistan. Cara and I didn't want to give you upsetting news when you were in the middle of a war on the front line. We didn't want to worry you when you were in danger."

"You're always thinking about me, Jess, and

Cara, too. Caring about me. But you could have told me."

She shook her head. "No, we didn't think that was the right thing to do."

"Did Harry know?"

"Eventually. Because he was coming over to see Dad, to stay here, and we felt it was only right to prepare him."

"Was it that bad?" I frowned, still focused on her intently.

"No, it wasn't. Most of the time Tommy was . . . Tommy. But he did have little lapses, and we needed Harry to be forewarned. For his own sake."

"I understand."

"Don't be angry with us."

"I'm not."

"When are you leaving me, Pidge?" she now asked, and there was a hint of sadness in her voice. I suddenly thought of Allen Lambert, glad that she now had a nice man in her life, who was seemingly devoted to her. I said, "I'll be back in July with Zac. But he and I will be worker bees during the day."

Her pealing laughter echoed along the terrace. "What a lovely term, worker bees. Well, you've prepared me for that already. So what can I say but that you'll have some lovely suppers to keep your strength up." My sister paused, and eyed me curiously. "You told me you and Zac will be getting married next year. I hope it will be here, that you'll have your wedding here?" It was a question.

"Where else? A bride gets married from her family home, doesn't she?"

"That's true," she agreed, her smile wide.

Cara was suddenly back with us, carrying a large tray, which she put down in the middle of the coffee table. She handed Jessica her lemonade, and I reached for my ginger ale. This had been Dad's antidote for a queasy stomach, and I hoped it still worked as I poured a little of it into my glass.

After gulping down some of the bottled water, Cara suddenly announced in that gloomy voice I dreaded, "You can't trust birth certificates, you know. They can be so easily doctored, especially by a doctor, and even more especially if you're a beautiful world-famous megastar with a certain amount of money to spend."

Jessica glared at her twin. She was furious, said angrily, "What's that supposed to mean, for God's sake?" She took a deep breath to steady herself. "What exactly are you getting at? What are you implying?"

"Nothing, don't get so het up," Cara answered in a sharp tone. "I think you should know that it's quite easy to doctor all kinds of documents . . . I'm simply alerting you, that's all."

Giving her a sharp look, Jessica snapped, "What

we should do is burn all the photographs and the damned captions, and forget they ever existed." Now, turning away, ignoring Cara, her eyes were fixed on mine. Jess said slowly, in a solemn voice, "You're our sister, do you hear, and Mom's daughter. Forget about Val . . . she never existed, as far as you're concerned."

I simply nodded. I didn't trust myself to speak. Jessica was so warm and loving, and loyal, I thought I might start to cry again.

Jessica had spoken firmly, confidently, in a positive tone, and she sat back in her chair, suddenly looking like the wise eldest sister. Well, she was the firstborn twin by ten minutes, and eight years older than me. The three of us were silent for a while, relaxing, sipping our drinks, lost in our thoughts. I knew the twins were endeavoring to control their tempers.

Suddenly, Cara spoke. She said, "You know, it's so easy for a woman to get pregnant, as long as she's got a man handy. All she has to do is lay down, open her legs, and let him do the hard work."

Unexpectedly, I wanted to laugh out loud but I didn't dare when I saw Jessica's face, noticed how she had cringed at Cara's blunt words. I knew how she abhorred coarseness.

I buried my laughter, took a sip of ginger ale.

Cara, unconcerned, went on, "It's no big deal at all. Nine months later she drops a baby, and that's that."

"We're all aware of the process," Jessica muttered, glaring at her again, swallowing her annoyance.

Cara paid no attention; she got up and came and sat in the chair next to me, took hold of my hand, stared into my eyes earnestly.

"Let me tell you what the big deal really is, Serena. It's raising that baby, loving it unconditionally, nurturing it, cherishing it, giving it the right values, making it feel secure, loved, protected, and important. It's called being a good mother. *And that's the big deal.* The biggest deal of all."

Leaning closer, Cara hugged me, then swiftly let me go. "I don't give a damn whose womb you popped out of. It's the woman that loved and raised you that counts. And that was Mom, and *she's* your mother, and don't you ever forget that!"

Her words so moved and touched me I began to cry. So did Cara, and Jessica too. We sat together on the terrace and wept. And sniffled and dried our eyes with tissues and wept again, and then quite unexpectedly Jessica began to chuckle. And so did I, because her laughter was always so infectious. And a moment later Cara was joining in our hilarity. We laughed uproariously until we were exhausted, and needed to rest for a moment or two.

I felt better. The gloomy mood lifted, and we relaxed with each other, knowing that we belonged. It was a moment later, as if inspired, that Jessica began to sing Mom's favorite song, her signature tune, in a sense.

Jessica's voice rang out, clear, beautiful and melodious as she began to sing "Everything's Coming Up Roses," the Stephen Sondheim song from *Gypsy*.

Cara and I joined in, and the three of us sang the tune to the very end, enjoying every minute and remembering so much of our lives which we had lived here together.

Cara and Jessica had been right in their own ways, and I saw the sense of their words . . . I had to relax, forget the photographs, and go on.

And later that day, when I was my usual calm self, and felt normal again, I did call Harry in New York after all.

The moment he came onto the line I told him about finding some pictures of Val Clifford taken in Venice, but I didn't mention the nude shots or the captions.

Before I'd even finished my story, he cut in. "I recall that day very well!" he exclaimed, and began to chuckle. "Tommy and I both shot pictures of Val in a grand palazzo on the Grand Canal. She wore a chiffon dress, it was an odd color, sort of greenish gray, and she danced around for all the world like a ballerina. The photographs were for her boyfriend, Jacques

Pelliter. Why are you suddenly interested in those photos? They're so old." He suddenly sounded curious—and instantly wary, I thought.

"It's not the photographs we're interested in," I explained. "But Val, Harry. Jessica and Cara were wondering what happened to her. She is our cousin after all, or rather, she was Mom's first cousin. I don't remember her at all, but they do. Actually, I have no clue about her. It was Cara who suggested I ask you, Harry, purely out of curiosity."

There was a silence, and then he said rather quickly, "I don't know, honey. I really don't know what became of Val. She and Jacques did get married. They lived in Rome, and then settled in Paris, that I can tell you."

"Are they still alive?"

"I've no idea, we lost touch. And now that you mention it, I realize I haven't seen their bylines for years. Why does this matter after all these years? My God, those photographs must have been taken well over thirty years ago!"

"It doesn't matter at all, Harry," I answered swiftly, brushing the matter aside, aware suddenly of a slight impatience on his part, a tetchiness echoing down the line. "Actually, the real reason I called is to tell you that I'm coming to New York on Friday. I've finished putting the Venice book together, and I'm sending it direct to Global by the same freight company."

"Now that is great news, Serena!" Harry exclaimed, suddenly sounding happy. "How about Rao's on Monday night? You and me for dinner? And Zac too, if he wants to come. I'm sure he can't wait to see you."

"You've got a deal, Harry."

Something awakened me in the middle of the night, and I sat up with a start. As I lay propped up against the pillows in the dark, thinking of the day's events, I had the feeling that Harry hadn't told me the truth about Val. How I knew this I don't know, but I was convinced he had lied.

But why? I knew the answer to that easily enough. To protect Mom, Dad, and, of course, me as well. I focused on Valentina Clifford. What had she meant to Harry? More important, what had she meant to Mom? And to Dad? Had my father slept with her to get that much-wanted baby he and Mom had longed for? Had she actually been a surrogate? Had she been carrying the baby—me—for them? Mom had been suffering from that rare form of osteoporosis. Would it have been risky, even dangerous for her to get pregnant? I had no answers for myself . . . and I realized I must let all of this go. Everybody was dead except for Harry, and it wasn't worth worrying about.

And I did have certain answers. Jessica and Cara both saw me here in this house, in Mom's arms in her bedroom, when I was two days old. Good enough for me. And as Cara had said, the woman who raised a child with love and devotion was the biggest deal of all. And certainly Mom had done that . . . she herself had been the biggest deal for me.

Thirty-five

When I arrived at the apartment in New York on Friday afternoon, I did three things immediately. The first was to go straight to the safe in the walk-in closet in Dad's den.

I had committed the code to memory, when Dad first gave it to me, and now I punched in the numbers and the safe opened with a click. Looking inside, I found my birth certificate at once. When I took it out of the envelope, a quick glance told me everything written on it was correct. I relaxed, and read it again slowly.

My mother was listed as Elizabeth Vasson Stone, my father as John Thomas Stone, and the place I was born was Jardin des Fleurs, with the full Nice address given. Listed as the obstetrician was Dr. Felix Legrange and the name of the nurse was Madame Annette Bertrand. My name and date of birth were also there in black and white, and obviously I was who I had always thought I was.

I felt a sense of immense relief, and I knew that Jessica would feel the same way when I phoned her later. With this worrisome matter taken care of, I immediately called Zac on his cell and told him I was at the apartment and waiting for him.

He was out on Long Island at his parents' home. Elated to hear my voice, he promised to be with me as soon as possible, certainly within two hours. He added that he was leaving immediately.

I next phoned Harry at Global's offices on Sixth Avenue to let him know I was safely back in Manhattan, and that was all I said to him. Except that I was looking forward to seeing him on Monday evening at Rao's, and that Zac was coming with me. Harry was obviously happy I was in Manhattan and said he couldn't wait to see me.

On the plane, crossing the Atlantic earlier today, I had contemplated telling Harry about the nude photographs of a very pregnant Valentina Clifford, but I suddenly changed my mind when we were on the phone. What was the point? The information on my birth certificate had eased some of my worrisome thoughts, and confirmed what my sisters believed to be the truth.

My third call was to Jessica in Nice. She was thrilled when I told her that she was absolutely right about my birth certificate, that all of the written details matched what she had told me.

And I was thrilled when she said that her doctor had just given Cara the results of our bone density tests. Neither of us had that rare form of osteoporosis which had so plagued our mother.

Jessica was relieved and happy that we would not suffer from this awful disease, which she would have to cope with for the rest of her life.

With these matters out of the way, I unpacked, had a shower, got dressed in a pale blue cotton tunic with narrow matching trousers, and then wandered around the apartment, checking everything out as I always did. And as Mom had usually done when returning here from Nice or L.A.

Mrs. Watledge had been in earlier, and everything was sparklingly clean, as pristine as ever, with flowers in the living room and plenty of food in the fridge. Including the Friday chicken from the butcher, I noticed, smiling to myself.

I checked the messages on my machine, and there were none. Then I reached for the stack of mail and went through it. There was nothing of any importance, except for a few bills.

Suddenly I was feeling hungry. I hadn't eaten anything since I'd left Nice this morning, except for a couple of apples. I never ate the food on the plane because I didn't like it; also, Dad and Harry constantly reminded me that the purpose of a plane was to get you somewhere, and that it was not a restaurant.

Zac had told me he was going to stop off and pick up Chinese when he reached Manhattan, and that we'd have an early dinner. I knew I'd better wait for him to arrive with the food. But wanting to stem my sudden hunger, I went into the kitchen, made a cup of tea, found a packet of plain cookies, and carried everything to my office on a small tray.

It was a glorious afternoon and the cream-and-peach room was filled with sunshine. The sky was the color of delphiniums, littered with floating white clouds, and the city sparkled in the brilliant light. It had never looked better on this June afternoon.

I put the tray on the coffee table and stepped over to the window, staring out at the East River, admiring the extraordinary panorama of Manhattan, suddenly happy to be back here.

I was looking forward to working again—with Zac on Dad's book *Courage,* and also picking up where I'd left off on the biography. Work was my pleasure, and it gave me enormous enjoyment, a sense of gratification.

The moment Zac walked into the apartment I knew that he had undergone a change. Harry had told me Zac was feeling much better, but I hadn't expected him to look as if he had had a miraculous transformation.

It was the old Zac who stepped into the foyer of the apartment, carrying a large bunch of pink roses, followed by one of the building's porters pushing a luggage trolley. On it were numerous shopping bags, an open cardboard box with bottles of wine standing up in it, plus Zac's backpack and camera bag.

Grinning at me as I eyed the trolley, he leaned forward and kissed my cheek, then handed me the roses.

"Thank you," I said as I took them from him, pushed my nose into them, smelled their scent.

"Welcome back, Pidge," he said. "Where should we put this stuff?"

"Right here is fine," I answered, smiling at the porter, who nodded and started to empty the trolley.

Zac tipped him, and once we were alone, he grabbed hold of me and held me close, his arms tight around me. "God, I've missed you," he murmured against my hair. "I never thought I could miss anyone so much, not even you, Serena."

"I've missed you too. You're crushing the flowers," I said, stepping away. "And thanks for the backhanded compliment."

He just grinned. "We'd better get the Chinese food into the kitchen." As he spoke he proceeded to pick up some of the shopping bags; I did the same.

Within seconds I had emptied the two cartons of won ton soup into a pan, which I put on the stove to be reheated later. I then looked at the other containers all marked with the contents; white rice, spring rolls, lobster Cantonese, chicken with vegetables, and sweet-and-sour pork. I placed everything in the oven, on a very low heat to keep all of it warm, thinking he had bought far too much food, just like Dad and Harry. But that was a man thing, wasn't it?

As I had been handling the cartons of food, Zac had put the three bottles of white wine in the fridge, and taken out a bottle which was cold, and opened it. Filling two glasses he said, "Come on, let's have a quick drink before dinner. In your mother's little sitting room."

"My office now," I corrected and followed him out of the kitchen.

"What a city!" he exclaimed as he walked down to the end of the room where the windows over-looked the East River. "There's nowhere quite like Manhattan anywhere in the world."

Clinking my glass to his, I said, "Cheers. And I couldn't agree more, I'm glad to be back."

"So am I. But then you know it's not the same without you."

Zac and I sat down next to each other on the sofa, and he went on, "In the last few days I've had a chance to spread out *Courage* in my apartment, and I think I might have to work over there, Serena, if you don't mind." He threw me a questioning look.

"That's fine," I replied quickly, although I had been taken aback for a split second. "I think you'll find it easier to write in a quiet place. I can always pop over when you've finished a section, glance at the final layouts, check things out. Anyway I trust you, and I know we were on the right track in Nice."

"I haven't changed anything, nor will I," Zac explained. "I like the way we arranged everything, following Tommy's lead. But you're right, I do need the solitude to write the introductions to each section, and the in-depth captions."

"No problem. And it doesn't take long to go back and forth between here and Central Park West."

"So how're your sisters? How's Jessica's ankle?" he asked and settled back against the cushions, sipping his wine.

"She's improving every day, and the soft cast has made things easier for her. She told me earlier today that Cara got our bone density tests back, and fortunately Cara and I haven't inherited osteoporosis from Mom."

"That's good news!" he exclaimed, and then made a face. "So it's only poor Jess who's stuck with it?"

"That's correct, but she has it under control with the best medication. She's being really good about it, and Allen Lambert has been very attentive lately. I think that relationship is going some-where."

"He's a lucky guy to have a woman like Jessica, she's terrific, and dare I ask about Cara? You haven't mentioned her for a while. I suppose Geoff is still in the picture?"

He said this in such a droll way I couldn't help laughing. "Sure, he's in the picture, and Jessica and I are very happy about that. Cara seems to have really taken to Geoff, and we want her to have a life, Zac. Her sadness these last two years has been awful, her depression about Jules's death unbearable to witness. She deserves a good man by her side."

"So do you, Pidge, and I'm right here . . . yours forever, if you'll have me. And if you think I'm a good man."

"I do, and you are. And I feel the same way," I said, studying Zac again, thinking that the change in him was not only in his physical well-being, but there was something else about him that was different. I endeavored to put my finger on it, but did not succeed.

Zac frowned. "What's wrong? You're staring at me."

"I was just thinking how great you look. You've put on a bit more weight, which suits you. You're relaxed. Actually, you seem to be your old self right down to having your self-confidence back." I settled in the corner of the sofa, then finished, "Something's happened to you while you've been back in New York."

"Only you would spot it, Serena, because you know me so well, and because I was such a wreck when you came to look after me in Venice. What with my exhaustion, my flashes of PTSD, and all that rotten stuff you had to cope with."

"I was glad to help, you know that. So what happened?"

"I grew up."

"What do you mean?"

"I suddenly understood that I had to become genuinely responsible, that I had to take charge of everything, handle the situation."

"But what about your father? And Danny and Stella?"

"When I went out to Long Island I realized immediately that there really was only me to deal with Mom and the situation. Danny was on the coast on business. Stella was a wreck, had been thrown for a loop by Mom's stroke. As for Dad, he was like a lost soul. He's always been so strong. I used to tell him he was as tough as an old boot. But he just fell apart when Mom was taken to the hospital. He simply couldn't cope. He wanted to help but he didn't know what to do. It was then I realized how much he had always relied on her, and what a strong woman she was."

"I've always known that about your mother, Zac."

"I suppose I had too. I'd just forgotten about it, being away so much. Anyway, I took charge. What was it that your mother used to call Tommy when he took over? Bossed everyone around?"

"Bismarck," I answered. "Sometimes the General. She used to say that going on vacation with him was like the German war maneuvers, because he had so many instructions about everything."

"However did she know about German war maneuvers?" he asked, and grinned. "The point is, *I* had to become Bismarck in order to get everything on the right track. With Mom's doctors, the hospital, everything. And so I finally had to grow up."

"I must say your grown-up-ness is very impressive," I said, finished my glass of wine, and stood up.

Zac followed me, remarking, "My mother sends her love to you, Pidge. She hopes you can go out and see her this weekend. You will come with me, won't you?"

"Of course I will. Now let's go and have something to eat. I'm starving."

"So am I," he said. "And in more ways than one."

We enjoyed our Chinese food and after dinner took our mugs of jasmine tea back to Mom's little sitting room, which Zac insisted on calling it, and sat watching the news for a while. But eventually he turned it off, and moving closer, he said, "My mother asked me if we're finally getting married, and I told her yes."

I simply stared at him.

Zac said, "Well, we are, aren't we?"

"Of course. Don't be so silly."

"I let you escape once. I'm not going to allow that to happen a second time."

"I guess both of our families have marriage on their minds . . . for us, I mean. Jessica asked me the same question the other day, and I said we were. Next year."

"When next year?" His eyes didn't leave my face.

"What about the spring?" I asked, and went on, "In Nice, at Jardin des Fleurs. That is all right, isn't it? You know it's tradition for the bride to get married from her home, and I think of that particular house as home."

"I'll get married wherever you want," he replied, and put his mug and mine on the coffee table. Wrapping his arms around me he held me close to him, telling me how much he loved me, how much he had missed me. Then he began to kiss me, and we were soon overwhelmed by our passion for each other, as we always were. Zac pulled off his sweater and I took off my tunic, and within seconds we were undressed and stretched out on the sofa, our bodies entwined.

At one moment, Zac pushed himself up on his elbows and looked down into my face. "There's only ever been you for me, Serena. I've never felt this about anyone else, or wanted a woman so completely, with such longing."

"I know," I whispered, touching his face. "It's the same for me."

He brought his face to mine and found my mouth, and we kissed tenderly at first, and then passion took hold once more and we were lost in each other. We touched and stroked each other, and kissed again, and there was great intimacy, a familiarity between us that transported us to a special place all our own.

"I can't wait, I want you now, Serena," Zac suddenly said against my neck, his voice unexpectedly hoarse.

"You don't have to wait." We drew even closer on the sofa, consumed by longing, and we became one, moving to our own rhythm, cresting together on waves of pleasure.

We had fallen asleep, and I awakened shivering. It had grown dark outside. I got up and took the wool throw from the end of the sofa. I went back to curl up against Zac, pulling the throw over us both to keep us warm.

My mind was racing. We were enemies last year at this time. Now we are friends. We are lovers. We are at peace with each other. The future is before us. We will be together, start a life. I thought of our marriage next spring. It seemed to have been decided without a lot of discussion. I was glad this reconciliation had happened.

My mother had once said we were meant to be,

Zac and I, and that we were well matched. It was true. We had a compatibility, one that was rather unique, and an understanding of each other. We were comfortable, at ease.

I pressed closer to him on the sofa, put my arm across his body. He was dozing, his breath even, steady. I hadn't slept very long because of the time change. I was thrown off balance slightly. And so here I was, suddenly wide awake. A second wind.

There was contentment in me, and a sense of belonging. He and I. Bound up for always . . . the prospect was pleasing.

Smiling to myself, I closed my eyes, let my thoughts drift . . .

Part Five

CANDID IMAGES

Libya, July/August

I would be true, for there are those who trust me;
I would be pure, for there are those who care;
I would be strong, for there is much to suffer;
I would be brave, for there is much to dare.
— Howard Arnold Walter: "My Creed"

I'll not listen to reason . . . Reason always
means what someone else has got to say.
— Elizabeth Gaskell

Thirty-six

L *ibya . . . Libya . . . Libya.*
It was never far from my thoughts. It surrounded me. Engulfed me. Overwhelmed me. On the front pages, the radio, the television. Zac remained glued to any set wherever he was, mesmerized by the coverage, zapping from network to network, trying to ingest everything in one big gulp. Except that the gulp lasted all day and into the night. His entire being was focused on it; his mind had been captured by it.

Libya also dominated the Global offices. Harry was grappling with it on a daily basis, moving the photographers and photojournalists around Libya, in and out of Libya, in order to get the greatest and most dramatic coverage, using Global's best.

Libya in Nice now, I thought, as I stared glumly at my BlackBerry. Cara had just texted: *Urgent. Call me. Libya looming. Cara.*

I knew Geoff Barnes wasn't going anywhere. Harry and I had already decided that days ago. Aside from the fact that he had proven to be a brilliant manager at the London bureau, and we needed him in place at all times, he had a child, and we both took that into consideration.

I texted my sister: *Geoff staying put. Forget Libya. Serena.*

I sighed under my breath because I was afraid *I*

couldn't forget Libya. I wasn't allowed to, because when Zac wasn't staring at the interminable television coverage, on all the different networks, he was discussing it with me. Or with me and Harry, if we were all together at Global, or out to dinner. He had become obsessed by the events evolving in Libya.

Zac had great insight into the Middle East, and was aware of what had been happening there for a long time. He understood the politics, the different factions, the motivations, and the aims. He had been following recent events ever since that troubled and desperate young man in Tunisia set himself on fire, in protest of the terrible inequities in his country.

It hadn't come as a surprise to Zac that the turmoil swiftly spread to Egypt, Libya, and into some of the countries surrounding them. Many had been infected by violence; some stringent and powerful dictatorships had managed to quell the uprisings, had encircled their people with iron bands of military control. But others had not, and bloodshed was rampant.

I had no idea what the outcome of the Libyan conflict would be, and neither did anyone else. I only worried, at times, that Zac would become even more involved than he was long distance. That he might get more emotionally caught up in the events in Tripoli, influenced by his fervent need to tell the world the truth.

And yet, as I worried that he might suddenly take off to cover another war, pumped up by the excitement of it all, adrenaline flowing, he seemed in fact quite content to be on the sidelines. An observer looking at it all, as if from another planet down a long telescope.

Since I had returned from Nice, Zac had been on an even keel. He had confided in me, when I first arrived, that there had been no sign of PTSD. He had then laughed, and added, "Perhaps I've just been too busy worrying about Mom to think of my PTSD. I guess I sort of shoved myself and my problems out of the way. To concentrate on her."

I understood what he meant, and for the past month, ever since I'd been back, there had been no blowups, no displays of temperament, no bad-boy behavior.

Zac had been swiftly drawn into Dad's book *Courage*, had worked on it tirelessly for long hours, and completed it brilliantly, writing the captions and introductions to the sections with a flair I never knew he possessed.

Courage was now with the publisher Harry knew, who had swiftly bought the rights to it, and it was currently in production, slated to come out next year. The spring of 2012.

The Venice picture book, *La Serenissima*, had just been snapped up by another publishing house, and it would go into production next month. It was going to be printed in China, where, we'd been informed, the best color reproductions of photographs were done. That I was thrilled was the understatement of the year. So was Zac . . . he said he was on cloud nine, and that we'd done Tommy proud.

Zac was living at my apartment full-time, although he had not yet given up his own on Central Park West. In fact he still went back and forth, as he had been doing all along, and it didn't bother me. I was comfortable with this arrangement, as was he, because it gave us both space, which we apparently seemed to need.

Much to my astonishment, and I must say pleasant surprise, Zac had actually started writing his much-talked-about memoir. He was still seeking a name for it, which troubled him, because he felt he must know what it was called in order to write it. I tried to help, but no good titles had yet come to mind. But nonetheless, he had started, was at his computer part of the day, every day.

I was working on my father's biography again, and I was making good progress, inspired by Zac's burst of enthusiasm for his own book; his wonderful energy was infectious.

In the evenings, we had been catching up on Broadway shows we wanted to see. We went to the movies also, and trotted off to restaurants, especially to Rao's with Harry, and, in general, we led what I called a normal life.

We had been having a bit of fun for once, and a great deal of sex. Zac was filled with enormous desire for me, and, not unnaturally, I responded with as much ardor as he was showing. We were young and in love, and we wanted a big chunk of life. The future looked bright for us after all our years on the front line.

The ringing phone interrupted my thoughts, and I picked it up, said, "Hello?"

"It's me, Pidge," Jessica answered, sounding as if she was around the corner.

This prompted me to say, "Hi, Jess, and where are you?"

"In my office at the house, why?"

"You sound so close I thought, no hoped, you might be in Manhattan."

"I'd love to be, but I'm afraid I have a few problems to cope with here at the moment."

"What kind of problems?" I asked, a hint of worry creeping into my voice.

"The roof has fallen in. And I do mean the roof of Jardin des Fleurs, and literally, not figuratively."

"Oh my God, no! How did that happen?"

"Remember that storm in April? The night of Dad's memorial dinner? And how it poured with rain until the next morning?"

"I do. It was like a mistral had blown up. Is that what caused the trouble? Damaged the roof? The slates?"

"So the roofing people tell me. However, it's not just a bit of roof, it really is a great chunk, and unfortunately a large part of the damage is over Mom's octagonal room."

"Oh no, Jess! I can't bear it!" I exclaimed, feeling a rush of sadness. "I hope not too much of it has been destroyed."

"A good bit of the ceiling and the top of one wall, but not near the fireplace."

"Thank God, otherwise the painting of Mom would have probably been damaged."

"That's safe. In fact all of the furnishings are. The damage is on the other side of the room, near the door. Anyway, the roofing guys will be coming in to start work on the house tomorrow. There's other damage to the roof, over the kitchen, and on the ceilings in two guest bedrooms. Quite a lot of work, Pidge."

"Do you want me to send you some money?" I asked at once.

"No, of course not. Cara and I can manage the down payment—"

"But I want to contribute," I cut in peremptorily.

"Listen, I didn't call just to give you bad news, Serena. I have some good news as well. A lucky break, you might call it."

"What kind of lucky break?" I asked, riddled with curiosity.

"*A man.* Whose wife was a big fan of Mom's when she was alive. Anyway, Rita Converse, that's the wife's name, was looking at Stone's Web site the other day, and saw the glamorous photograph of Mom I'd posted recently, announcing the auction of Mom's jewelry next year. In the photo Mom's wearing that gorgeous pearl-and-diamond Harry Winston necklace, earrings, ring, and bracelet. The whole suite. And the woman began to drool over it, seemingly. She told her husband she would love to have it for her wedding anniversary present. To cut to the chase, as Harry would say, Tom Converse wants to come and view the jewels, and make a preemptive bid *now*, long before the auction. He doesn't want to wait until next year."

"Hey, that's just great, Jess! A lucky break, indeed. When's he coming?"

"Sometime next week. The thing is, Pidge, the earrings which are a part of that set are the ones Mom left you. The diamond flowers with the pearl drops. They belong to you, Serena."

"No, they don't, they belong to the three of us. Anyway, you can't sell the necklace without the earrings. They go together, so go ahead and do it, and get as much as you can. Mom left us all some of her jewelry for a rainy day, and that was one helluva rainy night."

I was preparing dinner, stirring the meat, when I heard the front door slam, and a second later Zac was striding into the kitchen.

There was a huge smile on his face, and I couldn't help thinking how great he looked this afternoon. He was definitely his old self, as handsome as always, with his thick dark hair and those laughing green eyes. He had lost that starved look, which made him seem diminished, and last weekend, July Fourth weekend, out on Long Island, he had acquired a tan. He wasn't movie-star good-looking like his father, Patrick, was, but he cut quite a swathe, and had a unique aura about him.

"Hi, darling," he said, and grabbed hold of me, kissed me on the mouth, before I could greet him in return. In fact I was still holding the wooden spoon in one hand.

I saw the exuberance, the excitement in him, and I laughed as I stepped back, holding the spoon high, and explained, "I don't want to get meat sauce on your white shirt. And what's happened? You're certainly in a very happy mood."

"Pidge, I am. Really happy. Because I've come up with a great name for my book. At least, I think it's great. I don't know how you'll react, though."

"So go on, tell me, and you'll know what I think immediately, since you claim you can read me so well."

"Okay," he answered, leaning against the island in the middle of the kitchen, his eyes roaming over me for a moment, and appraisingly so. "You do look sexy in that short little dress, Pidge. Good enough to eat. You make my mouth water."

I knew he was teasing me, that he was in a playful mood, but then when he moved toward me I realized he was intent on pulling me into his arms, had more serious intentions.

I dodged him, exclaimed, "Don't come near me. You know I'll succumb to your charms instantly. And then you won't have any dinner tonight."

"I don't care, I'll make do with you," he shot back, and winked.

"I'm making a cottage pie, one of your favorites. So come on, tell me the title you've come up with."

He nodded. "It's *Semper Fi.*"

I stared at him for a split second, puzzled, and then I exclaimed, "Oh, that has to do with the Marines, doesn't it?"

"Yes. It's short for *Semper Fidelis*, which is Latin for 'always faithful,' the Marine Corps motto. What it actually means is: *always faithful to the country's call.* But for all Marines it means faithful to each other. Let's not forget that Marines never leave their buddies behind . . . they bring out their dead. As well as their wounded. I've almost always been standing next to a Marine on the front line, and I admire them greatly. And my memoir is mostly about my days on the battlegrounds . . . with Marines as my buddies. So it works for me."

"I do know that, Zac, and the title is most appropriate. I like it a lot. No, correction, I love it." I put the spoon down, and took off my apron.

I walked toward the fridge. "It's a wonderful title. Works for me, too. And so we must toast it right now."

I reached into the fridge, took out the bottle of pink Veuve Clicquot, and handed it to Zac. "Please open it, and I'll drain the potatoes for the pie, so they don't disintegrate."

He had a huge smile on his face once again, as he popped the champagne cork, then took two crystal flutes out of the cupboard.

"I'm so glad you think the title works, Serena. I trust your judgment. I'll try it on Harry later, but since you like it so much, that's it for me. *Semper Fi* it is."

We clinked glasses, and drank some champagne, and then Zac said, "Let's go into your mom's sitting room for a minute or two, there's something else I want to tell you." He picked up the bottle of champagne.

I simply nodded, and followed him out of the kitchen, holding my glass.

We settled on the sofa, and Zac said in a more serious, somewhat subdued voice, "I know you're not going to like hearing this, Serena, but I feel I have to go to Libya, to cover the uprising, and—"

"Oh Zac, no!" I cried, taken by surprise, my heart dropping. "You promised you'd never go back to the front line. I won't let you, you can't." I sat staring at him, aghast.

"But it's not like the usual front line, it's an uprising, taking place in the streets of Tripoli. I want to go, just for a week or two. I thought—"

"But what about your book?" I interjected again, cutting him off once more.

"I'll put it on one side for a couple of weeks, and what I was starting to say was that I want you to come with me. Let's do it, Pidge. For old times' sake. One last assignment together as photojournalists, sort of like one last throw of the dice."

"It might well be one last throw of the dice in the worst way. We might get killed. You've lost your edge, and so have I. And anyway, Harry would never let us go. He'd block us. He's afraid for us, Zac, I know that. He wants us to have a happy life together." I paused, tears coming into my eyes, but I swallowed them back.

He put down his glass, and drew closer, put his arm around my shoulders, held me tightly. "Nothing's going to happen to us, Serena. We'll go in and out. Two weeks max. Come on, say yes, come with me, be my old buddy, as you've always been. I'll have your back, you'll have mine, and we'll do a great job together. And then we'll come out, and stay out. Forever."

When I was silent, he said again, "I promise."

I drew back, stared at him coldly. "You

promised you'd quit, that the front line would never tempt you again."

"I know. But this is not the usual kind of front line, and you're aware of that. This is an uprising. The people against an overbearing government. Against the Gaddafi regime."

"There are many uprisings, not just one in Tripoli . . . they're springing up all over Libya."

"I want to get the truth out. The world must know what's going on there."

"Other war correspondents and war photographers are doing that, Zac. We're not needed. Let others risk their lives."

"Yes, we are needed. We're not just the best, we're better. Harry will let us go. Come on, relent, say yes. We've always been a team, like Harry and Tommy were."

Not quite, I thought, and remained silent. I wondered how long Zac had been planning this little speech, and then decided he hadn't planned it. He had said all of this on the spur of the moment. He was manipulative at times, and he had an easy, very persuasive charm, but he was not calculating. I was certain of that.

"Why are you so quiet?" he asked, turning my face to his, looking into my eyes, his own loving and warm.

"I don't think I can make a decision at this moment," I said at last. "I have to think about it."

Thirty-seven

I think there is a fine line being drawn here," I
said quietly, and shifted slightly in the chair,
adjusting my linen jacket.

"I'm not sure what you mean," Harry answered,
puzzlement flickering in his blue eyes. "Who is
drawing the fine line?"

"Zac is." I paused, then half smiled. "Or perhaps
it's me, maybe I'm the one doing it."

I realized he still didn't quite understand what I
was getting at, and added, "Zac says that going to
Libya is not going back to the front line, because
it's an uprising in the streets, civilians confronting
soldiers. I say it is a front line, because the
civilians are armed like soldiers. That it's a
dangerous place, and our lives are at risk. But he
won't have any of that."

"Well, he's wrong, Serena, and you're right. I'm
not sure I'd call it drawing a fine line, though, I
think it's more like splitting hairs. But whatever
we call it, Tripoli, Benghazi, Sirte, and all those
other Libyan cities are indeed front lines, and
highly dangerous places to be. I certainly won't
allow you to go. And I won't allow Zac to go on
his own either. It's too soon after leaving
Afghanistan for him to be in the line of fire. He's
not ready yet, in fact he might never be ready.
He's lost his edge."

"So we're on the same page, Harry. But try and convince him we're right. You won't succeed. He's very stubborn, and once again possessed of that supreme self-confidence. He's sure he knows better than anyone else."

I shook my head. "It's only a few months since I was flying off to Venice, to help him recover his health and well-being, and to cope with his bouts of PTSD."

"I know. He told me he didn't want to be a war photographer any longer, wanted a normal life. With you." Harry raised an eyebrow, the expression in his eyes quizzical. He also seemed concerned, to me, but then I was important to him, and he wanted only the best for me.

There was a moment of silence, and then I said, "He actually made a promise to me, Harry. Zac said he would never go back to the front line. And now he's broken that promise. And can you believe it, he doesn't understand why I'm upset? Actually, 'disappointed' would be a better word to use."

"Oh, now I understand. I see what you're getting at. Zac thinks he didn't break his promise to you, because he's not actually going to the front line . . . just to Tripoli, a city in disarray. Is that it, honey?" He leaned back in his chair, his loving gaze on me.

"Yep, that's it," I answered. "Listen, I'm not only disappointed. To be honest, I'm not sure that I can trust him again."

"That's understandable, but let's not be too hasty, Serena. He hasn't left yet. And where do you two stand, actually? How's your relationship?"

"It's okay, because we didn't quarrel last night. He told me he wanted to go to Libya, to cover what's happening there, and added that he wanted me to come with him. When I said I'd have to think about that, because I wasn't at all sure we should do it, he let it drop. I told him I'd give him a decision later."

"So no big rows?" Harry asked softly.

"No, not at all. To be honest, I was so shocked when he mentioned Libya I was incapable of saying very much. So I just let the evening roll along. We had supper, watched a movie, went to bed. Everything was normal. This morning, when I was leaving, he was just getting up. I said I had a lot of errands. He simply said, 'See you later,' and gave me a big hug. And I left."

The phone on Harry's desk began to ring, and he answered it. I sat back in the chair, glancing around, looking at all the familiar photographs on the wall and Harry's awards. My office here at Global Images was pretty much the same; it had been Dad's, and was filled with all of his mementos, awards, and pictures; I felt very at home in it. But then I'd known it all of my life. I now owned this company with Harry, but that never sank in. I let him run it the way he wanted, as he and Dad had run it always.

Harry hung up and went on, "So he's not made a song and dance about it, and that's good. Perhaps he's not as self-confident as you think. The other thing is, he does have to talk to me, be accredited to the agency, and we have to make all the arrangements for him to fly off. He can't just do it all on his own, and you know that."

"And when he does show up, to announce that he wants to go to Libya, what will you say?" I asked.

"*No.* That's what I'm going to say. No, he can't go. I'm going to tell him I won't allow it. First, I'll remind him that he gave up war photography, and had more or less retired from that area of journalism. Next, I'll point out that he made a commitment to you, promised he wouldn't go back to battlegrounds. I shall also explain that, in my opinion, he's not ready to be in the line of fire, that it's too soon after his trials in Afghanistan."

There was a small pause, and then Harry continued. "To be very honest with you, Serena, I would be extremely worried about Zac's safety. It's very chaotic out there, from what I'm hearing from our guys. Don't fret, honey, Zac will get the absolute truth from me. No holds barred."

"Oh, I know he will, Harry. And listen, I've had another thought." I leaned over his desk, and said slowly, "It could be a bit of bravado on his part. A longing to be back at the front, yet knowing he's not really up to it." I flashed Harry a smile. "It'll turn out all right, you'll see."

"I've no doubt about that, honey. So come on, let's go to lunch. It's not often that I get that pleasure."

I don't suppose I will ever forget the date: July 14. Because that's when I knew for sure that Valentina Clifford, Mom's first cousin, was alive. Not only alive, but alive and kicking and still working as a war photographer.

Always an early riser, I was up at six o'clock the next morning and drinking a cup of coffee in the kitchen. And looking at *The New York Times*. On page A6 of the International Pages a photograph of a group of women caught my eye. Actually, it was the face of Marie Colvin that drew my attention. There was no missing her with her famous eyepatch.

And then I noticed the woman standing next to her. It was Valentina Clifford. At least that was what the caption said. The two women were part of a group of war correspondents and war photographers, six of them altogether. They had just arrived in Tripoli to cover the fighting between the armed civilians and soldiers . . . the uprisings all over the country.

Startled, even shocked, I dropped the paper on the floor and sat back in my chair, endeavoring to calm myself. It was then that I realized my heart was thudding and I felt slightly sick.

After a few minutes, I reached down and picked

up the paper. Turning back to A6, I studied the photograph intently. To be truthful, it wasn't a very good shot; it was rather hazy in fact. And if Marie Colvin's face, and her eyepatch, weren't so well known I might have missed it altogether.

The famous war correspondent for the London *Sunday Times* was an international star, much admired. Marie was American-born and had been brought up on Long Island. Zac was probably her greatest admirer. He had always called her "the brave and brilliant Marie," and I think that was the way the whole world thought of her. Certainly I did.

I folded the A section of the newspaper, picked up my mug of coffee, and took both to my little office overlooking the East River. I sat down on the sofa and sipped the coffee, my mind racing. I sat there for a long time, wondering what to do.

The game had changed, hadn't it? Now there was another player in it. A player I had assumed was dead.

Thirty-eight

I want to talk to you about Libya," I said to Zac, a little later that morning, after we'd had breakfast together.

Immediately his eyes brightened, and he beamed at me. "So you've made a decision, you are coming with me," he exclaimed, reaching across the kitchen table, grasping my hand. "I knew you would in the end."

"Well, I haven't actually said I'm coming," I said, staring hard at him. "I just want to talk to you about Libya."

He was surprised at my comment, and he sat back in his chair, looking at me intently. "Okay, go ahead. I'm listening."

When I remained silent, he smiled at me, in an encouraging way, I thought.

I said, "First of all, I want to remind you that you made a promise to me. You said you would never go back to the front line. But that is exactly what you want to do. Have you forgotten that promise, Zac?"

"No, of course I haven't," he said, eyeing me warily. "And going to Tripoli is not going to the front line. It's—"

"Stop right there!" I said in a tough voice. "You're splitting hairs. You don't want to admit that you've broken a promise, and so you fudge everything. By claiming that the events unfolding in Libya are civilians rioting, fighting the soldiers, that it's just an uprising. And maybe you're right. But it's still the front line, because it's dangerous, and we could as easily get killed there as we could in Helmand Province. Why won't you admit it's the front line? Certainly we know it's a bloody awful battleground, and that people are dying."

His face changed, became more serious, and he said quietly, "Okay, you're right. It's really bad, from what I've been seeing on television, but in all honesty, Pidge, I don't think of it as a front line."

"Then you'd better start, if you want me to go with you. I'm not going if we can't be brutally honest with each other. Tell each other the truth at all times."

He knew I was angry, and that I had a very strong will, and so he was smart enough to simply nod, and he did so swiftly, and vehemently.

I said, "I will go with you, Zac, on certain conditions."

"Okay, fine, anything you want, just tell me." He sounded eager.

"This has to be the last time we put ourselves in danger. If you ever want to do this again—go to a front line—it's over between us. I don't even want you to promise me. I just want you to truly know that I mean what I say." I leaned forward. "Tell me you understand, Zac."

"I do. And I know you mean every word. Okay, it's a deal. This is our last time." I knew he was sincere—and I noticed the apprehension in his eyes. "I love you, Serena, very much. I don't want to lose you. We must be together always," he said, and he meant it.

"We will be, as long as you stick to this deal." I smiled at him. "And I love you, too."

"Thank God. You said conditions. What are the others?"

"I want you to help me find this woman, when we're in Tripoli," I replied, handing him *The New York Times*, folded to the International Pages on A6.

He looked at it and then at me. "Do you mean Marie?" He was frowning. "I thought you'd met her."

"I did a long time ago, with you and Dad. But I'm referring to the woman standing next to her. Valentina Clifford."

He glanced at the newspaper again and shook his head. "But I don't know her. Who is she?"

"She is Mom's first cousin, and we, meaning my sisters and I, lost touch with her. We didn't know whether she was still alive. And neither did Harry. She's a war photographer. Anyway, there she is this morning, staring out at us from a newspaper."

"Okay, fine, but why do you want to meet up with her? I guess that's a stupid question. Because she's long-lost family, right?"

"Yes, that's one reason."

"You mean there are others?" he asked, baffled.

"Yes. I need to clear something up with her."

"What? Is it to do with your family?"

"Yes, and with me." I paused for a moment, and then I got up, went to one of the kitchen drawers, and took out the blue folder from Dad's studio in Nice, where I had put it an hour ago. I then told him the story about finding it, and showed him the pictures and the captions on the back of them, explained that Harry had been at the dancing shoot.

He scowled when he saw the photographs of a very pregnant Val, and immediately read the captions. He looked up at me, and exclaimed, "Why is your name in the captions? Are you the Serena referred to? Another stupid question, since your mother was Elizabeth." There was a moment's pause. He gazed at me, opened his mouth to make a remark, and then closed it, obviously changing his mind.

I said, "Yes, Mom was my mother. I have my birth certificate in the safe. And my sisters confirm everything. But there's just something strangely odd about these pictures, Zac, and now that I know she's alive, I want to talk to her."

"I can't say I blame you. However, you just said Harry was with Tommy the day he took the dancing photos. What did Harry tell you about the pregnant shots?"

I grimaced. "I didn't tell him about them, nor did I show them to him. Whatever he knows, if there's anything to know, he would never reveal. He'll take any Stone family secrets to the grave. And you must know that, after all these years."

"Yeah, I guess you're right, Pidge. And I must admit, they are odd captions. But oh boy, was Tommy before his time! I've never forgotten those photographs of Demi Moore, a very pregnant Demi, in *Vanity Fair*, and so Tommy was very daring, wasn't he, and so much earlier."

I nodded. "So you agree to help me meet up with Valentina Clifford, do you, Zac?"

"Sure I will, Pidge, no problem. And she won't be hard to find. You know as well as I do that journos hang out together." He took hold of my hand, and looked into my eyes, his own questioning. "But what are you going to ask her?"

"Who Serena was, or is. The Serena referred to in the captions."

A look of sudden comprehension flitted across his face. "Surely you know it can't possibly be you?"

"I do know that, but I still want to ask the question. I want to solve the mystery. Not knowing bothers me."

Later that same morning I went to Global Images on Sixth Avenue. After putting my things in my office, I took the blue folder out of my bag, and went to Harry's office next door.

I knocked on the door, opened it, and put my head inside the room. "Can I come in?" I did so before he had even responded.

"Of course," he said, rising, coming over to hug me. Then he indicated the sofa. "Let's sit over there." Once we were seated, he went on, "I guess you saw the photograph of Val Clifford in *The*

Times this morning. So now we know she is alive, after all."

"And still working. For a French photo news agency. According to the paper." Not wanting to waste any time, I held out the blue folder. "Take a look at these pictures, will you, please? Not the dancing ones, you know all about those. But the two others, showing a pregnant woman."

Harry appeared to be taken aback as I handed the folder to him, and even more surprised when he saw the photos. He studied them, then turned them over, read the captions.

I had known this man for my entire life, and I realized at once that he had never seen them before. He looked shocked.

He shook his head, silent for a moment or two, and there was no question in my mind that he was flabbergasted.

After a few seconds he said, "I wasn't present when Tommy took these, Serena. As a matter of fact they must have been taken some months later. Because when Tommy and I shot these dancing pictures for Jacques Pelliter, Val's boyfriend, she wasn't pregnant. Well, let me amend that. She might have been, but it certainly didn't show."

"I understand, but why is the name 'Serena' on the back of those two pictures, Harry? What do you think?"

"I have no idea, and that's the truth. But it's certainly not a reference to you, honey."

"How do you know that?"

"Oh come on, Serena, don't be ridiculous! Elizabeth was your mother, and you know that as well as I do. Take a look at your birth certificate, which will tell you everything. I was there when you were born at Jardin des Fleurs, and so were the twins. Your sisters will confirm this."

"Oh, they have, and they're a bit puzzled too."

"It's not a reference to you," he insisted, and sat back against the cushions, looking troubled.

We sat there for a few minutes, enfolded in silence, lost in our own thoughts. Finally I spoke. "Harry, listen to me, I've decided to go to Tripoli with Zac." I announced this in a calm but firm voice.

He turned to me at once, astonishment flashing across his lean, handsome face. "For God's sake, why? It's far too dangerous. The battle is heating up, people are dying in droves, and the press are not immune. From what Yusuf Aronson tells me, the press are actually targeted by some elements there. I won't let you go, Serena. I can't take that chance, not with your life."

I looked into those bright blue eyes. "Please listen to me, let me explain. I have to go, because of Zac. He's hell-bent on covering Tripoli, and if I stay behind it will be the end of our relationship. Really the end. He will see it as willful desertion on my part. A betrayal." I took a deep breath. "God knows, I'm sure you and

Tommy experienced the same rush of adrenaline, the compulsion, the overwhelming need to be in the middle of the action, wherever it was. Reporting to the world what you were seeing, telling the world the truth, taking those pictures that didn't lie."

"Yes," was all he said, and he shook his head, his expression dismayed, his blue eyes suddenly moist. He blinked several times, and expelled his breath. He said slowly, "Will it really kill your relationship with him if you don't go, Serena? Are you absolutely sure about that?"

"I'm positive. Besides, I need to have his back."

Harry groaned, helplessly shaking his head once more. "And he must certainly have yours. I have to see Zac later today or tomorrow, especially since you're both determined to have this assignment, and obviously want to leave immediately. There's paperwork, other things to do. However, I also want to make sure he understands he's got to have your back at all times."

"He's always known that." I studied him for a second, then asked, "So are you agreeing we can go?"

"Do I have an alternative?"

"You could still say no."

There was a short pause before he said slowly, in a cautious voice, "This desire on your part to cover Tripoli doesn't have anything to do with Val Clifford, does it?"

"Don't be silly, it's all about Zac. I love him, and I want it to work. And listen, it will be our last trip to the front line. I've explained this to Zac, and he's agreed. We'll give up war coverage after Libya."

"I think that would be most wise." Harry stood up, strode over to his desk. I also rose, followed him, holding the blue folder, sat down in the chair opposite him.

He said, "I've some conditions, and you must meet them, Serena. Otherwise I won't sanction this assignment, not for *you*."

I nodded.

Harry said, "I'm putting Yusuf Aronson on your case. He'll never leave your side. Understand? Never. Not under any circumstances. He'll be your shadow. *Understood?*"

"Yes. Yusuf will be with me twenty-four hours a day. Whether Zac likes it or not."

"Correct. And you'll check in with me every day, twice a day, if I deem it necessary. And you'll listen to Yusuf. Do as he says, especially if he thinks there's danger. Okay?"

"Yes, Harry, and you know I admire Yusuf, trust his judgment. No problems about that. And there'll be no problems with Zac."

"There better not be. He's got to understand that Yusuf is there to protect you. Got it?"

"Yes," I answered. "And thank you. Thanks for letting us go."

"Reluctantly," he said.

· · ·

I was fully aware how worried Harry was about letting us fly out to Libya. He obviously knew so much more than we did about the situation out there. Television coverage told you only so much. Being on the ground, amidst the chaos and destruction, was an entirely different matter.

I also understood why he was insisting Yusuf Aronson was with me at all times. He was my protection. Not Zac's or anyone else's. Mine. And Harry didn't care that Zac might resent the intrusion. There would be no privacy with Yusuf around.

But I wasn't going to argue with Harry. His rules were my rules. They always had been. Also, I had another problem to contend with. I was fairly certain I was pregnant. Several days ago I realized, with a shock, that I had just missed my second period. I had also experienced certain changes in my body this past week; my breasts were not only larger, but tender. And I felt queasy at different times during the day. But no morning sickness as yet.

On my way home I stopped off at a Duane Reade pharmacy to pick up various items I needed for the trip. And a pregnancy home test kit. I bought two in the end, wanting to make doubly sure of the results.

A short while later, back at the apartment, I used the first kit, which showed *positive.* And so did the second. There was no question about it anymore. I was pregnant. And going to the front line in Libya.

Or should I tell Zac about the baby, and stay at home?

I was now facing another dilemma and I didn't know what to do. Go or stay? If I went was I risking the baby? If I stayed here would I lose Zac?

Thirty-nine

Yusuf Aronson was ten feet tall. Well, not really. He was only six feet three inches in his stocking feet, to be precise. However, he frequently stood on a set of small folding steps that instantly shoved him up higher than everyone else. But he only ever made use of them in a situation like this.

So naturally, I saw him first.

Then he suddenly spotted me, shouted, "Pidge! Pidge!" at the top of his voice, and began to wave his large white hankie, which he always used to attract attention to himself. He had once told me he never waved a red one, in case it attracted a bull; he had a great sense of humor.

Zac and I were standing in the arrivals area of Tripoli's international airport. We had passed through passport control, and collected our checked luggage, which wasn't much, and now we were in the middle of a wobbling mass of human flesh. Crowds of people, waiting for family and friends, I supposed. And in a sense we were trapped. Yusuf was on the outer edge of the crowds.

He was shouting to me once more. "Pidge! Start moving! Go to the right, to your right! As far as you can go."

"Okay!" I screamed back, waving my scarf, and grabbed Zac's arm. "Come on, let's try and do what he wants. He always has a reason."

"He's a good guy," Zac muttered, and walked ahead of me, squeezing, pushing, wriggling, shoving, getting through the people somehow, and following Yusuf's instructions, we kept on moving to the right. It seemed to take forever, but finally we had gone as far as we could . . . we were now at a wall. There was a metal door set in it at one end; I tried the handle, but the door was locked from the other side. No way out.

It swung open a moment later, and there was Yusuf, a wide grin on his face, and behind him stood Ahmed and Jamal, his two sidekicks. That was what I called them. He said they were his handlers . . . because they handled anything and everything for him. Zac had dubbed them gofers. I noticed Jamal was holding the folded steps, and smiled to myself.

Yusuf opened his arms to me, and I stepped into them. He hugged me tightly for a few seconds, and then released me, turned to Zac. "Well, hello, old chap, it's great to see you," he said, in his lovely English voice, thrusting out his hand, still grinning. Due to his Lebanese mother, a Swedish father, and an English-Swedish-Arabic-French education, I considered Yusuf to be an international polyglot of the first order. Altogether he spoke six languages, and could write in all of them.

Glancing around, Zac said, "Where the hell are we, Yusuf?"

"In a corner of the parking lot. Through a connection I have a key. Come on, my van is over there." Leading the way, Yusuf took us quickly to a large black van, and as Jamal and Ahmed handled the luggage he helped me inside and onto the backseat. Zac followed, and then Yusuf got in himself. A moment later, Ahmed jumped in the front, took the wheel, with Jamal next to him, and we were driven out of the airport, heading for Tripoli.

"We'll be staying at the Rixos hotel," Yusuf said. "It's one of the best. You'll like it, and the good thing is, it's not too near the fighting."

"I've heard of the Rixos," Zac said. "It's very luxurious, isn't it?"

"That's right. I like it because there're quite a lot of journos staying there, and it's good to mingle, have a drink. You can pick up a lot of information. Mind you, I'm usually ahead of the game."

"Who's staying there, anyone we know?" I asked, hoping that he might pinpoint the group of six women war correspondents and photographers I'd seen in *The New York Times* a few days ago.

"Quite a few TV correspondents. CNN guys, BBC and ITV chaps from London, some French and Italian correspondents. It's quite an international lot, and all the wire services are here, naturally."

"Is Marie Colvin staying at the Rixos?" Zac asked, always interested in her whereabouts, really thrilled if he ran into her. She was not only charismatic but very friendly, and helpful to all of us. A good woman as well as a brilliant war correspondent.

Yusuf shook his head. "No, she's not. I don't know where Marie stays, actually. A lot of women correspondents are in Libya, though. By the way, I've got stuff at the hotel for you. Flak jackets, helmets, the usual, and you're going to need it all. The fighting's nonstop now, around the clock, and personally I think it's going to get worse. This is one hell of a revolution, and the rebels are intent on winning, determined, you know, and they're extremely well armed. A lot of foreign weaponry, by the way."

"What do you think will happen?" I asked, well aware that Yusuf had great judgment, and could call it as it was, or how it might be.

"I don't know, to be honest. Frankly, Gaddafi is

as tough as an old boot, a wily bugger, and he's got the army and the guns and the determination. Equally, the rebels are deadly, and out to get him. They want him ousted, want a new government."

"And how different will it be in the end, if the rebels win?" Zac asked in a low voice. "How much is going to be different? Look at Egypt."

"Yes, I know what you mean, the Brotherhood has a strong foothold there." Yusuf shook his head. "The Arab Spring, they're calling it. It might run into the Arab Winter, in point of fact. There's a strong feeling here that Gaddafi will fight to the bitter end, that he'll sustain the conflict forever."

"So you don't think he'll be defeated?" I asked.

"I just don't know. No one does. I'll tell you this, there's great hatred for him, and the family, and especially his sons. Most especially Saif." Yusuf chuckled. "They call him the Playboy of London, you know . . . in the streets. That's where you learn a lot. On the Arab street."

The Rixos hotel was indeed palatial. The huge lobby and the atrium were all marble, mirror, and glass, with glittering crystal chandeliers everywhere. A wide staircase with red carpeting and a brass handrail led up to the higher floors; there were potted trees standing next to the balconies of the atrium—a truly grand open area.

Once we had registered, Yusuf took us up in the

elevator to our rooms, followed by the bellboy with the luggage cart. Yusuf tipped him, the bellboy deposited the bags and left.

"My God, you've gone mad!" I exclaimed, as we walked into the sitting room of the suite, which was enormous. My eyes swung around the room, and I noted the handsome furnishings, the beautiful fabrics, the antiques, the luxury in general. "Has Harry gone mad also?" I wondered aloud.

Yusuf chuckled. "No, and to be truthful, I didn't have much option but to book us all in here. The other hotels are jammed, and anyway, since I was instructed not to take my eyes off you, Serena, I absolutely needed this set of rooms." He waved a hand at the double doors at the far end, then went and threw them open. "This is the bedroom. For you and Zac. And I shall sleep on that divan over there in the sitting room. Actually, it's a single bed."

"I see," I said.

Zac was silent. He walked over to another door, and opened it, looked inside. "But here's another bedroom," he said, swinging around, staring at Yusuf. "With two single beds."

"Yes, I know. That room's for my lads."

"We're going to be quite a crowd, now aren't we just?" Zac said, a little too sharply.

Whatever he thought, Yusuf ignored the tone, answered in his cultured, Oxford-educated voice,

"We are, but those are Harry's instructions, and he's the boss. And remember, he can pull us all out of here whenever he wishes. He's in charge long-distance. And I'm in charge here."

"And I'm glad you are," I said swiftly. "You know this place far better than we do, and we'll listen to you, Yusuf, please be assured of that. We couldn't manage without you."

"Oh you could, Serena. However, I can help make things easier for you, and I've got a lot of access to a lot of people. In the government and the military, so you've nothing to worry about. I've even got some good contacts in the rebel army."

I nodded, then asked, "By the way, why were you calling me Pidge? You've never used Jessica's nickname for me before. Why today?"

His blue eyes sparkled, looked mischievous for a moment. Then he explained, "I didn't want to be shouting out 'Serena.' Everyone knows that's a girl's name. It suddenly occurred to me that no one would understand what Pidge meant, but that you would recognize it immediately." He shook his head. "I don't even know what Pidge actually means."

"Nobody does," Zac said in a nicer voice, and walked into the bedroom, looking around, then disappearing into what obviously must be the bathroom.

I sat down, and said, "Are you going to be

comfortable out here on that divan? It looks awfully short." I made a face.

"I'll be fine, and there's nothing I can do about this situation. Harry has entrusted me with your life, Serena. I daren't leave anything to chance. But obviously you can close the bedroom door at night." Yusuf suddenly grinned at me. "Even though Harry told me I must not take my eyes off you."

I burst out laughing. "He's just too much."

"He loves you like a father," Yusuf said.

"I know, and I feel the same way. About him." I looked around, frowned. "What happened to Jamal and Ahmed?"

"They've gone to do a few errands for me. Now, what about something to eat? You must be famished."

"I am, even though we had a good breakfast in Venice before we left this morning. I'm glad you suggested we should spend the night there, break the trip from New York. I'm much less jet-lagged."

"I always do that when I come to the Middle East from New York, it makes life easier. Let's order the food, and then I'd like to go over a few things with you and Zac, ready for tomorrow."

"Aren't we going out this afternoon?" Zac asked from the doorway of the bedroom.

"There's no reason to go now, or later. I want you fed and rested before we venture out," Yusuf said in a careful tone.

"Fine by me," I replied.

Zac was silent, went over to get his camera bag and his roller suitcase.

It struck me that he was suddenly being a sourpuss, and I instantly realized why. He didn't like the idea of Yusuf being with us all the time. But there was nothing I could do about that. I was following Harry's rules and conditions. And I aimed to continue doing that, whatever Zac thought. I'd managed to get him where he wanted to be, and he was going to have to live with the conditions no matter what.

Yusuf suggested we order club sandwiches, explaining they were one of the best things on the menu, and hot lemon tea. Zac nodded, as did I, and asked Yusuf to also order me a Coke. I then excused myself.

I left the two men talking about the situation in Libya, and rolled my suitcase into the bedroom and closed the door.

I unpacked, putting items in the chest of drawers. Everything I had brought with me was made of cotton because of the extreme heat in this country. Lots of underwear, two pairs of strong but comfortable trainers and plenty of white ankle socks, plus five pairs of black cotton pants and ten black T-shirts. Following Dad's instructions, I always wore black on the front lines, because light or bright colors drew attention. I had also packed a few pieces of khaki clothing, just in case I needed them.

Picking up my shoulder bag, I took out my satellite phone, two BlackBerrys, and two cell phones, put them on my bedside table, then checked my camera bag. Everything was in order. Once I'd taken my toilet bag to the bathroom, I went to lay down on the bed. I felt a little queasy, maybe from the heat, although the air-conditioning was working. I was also hungry. Hopefully I would feel better after some food.

I smiled to myself when I thought of Harry and all of his instructions to Yusuf, who I must talk to later. I had decided it would be wiser if he found a room elsewhere in the hotel for Jamal and Ahmed; he could then move into the other bedroom. It would make Zac happier, and I would prefer this myself.

I had soon realized that Yusuf was teasing Zac a little about not taking his eyes off me. Obviously, Harry had meant out in the war zone, not here in the hotel. I was perfectly safe in this suite, and we all knew it.

I focused on Yusuf Aronson. He was a good man. He was forty-one and had worked for Global Images for seventeen years, had started as an assistant to Harry when he was twenty-four, after graduating from Oxford. He was a great photojournalist, and because he spoke English, Swedish, Arabic, French, Spanish, and Italian he was an enormous asset.

There was something extremely cosmopolitan

about him. His mother, who had been born in Beirut, had spent her youth in Paris, where her father owned various businesses. Very beautiful, she had been a Dior model for a time, had married Sven Aronson in 1970. He was a Swedish diplomat. Yusuf was their only son; he had a sister, Leyla, who created beautiful handmade clothes, which were works of art almost, and very costly. They were a close family, like ours.

Yusuf and his wife, Carlotta, lived in Paris, but Yusuf traveled the world a lot of the time. Harry called him Global's Roving Ambassador, but I was well aware he was Global's Major Trouble Shooter. He was a good manager, as well as an excellent photojournalist, and when it was necessary Harry sent him in to other countries to take over one of our bureaus, usually to get it back into shape.

I fully understood that having been assigned by Harry to cover Libya in February, he was now the Trouble Shooter at the moment, given the task of protecting me, and helping in any way he could. I had always liked Yusuf, with his bright blue eyes, slender build, and amazing height, obviously inherited from his Swedish father, while his dark, curly hair and dusky skin came from his Lebanese mother. He was a lovely mixture, I thought, and always made light of difficult situations, usually managing to solve them with the minimum of fuss and a lot of success. Furthermore, he was always calm, cool, and did not allow anything to rattle him.

I was fully aware that I had several imperatives at the moment. I must not let Zac and Yusuf know I was pregnant; I had to look after my health and be extra careful; and I must not mention Valentina Clifford to Yusuf. It might get back to Harry if I did. I had better warn Zac later, although I knew that wasn't really necessary. Zac usually played everything close to the vest, and tended to be a very private person.

A short while later, Zac tapped on the bedroom door and looked in. "Are you all right, Pidge?" he asked, his good humor restored. He sounded worried about me, his expression full of concern.

I pushed myself up on the bed. "I'm fine. I felt a bit jet-lagged, but I'm good now."

He smiled, relief reflected in his eyes. "The food's here. Come and eat something, you'll feel better. Then Yusuf is going to show us around the hotel. We'll meet some of the other journos, have a drink with them."

"That's great," I said, getting up off the bed. "I'll be out in a minute." As I freshened up, I wondered if we might run into Val Clifford here at the Rixos.

When we went down to the lobby much later I realized that the Rixos hotel was crammed with war correspondents and photographers from all over the world. I recognized a few of them, and spoke to some briefly. We had drinks with several others with whom Yusuf was friendly, but as the evening progressed I started to get worried. From the conversations it was becoming apparent to me that we were not merely on a front line, but on many front lines. There were rebel armies in many other Libyan cities who were heavily armed and fighting ferociously, their own war against Gaddafi's dreaded regime growing worse. Violence prevailed, apparently.

There was a moment when I was gripped by apprehension, as I suddenly wondered if I'd made a horrible mistake in coming here to please Zac. And seek out Val Clifford.

I then acknowledged the fact that I could so easily be injured or maimed. Or worse. I could be killed.

I had never felt this sense of apprehension so intensely before, and I accepted that it was because of the baby I was carrying. I was at risk, wasn't I?

Forty

We went out early the next morning.

It was Sunday, July 24, and our first day on the streets of a war-torn Tripoli.

The ongoing battle had been raging since February, and it showed. Broken-down walls, shattered windows, buildings in ruins. Destruction and death everywhere. And hatred.

The air was misty. The heat was already rising. It would be cruelly hot today. I was relieved I was wearing cotton clothes and comfortable trainers.

Yusuf told us over breakfast that we would head for Green Square, where there was constant conflict between the rebels and Gaddafi's army, who were well equipped in every way.

We were wearing our flak jackets of deep blue, marked PRESS in huge white letters. Our helmets were also deep blue, again with large bright white letters: PRESS. No way to misunderstand who we were. I noticed some other correspondents arriving, also with blue flak jackets and helmets. A couple of them had made the letters TV out of lengths of white tape, and stuck the tape on their backs. Clever, I thought, as I moved forward with my crew.

I had two cameras slung around my neck; my shoulder bag, with the strap across my chest, held a notebook, pens, my satellite phone, the four other phones, my press credentials, passport, credit cards, and extra cash. I had additional cash in my trouser pockets. Tommy and Harry had both drilled this into me years ago. I must keep these items on my person, in case I had to flee immediately without returning to the hotel. I could leave right now if I had to, and go wherever

I wanted in the world, because I had everything I needed on me.

Zac was silent, as usual, alert, glancing about as we moved cautiously down a street toward the square. I was alongside him, Yusuf just behind me, with Ahmed and Jamal in the rear.

I knew we were almost at Green Square. I could hear the incessant rapid gunfire, explosions, loud blasts, shouting and screaming, yells and whoops, and within a few seconds we were part of a mob of people.

Yusuf moved closer to me, took my arm, led me to the left. "Rebel forces are over here," he explained. "Safer for us."

I followed the direction of his hand, saw where he was pointing. I shook my head. "They don't look like a rebel army. What a ragtag bunch. And are all the rebel armies so disorganized?"

"Afraid so. But what they lack in organization they make up for in enthusiasm and determination, and they're all good shots, I might add."

His words were drowned out by a burst of machine gun fire. A pickup truck came careening around a corner, very fast, a machine gun mounted on it. It was being manned by a soldier in uniform, and several more trucks followed, also manned by Gaddafi forces. Men on flat-roofed buildings were shooting, and jumping to the next building, taking aim at the soldiers driving the pickup trucks. Waving their rifles, shouting, shooting.

Some of the rebels in the square began to run, as we did, shepherded by Yusuf to a safer area, a corner of a street off Green Square.

I happened to look down that narrow alley, and saw two frightened women in black, huddled against a wall. Another woman was prone on the ground, appeared to be totally helpless.

With them was a small girl with huge black eyes, black curls, and a dirty face, in a T-shirt that was too big for her, wearing it as a dress. She was staring at me, and looked to be about three years old.

I smiled at her.

She smiled back. Then she raised her small grubby hand and waved to me, still smiling as I lifted my camera and got that lovely shot of her. And several more.

The two women were staring hard at me, anxiety written across their faces. I moved slowly into the alley, wary as always, very cautious. I then saw that the woman on the ground was older. Her face was full of immense sorrow, her dark eyes filled with tears. Blood was pooling around her. I realized that she was probably dying. Oh my God.

"Please," one of the women said. "Please. Help us."

"Okay," I answered swiftly, nodding. "Okay."

As I turned, I saw Yusuf waiting for me. "One of those women has been shot. She's in a bad way," I told him.

"I'll phone Emergency at the hospital. Sometimes they have ambulances in this area." He shook his head, added, "But the hospitals are full, bursting at the seams with the wounded. That's one of the many problems. The wounded and the dying."

Together he and I walked back to Green Square, where I almost gagged on the smell of gunpowder, blood, sweat, and burned flesh. I swallowed. "God, it's an awful stench," I muttered to myself.

"Don't I know it," Yusuf said, glancing at me. "It's the smell of war, hatred, and fear . . . all mingled together."

Yusuf took out his cell, called the hospital, and told them about the woman, gave the name of the street as well as his name. Then he glanced at me, and said, "Whether they'll come or not I don't know, your guess is as good as mine." He pulled me into a doorway, where we stood huddled together, scanning the square, dodging bullets.

I suddenly thought: I'm in the middle of a civil war. Two factions in the same country and filled with anger and hatred for each other. A country so rich, from massive oil revenues, and yet the majority of the people are so poor . . . with nothing. No wonder they have risen up, caused a revolution.

It was directed at Gaddafi, their leader for forty-two years, stealer of their wealth, their health, their welfare, and their happiness. Not to mention human rights on every level.

Yes, I was on the front line, no doubt about it, whatever Zac wanted to call it. The front line of a civil war. Who would win, I had no idea. I had to hope it was the rebels, because they had been cheated, were the downtrodden. They should have freedom and equality. But I wasn't sure they could win, however enthusiastic they were, and such good shots, according to Yusuf.

I wanted to stay in the square longer, needing to know if the ambulance came. But Yusuf was adamant. We had to keep moving. He wanted to get us away from this ongoing violence. People were on edge, angry, ready to kill anyone. He said the mob might soon be out of control.

Zac was behind me as we set off, shooting pictures, capturing vivid images on film. He was being tailed by Ahmed and Jamal; protecting him, I thought. Watching his back. I knew that the two lads, as Yusuf called them, had guns. I'd noticed them this morning. But I had kept quiet. It was none of my business. Yusuf was in charge.

The gunfire unexpectedly increased, seemed to become overwhelming. The crowds were yelling and screaming, growing more restless and resentful, and it wasn't yet noon.

Within a few minutes Yusuf was hurrying us out of the square, moving us along quickly. "Too many people. It's chaos. And it's going to get worse, there'll be a lot of people killed. It's a bad day."

"Bad day at black rock," I said, and squinted in the sunlight as I looked up at Yusuf.

"Good movie though," he responded, his face straight. Then he winked.

Zac fell into step with us. "Some of these rebels are just kids," he exclaimed, staring at Yusuf. "Very young . . . teenagers."

"And inexperienced, no training, nothing, just a desire to be free of the yoke . . . free of the Gaddafi government. It's quite amazing that they have managed to hold parts of this city, and other cities as well."

"Benghazi," Zac said. "I watched it all on television back home. CNN did some great coverage."

"That city was almost defeated," Yusuf replied. "If it hadn't been for the NATO strikes it wouldn't exist today . . . fighting between the rebels and the loyalists was incredible, violent, brutal, incessant."

"And some of them are just kids," Zac said yet again, amazement lingering on his face.

"Students, oil workers, doctors, engineers, teachers, farmers, lawyers . . . in other words, civilians. They're the ragtag militias facing Colonel Gaddafi's much better trained and armed forces. Land, sea, and air forces, at that. In a way you've got to take your hat off to the militias. They're brave, stalwart," Yusuf finished.

None of us disagreed.

For the next week we went back to Green Square from time to time, but we also covered outlying districts and the suburbs of Tripoli, also some of the desert villages farther away from the city. Fighting was in progress everywhere. Violently so.

It seemed to me that this whole land was consumed by the revolution, new militias springing up every day, rebels arming themselves. No one could tell us where all the guns were coming from, but I had seen a lot of Gaddafi's soldiers with Kalashnikov rifles. It was like a world on fire . . . a burning hell . . .

Both Yusuf and Zac kept referring to the social networks, and how word spread so fast these days everything changed from minute to minute. No time to think, I thought, silently agreeing with them.

The brutality, the noise, the deaths . . . all began to take their toll on me, and everyone else in our little group. Even the lads, Ahmed and Jamal, had started to look weary, their faces grim. They never said much; when they did speak they were extremely polite. And always wanted to help.

Every night I insisted we have a rest, get cleaned up, and go downstairs for dinner. Of course, all of this happened after Yusuf had checked in with Harry, and Zac and I had also talked to him.

Sometimes we didn't feel like leaving the Rixos, other times we did. In this instance, we visited the Corinthia Hotel, and a few others, hoping to see other journalists we knew. Mostly Ahmed and Jamal went off on their own, but not always. We considered ourselves a team.

Whenever I was with other journos, I wanted to ask about Val Clifford, but didn't dare. And so Zac volunteered to do this for me. He usually began his conversation by inquiring about friends of his, not mentioning her until later. And one night he got an answer.

A war correspondent from a French network, whom Zac knew, Henri Brillet, said he'd heard that a group of women journalists had gone to Sirte. He specifically said that Val Clifford and a Frenchwoman, Ariel Salle, were two of them. And perhaps Marie Colvin. But Zac said he doubted that Marie would go there, because she was too smart. It was such a dangerous area few journalists ventured into that town.

Later that night, when we were alone in the bedroom, I said to Zac, "Let's go to Sirte, see if we can contact Val Clifford."

Zac nodded, then sighed. "Well, why not. I wouldn't mind shooting in another city. We might even get some iconic pictures. It's Gaddafi's hometown, where he was born, and it could be interesting, especially if we talk to some of his people." He half laughed. "They're all his people in Sirte, which is the main reason why we should stay away. It is very, very dangerous, Pidge."

Wanting to encourage Zac, I exclaimed, "But we could get some really unique pictures! It's worth a try. And I think you should bring it up with Yusuf. You'll have to do it, Zac."

"No, no, no," he said, giving me a hard stare. "He'd always favor you first. He's got a thing about you." He laughed after saying this, just so I wouldn't think he was jealous of Yusuf. But I knew he was.

"It's better you do it, honestly," I insisted. "He'll tell Harry I wanted to go, and Harry might put two and two together and come up with ten. He also might well know Val Clifford is there."

"How could he possibly know that!" Zac sat back, shaking his head, frowning, and looking suddenly exasperated. "We've only got the idea she is in Sirte from Henri Brillet, and he wasn't all that positive."

"Yes, you're right, probably it's better that we don't go. Couldn't you ask him though, tomorrow, Zac? Please."

Naturally the answer was a resounding NO, when, next morning at breakfast, Zac broached the idea of making a trip to Sirte.

"Too dangerous, especially for the press. Dangerous for anyone, except Gaddafi's soldiers, family, hangers-on, his cronies. That place is rife with loyalists, they'd shoot us as easily as looking at us. We're the foreign press, remember, they don't trust us."

I knew Yusuf well, and I understood at once that there was no point in arguing with him. And it would get back to Harry, who would, no doubt, be immediately suspicious of my motives.

So I let the idea go. Much to Zac's relief, I think.

A few days later I started to feel ill. It was mostly a nauseous feeling that really hit me one afternoon. I told Yusuf and Zac I needed to go back to the hotel to rest, that I was overtired.

They both agreed immediately, and we left the area on the outskirts of Tripoli, a desert village where we were taking pictures, returned to the Rixos hotel. They were both concerned about me, and wanted to help me in any way they could.

The strange thing was, I still didn't suffer from morning sickness. However, some afternoons and evenings I experienced a queasiness . . . it was like being seasick. But on this particular afternoon I became violently ill when I got back to the hotel, and vomited for some time. This was unusual for me. On the other hand, I was pregnant, and thought this was probably the reason for the nausea.

To explain my upset stomach, I told Zac I might have eaten something which disagreed with me, and he accepted that. He also said he wasn't feeling well himself. And then Yusuf had a similar upset stomach that evening. I relaxed, decided we had all eaten food that had been contaminated, and were suffering from food poisoning.

Late one afternoon Zac, Yusuf, and I were sitting downstairs at the Rixos, having cold drinks. It was an extremely hot day, scorching, and we had decided to take a break from filming. The air-conditioning in the hotel and the tall glasses of iced tea helped us to cool off, feel refreshed. It was good to take it easy for once.

We were talking about Gaddafi, who we knew was still in Tripoli. At least, we believed all the reports that said he was. But he was on the run, in hiding, as were his family. And also his grown sons.

There was a great deal of speculation amongst the three of us. Yusuf threw out the idea that the dictator might attempt to get his wife and younger children out to another country, more than likely Algeria. Zac agreed; I did, too.

Unexpectedly, I saw Henri Brillet, the French war correspondent, approaching our table. I looked at Zac, and touched his arm. "Henri looks very serious," I murmured. "He's coming over here."

A moment later Henri arrived at our table, and I asked him if he would like to join us.

He smiled, shook his head, declined politely, and focused his attention on Zac. "I heard that Val Clifford and Ariel Salle, and two male journalists from the UK, were killed today. Very bad news, tragic."

I sat very still, listened without saying a word. I was shocked, speechless.

Zac exclaimed, "Henri, this is terrible! Are you sure?"

"I am. It came from a good source. One of the cameramen I know. From the BBC. The two men who also died were British, as I said."

"How awful, how very sad," I said in a low voice. "I hate it when journalists die in battle. We're only here to report, not to fight. We're just seeking the truth."

Yusuf nodded. "*C'est la vie,*" he said, looking grim as he spoke.

Henri inclined his head. "I wanted you to know, Zac." He added something in French that I didn't quite catch, and left, heading toward French colleagues who were at another table.

The three of us were silent for a moment or two, and I was about to make a comment about Val Clifford's death, when my BlackBerry buzzed. I saw from the screen that it was Harry calling from New York.

"Hi, Harry," I said.

"Hi, honey. Are you all okay?"

"We are, yes. I wanted—"

He cut in. "Val Clifford was killed today. Along with some other journalists, Serena. Outside Sirte. On a desert road. It's already on all the wires."

"We just heard about it," I answered. "It's very sad when a colleague goes like that. Tragic."

"It is indeed, Serena. But she died doing what she loved." There was a slight pause before he added, "We all take a chance when we go to the front lines. So just take care of yourself, Serena, don't do anything risky. What's happening there?"

I filled him in swiftly, and then passed the phone to Zac, who needed to ask him about a certain photograph. And then Zac handed my BlackBerry to Yusuf, who spoke to Harry at length, standing up, walking away from us, heading into the lobby.

Zac stared at me, and raised a brow without saying anything.

I reached out, took hold of his hand. "I'm okay, Zac. I'm just very, very sad a war photographer got killed in battle. I never knew her, you know. Even though she was Mom's first cousin, I have no recollection of Val, but it's another member of the family gone, isn't it?"

He nodded, squeezed my hand, remained silent.

I sat back in the chair, thinking about Valentina Clifford for a moment. I had wanted to meet her, ask her questions about those strange, disturbing photographs. Now that was no longer possible. And perhaps it was just as well. As Harry had said to me in New York, I knew everything I needed to know about myself. Why had I thought I didn't know enough? Perhaps because I was a photojournalist and always wanted to get to the bottom of a story, find the meaning behind it? The knowledge that I would now never know what the photographs were all about frustrated me. Also, I'd liked the thought of meeting Mom's cousin, who had known her all of her life. I sighed and wished, for a moment, that I'd met Val years ago.

Forty-one

I just know I can't make it," I said to Zac, leaning against the doorjamb of the bathroom.

He was shaving and turned a soap-covered face to me, the razor in his hand, and asked, "But why not, Serena? You've been looking forward to this evening, this little party. It'll do you good."

I shook my head. "I can't. Really."

"Oh come on, Pidge, all you have to do is slap on some makeup, get dressed, and take the elevator downstairs. It's not such a long trek, you know. There have been times when you've gone much farther for a party. I know that only too well." He began to laugh, and started to run the razor over his cheek.

I laughed with him, and said, "Oh, yes, I'm guilty of that. But I won't be able to make it tonight. I can barely make it back to bed."

Again he turned to look at me, a scowl

appearing. "But why not? What's wrong with you? Are you sick again?"

"If you mean nauseous, yes, I am. But I feel totally drained as well. Also, I've got pains in my stomach."

"Oh God, don't tell me you've been poisoned a second time. What have we eaten? I got sick too the last time and so did Yusuf."

I shook my head. "I haven't eaten very much at all, either yesterday or today. Listen, I know my own body, just as you know yours, and I feel lousy. So I can't go to the party the guys from CNN are giving. I'm sorry, Zac, but that's the way it is."

I walked away from the bathroom doorway, and got into bed, pulling the sheets over me, lay propped up against the pillows. I was mostly worried about the stomach pains. I was wondering if I *had* eaten some bad food. I hoped not. Vomiting always did me in.

A few minutes later Zac came and sat down on the bed next to me. He was shaved and his hair was combed. Leaning closer, he touched my face gently. "I'm sorry you're not well, and God knows why I'm arguing with you. If you don't feel good you've got to be right where you are. Who cares about a party? There's always another. Look, do you need a doctor?"

"No thanks, Zac. And I'm glad you understand. Give Tim Gordon my apologies, won't you?"

"I sure will. I'd better get dressed." He put on a fresh white T-shirt, clean blue jeans, and slipped his feet into his brown penny loafers. Unlike me, he always brought a pair of shoes with him, as Dad had and Harry still did. It always amused me that they thought they needed loafers on the front line. I'd always settled for trainers or combat boots, which they usually wore also when working.

He came back to the bed and kissed my cheek, just as Yusuf tapped on the bedroom door. Striding over to open it, Zac said, "Come in, Yusuf. Serena's not feeling good, so she's not coming to the CNN party after all."

Instantly looking concerned, Yusuf asked, "Are you nauseous? I hope you've not eaten the wrong thing."

"I don't think so, and I'll be fine. Frankly, I feel bone tired tonight, and I just want to relax in bed, watch the TV, drink my Coke. Sorry to miss the party, but as Zac just said, there's always going to be another."

"He's right, and it's best that you stay here resting. Is there anything I can get you? What about a doctor?"

"No, I'm fine, thanks anyway. Oh, put the Do Not Disturb sign on the door, will you, please?"

"I will, Serena." He grinned at me. "And I won't tell Harry I took my eyes off you for a few hours, if you won't."

"I'm very safe here, behind a locked door, so

please don't suggest sending up the lads to watch over me," I replied with a smile.

"I wouldn't dream of it." He planted a kiss on my forehead, and left the room.

Zac bent over and kissed my cheek. "Call me if you need me. On my cell. That's the easiest."

"Good idea, and please give me my BlackBerry. I'll keep it next to me on the bed."

It was true that I felt tired, and I fell asleep almost immediately. I must have slept for several hours, because when I woke it was already half past nine. I pushed myself up in bed, and reached for the Coca-Cola. I'd only taken a few sips of it when I quickly put it back on the bedside table. A sharp pain had ripped through me. I bent over, holding my stomach, and then instantly I got out of bed and rushed to the bathroom.

I just made it to the toilet in time. Blood was gushing out of me, and clots of blood as well. I was in great pain, spasming at times, and I knew I was having a miscarriage. I sat there groaning to myself for the longest time, feeling as if all of my innards were leaving me. And I think they were . . . some of them anyway. The pains were acute, the clots thick.

I began to cry, and eventually I got up, went to find some tissues. I noticed that blood had dripped onto the floor, and I quickly bent over, cleaned it up with the tissues.

It struck me immediately that I had to stay in the bathroom for as long as it took. Once I was certain the bleeding had properly stopped, I would clean up. The bathroom as well as myself.

I was still wearing my stained nightgown, on my knees on the bathroom floor, cleaning the marble as best I could with a wet towel. I already had one soaking in the tub, hoping it would soon be clean.

"What the hell are you doing?" Zac asked from the doorway.

I was startled, swung my head, and exclaimed, "I'm just tidying up!" Then I stood, grabbed a large bath towel and wrapped it around myself like a sarong.

"What's happened?" he asked, sounding baffled and also disturbed. He was gaping at me.

I didn't answer the question. "Is the party over already?" I asked, staring back at him, pushing my wet hair away from my face. I knew I looked a mess, sweaty and damp, and probably there was blood on me somewhere.

"No, it isn't over. I was worried about you, Pidge. I came up to check on you. There's a lot of drinking going on, we haven't even had dinner yet. I wanted to tell you I'd be late."

"Then go back, go back, enjoy it," I said in a warm voice, just wanting him to leave so I could make myself look halfway decent. Forgetting that I was holding the towel around me, I waved my hand, shooing him out, and the towel fell to the floor. As I swiftly bent down and grabbed it I heard him gasp.

"Jesus, what's happened?" he cried, coming into the bathroom, grabbing my arm. "You've got blood all over your legs."

I knew there was only one thing to do. I had to tell him the truth. I took a deep breath, and said, "I think I just had a miscarriage."

"*Think* you had a miscarriage. Don't you know?" he shouted, sounding shocked.

"Well, yes, I do. I did have a miscarriage."

"Was the baby mine?" he asked, his voice unexpectedly hard, tight in his throat.

"Of course it was yours," I said coldly, angry that he would think otherwise.

"And obviously you were pregnant when we left New York?" he shot back at me, the anger still echoing.

"Yes, I was."

"And you decided to come here, to the front line, when you were pregnant? Are you crazy? What were you thinking?"

I was so startled by his loud voice, the hardness in it, the look of fury on his face, that I was stupefied for a few seconds. Then I exclaimed, "I was thinking of you, Zac, knowing how much you wanted me to come with you. I decided to stay with our plans. I was only two months pregnant."

"You took a chance, put yourself at risk!" he answered in an icy tone, turned, went out of the bathroom without another word.

I followed him, saying, in a slightly calmer voice, "I'm strong and healthy, and I didn't think it was a risk."

"You were wrong, weren't you?" he snapped, glaring at me.

I was silent for a moment. Then I said, "Seemingly so."

"How could you do that? Take such a chance?" He was so furious now he could hardly speak and his face was congested. "You risked our child. And by coming to Libya it died. All your fault."

His words inflamed me, and I shouted, "How dare you say that to me! It's a rotten thing to say, Zac."

He stepped forward, took hold of my shoulders, and shook me. I noticed that his fury had not abated at all. I remembered that night when we had broken up, just over a year ago now, in Nice. He had been gripped by a similar anger. I had sensed a violence in him then and I did now.

I pushed him away. "Zac, I love you, and I loved that I was pregnant with your child. I didn't tell you because I believed everything would be all right. I'm young, healthy, strong. This was a fluke . . . my having a miscarriage."

When he remained totally silent, I said softly, "But maybe I should have told you."

"Yes, maybe you should have," he said in that hard, icy voice.

I stood staring at him, gripping the towel around me.

He turned on his heels and left the bedroom. For a split second I wanted to run after him, call for him to come back, but I didn't. I knew him well enough to understand that I had to let him cool off.

He would be better in a few hours, of that I was quite certain.

I finished cleaning the bathroom, washed the towels and my nightgown, had a shower, washed my hair and dried it. Then I put on a clean nightgown and went to bed.

After watching television for half an hour, I turned it off. But I lay awake for a long time, cursing myself under my breath for being so silly, stupid for not having told him I was pregnant when we were in New York.

I woke up in the middle of the night, and reached out, feeling for Zac. But he wasn't there. I sat up immediately, glanced around the room, and got out of bed. My legs felt weak, and I was a little woozy. And still slightly nauseous, which didn't surprise me. I'd just been through an ordeal.

Zac was not in the bathroom. Nor was he in the sitting room. For a moment I had expected to see him sleeping on the divan. When I glanced at my watch I saw that it was four in the morning.

Where the hell was Zac?

Part Six

OUT OF FILM
Venice, August

How sad and bad and mad it was,
But then, how it was sweet!
—Robert Browning:
"Confessions"

Give all to love;
Obey thy heart;
Friends, kindred, days
Estate, good fame,
Plans, credit and the Muse,
Nothing refuse.
—Ralph Waldo Emerson:
"Give All to Love"

Forty-two

Yusuf Aronson got me off the front line and out of Libya. It was a swift, smooth, and highly professional operation that impressed me.

As usual, Yusuf was calm, efficient, discreet, and kind, and I was very grateful to him. He had proved to be the good friend I had always believed he was, had asked no questions, just agreed to get me out immediately, once I'd told him I wanted to go. ASAP . . . as soon as possible, to quote Tommy Stone . . .

Now, here I was, sitting on a private jet, a Cessna Mustang, and fastening my seat belt. Moments later, as we soared up into the air, I breathed a sigh of relief. I was free. Free of Libya. Free of war. Free of Zac.

Although I was sad, and filled with guilt, and also blamed myself for the miscarriage, I thought Zac's behavior had been reprehensible. He had shouted and screamed at me, losing control, letting his temper flare. He had also displayed the signs of violence that had so alarmed me in the past.

The scene he made when he found me cleaning the bathroom was reminiscent of his angry performance after Dad's funeral in Nice last year. I still found it hard to believe that he had taken hold of my shoulders and shaken me so hard last night, when he knew I had just been through a difficult physical and emotional ordeal.

The plane leveled off. We floated through the clouds and I stared out of the window; the bright blue sky was filled with sunlight, and I hoped I would feel better soon, less tense.

In exactly two hours from now I would be landing at Marco Polo airport in Venice. I would head straight for the bolthole, where I would try to recoup my strength and collect myself.

When I felt well enough, I would go to Nice. I wanted to be with Jessica and Cara at Jardin des Fleurs, needed to be with my caring sisters, surrounded by their love.

I was aware that I loved Zac; I suppose I always would. And I cared about him, worried about him, as well. Strong feelings didn't stop just like that. However, I was no longer sure that our relationship would work, or that we had a future together.

I had told Harry in New York that I wasn't sure that I could trust Zac again, after he had broken his promise not to go back to a war zone. And I wondered about that now. Hadn't I been stupid, agreeing to go with him to Libya? But there had been another reason: Valentina Clifford. I had been stupid about her, too. There wasn't anything I needed to hear from her . . . I knew exactly who I was.

I had long been aware that Zac had a short fuse.

However, I had forgotten how impatient and juvenile he was when it came to a problem between the two of us. When he learned about my miscarriage last night he had flown into a rage, shown no concern for my well-being, nor had he even wanted to discuss the matter further. Instead he had turned on his heels and stalked out of the suite in an angry huff.

Several years ago, Cara, my lovely sister who was often the bearer of bad news, had told me to beware, that Zac was self-involved and selfish. It was "all about Zac," was the succinct way she put it. I think I'd always known this, deep down. On the other hand, I was also a little self-involved, as were most people.

Yet I did not lose my temper or my control, and I always endeavored to see other people's point of view. I liked to give them the benefit of the doubt, and I prided myself on my sense of fair play.

I sighed under my breath, filled with regret. I should have told him I was pregnant before we left for Tripoli. I realized that now. But he had so desperately wanted to be on the front line, with me by his side, I hadn't had the heart to disappoint him. We had been apart for a year, and I was truly happy that we had reconciled. And so was he. There was no question in my mind that he had been looking forward to a future together, as had I.

Well, he was the one who strode out without a backward glance, filled with anger and indignation, I suddenly thought. Still, I had allowed him to go, believing he would cool down, that we would talk it through later. But he hadn't come back by four o'clock, and this had worried me.

At five this morning I was even more anxious about him. I had gone to the sitting room to see if he was sleeping on the divan, found Yusuf instead. He was sitting at the desk, using his laptop, and had looked up when I had appeared, and greeted me affectionately.

I asked him if he knew where Zac was, and he had quickly explained that he had put Zac to bed in the room which Ahmed and Jamal shared on another floor. "Because he was very drunk, really out of it," Yusuf had continued. "I thought this was the best thing to do. You weren't feeling well when we'd gone off to the CNN party. Also later, after he'd been to see if you were okay, he came back to the party in a rage. He told me you and he had had a nasty quarrel. He was still seething about it."

It was while Yusuf was telling me all this that I began to shake inside; tears welled. I understood I must leave at once. I no longer wanted to be in Libya covering a war. It was all too much for me now. Nor did I wish to share a suite with Zac, considering the angry mood he was in, and the way he had behaved toward me. My emotions were flaring. I endeavored to get ahold of myself, not wanting to break down in front of Yusuf.

Once Yusuf knew how anxious I was to leave, he had made everything happen with great speed. He had chartered the private plane from the company Global used in Europe. This had been flown into Tripoli, without delay, with a turn-around time of four hours. I had been dressed, packed, and out of the Rixos hotel before Zac had even woken up.

On the drive to the airport Yusuf had been the soul of discretion, and we had talked about other things; Zac was not mentioned at all. I held myself in check; my heart ached. I called Claudia in Venice and told her I would be arriving at the bolthole later today, and I spoke to Harry in New York, once we got to the airport.

It was six o'clock in the morning there, but he was an early riser and answered the phone immediately. I filled him in, said that I still wasn't feeling great after my bout with food poisoning, and thought it wiser that I left the war zone.

He agreed at once, and was pleased Yusuf had chartered a plane. I told him Zac was staying on to continue covering the revolution, then handed the BlackBerry to Yusuf.

They talked for a few seconds about the situation in general in Tripoli, and then Yusuf clicked off and gave the BlackBerry back to me.

"Harry didn't say it, but you've just made his

day, Serena. He's delighted you're putting distance between yourself and the war."

"You'd better believe it," I said, smiling at my old friend.

I tried to take a nap, but I found that to be impossible. I was far too agitated inside, pent up, not calm at all. Just the opposite. I would have liked to shout and jump up and down, have a real tantrum. Release the anger inside. I wished I had a copper frying pan. I wanted to bash something hard, over and over again. The windows? That wasn't possible, of course. The plane would crash.

I began to realize that my rage with Zac was surfacing. Until now I had played it cool. Suddenly I wanted to let it all out. He had been so wrong. I had wanted, no needed, his comfort, not his criticism.

I began to shake inside once more. He'd hurt me, hurt my feelings. I sat back in the seat and closed my eyes. I felt the tears pricking behind my lids. I struggled not to cry. If truth be known, I was angry with myself. I had hurt myself, so it was a double hurt. And all because I had gone to Libya. I should not have been so hell-bent on pleasing Zac. I should have given more thought to myself, to the baby. The tears started, trickled down my face. I felt my sense of despair . . . I'd lost my baby.

• • •

Yusuf had thought of everything, and once the Cessna Mustang landed at Marco Polo airport and I had been through passport control, I was met by a young woman who often worked for him. He had told me to expect her, to look for her in Arrivals. She was a travel agent, and carried a large white card with the name PIDGE written on it in black letters.

I smiled inwardly as I greeted her. We shook hands, and, calling me Miss Pidge, she led me outside to a water taxi she had waiting for us. Her name was Lucrezia and she insisted on riding into Venice with me, explaining that Yusuf had instructed her to take me right to my front door.

There was no point arguing, because she was adamant, so I settled back in the speedboat and chatted to her as we headed toward La Serenissima. It was a typical August day, sunny and hot under a blameless blue sky, and I enjoyed the ride and the familiar sights. In a way, it was like coming home.

Once we arrived at the Piazza San Marco, I was glad Lucrezia was with me. It was tourist time again, and on this Sunday afternoon, the piazza was full of people from all over the world, milling around. She insisted on pulling my roller suitcase, and I carried my camera bag, with my shoulder bag filled with all my credentials and money slung over my shoulder and across my chest, for safety.

Yusuf had been right. Lucrezia had made my life easier, and I thanked her profusely once we were finally standing outside the bolthole door. She left with a cheery good-bye and a smile, and I unlocked the door of the apartment and went inside, bracing myself.

I had expected the bolthole to be full of Zac and me, and the aura of sex, after our last visit en route to Libya. But this was not so. It was redolent of Dad and Harry and Mom, and me and my sisters, when I was a child. Memories of the past assailed me, welcomed me, comforted me; all the visits we had made here rushed back . . .

Closing the door behind me, I stood for a moment looking around. The living room was fragrant with the scent of fresh roses, and I noticed the big bowl of them on the coffee table, pink and white and in full bloom. And mingling in with their perfume was the citrus smell of Jo Malone's grapefruit-and-rosemary room cologne, which I loved.

On the dining table stood a large plate of fresh fruit, and all this was due to Claudia's thoughtfulness, her kindness. I knew that the fridge would have all the right food in it; she always stocked up when she knew someone from Global was coming to stay, whether it was me or Harry, or some other photographers exiting a war.

The apartment was so familiar and welcoming, I relaxed. And I felt it embracing me, or rather, it was the memories of long ago that were taking over, putting their arms around me. I had toyed with the idea of staying at the Bauer Palazzo, when I realized I had to get out of Tripoli. Now I was glad I hadn't booked a room there. This was the only place to be because it was ours.

Wheeling my suitcase into my parents' former bedroom, I sat down on the bed, took out my BlackBerry, and dialed Harry at Global in New York.

When he answered his cell, I said, "Harry, it's me, and I'm here. In the bolthole, and I'm fine. Everything is fine."

"Thank God you're out of the war zone!" he exclaimed, sounding happier than he had for weeks. "I worried so much about your safety, even though I had Yusuf and his lads surrounding you."

"He's the best, but then you know that," I answered.

"I do indeed, but how are you feeling, Serena? Do you think you ought to go and see a doctor? The earlier bout of food poisoning might not have been that at all. You could have picked up some sort of parasite."

"I don't think so, Harry. Zac and Yusuf were hit with it, too, and as far as I'm concerned, I do believe a lot of stress and tension fed into it, didn't help me. My stomach feels pretty much settled down today, honestly. I'm okay."

"You know best, just take care of yourself, relax and enjoy Venice. I'll talk to you later."

"I'll be right here," I answered. "And thanks, Harry, for pulling me out."

"Now you know very well that was all Yusuf's doing," he said in a cheerful voice. I sensed his relief that I was on safe ground. I was relieved myself.

After we had hung up, I called Jessica in Nice to tell her I was off the front line and in Venice, but her answering service kicked in. So I left a message, began to unpack, and put everything away. I didn't have any plans for the next few days. I just wanted to rest, calm myself, and take stock of my life. I thought of Zac and my throat tightened. Don't go there, I warned myself, and jumped up, left the bedroom.

I noticed a note on the coffee table next to the roses, and went and read it. Claudia had welcomed me, and suggested we have coffee tomorrow. I would do that. I wanted to see her, and also to thank her for all she had done to spruce up the bolthole, and for the flowers and food. And to settle my bill with her for the food.

In the kitchen, I made a mug of lemon tea and a ham-and-cheese sandwich, and sat at the small table eating it. I happened to glance up, noticed the copper frying pan hanging on the wall opposite me, along with some other copper items.

I shuddered when I thought of Zac destroying

the TV with it, and wondered yet again why I had not known we owned such a thing. I had probably never paid any attention to it, nor even noticed it amongst the other pieces of copper. Oddly enough, now I understood his need to bash something to pieces out of frustration and anger.

My mind zeroed in on Zac's post-traumatic stress disorder, and I reminded myself that this caused much of his anger. And his incipient violence at times? *Possibly.*

He had been a war photographer for sixteen years, always in combat, actually, and had most likely suffered from PTSD for longer than Harry and I understood. As I continued to focus on his condition, caused by war, I accepted that I wasn't afraid of Zac harming me physically. The undercurrent of violence was more verbal than anything else. Nonetheless, he did shake me, holding me by the shoulders last night, and that had upset me.

Sighing, I took the dishes to the sink, rinsed them, and went back to the bedroom, suddenly feeling tired. I lay down on the bed, hoping to fall asleep, but this didn't happen. Instead, I began to think of the miscarriage, and instantly started to cry. Now that I was alone I could finally let go.

I wept into the pillow for a long time, for the baby I had lost, would never know, never see grow up. I was overwhelmed by my loss, and the sadness, and I again chastised myself for going to Libya in the first place.

As the weeping abated, finally, I began to retrace my steps, thinking of every day I had been in the war zone. I quickly came to understand that I had done nothing untoward. I had not put myself at risk. Yusuf had always been with me, protecting me, along with Jamal and Ahmed. And Zac. I'd been fully aware that he always had my back, even when he was in the thick of taking pictures.

I had not done anything hectic physically, like jumping off walls, Jeeps, and trucks, as I had done very often in the past. Food poisoning aside, I had eaten very carefully, and had watched myself at all times, fully conscious of the baby, not wishing to harm it in any way.

In the inner recesses of my mind, words echoed, words I'd heard long ago. I concentrated, heard them again: *A woman can have a miscarriage for no reason at all. It just happens. Don't worry, you'll get pregnant again.*

The voice had been my mother's, and I remembered now that she had been talking to Jessica when she was still married to Roger. And I had been with them on the terrace at Jardin des Fleurs.

I felt unexpectedly comforted. Sometimes things like that happen . . . remembered incidents come to mind, little rays of happiness shining out in the darkness, like sunlight glinting through deep water.

• • •

I must have fallen asleep. The buzzing of my BlackBerry on the bedside table awakened me. I grabbed it, saw that it was Harry, and pushed myself up into a sitting position.

"Hello?" I said, realizing I sounded groggy.

"It's me," Harry said. "Are you all right? You sound funny."

"I'm great, Harry, I've been resting. I didn't get much sleep last night."

"I'm not surprised," he exclaimed. "I understand that you and Zac had a terrible row, that he was shouting and screaming at you."

I stiffened slightly on the bed, and exclaimed, "Yusuf must have told you." As I said these words, I couldn't believe he would do such a thing, not my good old friend.

Harry confirmed this, when he said, "Of course it wasn't Yusuf who blabbed. He's too discreet. Zac told me."

"When?"

"Just a short time ago. He phoned me from Tripoli. He said you hadn't been well when he left for the CNN party, that he'd come back to check on you, and you'd quarreled. He sounded so down in the dumps, I wondered if you'd broken off with him?"

"I didn't actually say that to him, that it was over, nor did he. But it could be that it is—" I stopped speaking. My throat had tightened, and I was choked up.

"Surely not! You've been so good together, Serena. Don't you want to make up with him? Give it a try?" Harry sounded worried.

"I don't know," I muttered.

"Why did you have such a big row? It can't be that bad, can it?" he asked, anxiousness lingering in his voice.

"I think it is," I answered, my own voice suddenly wobbling. There was a silence on my part for a moment, and then I said, "I had a miscarriage on Saturday night, Harry—" I did not finish my sentence, started to weep. But somehow I managed to control myself within seconds. And I then told Harry all about the events in the suite at the Rixos hotel.

He listened, not interrupting. When I'd finished he said, "I understand, understand everything. I'm sorry this happened to you, that you lost the baby, Serena. But I must admit, from what you've told me, I don't think you should have gone. If I had known you were pregnant I would have forbidden it."

I was startled, and I heard the annoyance in Harry's voice.

"Zac blames me, and says it's my fault," I explained, "and he behaved very badly."

"I suppose it was natural, he must have been very shocked, maybe even hurt you hadn't told him you were expecting his child. The first he heard of it was when you'd lost it. I can well imagine how he felt, and why he reacted." Harry sighed heavily.

I remained silent, surprised by his words. I knew he was shocked and disapproving of me. "I'm sorry," I said. "So sorry, Harry."

"I see from my watch that it's nine o'clock over there," Harry went on. "Let's talk tomorrow and decide what you should do."

"All right," I replied, filled with exhaustion and disappointment. "Good night." I paused, then added, "I love you."

"I love you, too, Serena."

As I hung up I was aware that I did not feel better. Talking to Harry had not really helped me, or comforted me, because I knew I'd displeased him by going to Libya in my condition. He had made it plain, though he had not chastised me. I felt more alone than ever.

It wasn't very often that the landline rang in the bolthole, but suddenly it was shrilling. Once again I pushed myself up on the bed and grabbed the phone.

"Hello?"

"Hi, Pidge, it's Jess. Your cell's been busy for ages."

"I was talking to Harry. I just hung up."

"Pidge, darling, we're so relieved you're out of Libya! I bet Harry is too."

"He is, and so am I. Are you there with Cara?" I asked.

"Yes, she is here, and she's grabbing the phone from me."

Suddenly Cara was saying, "We can now admit that we've been very worried about you, Serena. In fact we've had mental images of you coming home in a body bag."

This was said in that gloomy voice of Cara's, which I so dreaded, and I exclaimed, "I'm sure that horrible image was in your head, Cara, and not Jessica's."

Cara laughed. "You know she worries about you all the time, and a bit more than I do, baby sister. But she wants a word again, here she is."

Jess said, "I do hope you're coming to Nice soon. There's no real reason to linger in Venice, is there? And you are all right, aren't you? You're not wounded, or anything like that?"

"No, I'm not, I'm fine," I said in a quiet voice, suddenly feeling low, down in the dumps. In a way, I *was* wounded, at least emotionally. Taking a deep breath, I added, "I'm getting it together. I'm alive and well and kicking."

"You don't sound it," Jessica answered softly, able to pick up on my moods as usual, since my childhood. "Just the opposite. So what's wrong? Tell me, Pidge, it helps to get things out."

"There's nothing wrong, honestly," I replied, and in the strongest tone I could muster.

There was a moment of silence at the other end of the phone, then Jessica made an aside to Cara.

They were talking together, but I couldn't quite hear what they were saying.

I waited for a moment, then exclaimed in a shrill voice, "What's going on?"

Jessica said, "Cara wants to know if Zac is with you? Did you come out together?"

For a moment I hesitated. "No," I managed to say. "He stayed behind in Libya."

"I see. So why have you come out alone, Serena? The reason you went to Tripoli in the first place was because of him, remember? You didn't want to upset him by staying in Manhattan."

I exclaimed, "Yes, that's correct. I went. And now I've left." My thoughts whirled around in my head, and I improvised, "I've had food poisoning, and it's left me feeling a bit low, not in top form."

"Oh, I see." Jessica cleared her throat. "Have you and Zac had a row?"

I was stunned for a moment that Jessica had guessed, but perhaps it was Cara who had put the idea in her head. Then I instantly reminded myself that these two knew me better than anybody else. I still did not answer, wondering whether to confide everything on the phone, tell them about the miscarriage.

"Are you there, Serena?"

"Yes," I answered miserably.

"Your silence seems to confirm our suspicions. You did have a row with him, didn't you?"

"Yes," I admitted. "It was rather upsetting, and I decided I wanted to come out. Especially since the food poisoning had debilitated me a bit."

"I understand. Cara's bugging me, she wants to know what the quarrel was about."

"Not anything important," I said, and instantly realized my voice was wobbling. I swallowed, felt myself choking up, and I was trembling inside, losing it altogether.

"Oh Pidge, something is terribly wrong, darling," Jessica said softly, in that warm and loving voice of hers, which had soothed me when I had been upset as a child. It got to me, and I burst into tears, began to sob into the phone.

I grasped the receiver tightly in one hand, groped for the box of tissues with the other. I endeavored to stem the tears, wipe my eyes. I wanted to get control of myself.

Jessica was saying, "I'm here for you, so let it all out, Pidge. I'll wait until you're able to speak, take your time."

"I'm sorry," I managed to say in a tearful voice a few seconds later, and then after a moment I did get a grip on myself. "I didn't mean to break down like that."

"What is it? Did you and Zac split up?"

"Possibly, probably . . ."

"But why? I thought everything was going so well with you both. You seemed so happy together when you were here."

"He's . . . sort of annoyed with me," I began, and stopped.

"What about?" Jessica probed.

I began to shake, and I said in a rush of words, "I had a miscarriage, Jessica, and he blames me, he's very angry."

"Oh how terrible for you, Serena, to lose your baby! It's so upsetting, heartbreaking. I know that only too well. I've been there."

"I remembered some words of Mom's the other day," I confided. "She was consoling you on the terrace, long ago, when you were still married to Roger."

"She did console me, and she said a woman can have a miscarriage without doing anything wrong. It can just happen. So I hope you're not blaming yourself."

"I am," I replied, swallowing back the tears. "I shouldn't have gone to Libya. That's what Zac said, and he's right. I put the baby at risk."

"Knowing you, I believe you would have been very careful, handled yourself well, so I don't agree with him," Jessica said. "You could easily have had a miscarriage in New York, or anywhere for that matter." She then added, her tone loving, reassuring, "You must be positive, and look to the future. You'll get pregnant again, you'll see."

"I hope so, Jess, I really do. One of the reasons Zac is mad at me is because he didn't know I was pregnant."

There was a silence at the other end of the phone, and I realized Jessica was startled.

I said, "I didn't tell him, because I thought I should go to Libya. I didn't want to disappoint him, because he was so keen to have me by his side."

"I see," Jessica murmured, and then went on in a stronger voice, "Well, I can understand why he's angry, Pidge."

"I had the best of intentions—"

"And that's the road paved to hell," she cut across me.

I began to cry once more, but managed somehow to tell her about my miscarriage and everything that had happened. And she was, as always, loving and sympathetic. When I'd finished, she said, "My heart goes out to you, Serena, I've been where you are now, although not quite in the same circumstances. And I really do empathize with your dreadful sense of loss, your pain."

"Thank you, Jess, thank you for being so understanding. It helps to know I have you and Cara."

"Cara wants to talk to you. Here she is, Pidge."

"Serena, listen to me, I got the gist of all that from Jessica's end of the conversation, and I just want you to know that we are here for you. This is a miserable time for you, and what you need is a little tender loving care. So come home to us, as soon as you can, so that we can look after you."

"I will," I answered. "I'll be there in a few days."

Forty-three

"Harry! Harry!" I shouted at the top of my voice, increasing my pace, hurrying faster up the street. I could hardly believe my eyes. There was Harry, pulling his roller behind him, about to enter the bolthole building. I hoped he wasn't going to chastise me again for going to Libya.

He turned around immediately, a smile spreading across his face as I sped toward him, and fell into his arms, clutching him tightly. "I can't believe you're here! But I'm so happy you are."

"I am too, honey," he said, still holding me close.

Finally I stepped away, and looked at him questioningly. "Why didn't you tell me you were coming when we spoke on the phone yesterday?"

"I wanted to surprise you, Serena."

"Well, you sure have. You're so busy, why did you come?" I frowned. "Are you still angry with me?"

"I was never angry. Only sorry for you. Sorry you'd gone to the front. I came to make sure you were all right, emotionally and physically. But let's go inside, it's grilling hot out here."

"August is a wicked month," I said, quoting the title of a favorite book.

"I, too, have read Edna O'Brien."

Once we got into the bolthole, Harry let out a sigh of relief. "Thank God for air-conditioning.

Whatever did people do without it?" As he spoke he went into the kitchen, took a bottle of water out of the fridge, and returned to the living room.

"Thank you for coming, Harry, I really appreciate it," I said.

"I felt I should be with you at this sad time, Serena, I knew how upset you were. You're all I have, you know, and I love you very much."

"I feel the same. You've been there for me in times of trouble, I don't know what I'd do without you." I felt my eyes growing moist, and I blinked back the incipient, and unexpected, tears. I was very touched that he had come all this way because he cared. His presence was comforting to me.

"Has Zac called you?" he asked, after a few swigs from the bottle of water, his bright blue eyes fastened on my face.

"No, he hasn't. I suppose he guessed I was in the bolthole, right?"

"He did assume it, naturally, and I wasn't going to lie. I confirmed it. He said he was staying there, in Tripoli, that he didn't want to come out yet, wanted to be at the front, in the action."

I nodded but did not respond.

"I'm really sorry you quarreled," Harry said quietly, his expression sympathetic. "I thought everything was on an even keel with him, and you'd done a lot to help him in every way, got him better."

I ignored this remark. "So he never mentioned that I'd had a miscarriage?" I said, giving Harry a penetrating look.

"No, he didn't, but you know he's discreet, plays everything close to the vest. Listen, let's not sit here chatting. I want to take you out to lunch, enjoy the few days I'm here with you. But I'm going to take a shower first, okay?"

"Very okay. I'll go and change into something else. I'm sick of my all-black front-line uniform. Where do you want to go? The Bauer Palazzo terrace?"

"Why not? It's nice on the Grand Canal, and there's always a bit of a breeze. Ten minutes?"

I nodded, went into my bedroom, where I searched through the big closet. I soon found a white cotton dress I'd bought several years ago, and forgotten, and quickly changed into it. Then I remembered I had red sandals and a red bag, and I found these immediately.

I brushed my hair, put on mascara and red lipstick, and sprayed myself with Ma Griffe. I threw a few things in the handbag, picked up my dark glasses, and went to tell Harry I was ready, all set to go.

It was two o'clock by the time we arrived at the Bauer Palazzo hotel, and the terrace restaurant was busy. There was only a small table left, close to the canal, and we took it at once. A little later, when we sat sipping our Bellinis and relaxing, I told Harry how impressed I'd been by Yusuf and the speedy way he got me out to safety.

"That's the way he is," Harry answered. "He has enough self-confidence to do what he's certain will work, and chartering the private plane was mandatory. He didn't even ask me if he could, he just did it, because it was the only way to go. He had no option. He'd have never been able to get you on a commercial flight. All the airlines are overbooked."

"I know, because of the world press descending on Libya, and leaving." I shook my head. "And a lot of the correspondents are very famous. But then you know that." I picked up the menu, scanned it. "What shall we have for lunch?"

"I'm going to start with tomato salad and then the branzino. The fish is always good here," Harry said.

"I'll have exactly the same."

Once Harry had ordered, I said, "I'm glad Geoff Barnes is doing so well. He seems to love running the London bureau, doesn't he?"

"He's found his niche in life, and his girl," Harry remarked. He threw me a pointed look, added, "He's a much happier guy, thanks to Cara."

"And so is Cara, happier I mean, according to Jess. We're both glad their relationship is working, he's an authentic guy, and trustworthy."

"I'll tell you something else, Serena, I think

Geoff has come to understand that there would have never been a reconciliation with his ex-wife. It just wasn't in the cards."

"I'm quite sure my sister made him understand that," I volunteered.

"I bet she did." Sitting back in the chair, giving me a long look, Harry suddenly asked, "Why didn't you tell Zac you were pregnant, before you went to Libya? Because you wanted to go yourself?"

I shook my head, and answered, "I'm not sure. And anyway, I didn't think I was in any danger. Also, I didn't want to disappoint Zac."

"So you thought he'd want you to stay in New York had he known you were pregnant? And that I would, too?"

"I guess so . . . well, he might have, and so would you."

Harry sipped his drink, looking thoughtful. After a moment, he asked, "Is Val Clifford one of the reasons you wanted to go to Libya? You knew she was already there. After all, you'd seen the picture of her in *The Times*."

I realized I was trapped. It would be hard for me to wriggle out of this one . . . I had to tell him the truth. He knew me far too well. I said, "Partially. I did want to meet Val Clifford, to talk to her."

Harry peered at me. "But why?"

"Those pictures of her pregnant really puzzled me, Harry, and the captions were . . . *lethal*. Yes, that's the word, to me they were peculiar. Why was my name on them?"

"I don't know, and I never will, and neither will you. But surely you knew enough about yourself, from your sisters, and me. What could Val have told you?"

"That's the point, I don't know."

He nodded. "That makes two of us."

I didn't reply, and he let it go. We went on talking about other things, and we enjoyed our lunch, and being together. We needed each other . . . we were each other's link to Dad and Mom and the past. I was aware that this comforted Harry. It also comforted me.

When we got back to the bolthole, Harry excused himself and went to have a nap. Before doing so, he suggested I make a reservation for that evening at Harry's Bar. "But not before nine-thirty," he instructed, as he disappeared into his bedroom.

Once I had phoned the restaurant and booked a table, I got undressed, put on a cotton robe, and lay down on the bed. The drinks at lunch had made me feel sleepy, and I decided a rest would do me good.

I didn't fall asleep at once. I kept thinking about the future. My future. Without Zac. He obviously hadn't said much about me to Harry, because Harry would have told me if he had. I was aware

Zac blamed me for the miscarriage, and perhaps he wouldn't be able to get over that. I just didn't know. The future looked glum. I had Dad's biography to finish. After that, what? What was I going to do for the rest of my life?

I decided to get dressed up for dinner. Like Dad, Harry loved to have an attractive woman on his arm, and so I selected one of my nicest outfits. It was a white gazar jacket, very light and floaty, which I wore over a slender red dress. The red sandals and handbag went well with it, and I added Cara's fake pearl necklace and earrings, which she'd left behind in a drawer last year.

When I went out into the living room, all set to go to the restaurant, I noticed that Harry had spruced himself up too. He was in a fresh white shirt, open at the collar, black slacks, and black penny loafers.

When he saw me, he exclaimed, "Well, don't you look beautiful, Serena!" Then he grinned. "And am I glad you ditched your all-black uniform!"

He was standing at the table, pouring white wine into two glasses, and continued, "I thought we might have a drink here before we go to dinner."

"Why not." I sat down in one of the chairs, and accepted the glass of wine from him.

He clicked his glass to mine, and took the other

chair. After several sips, he said, "I want to talk to you about Val. She was in touch with me some months ago, Serena."

His words made me sit up straighter in the chair. He had my entire attention. I stared at him, flabbergasted.

"I told you the truth when I said Val Clifford had dropped off my radar screen years ago. However, she wrote to me four months ago."

"Why was she suddenly in touch? What was it all about?" I asked, my voice rising.

"She was an old friend who wanted a small favor from me."

"What kind of favor?" I asked, riddled with curiosity, and still taken aback.

"First I'd like to explain something about those years just before you were born. And about your father."

"Tell me," I said.

And he did.

Forty-four

F or a couple of years before you were born, your father was going through a very bad time, Serena. I tried to help him, but it was hard," Harry said. "No one could help him really."

"Why? What was wrong?" I spoke quietly, wanting to know everything. His announcement that Val Clifford had been in touch had surprised and startled me. Now I was composed and wanting to know more.

Harry sipped his drink, then continued. "It was a difficult period, and the years 1978 and 1979 were rough on him. And so was the beginning of 1980. We'd been a lot on the various front lines, also in El Salvador, covering the war there. And your mother hadn't been well. He worried about her a lot, he loved her so much. One time, when we got out of El Salvador for a few weeks, I thought he was going to have a breakdown, he was at his wits' end. Exhausted, on his last legs, and suffering from PTSD, but I only realized that later. I was, too, as it happens. He was also wracked with worry about Elizabeth. Her osteoporosis had debilitated her more than ever. You know yourself how much she suffered at different times."

"I do, and having that condition can be very confining. I know when I was little she had to stay in bed a lot."

"In 1980, around November, your father was truly down in the dumps, depressed, worried about your mother. He had a bad case of the blues. So, once we were off the front line, I talked him into spending a short period of time in Venice, at the bolthole, having a bit of R & R." Tommy paused, took a gulp of white wine, added, "Before going home to Nice."

"I know what you're going to say," I announced.

"He got involved with Val Clifford." I sat staring at him, nursing my glass of wine.

Harry stared back at me, and then he said carefully, "Briefly. Very briefly. So, can I continue?" His eyes were questioning.

I nodded, and held myself still in the chair. I felt slightly queasy.

Harry went on, "Tommy and I took the dancing pictures of Val for her boyfriend, Jacques Pelliter, at that particular time. Val had known Tommy ever since his marriage to Elizabeth. After all, she was her first cousin. Val was a talented, gifted photographer, actually, and we gave her a job at Global. She loved the front line, the danger, the excitement of being in the middle of the action. She reveled in it . . . loved being one of the guys in combat boots and camouflage. She worked for us for a few years, but she hadn't been in El Salvador with us because she'd had bronchitis at the time. Anyway, I was very aware that she had a crush on Tommy. He ignored it. But that November, in 1980, in Venice, he succumbed. She was attractive, charming, shared his interests, and adored him. And he was at a really low ebb."

"I understand, I'm not going to judge him, Harry," I said, needing him to continue, and wanting to encourage him.

He nodded, said yet again, "Tommy worshipped your mother. He only had eyes for her. It *was* that grand love affair. Always was. But he didn't have a sex life with her, because of her osteoporosis. He was handsome, charming, virile. He was only thirty-nine, Serena. He was also the most daring and fearless war photographer in the world. Famous, a celebrity, much admired. Women threw themselves at him. And so—"

"He slept with Val," I said softly, interrupting the flow of his story.

"Yes, he did," Harry answered, his voice as low as mine had been.

"You said the word 'briefly,' before. Was it a one-night stand?" I asked.

"More like a two-week stand. And then it was over. He couldn't continue it, he told me, because of his love for Elizabeth. He was riddled with guilt, contrite. He'd never strayed before, and it troubled him that he had been unfaithful with Val."

"But she was pregnant with me. Am I right?"

"She was, yes."

There was a long silence.

Finally I broke it when I said, "So Val Clifford was my mother."

"She gave birth to you, Serena. Elizabeth was your mother," Harry corrected me. "From the day you were born."

"So Val wasn't actually a surrogate?" I gave him a piercing look.

"Not really, not in the sense you mean."

"Didn't Val want me?" I asked.

"Of course she did, but she had a problem. Remember this was thirty years ago, and she was afraid of being a single mother. Single mothers weren't that common in those days. And were even disapproved of. Basically, she thought she couldn't cut it. Also, she didn't know how she could have you and continue her work. War photography was her great passion. She realized she would find it hard to give that up. In general she was nervous, insecure, worried, doubted her ability to bring up a child properly."

"Did she want to abort me, Harry?"

"Absolutely not! And your father didn't either. They'd both seen too much death and destruction as war photographers. They wouldn't take a life, so there was never any discussion about an abortion. The mere idea was abhorrent to them."

"So what happened ultimately?" I sat back, anxious to know the rest.

"He and I discussed it. And then Val became part of the discussion about the situation. Tommy said he had to tell Elizabeth the truth, and also explain that Val was pregnant with his child. He felt compelled to do this because of the importance of his relationship with Elizabeth. He wanted to remain married to her. There was no question of a divorce. He liked Val, but it was his wife he loved."

"And you encouraged that, and Dad told her. Am I correct?" I asked, and for the first time I relaxed, reached out, touched Harry's hand. "It's okay," I said. "I'm okay about this." And I really was.

Harry looked relieved. "He and I flew to Nice, and he told Elizabeth everything, asked her to forgive him. Later, he said that your mother was wonderful. She completely understood the situation, how it had come about. Elizabeth was a worldly woman, and she realized that your father's predicament was untenable, and all because of her illness."

"Yes, Mom would've been understanding. She was a very sophisticated woman, and so very intelligent. I bet Dad asked her if she wanted the baby?"

Harry shook his head, a half smile on his lips. "Trust you to get it all. You're too much at times, Serena, too bright for your own good." He drank the last of his wine, and said, "And you're correct. Tommy did ask Elizabeth if she wanted the baby, and apparently she was thrilled at the idea. If Val agreed to it, that apparently was her only stipulation."

"And Val did agree. And so all's well that ends well."

Glancing at his watch, Harry said, "I think we have to go to the restaurant, Serena. Otherwise we might not have a table. It's getting late."

"I've lots of questions, Harry, but I suppose we'd better leave."

"You're right. And that's the story . . . you know the rest, honey."

"Not all of it." I stood up, reached for my handbag. "Just one question now, Harry, before we go. Okay?"

"Go ahead."

"When Val contacted you recently, what favor did she want from you?"

"She wanted me to be the executor of her will."

"Oh," was all I said, yet again totally surprised.

"And I agreed." He took hold of my arm and led me to the door. "The rest over dinner at Harry's Bar."

Like everyone else, Harry had his faults, but many more good qualities, one of which was his graciousness. He was nice to people, whoever they were. This never varied, and it was natural, endeared him to everyone.

The moment we walked into Harry's Bar we were instantly greeted with great affection by Arrigo Cipriani, the owner, and then by some of the head waiters. I had booked the table in his name, so his favorite spot in a corner at the back of the room was waiting for us.

Once we were seated at the table, Bellinis began to arrive along with his favorite small rounds of toast, breadsticks, butter, and sparkling water.

"You're like the king here," I said, picking up my Bellini, holding it toward him.

He touched his glass to mine. "Tommy always used to kid me about that, and once tried to persuade me that the restaurant had been named after me. But I knew that this wasn't true, since it has been called Harry's Bar since Hemingway's day. Anyway, they're all very nice, and this is one of my favorite places in the world."

"I know. You came here a lot with Dad and Mom, didn't you?"

He nodded. "Many a great evening was spent here, the three of us laughing our heads off and enjoying life. Or the four of us if I had a girlfriend in tow." He took a sip of his drink, went on, "Can I explain why Val Clifford asked me to be executor of her will?"

"Yes, I want to know." I leaned closer to him.

"As you are already aware, she did marry Jacques Pelliter several years after you were born. He died some years ago, and she never remarried. And she never had any children, because of her career as a war photographer. At least, that's what I believe played a major part in her decision not to have children. And so she made you her sole heir. I have a copy of her will."

"Oh my God!" I exclaimed, and immediately fell silent, totally stunned by his announcement.

"I can see you're surprised, Serena, but it sort of makes sense really. She did carry you for nine months, did give birth to you, and she and your mother were first cousins, she was your great-aunt

Dora's daughter, as you know. And Dora was your grandmother's twin sister . . . so you're truly family. Who else could be her heir?"

"My sisters? As well as me?" I suggested, a brow lifting.

"She also thought of that possibility, and said she was leaving everything to you because, like her, you were a war photographer, as well as the child she had carried."

I looked at him, and made a slight grimace, but said nothing. I was still stunned about Val's bequest to me.

There was a small silence, and then turning to me, he continued. "She's left you her studio, the possessions in it, and all rights to her photographic archive."

"Oh." I sat there biting my lip, feeling suddenly overwhelmed by this information. "It's generous of her," I finally said, not knowing what else to say. Moving on, I gave Harry a small smile. "Listen, I want to ask you a few questions. Is that all right with you?"

"Of course. What do you want to know?"

"How was my birth certificate faked?" When he didn't respond immediately, I continued. "It must have been faked, Harry, because Elizabeth is named as my mother, when she didn't actually give birth to me. Val did that. Cara told Jessica and me that birth certificates could be faked, as well as other documents."

"She would say that," he exclaimed, and then reached out, squeezed my hand. "Val gave birth to you at Jardin des Fleurs. Dr. Felix Legrange and the nurse Madame Annette Bertrand were present at the time. The next day you were in Elizabeth's arms, and Tommy and I took Val back to the Negresco hotel, where she had a suite. She stayed a couple of days, resting, and then went to Paris, where she lived at that time. Dr. Lagrange filled out the required form, and that information he supplied went on your official birth certificate."

"Just as I suspected. I knew the doctor must have been in on it."

Harry looked taken aback at my comment, and said swiftly, "Nobody was 'in' on anything, as you call it. Dr. Legrange knew how desperately your mother wanted another child, and he helped to facilitate it. The birth was uncomplicated, very easy. Val left. Your mother took over. Everyone was happy, and neither the doctor nor the nurse took any money at all."

"Because Mom was a famous movie star, and—"

"That was not the reason!" he cut in peremptorily, in a sharp tone for him. "They did what they did because your mother was a nice woman, sweet, caring, kind to everyone she knew. Also, Dr. Legrange was a smart man, and he was very well aware that Val was unequipped emotionally to be a full-time mother. He recognized that her career as a war photographer came first, and also truly understood that Elizabeth and Tommy would give you a much better life than she could. A happy and secure life. And they did."

I gazed at him, slightly chagrined, and somewhat chastised. "Sorry, Harry, I shouldn't have said that. And you're right, they were wonderful parents."

"And then some," he exclaimed. "Never forget that you were the much-longed-for baby, and cherished."

"Cara said exactly that. She told me it was easy for a woman to give birth, but what truly mattered was the care and love a woman gave to the baby after it was born, and forever."

"Elizabeth Vasson *was* your mother, and don't you ever forget that, Serena."

"I promise I won't," I said. "I couldn't, even if I tried. Elizabeth made me who I am."

"As did Tommy," Harry pointed out, and squeezed my hand again. "You were one lucky girl."

After this discussion, we ordered dinner. I didn't really feel like eating, and when Harry said he was starting with shrimp, then would have the specialty of the restaurant, liver Veniziana, I said I would have the same.

On the walk home I suddenly said to Harry, "If I hadn't found those pictures of the very pregnant Val, I would have never known any of this."

Harry didn't answer at first, and then after a few minutes he said, "When Val got in touch with me recently, she said I could tell you she'd made you her heir because you were family. And also because you were both in the same profession. Or I could tell you the truth about your actual birth. She said it was up to me. I should do what I thought was the best for you. She didn't want you to be upset, she said that several times."

I was taken aback, and then I asked, "And what would you have done, Harry, if I hadn't found the pictures?"

Again he was silent, and then he unexpectedly stopped walking in the middle of the Piazza San Marco, and looked at me intently. "I'm still not sure, Serena." A deep sigh escaped him. "I might have told you the truth. On the other hand, Elizabeth and Tommy never did that, and so perhaps I would have honored their decision, and kept their secret. I honestly thought it really wasn't my place, and Val seemed to be against it when she spoke about her will."

I put my arms around him, and hugged him tightly. "It doesn't matter, honestly. I love you very much, and I know you have my best interests at heart. I have always trusted you, and I still do. And I always will."

"Thanks for that, Serena. There is just one more thing I want to say. I don't want you to think badly of Tommy because he slept with Val. The pressure was always on him, he was stressed, and he did love Elizabeth so very much—"

"How could I ever think badly of Dad? He was the most wonderful man, my magic man, a very special father, not only to me, but to Jessica and Cara as well. And he was a loving and caring husband . . ." I paused, and added, "I was there, you know. Also, I'm thirty years old, a grown-up, Harry. I realize how difficult and frustrating things must have been for him at times, because of Mom's illness. And thank God she did get much better eventually, because of the new drugs for osteoporosis. And things normalized for them . . ."

"Yes. They did. And *they* loved *you,* and this also helped to sustain them even more. You were a blessing, Serena."

Forty-five

When I went into the living room the following morning, Harry was already working on his laptop, and drinking a mug of coffee.

He glanced up, smiled when he saw me, and exclaimed, "You look as fresh as a daisy, and very pretty, Serena. How about coffee?"

"That would be nice and thanks for those compliments. I took your words to heart, about my all-black front-line uniform. I've ditched it permanently. White suits me better, don't you think?" I said, looking down at my white T-shirt and white jeans.

"It sure does," he said and walked into the kitchen.

I sat down at the table, and a moment later he returned with a mug of coffee for me.

"Thanks. And thanks for last night," I said. "And for telling me all about Val and Dad and Mom, and my birth. I'm going to explain everything to Jessica and Cara, but I prefer to do it in person when I go to Nice."

"They should know, Serena," he replied. "I'm certain they'll understand just the way you have. They're both as levelheaded as you are, and know that we're all human beings, with human frailties."

"They won't have any problems about it," I said, smiling at him. I took a sip of my coffee, and asked, "What would you like to do today?"

An answer wasn't forthcoming for a moment, and then he said, "You haven't said a word about Val's bequest to you, but I thought we ought to go there this morning . . . go and see it. What do you think?" He looked at me expectantly, his blue eyes twinkling, and a faint smile crossed his face.

Once more I was taken by surprise, and I gaped at him. Finally, I said, "Do you mean the studio is here? In Venice?"

"Yes, it is." Rising, he went into his bedroom, came back a second later, carrying an envelope.

He handed it to me and sat down, explaining, "Val sent this to me before she went to Tripoli, and told me to give it to you only if I told you the truth. It's a letter to you. And here's the key to her studio. Which is on the Grand Canal, by the way, and not far from the Bauer Palazzo." He put the key on the table.

I was dumbstruck for a moment, filled with amazement, and I just sat there clutching the envelope and continuing to stare at Harry.

He said, "Aren't you going to open it?"

"Of course," I answered. I took out the letter, and began to read:

Dear Serena:

I am fully aware that by going to Libya I'm risking my life on the front line, as I always have. Being a war photographer has always been my one great passion, and it has dominated my life. So if you are reading this letter you will know that I didn't make it, that I died doing what I loved the most.

I also wanted you to know that I have always loved you, held you dear, in my heart. Giving you to Elizabeth and Tommy was an act of love on my part. It was my way of securing your life, making sure you had everything, and most especially their abiding love. I want you to truly understand that I loved Elizabeth and Tommy, and trusted them implicitly.

I saw you several times when you were little, and I thought you were the most beautiful girl in the world. I was so proud of you, and even prouder when you became a war photographer yourself. I like to think you've inherited some talent from me as well as from Tommy.

Take care of yourself always.

Love,

Val

Tears came into my eyes as I was reading the letter. I was touched by it, and my hand trembled slightly as I gave it to Harry without saying a word.

He took it and began to read.

I wiped the tears from my eyes with my fingertips, and stood up, went over to the window and looked out at the piazza.

A moment later Harry was enfolding me in his arms, and holding me close. He didn't say anything, because there was nothing to say. That this woman had loved me in her own way was undeniable, and I think Harry knew that too, had probably always known it.

We sat in Florian's, having a coffee and croissants, and cooling off in the air-conditioning. Harry and

I had walked down to the piazza from the bolthole, and come in here for breakfast, before going to Val's studio. The heat was intense outside this morning, and I'd even brought a cotton hat with me.

Harry knew I was still feeling emotional, and he did not mention Val, or Mom and Dad. Instead he started to talk about my grandparents, Dave and Greta Stone.

"They saved my life, you know," he announced at one moment.

"No, I didn't know that," I said, looking across the table at him. "No one ever told me."

"I was seven, sad and lonely, a lost little boy, really," he began. "My father was a serial womanizer of the worst kind, because he boasted about it. My mother was an alcoholic because of his boasting. My father had a trust fund, so we weren't poor. Except when it came to feelings and giving love and attention to their child. Me. My parents were awful."

Harry paused to sip his coffee, and looked at me. "Tommy and I met at school, and he sort of adopted me, took me under his wing. Once, after he'd come home with me, to our apartment on Eighty-sixth Street, he had been horrified. It wasn't messy or neglected. Just cold, seemingly deserted, and a little bit frightening to him, I guess."

"Harry, what a terrible thing for you! Growing

up like that," I sympathized. "And I bet Dad was appalled, because he was so empathetic."

He went on, "So much so, he started inviting me to his parents' apartment for dinner. We'd do our homework, and then we'd have lovely food, cooked by your marvelous, generous grandmother. It was heaven for me. At weekends Tommy always included me in their little jaunts, to the movies, sometimes to the theater, even out to dinner. In the end, I became part of the family, spent all my time with them."

"And you became like brothers, didn't you? Since you were both only children."

"That's true. And do you know, Serena, in all the years I knew Tommy, and that was right up to his death last year, we never had a row. Sixty-two years." He gave me a look that was full of amazement.

I laughed. "That must be one helluva record."

He also laughed. "I think it was."

I was a little nervous when I put the key in the lock and opened the front door to Val's studio, in an old palazzo on the Grand Canal.

Harry and I stood there in the doorway for a moment or two, glancing around. We stood facing a large space, obviously the living room, with tall windows at the far end, overlooking the canal. It was quite impressive.

"Come on," Harry said, closing the door behind

us. We both stepped forward, and I turned on a couple of lamps, while Harry headed for the air conditioner, and adjusted it to high. "It was on low," he said.

Slowly, I walked around this main room.

It had a highly polished parquet floor, and several large sofas and chairs, all of them upholstered in a dark fir-green fabric. The walls were painted cream, and the other woodwork was a buttery color.

It was an airy room, with lots of daylight, and an ornate Venetian glass chandelier hanging from the ceiling. There were several glass coffee tables, and some nice pieces of sculpture. Along one wall there was a series of tall bookshelves. On some shelves there were photographic books as well as novels.

For the most part, the shelves were filled with photographs . . . of me at different ages, alone, and with the twins, of Mom and Dad with me, Mom and Dad with Val and Harry, photographs of Jessica and Cara. All in beautiful frames, so many of them, and they told their own story. And Val's story, and how she felt about us all. She had loved us, there was no question in my mind about that.

My attention was taken by a photograph of Mom and Dad, with Harry standing off to one side. My mother, as usual, looked incandescent, and so gorgeous she was breathtaking. As I continued to study this picture, I noticed the look on Harry's face, and I thought: Oh my God, a single frame does tell it all. *Harry had been in love with my mother.* I knew that at once.

I turned around quickly, and he was staring at me intently. He must have seen the look of comprehension reflected on my face, because his expression changed slightly.

"Yes, I was," he said, coming closer, looking again at the photograph, and then at me. "Always. It's probably why my two marriages never worked. And none of my other relationships with other women."

"Did Mom know how you felt about her?" I asked, sounding slightly breathless, once more full of amazement and wonder. How little we know about secrets from the past.

"I'm not sure, Serena," Harry said softly. "Certainly never from me. But Elizabeth might have known I was in love with her. Women are intuitive about these things."

"And Tommy? Did he know? Or perhaps guess?"

"No, he didn't."

"And Val?"

"Maybe." Harry shook his head. "I was in love with your mother, but I also loved Tommy. And anyway, Elizabeth worshipped your father. From the day she met him . . . an hour before I strolled onto the scene and also fell for her."

"Oh, Harry . . ." I stared at him. "I'm so sorry."

"You don't have to be." He smiled and his eyes

were warm, loving. "I didn't fare too badly, you know, and you were always like the daughter I never had, and still are."

I slipped my arm through his and led him away from the bookshelves. "Let's look around the studio, I think there must be other rooms, perhaps through that door over there."

We spent another twenty minutes viewing the charming studio. There was a bedroom, also overlooking the canal, a small kitchen, a bathroom, and another medium-sized room, which obviously Val had used as an office. The studio was compact, nicely furnished, and well kept, with a fantastic view from the large living room.

"I think I'd like to go now," I said after a short time. "I'll come back another day, Harry. I certainly don't feel like poking around in cupboards and opening drawers. It would seem like an intrusion. And I'm not up to it just yet."

"I understand completely," Harry answered. "Let's go and have a drink somewhere, and then I'll check in with Geoff in London, touch base with Yusuf. See what's going on in the rest of the world."

"Lots of people killing people, if you want my guess," I said, sounding as gloomy as Cara.

Forty-six

The upstairs room at Harry's Bar was large and comfortable and it was air-conditioned. And that's where we ended up. The heat in the streets was unbearable by noon, and we craved coolness after walking all the way back to the piazza, from Val's studio.

I was slightly overwhelmed by everything I'd discovered in the last twenty-four hours. I needed time to think, sort out my emotions. At one moment, when Harry was talking to Geoff in London, I thought: Secrets. All families must have secrets. It can't just be ours.

I sat back in the chair, and drank the entire glass of sparkling water, I was so thirsty. I looked across at Harry, sitting near a window, talking on his BlackBerry. Dad had been the same, always dealing with business, ever efficient, never neglectful. That's why Global had been such a great success. Harry was on top of everything, knew where every photographer was, and what they were doing.

Unrequited love, I thought. That was a real bummer. Well, it wasn't really unrequited love, rather, *unspoken love,* I decided, focused on Harry. Mom might have guessed how Harry really felt about her, because she had been extremely bright, very intuitive. However, her heart had been taken by Tommy Stone the moment she met him; she had never looked at another man.

A long sigh escaped me. Life wasn't easy, was it? I heard a voice at the back of my head. It was my mother's, and she was talking to Cara: *Life is hard, it's always been hard and it always will be,* she had said, had added, *and the important thing is to beat life at its own game.*

I wondered how you beat life at its own game. I had no idea, at least not at this moment. I wished Mom were here to tell me. I wished Mom were here, period.

Harry was heading across the room, and he appeared to be excited, his face animated. "More rebels winning in various areas of Tripoli! It looks like Gaddafi's loyalist troops are laying down their arms, quitting."

"Hey, Harry, that's great. You just spoke to Yusuf?"

"No, to Geoff. And he said to say hello, by the way, sends his best. I'm going to speak to Yusuf now. I'll go back over there, the reception's better."

"That's fine. I'm just sitting here, trying to absorb everything that I've learned since you arrived in Venice. I could write a book about it all."

Harry threw me an amused look, chuckling to himself as he hurried over to the window.

I drank some more water, and then picked up the menu for lunch. As my eyes roamed over it, I was so startled to see the date, I did a double take. It was Thursday, August 18. I could hardly believe it. The last few days had just slipped through my fingers.

My mind went to Val, and I wondered about her life, what it had been like. I felt sad for her, and then brushed that feeling away. Perhaps she had been fulfilled. And she *had* chosen her life. Knowing Dad, I felt sure he would have supported her financially, if she'd wanted to keep me, and had been prepared to give up her career. I also was positive he would never have left Elizabeth. She was the love of his life. And I was the winner in the end, wasn't I? I had had the best parents anyone could hope for. I had been blessed.

It was very generous of Val to make me her heir. My thoughts now strayed to the beautiful studio on the Grand Canal. Once the lawyers in New York and here in Venice had completed the last of the documents, I could take possession of the studio. Harry had told me this as we had walked back here.

In the meantime, I could go in and out as much as I wished, because I did own it and had the key. Did I want to keep the studio? To stay there occasionally? I wasn't sure. I might miss the bolthole. That funny old place was full of memories, full of the past, full of my family. Well, there was no hurry. I would wait and see, make a decision later.

I knew I didn't want to go back to the studio this week, to look around again. I wanted time to elapse. It had felt like an intrusion on Val's privacy earlier this morning. Her death in Libya was far too close in time. Later, I would come back to Venice, perhaps in September, look at it again. It was truly beautiful, tasteful in every way, and it told me much about this woman who had played such an important role in my life. Without her I would not have been here.

Harry strode over, and handed me his BlackBerry. "Have a word with Yusuf, honey, he's been asking for you."

I took the phone, and exclaimed, "Yusuf, how are you?"

"I'm great. And how're you, my darling?"

"Much better, rested, being well fed by Harry and enjoying that much-needed relaxation. I bet you miss me in that great big fancy suite. You do, don't you?"

"I always miss you, Serena. However, I gave up the Rixos suite the other day. It was far too big. Four rooms suddenly became available at the Corinthia Hotel, so I grabbed them for Zac, me, and the lads. Much better. Also much cheaper." His chuckle echoed down the line.

"Good for you," I said, and went on. "It looks as

if things have started to change . . . the rebels are winning."

"That's how it seems, but looks can be deceptive. The Gaddafi soldiers haven't given up, there's still fighting in many of the suburbs, and other cities. But the rebel interim government, the National Transitional Council, appear to have their priorities well defined. Make no mistake, it continues to be a most dangerous place. I'm glad you're out of here."

"So am I, Yusuf. Good talking to you, stay in touch. Do you want to speak to Harry again?"

"Not at the moment. We'll be having our usual evening chat later. So long, Serena." He clicked off.

I handed the BlackBerry to Harry, who was now seated at the table with me. "What do you think? Is it the endgame?" I asked him.

"Not just yet. The endgame of war will not play yet. The Colonel lurks somewhere in the country, as do his sons. His cronies want to hold on to the power. The army has not really surrendered yet. There's a lot of continuous looting. Almost every man and boy has a gun in his possession. That spells danger. And everyone in the West is wondering if the National Transitional Council can run the country, function as a viable government. So, we'll wait and see."

"It's always the same, isn't it? Anyway, it was nice to have a word with Yusuf, and thank God he moved everyone to the Corinthia. That suite at the

Rixos was awful. I needed roller skates to get around."

Harry chuckled, then asked, "Shall we stay here? Have a glass of wine or a Bellini, and order lunch later? Something light."

"I think so, it's cool up here, and most of the posh tourists are downstairs. Who wants to drag around Venice in this heat? Not me."

"I agree." He poured himself a glass of sparkling water, and leaned back, eyeing me carefully. After a moment he said, "You didn't ask Yusuf about Zac."

"No, because I haven't heard from him, and anyway, he obviously wants to stick it out there in Libya, especially now with these sudden changes happening . . . he'll be out there in the streets, seeking his iconic pictures."

Harry gave me a knowing smile, and said, "Only too true."

"Can I ask you something, Harry?"

"You know you can, certainly after yesterday and today . . . I have no secrets from you anymore, Serena."

"You all stayed friends, didn't you? Mom and Dad and you? With Val, that's what I mean."

"Yes, we did, as a matter of fact."

"I've been wondering about that, obviously because of all those photographs in her studio. They do convey a continuing friendship. But why did you remain friendly with her?"

"First of all, there was no animosity in anyone. Tommy, Elizabeth, and Val were all in agreement about the situation, and what to do. How to handle it. Secondly, Elizabeth preferred it that way. She didn't want Val to feel cut off from the family, or out of the family. However, we saw less of Val after she married Jacques. Also, she had left Global during her pregnancy. She just never came back. It was for the best."

"That's understandable. And what about Jacques Pelliter? She broke up with him for several years, didn't she?"

"Yes. Then they began to see each other again, when Jacques quit working as a war correspondent. Eventually she did marry him. Even though your great-aunt Dora didn't approve of him."

I began to laugh, and told Harry about Cara's story, adding, "And she said Val had put the cat among the pigeons when she got engaged to Jacques."

"Oh God, Granny's old sayings did seem to attract Cara. I can't believe she still uses them." Harry grimaced but his eyes twinkled.

"Oh yes, she certainly does." I paused, sipped the water. "Another question. Is that okay?" I said.

He inclined his head, gave me one of his loving smiles.

"Why do you think Dad took those pictures of Val when she was pregnant?"

"Honestly, Serena, I have no idea. I was never aware he had taken them, posed her in that condition. I've wondered about it myself, since you showed them to me. I finally came to the conclusion that Val herself wanted them."

"Maybe you're right. One other thing. Did Jacques ever know anything about . . . the situation?"

"Absolutely not! No one did. Except for the four of us, plus the doctor and the nurse. It was an enormous secret and we all kept it," Harry finished.

One of the waiters came over, and Harry ordered Bellinis. Then we looked at the lunch menu, ordered green salad and little fried fish with lemons. As usual, I followed Harry's lead.

It was toward the end of lunch that Harry's BlackBerry began to buzz, and he answered it at once. "Hello, Yusuf," he said, speaking in a low voice. That was all he said. He just sat and listened attentively for a few minutes and then told Yusuf he would call him back shortly.

Clicking off the BlackBerry, Harry looked across at me, and said, "Zac wants to come out."

"Oh." I sat back in my chair, trying to read Harry's expression. But it was bland, told me nothing.

"Why does he want to come out? Now?" I asked. "It's going to be an interesting time, what with the rebel militias winning, and all that stuff."

"He told Yusuf he had lost his concentration. That he couldn't properly focus anymore because of your terrible quarrel. He believes he's lost his edge."

"Zac said he'd lost his edge when he came out of Afghanistan. And he had," I said.

Harry threw me a penetrating look. "And did he get his edge back in Libya?"

"Yes, he did, and so did I. It's funny how everything suddenly kicks in again, and you're really on top of it, and working at your best. But then you know that better than I do, Harry, you've been there, and long before I was."

"Yusuf is arranging a private jet for Zac, and we'll have him out tomorrow."

I simply nodded.

Harry went on, "The thing is, Zac told Yusuf that he wanted to come here to Venice and—"

"Oh God!" I exclaimed, cutting across Harry. "It'll be a bit crowded in the bolthole, don't you think?"

"Oh no, he doesn't want to come to the bolthole, Serena. He asked Yusuf to get him a room at the Bauer. He apparently doesn't want to intrude on you. However, he does want to see you, to discuss what happened in Tripoli."

I was silent.

Harry leaned closer, and gave me a direct look. "Don't you want to see him, honey? Just tell me what you want, and I'll arrange it. The jet can fly him to Rome, Paris, London, wherever he wants to go, and from there he can make a connection to New York."

"I suppose I ought to see him. Everything was left sort of hanging in the air . . . he stalked out, I didn't call him back, and then I left without talking about what happened. I'd better meet with him."

"I agree with you, Serena. See him, talk to him, and if you're going to end it with Zac, do so in a civilized way. You'll feel better later, if you keep your dignity."

"I'm still mad at him, actually rather angry, Harry. Because he behaved so badly. He was juvenile, and there are a few things I have to get off my chest." I became tense in the chair, my face taut.

He smiled at me, leaned closer, kissed my cheek. "I know you so well, and you'll handle it properly. And just remember this, do the right thing for *you*. It's your life I'm concerned about, not anyone else's. All right, honey?"

I grabbed his hand, held on to it. "Oh, Harry, whatever would I do without you. You're my rock. And I'll be fine, seeing him. So call Yusuf back right now and make the arrangements. Before I change my mind."

A moment later, Harry was talking to Yusuf in Tripoli. He said, "Okay. We're on. Serena has agreed to meet Zac. What time is he getting in?" Harry listened for a moment and then said, "I'll tell her that, and tell him to stay at the Bauer. And come to the bolthole around six o'clock. Confirm everything with me, and thanks, Yusuf."

On Friday evening I paid careful attention to my appearance. I took time doing my hair and makeup, and put on the slim red silk dress. After spraying myself with my favorite Ma Griffe, I added Cara's fake pearl necklace and earrings. Then I stepped into a pair of black patent high-heeled shoes.

Standing in front of the long mirror, I nodded to myself. My need to look good when confronting Zac was part pride, part upbringing. Mom was one of the world's greatest movie stars, she had always drilled it into Jessica, Cara, and me that we should look great and go out there and "kill 'em," as she said. Her theory was that people were genuinely intimidated and impressed by appearance, voice, and demeanor. Looking great, sounding good, and acting elegantly gave a woman the upper hand, she believed. And I did too.

Glancing at my watch, I saw that it was fifteen minutes to six. That was when Zac was due at the bolthole. Glancing at myself once more, I went out into the living room, seeking Harry's approval.

He turned around when he heard the clicking of my high heels on the wood floor, and was obviously startled for a moment. Then he said, "Good girl! You look wonderful, Serena. You'll knock him dead."

I smiled, and reminded him who my teacher had been. "That's what Mom taught us . . . to go out there and knock 'em dead. The last time Zac saw me, I was kneeling on a bathroom floor, cleaning it, and I looked a mess. I was sweating, had blood on my legs, and wet hair. That was his last memory of me, Harry."

"And if you break up with him tonight, he'll have quite a different memory of you, won't he, Serena? The glamour-puss personified, not the cleaning woman, and—"

"Oh, God, do you think I've overdone it, Harry?" I broke in. "Shall I go and take Cara's fake pearls off? Or the high heels?"

"I don't want you to change a thing. You look perfect . . . and perfectly beautiful." He walked over to me and kissed my cheek, and then stood staring at me.

I saw his eyes grow moist, as he added, "You think you don't look like Elizabeth, but you do, sometimes. It's a certain gleam in your eyes, an expression on your face . . . you remind me of her a lot."

"Zac has said that, and I think it's probably a family resemblance. I have a bit of Granny in me, and she was Great-Aunt Dora's twin . . ." I let my voice trail off, then asked, "So what's the plan of action?"

"When Zac arrives I shall offer him a drink, chat with you both for a short while, and then excuse myself. I'll amble off, disappear, and you and he can be alone. That's the only way this situation can be handled. You don't need an audience."

"That's true." I went over to the ice bucket on the table, lifted out the bottle of white wine, poured us both a drink. I said, in a confiding tone, "I do love Zac, and I suppose I always will. The thing is, can I live with him?"

"That's always the million-dollar question, Serena." Harry picked up the glass of wine. "Keep an open mind. Let him do the talking first. Remember, he's the one who asked to see *you*."

"I will. Listen, Harry, you look dashing tonight. Very much so. Do you have a date?"

He burst out laughing. "Who with, for God's sake? So no, I don't, but I'm going down to Harry's Bar to have a drink with Amos Haversmith, who retired here some years ago. You remember him, your mother always liked his paintings. I usually give him a call when I'm here."

"I do remember, and I know where you'll be if I need you." I sat down, took a sip of my drink. "I can't believe all that stuff that's happening at the Rixos. It's just awful. Frightening."

"It sure as hell is. Yusuf was smart, and made all

the right moves, as usual. He's got such a knack for that."

There was a knock on the door. I stood up instantly, went over to the TV, hovering there, suddenly feeling nervous.

Harry opened the front door, and exclaimed, "Zac! Hello! Come on in, I'm glad you made it out of Libya okay. And just in time. You had a narrow escape."

The two of them embraced.

"I know I did," Zac responded, and began to walk toward me, then hesitated, stopped in the middle of the floor.

His face was serious, but he looked healthy. I smiled inwardly, because he too was well dressed tonight, wearing a pale blue shirt, navy jeans, and the brown penny loafers.

I felt that same rush of excitement I experienced whenever I saw him after an absence, and hoped he wouldn't hear my heart thudding.

Walking toward him, I gave him a quick peck on the cheek, stepped back. I said, "Would you like a glass of wine?"

"Thanks, I would," he answered and turned to Harry. "What a fluke it was that Yusuf decided to move us from the Rixos to the Corinthia. If he hadn't, I certainly wouldn't be standing here tonight. I'd be one of the hostages in the Rixos, and so would Yusuf and the lads."

Harry said, "I was stunned when I heard about it

on the news this afternoon. Over thirty journalists being held, not allowed to leave. It's madness. Those loyalist Gaddafi soldiers waving around Kalashnikovs don't seem to understand that there's a cease-fire."

"What I worry about is that most of the hotel staff have fled the Rixos. There's no one to run anything. It could develop into a dangerous situation. The hotel won't be operating properly," Zac pointed out.

"You're not kidding." Harry sat down, and so did I, next to him. Zac took the other chair. We went on chatting about this unexpected and serious development at the hotel in Tripoli. Harry was right. Zac, Yusuf, and the lads had really had a narrow escape.

Zac crossed his legs, and turning to Harry, he explained, "There's got to be some intervention. Maybe by the Red Cross. Or perhaps one of the rebel militias. I just hope there's no bloodshed. About thirty-five journalists held captive in the Rixos, and to what purpose?"

Harry announced, "It gives us a taste of what might happen once this civil war is over. Chaos."

"Jesus, I daren't think about it," Zac exclaimed, and took a swig of wine.

Harry had left and we were alone.

I was relieved I was in a chair, and not on the sofa. I didn't want Zac to come and sit next to me.

I had felt that sexual pull toward him when he had walked into the bolthole. And immediately. There was something about him that was irresistible. He excited me, made me want to be with him. In every way.

Remembering what Harry had told me, I didn't say a word. I just sat there, sipping my drink. My long silence finally forced him to speak first.

His head on one side, his eyes riveted on me, he said in a soft voice, "You look wonderful, Serena. So you must be feeling better."

"I am. Harry's been spoiling me all this week, and generally fussing over me. He reminds me of Dad."

"I know what you mean. Can I have another drink?"

"Of course."

"Thanks." He went over to the table and poured the wine. "How about you?" he asked without turning around.

"No thanks," I said, swallowing hard. I hoped he wasn't just going to sit here, guzzling the wine. I wanted to get on with it, discuss what had happened in Tripoli, and be finished with the whole messy affair.

Returning to the chair, Zac put the glass on the coffee table. He said, "I know you're angry with me, and I don't blame you. I behaved like a shit. I have no real excuse for my behavior. I was rude, nasty, unfeeling, and cruel to you, showed no love or affection whatsoever. And I'm sorry. So very sorry, Serena."

I didn't answer, I just sat there like a statue. Immobile. I wanted to make him understand I was not going to be a pushover. I would be relentless.

He said, "I'd been drinking when I came up to check on you that night. I just wasn't myself."

"Yes, you were yourself," I shot back, my voice cold. "Because you repeated the way you behaved last year, after my father's funeral in Nice. There was violence in you then, Zac. And again last weekend. That undercurrent of violence frightens me. Because I don't know what brings it on."

He shook his head. He had turned pale, and his green eyes were stricken. It struck me that he didn't know how violent he could be, and perhaps it frightened him, too.

Finding his voice, he said, "But I'm not a violent person, Serena, and you know that. I've never struck you, never hurt you. Or any other woman. Only cowardly men strike women. I'm not a coward."

"What you say is true. So let me amend what I said. You *sound* violent. You seem to have a pent-up fury inside you. And so it makes me expect a violent act from you. It's an awful feeling, scary."

"Maybe it's the booze. I guess I should watch my intake." He started to reach for the wine and pulled back, left the glass on the table.

"You shouldn't drink at all, in my opinion," I said icily, giving him a hard stare.

"Why not?"

"Because you have PTSD, and abstinence is better for you right now. I think booze fuels the anger you're feeling because of all you've witnessed on the front lines."

"Maybe you're right. I sound violent perhaps, but I never would do anything to hurt you or anyone else. As for the front lines, I'm never going to set foot on a battleground again. It's over for me. I'm retiring from war."

"You said that when you came out of Afghanistan. But as soon as I'd helped you to get better, you got all excited about the Arab Spring, and just had to rush off to Libya, because your adrenaline was high and you wanted to be in the middle of it all."

"I know. I broke my promise to you. I'm so sorry about everything . . . breaking my promise, screaming at you, showing no compassion. I guess I just lost it, and the drink didn't help." There was a sorrowful look in his eyes and he had tensed in the chair.

I was taken by surprise when I noticed, suddenly, the tears glittering in his eyes. But I made no comment. After a long moment of silence, I finally said, "You never gave me a chance to explain anything. You stalked off in a fury, treated me like dirt."

"I know. It was wrong. I was so heartless. I don't know how I could behave that way toward you of all people. You're the only woman I've ever loved, Serena. I really mean that. You must know I adore you."

When I still said nothing, he pulled his chair closer to mine, and reached for my hand. "Please, please forgive me, Pidge. *Please.* I can't live without you. There's nothing in this world for me without you." His voice broke, much to my astonishment, and he jumped up, unexpectedly, and strode to the window.

I realized then how sincere he was being; he meant every word. And he was chastened, contrite, and obviously he had a conscience. He was fully aware how mean he had been, and it troubled him. Because deep down inside, he was a decent man, a good human being. Rising, I walked across the room and stood next to him. He didn't speak, and neither did I. And then I became aware he was crying. Tears were rolling down his cheeks.

Staring straight ahead, looking out of the window at the piazza, not wanting him to know I'd noticed his tears, I put one hand on his arm. Very softly, I said, "I accept your apology, Zac."

"But do you forgive me?" he asked, in a low voice, without looking at me either.

"I want to, I'll try. The problem is that you more or less said I'd killed our child, and you blamed

461

me. You said it was my fault that I'd had the miscarriage. And it wasn't. I'd been so careful, and a woman can have a miscarriage without doing anything hectic, or careless. It just happens. Mom always told me that. And it's true."

"I was so wrong. And I'm truly sorry. I think I'm going to live to regret everything I said to you for the rest of my life, which will be meaningless without you."

"Can I explain something, Zac?"

He nodded, did not speak, and I knew why. He couldn't. The tears were still trickling out of his eyes.

"When I discovered I was pregnant, it was literally just before we were leaving for Tripoli," I confided. "I did wonder if I should tell you. And I almost did. I wanted to share my happiness with you, hoped you'd be happy. But—"

"I would have been thrilled," he interrupted swiftly. "I want a child with you."

"I believed you would be happy, Zac. Then I knew how disappointed you'd be if we decided I couldn't, or rather, shouldn't, go to Tripoli. I guess I wanted to please you, and that's why I never told you about the baby. I took care of myself in Libya. I didn't do anything hectic. Nor did I jump about as I normally do, off trucks and Jeeps. It was a fluke, I guess. And I'm sorry, too. I really wanted that baby of ours." I realized my voice had softened, and it had quavered with emotion as well.

462

He wiped his cheeks with his hands, and turned to look at me at last. "Sorry about that, getting so emotional. But I love you. I can't imagine being without you for the rest of my life."

When I didn't respond, stood there, looking up at him, he said, "Don't you love me anymore?"

"Of course I love you, and with all my heart!" I cried, before I could stop myself.

He reached for me, pulled me into his arms, and began to kiss me, carefully at first, on my cheeks and neck, and then his mouth found mine. I clung to him, returning those kisses, and I understood that I was lost.

As it had months ago, something shifted inside me, and I knew this was the only man I could be truly happy with. To be with anyone else would be ridiculous.

When we stood apart, he gently stroked my face. "Let's start again . . . you know we're meant to be together."

I took hold of Zac's hand and led him back to the chairs, where we sat down. "I forgive you," I said sotto voce. "And I want us to be together. And to get married as we planned. However, I need to say something, and you might not like it."

"You're going to give me conditions. I'll agree to whatever you want, Pidge," he cried, his face brightening, his eyes suddenly sparkling.

"I want you to limit your drinking. Especially hard liquor. I want you to get medical attention for your post-traumatic stress disorder. And I absolutely insist you must never go to a war zone again."

"I agree. To everything. I'd like to be in Nice, because I think Dr. Biron is the best there is for my problems. Is that all right?"

I smiled, and then I started to laugh, shaking my head.

"What is it?" he asked. "What's wrong?"

"I think Harry knew this was going to happen. I realize now that he went out of the bolthole looking rather happy, not worried at all."

"I only have eyes for you," Zac said softly. "Are we going to get married in Nice, next spring as we planned?"

I simply gave him a beatific smile.

He suddenly said, "Oh, I want to apologize for something else. Not helping more to find Val Clifford."

"That's all right."

"I always had a strange feeling you thought she was your mother, and that you had a need to find her, to meet her."

"I happen to have all the answers now. She wasn't my mother, Zac, but she did give birth to me. Elizabeth Vasson Stone was my mother. She took me into her arms when I was just a day old, and she loved me, nurtured me, cherished me for twenty-six years, until the day she died."

"Yes, Mom was your mom, I know that. The

beautiful Elizabeth adored you. How did you find out that Val was your biological mother?"

"She contacted Harry, who was an old friend. She wanted a favor. She asked him to be the executor of her will." I stood up. "Back in a minute," I said.

When I returned to the living room, I was holding the letter from Val. I handed it to him silently.

Zac sat reading it, and when he had finished he looked at me, his face sad. "How very moving," he said. "And so sincere."

I told him everything I had learned from Harry, and when I'd finished he said slowly, "Isn't it odd, though, that you always thought there was some sort of secret? After you found those pregnant pictures."

"It was seeing my name on Dad's captions that alerted me."

"I loved your father. He was the very best person I've ever known." Zac gave me an odd little smile. "Whatever happened, ever so briefly with Val, he was, nevertheless, still a one-woman man, you know."

I looked into Zac's eyes, and nodded my head rather vehemently. "Remember, I grew up with them, and he sure was a one-woman man. I can testify to that!"

"And so am I," Zac responded. "I'm *your* one-woman man."

"For the rest of your life," I murmured.

"And even afterward," he added, and stood up, pulled me to my feet. He led me to the window, where we stood looking out at Venice. He put his arms around me, held me tight, and when he released me finally, he looked deeply into my eyes. "I can't believe you're going to be my wife, Pidge," he said, a sense of wonder in his voice, and anticipation.

"I am," I answered, feeling his love surrounding me.

"Then let's go and tell Harry."

And we did.

Epilogue

Nice, October 2011

It was Friday, October 14. Jessica and Cara were thirty-nine years old, and we were celebrating with a small dinner party here at the house tonight.

Jessica, who always did the cooking, had been forbidden by Adeline to enter the kitchen. She and her sister, Magali, would prepare the special birthday supper, both of them insisting that Jessica could not slave over a stove on her birthday.

It had been a gorgeous Indian summer day, but the weather had changed abruptly, had turned cool; as I walked into the peach sitting room I decided we needed a fire. After lighting it, and the small votive candles scattered about, I glanced around. Cara had placed some of her exotic orchids on various tables, and the room looked warm and welcoming.

I went over to the French doors, opened them, and stepped onto the terrace. I glanced up at the sky. It was dark but clear, littered with bright stars, and there was a huge full moon. It was a beautiful Mediterranean night, but really chilly. Swiftly, I went back inside and hurried over to the fireplace.

I felt relaxed, at ease, as I stood with my back to the fire blazing up the chimney. There was something uniquely peaceful about Jardin des Fleurs. I smiled to myself. Mom had always known that. It had been her safe haven. And it was mine.

Zac and I had been here for a few weeks. The tranquility had done wonders for me, and although my miscarriage had been a shattering blow, my sadness had begun to recede. Zac was loving, understanding, and considerate, which had helped me to mend, and continued to give me comfort.

Jessica and Allen Lambert had just become engaged, and he was now considered a member of the family. Even Cara had come to realize they were perfectly suited, made a great couple. I was thrilled to see Jessica so happy and radiant, and so was her twin.

I glanced at my watch. My sisters would be joining me any moment now. I had suggested we have a quiet drink together before the men arrived. Allen, of course, would be driving over from Nice, but Harry and Geoff were at the house, having arrived from London last night. I had told Zac not to bring them down for another half hour.

A moment later Jessica and Cara came walking in together, as glamorous as usual, true to Stone tradition. They had chosen silk dresses, as had I. Mine was red, Jessica wore royal blue, and Cara was in emerald green. We were a colorful trio.

I noticed at once that they were wearing their birthday gifts. Harry, Zac, and I had given them gold earrings, of a different design to suit their individual taste. Allen's gift to Jessica had been a string of pearls, and he had given Cara a smart evening bag. Geoff's present to Cara was a gold locket on a chain, and I smiled to myself, remembering the one I had bought for Jessica when I first started working, because, as Mom had said, she had a "heart of gold." Geoff's gift for Jessica was a beautiful blue silk shawl, perfect for her because it was her favorite color.

Cara came to join me near the fireplace, and Jessica went to open the bottle of champagne in the ice bucket. A moment later I was toasting them.

After my first sip, I said, "I've made a decision about the studio in Venice. I'm going to sell it."

My sisters were obviously taken aback. I could see that from the expressions on their faces.

Before I could continue, Jessica asked, "But why? You'd decided it would be the ideal place for you and Zac to live for the next year, while you finish your book about Dad, and he writes his memoir."

"I want to sell the studio to contribute to the cost of the repairs to the house. A whole new red-tile roof, for God's sake! And what about all those floors and walls which have been damaged by water? And Mom's octagonal room partially ruined. The bills are staggering already."

They stared at me, both of them speechless. Then Cara said, "You don't have to contribute to the repairs, Serena. We can manage it between us."

"But I—"

"Now, Pidge, be quiet!" Jessica exclaimed in a firm tone. "Mr. Converse finally bought Mom's pearl-and-diamond necklace for his wife. In fact he bought the whole set, and I got a good price. And there's the auction of Mom's other stuff coming up next year. That will bring in good money. We'll be fine."

"Is it because the studio was Val's? Is something troubling you about that?" Cara asked.

"Don't be silly!" I replied. "I was never angry about Val, or upset by what I found out."

"And neither were we," Jessica volunteered. "I can't even remember Val. But what I do remember is coming home from boarding school with Cara for the summer vacation, and finding Mom confined to her bed and about to give birth to you."

"We knew she was expecting our baby sister, and we were thrilled to have you at last," Cara said.

"Let's get back to the studio," Jessica interjected. "Zac told me he would be glad to settle in Venice for a while, not roaming the world covering wars."

Before I could answer, Cara cried, "Oh what the hell, Serena! Do what you want. It's yours, it belongs to you. So it's your decision, not ours."

"Yes, it is, Pidge," Jessica agreed. "Let's leave it at that."

I looked from one to the other. "If you don't need the money to help with the repairs, then I guess I might as well keep the studio. A year in Venice *will* be good for me and Zac."

"It will indeed." Jessica beamed at me, added, "And you know how happy and relieved we are that you have both left the front lines."

"Zac and I are too, and so is Harry." I grinned at them. "Especially Harry. Oh look, here he is now."

"Good evening, ladies," Harry said, adopting a tone of mock formality, coming to a standstill at the fireplace. "And you all look beautiful tonight, as usual." An affectionate smile played around his mouth as he said this, and then added, "I'd love a drop of that champagne."

"I'll get it for you," Jessica responded, and went over to the ice bucket, poured a flute of Veuve Clicquot for him.

Before I had a chance to start a conversation with Harry, Geoff arrived with Zac, and they both came over to join us. After hugging me, Geoff went to Cara, enclosed her in his arms, kissed her cheek. She smiled up at him, her dark eyes shining; he looked down at her adoringly.

Being in love, I thought, it's all about being in love. That's what makes the world go round. How strange life is . . . I thought of the way Geoff and Cara had met here in this house, her home. How they had immediately "glommed on to each other," as Cara had put it to me, and I had retorted, "No kidding!" wondering at the time how she thought anyone could have missed their reaction to each other. It had been mesmerizing for a few seconds.

I glanced toward the hall, and there was Allen Lambert heading toward the peach sitting room. Jessica saw him the moment I did, had no doubt been watching for him. She rushed across the room, hurrying out to meet him. It was so obvious they were in love. He swept her into his arms, and off her feet, holding her tightly to him. Jessica had a dreamy look on her face. As for Allen, he was beaming, staring at her as if he was enchanted. A happy man. But then we were all happy tonight.

I knew it was going to be one of those lovely occasions when everyone was at ease with one another. No dramas on the horizon, I thought.

I was growing too warm in front of the blazing fire, and edged away. After going to greet Allen, I went over to the French doors and sat down in a chair.

I am a camera with its shutter open, quite passive, recording, not thinking.

As those words, written by Christopher Isherwood so long ago, flew into my mind, I knew that was exactly how I was feeling at this moment in time.

I was the camera mentally recording everything and needed to remember about this special evening long after it had ended. Then I would have those memories to add to those already stored in the computer in my head. So many memories . . . of growing up in this marvelous old house . . . of Mom and Dad . . . of Jessica and Cara. I truly believed that memories were important to all of us, no, vital, because they helped to ease the pain, healed the many losses we all suffered in life. Memories helped to make us whole again.

We had gathered here to celebrate my sisters' birthday, and now as I sat here I could see the future, in a certain sense. My eyes roamed around the room, taking it all in, photographic images which would last forever. Splashes of vibrant color were alive in the exotic orchids . . . the votive candles were flickering, bright pools of light on polished wood tables and standing in a line on the mantelpiece . . . the cheerful fire . . . the men all spruced up, casual but smart.

I felt quiet within myself, had a sense of calmness. I scanned the future at this moment and it looked hopeful . . . Two marriages, at least. Zac and mine in the spring, Jessica and Allen's in the summer. But what of Cara and Geoff? How would they fare? My eyes focused on them.

They were sitting on the sofa. She was talking, he was listening attentively. His love for her was reflected in his face, in his entire body.

Whether they would marry or not I did not know. For the moment they were together, and if they truly loved each other they would be able to work it out. The logistics of their different lives in two countries, a child called Chloe, Cara's huge commitment to her business, the business of orchids. So many things to be dealt with, but they would manage.

My gaze rested on Harry. He was in the best of health, handsome, looked twenty years younger than he was. Perhaps he would meet a new woman. The last one had sadly died of leukemia three years ago, and there had been no one else since. But like my father, he attracted women in droves, and two failed marriages hadn't stopped him from becoming involved before. Harry would be fine, I felt it in my bones.

I saw Zac walking toward me, looking purposeful, intent on some kind of business. Drawing to a standstill in front of me, he said, "You look very pensive. A penny for your thoughts."

My mouth twitched with hidden laughter. I said, "They're not even worth a penny, you can have them for nothing, and I'm not pensive, I was just thinking of the future, what was going to happen to us all. But of course that's not really possible."

"No, it isn't," he agreed. "Life gets in the way occasionally. As we both know. But, come on, come with me. I think you have to make a toast to your sisters before we go in for dinner."

"You're right." I stood up. Taking my arm, Zac led me across the room.

I went to Jessica and Cara, stood next to them. Smiling, filled with a sudden rush of happiness, I said, "Happy birthday, Jessica, happy birthday, Cara. You're the best sisters anyone could have. As I look back, I know you've both always been there for me, as I have for you." I smiled, but my smile quavered slightly, and my throat tightened with a flood of nostalgia and emotion.

I took a deep breath, and went on. "Do you remember when I was quite little I used to mangle a certain phrase, couldn't quite get it out right?"

They both nodded, laughter brimming in their dark eyes, which suddenly looked moist to me. And I knew they understood exactly what I was referring to.

"I meant it then, and I mean it now." I put an arm around each of them and drew them closer to me. "We love arch others," I said.

"We certainly do," they answered in unison.

Loving each other, that's what family is all

about, I thought, and it always will be. I raised my glass to my sisters, and said, "To family!"

"To family!" the whole room repeated.

May it last forever, I thought, as my sisters wrapped their arms around me and held me safe in their love.

Acknowledgments

M any of my friends often feel the need to sympathize with me, because they think I lead a lonely life as a writer. I immediately point out that it's a solitary profession rather than a lonely one, because I have so many people bouncing around in my head. They soon go from characters in my imagination to living, breathing people, and that's when they enter the room where I work, fully formed, demanding to be heard.

I live with them happily for months on end, as I create their complicated lives, force them to deal with their problems, and help them to survive the dramatic events that invariably engulf them.

By the time the book is finished they truly are *real* people to me; I believe they actually exist, and because I have made them come alive, apparently so realistically, they not only ring true for me but seemingly for my readers as well. And that pleases me. I never lose those characters. They stay with me forever, like old friends I care about.

But once the finished manuscript is on my desk, truly complete, my solitary life ends. I am then joined by a lot of other people, whose job it is to see that the manuscript is properly edited, designed, and finally sent off to the printer. That's when I finally sigh with relief.

I must now mention all those people who are involved with my books. I owe special thanks to Jennifer Enderlin, VP and Executive Editor of St. Martin's Press, my superb editor and sounding board. Her ideas and suggestions are always on target, and her enthusiasm for all of my books is much appreciated. Thanks are also due to Sara Goodman, Associate Editor, who handles all the nitty-gritty. I want to thank Sally Richardson, President and Publisher, and Matthew Shear, Senior Vice President and Publisher, for their continuing support of my books.

I have to thank Lonnie Ostrow of Bradford Enterprises for his help with preparing the manuscript for publication. A computer whiz, he gets all of my numerous rewrites and edits onto the computer with good humor, and helps with my research as well. My thanks to Linda Sullivan of WordSmart, the best typist I ever had, who is willing to work weekends when required, which is often, I must admit.

It is always my husband, Robert Bradford, who gets thanked last, but he really should come first. He is as much a part of my novels as I am myself, listening to plot lines endlessly and without complaint. His insights are invaluable. He is a true partner in every sense, taking care of a huge part of my career. He does so with the skill of a businessman and the creativity of a movie producer. I am lucky that I have his support, love, and devotion, and that he never gets upset when a book consumes me and seems to take over the entire household. And he always manages to make me laugh every day, even if it's at myself.

Center Point Large Print
600 Brooks Road / PO Box 1
Thorndike ME 04986-0001 USA

(207) 568-3717

US & Canada:
1 800 929-9108
www.centerpointlargeprint.com